SCARLET
IN BLUE

ALSO BY JENNIFER MURPHY

I Love You More

SCARLET
IN BLUE

A Novel

Jennifer Murphy

DUTTON

DUTTON

An imprint of Penguin Random House LLC

penguinrandomhouse.com

DUTTON and the D colophon are registered trademarks of
Penguin Random House LLC.

LIBRARY OF CONGRESS CATALOGING-IN-PUBLICATION DATA
has been applied for.

ISBN 9780593183465 (hardcover)
ISBN 9780593183472 (ebook)

Printed in the United States of America
1 3 5 7 9 10 8 6 4 2

BOOK DESIGN BY ELKE SIGAL

To David and Madi

How do you know I'm mad?
   —LEWIS CARROLL, *Alice's Adventures in Wonderland*

I want a red to be sonorous, to sound like a bell.
   —PIERRE-AUGUSTE RENOIR

September 1968

We killed him today.

It was more difficult than I had imagined. Not the gory part—I relished watching the blood ooze from his flesh—but the lifting and dragging. He was heavy.

Now I paint.

The book on Impressionism lies open to the portrait by Renoir. I can't remember *Madame* ever looking so real, so alive. Everything is alive. Me, my surroundings, my canvas. Light drenches the room. Sheer curtains flutter and soar. My senses are crazy sharp. Distant waves roll and splash. A hummingbird's wings tick like a clock. Apron strings brush my bare flesh. The scents: a pungent stew of turpentine, linseed oil, and corpse. My palette a sea of glorious reds. Scarlets and roses, carmine and crimson. I can't help but swirl my fingers through the gooey mixture.

I study my canvas. Compare it to Renoir's *Madame*. Poor thing. Her reds had faded long ago, but I tell her not to worry. Because *now* I can fix that.

FEBRUARY 12, 2014

Chicago, Illinois

46 Years After the Murder

The Pianist

I see her there sometimes, inside that frozen wave. Floating, white nightgown billowing, blond hair swirling. Sometimes she's holding the knife she used to slit his throat. Sometimes it's she who is dead. When the bad images come, I try to replace them with good. Her smile, her playful spontaneity, the particular choreography of her body when she applied paint to canvas.

But these attempts don't always work.

It's cold and windy today, as it is most winter days in Chicago. Symphony practice just broke for lunch. I listen to Vivaldi through my newfangled earmuffs (a birthday gift to myself for a number I'd rather not discuss) as I cross Michigan Avenue. Who knew that one day they'd put miniature speakers inside fur? Like always, I slow my pace as I near the Art Institute. I never enter it. Yet I choose to walk by it every day. I tell myself I prefer the wide sidewalk that fronts it, admire its Beaux Arts architecture, appreciate the large green lion statues that flank its grand entrance, but I know those aren't the real reasons.

I glance at the colorful exhibition banners. They don't change much, every few months or so, but I see there's a new one. I try to make out the lettering. Squint.

Renoir's True Colors.

My heart beats fast and loud. I read the banner again to make sure. It is the exact title my mother had used for a lesson she gave me that final year on the little-known art term *fugitive pigment.*

Then, just like that, I'm propelled forward. I cross the plaza, pass under the arched doorways, file through the ticket line, wander along the maze of halls displaying works by Van Gogh and Matisse and Seurat until I stand before duplicate paintings of Pierre-Auguste Renoir's *Madame Léon Clapisson*.

I catch my breath, feel faint. I'm not certain I even know there is a bench behind me when my knees buckle.

For *Madame* was the painting on my mother's easel that day.

WINTER 1968

South Haven, Michigan

NINE MONTHS BEFORE THE MURDER

FUGITIVE PIGMENT: Pigment that either fades with prolonged exposure to light, is susceptible to atmospheric pollution, or tends to darken when mixed with other substances.

Blue

My eyes still burn from the thick cloud of cigarette smoke. We are walking home from dinner. A dark wood-paneled bar sporting dead animals. There's a menu item called popcorn shrimp I really like. My mother didn't eat. She rarely eats dinner, perhaps an apple or cheese and grapes, but she never skips her pinot or chardonnay. She insists she should have lived in Italy, where people consume more wine than water. It has just begun to snow. Christmas music pipes through the streets. Decorations are still up. Santa and his reindeer fly from building to building. Colorful lights wrap around trees and posts and boat masts. My mother, drunk, is even more animated than her normal not-normal self. Dressed all in white, she leaps and twirls along the sidewalk, her arms cupped above her head like a sugarplum fairy.

She inhales, sighs. "Do you smell that? How about we pick up some fresh scones and clotted cream from the bakery? I can make a mushroom omelet and new potatoes and berry tarts."

"Can we sleep first?" I ask.

She laughs. "Of course, silly."

My mother's favorite meal is breakfast. We often engage in long, leisurely morning feasts. We can enjoy this luxury because she doesn't have a day job. She is a painter. Nationally recognized. A gallery in New York exhibits her work.

She rushes ahead, motions me to follow. "Come on. Don't be such a stick-in-the-mud. It's a joyous night."

I don't like it when she calls me a stick-in-the-mud. "Circumspect," I say.

She doesn't hear me. She is in front of the bakery by now, peering through the window. I see what happens next in slow motion. *I see her reach for the door handle. I see her face distort. I see her recoil, slump to the ground.*

I run to her, help her to her feet. "What's wrong?"

"It's HIM."

HIM is the man who is chasing "us," meaning her and, by association, me. She refuses to utter his name because names, she says, give someone value. I have another name for him, the Shadow Man, because I've never actually seen him, and so, especially when I was a child, I imagined him lurking in shadows—around corners, behind doors, under my bed—waiting to devour me. I have yet to conquer my fear.

"Where?" I ask, my chest tightening, heart pounding. I see the clerk behind the counter. I see people sitting at tables. A family with two children. A blind woman with a German shepherd. No singular person stands out.

She points. "There. In the glass. His car."

"You mean a reflection?" I check the street. Nothing.

"We need to leave," she says. "Now." She grabs my hand and we run.

Once home, a small but clean apartment above the five-and-dime, she pulls the large rucksack out from under the bed, brushes off the dust that has accumulated over the past several months, and says what she does every time we move. "Grab your backpack. Remember, just five of your favorite outfits, a jacket and parka, a pair each of sandals, shoes, winter boots, and no more than three books and five valuables."

"What about my piano?" I ask. "And my sheet music?"

We'd found the piano the week we arrived in Erie. An upright with wheels. My mother pointed out it was next to a dumpster, a sure sign the owners meant to discard it. I had been stealing time on other people's pianos for years, and the thought of owning my own overshadowed my reticence. Everyone stared at us as we rolled the behemoth down the streets. We laughed so hard we peed our pants. It took four clerks at Woolworth to get it up the stairs.

"Don't be difficult," she says. "You know the routine."

I do, but don't want to. "My piano is valuable."

"I'm leaving my paintings behind," she retorts.

"That's not true," I say. "Won't your *gallery* come and get them?"

"Drop the tone."

I start to argue.

"Conversation over," she says.

She rolls her brushes in tinfoil, making sure to protect their hairs from separating or bending, puts her paints, turpentine, and linseed oil in plastic bags, places them in the rucksack's front pocket. I gather the assigned clothing, along with the blue ribbon I won when I was eleven for playing Pachelbel's *Canon in D* at the Indiana State Fair. Then I grab my three favorite books (worn from repeated readings), *Animal Farm* by George Orwell, *Silas Marner* by George Eliot, and *Sunset Gun* by Dorothy Parker, the only ones I actually own. I bought them three moves ago for one dollar each at a library book sale.

Just before we're ready to leave, as she does before every move, she retrieves the tattered box of sixty-four crayons from the dresser's top drawer.

"Close your eyes."

I hear the crayons hitting one another as they land on the bed, a waltz of hollow pings, their waxy scent comforting, and run my fingers through them. I never choose the first one I touch. I've convinced myself that the right one will find me, which it does. And in this moment, I stop being Maize, and become Blue.

Now we board a bus. It isn't the first bus we've boarded. I've lost track of how many journeys we have taken and how many places we have lived. My mother says the changing—our names, our towns, our story—is essential to our survival. She goes first. I climb the narrow steps, concentrate on my mukluks. During transitions, any form of communication is forbidden: talking, smiling, even eye contact. "It's important we aren't remembered," she always says.

"Happy New Year," the bus driver says. A fat man with round cheeks and a red nose. Jolly. "I have it on good authority that it's going to be a good one."

His smile is infectious. I note that my mother is already partway down the aisle. "Happy New Year," I say, and hurry past him.

She drops the rucksack on the floor, shoves it toward the window with her foot. Grabs thin blankets and small pillows from the overhead rack. I slide into the seat. Use the sack as an ottoman.

"You're going to want to sleep," she says. "We have a long journey ahead of us."

"How long?" I ask.

"Through the night."

"But it's snowing," I say. "I need to stay awake to make sure we don't slide off the road."

"You can't control that," she says.

I lean my backpack against the window, position the pillow atop it, snuggle into the blanket. Big snowflakes fall from the sky. I try counting them. Sound of engine revving. Smell of diesel fuel. The bus lumbers forward. A woman coughing somewhere behind me. Baby crying. Child singing. "Frère Jacques." I close my eyes . . .

A jolt. Screech of grinding gears. The bus stops. I don't remember falling asleep. I look out the window. Still dark. Still snowing. The crank and clap of the opening door.

"South Haven," the driver bellows.

Scarlet

The bus pulled to the side of the road.

"South Haven," the driver announced.

We gathered our backpacks and headed to the door.

"How far to town?" I asked the driver.

"About a mile," he said.

"A mile which way?" I hoped the question was clipped enough to avoid further conversation.

He pointed. "This here's Broadway. You'll turn left at the first traffic light. That's Phoenix. Best bundle up. It's cold out there."

We took our first steps onto new ground, a symbolic moment for me. None of the other towns had mattered. Town selection had always been an on-the-spot decision, made when buying our tickets. "Where to?" the clerk would ask. "Wherever your next bus is going," I'd say. But not this time. Though I'd known for several years that this town, and what would happen here, was my destiny, it hadn't been time yet. Now it finally was.

The bus drove away. There was no station or shelter, only a rectangular sign on a post. Better at least than some of our towns where merely a stick or a mound served as demarcation. A thin sheet of snow covered the ground. The wind was biting.

"Come on," my daughter said. "You're dilly-dallying. It's cold out here."

Dilly-dally. Those were my words. She'd been throwing some of my words back at me for a while now. When had it begun? Two moves ago? Three? She had always been shy, quiet. Easy. Never one to complain. All I needed to do was make our bus rides fun and adventurous. Every journey led to an imaginary place: Wonderland, Emerald City, the Enchanted Forest. We played the Map Game (which revealed the locations of long-buried treasures) or the Clap Game. "Close your eyes and clap three times," I'd say. And poof, there was the white rabbit checking his pocket watch while running ahead, or Dorothy and Toto skipping along, or Little Red Riding Hood picking flowers on the way to her grandmother's house while the Big Bad Wolf hid behind a tree. And there we were, mother and daughter, entering these imaginary worlds, losing ourselves inside them. Her face, her wide eyes and large smile, was enough for me to be transported right alongside her. To believe. Now, more often than not, she fought our moves. She refused to play I Spy or the Alphabet Game or any kind of pretend. And she was forever testing the Rules. Making eye contact with bus drivers, striking up conversations with strangers, playing the piano in the presence of adults. Five towns ago, when we lived in Savannah, Georgia, I caught her sneaking piano lessons from a teacher at her school. The same thing happened in Wilmington, Virginia Beach, and Charleston. If anyone was certain to remember us, it would be one of those teachers. My daughter wasn't merely talented; she was gifted like my father had been. My mother once said that when my father's fingers touched piano keys, they spun pure grace. How do you stop a child from spinning grace? How do you deprive the world of receiving it? But I had no choice. The Rules were not arbitrary. They were our life jackets. If we didn't follow them, we could die.

Blue (her new crayon name) ran ahead. I positioned the rucksack and followed. The mile felt more like ten. I hadn't slept. I was dragging. The straps dug into my shoulders.

"How much longer?" Blue asked.

"Just a few more blocks."

"Don't blocks usually have sidewalks?"

"Be grateful there are streetlights."

I didn't remember town being this far from the freeway, but it was so long ago that I'd come here with my parents.

"I rented a house downstate," my father had announced at dinner one night. "On the beach. I thought we could use a vacation." He had just won a big case.

"Vacation?" my mother asked. "Is that even a word? I don't think I've ever heard it before."

"Funny," my father said.

We stayed for a week.

It was the last vacation we took together before they died. It seemed fitting it would be the town where I carried out my plan.

As instructed, Blue and I took a left at the light. A slew of touristy stores and restaurants lined the two-lane road. The lights were on in one.

"The rental office won't be open for a while," I said. "Let's stop here and get something to eat."

"It's a drugstore," Blue said. "Do you plan to eat cough drops?"

Blue's newfound obstinance could be challenging, but although I chastised her sometimes, I tried not to do so too often. I liked that she spoke her mind. I considered it a sign of strength, and strong she needed to be as a girl in this world.

"It also has a soda fountain," I said.

"What's a soda fountain?"

"You'll see."

A bell rang when I opened the door.

There were tables, but we sat on the chrome and red leather-topped stools at the counter, and Blue, ever inquisitive, quickly learned that the stools could spin. For a brief time my little girl returned. It seemed the way of being fifteen: Sometimes she was old beyond her years. Sometimes she was a child.

The waitress popped over with menus.

"Fixing to get nasty out there," she said. "I'm sick and tired of snow. It's the third storm this month, for god's sake. One of these days I'm going to surprise everybody and up and move down to Florida."

"How can you move both up and down?" Blue asked. "Florida's down, right?"

"*Up and move* is a figure of speech," the waitress said.

"What's your name?" Blue asked. "Don't waitresses usually wear name tags?"

"Mind your manners," I said to Blue.

"She's fine," the waitress said. "I'm not really the manners type myself. It's Shelley. But people call me Sunshine."

"Why?" Blue asked.

"You mean to say you're not blinded by my sunny disposition? What's your name?"

"Blue." I noted that she'd hesitated. It always took her a few days to get used to a new name.

"Well then, what can I get you, Blue?"

"I'll have a hamburger."

"For breakfast?" I asked.

"Why not? Is there some sort of law against it?"

"You want a blueberry malted with that?" Sunshine asked. "It's our specialty. This here's the blueberry capital."

"Capital of what?" Blue asked.

"America," Sunshine said.

"Really?"

"Yup."

"Sure."

"How about you?" Sunshine asked me.

"Eggs," I said.

"Just eggs? Our bacon is world-class."

"No bacon. Just the eggs."

"How do you like them?"

"Scrambled is good," I said.

"Just brewed a fresh pot of coffee."

"Do you have hot tea?"

"Sure do."

We ate in silence like we always did. Neither one of us was a big talker. We lived in our heads. Any deep or intellectual conversations we had generally took place during Blue's daily lessons. Before she could even walk, I began teaching her about art history, the Great Masters, and how to use a paintbrush. Aside from that, we were like an old married couple, content to be in each other's company.

Sunshine returned to clear our plates. "Looks like you enjoyed the malted."

"It was really good," Blue said. "It tasted just like mashed berries and whipped cream.

"Yup, that's what everybody says. Anything else I can get you?"

"Just the check," I said.

She reached into her apron pocket, handed me the ticket. "I haven't seen you around here before. Passing through? You chose a bad time to come. What with the storm coming and all."

"We'll be staying," I said.

"Well then, I guess I'll see you again," Sunshine said. "You should head down to the water. The waves are frozen in place. Taller and wider than tractor-trailers. That only happens once in a blue moon. I figure it's a sign."

"Of what?" Blue asked.

"Hard to say. But mark my word, Mother Nature's got something in mind."

"Thank you for the hospitality," I said.

"My pleasure. Welcome to South Haven."

A woman was unlocking the door to South Haven Realty when we arrived. She wore a green stocking hat that sported the word SPARTANS. "Hello," she said. "I'm Theresa."

"Scarlet Lake," I said. "I left a message. About rental properties? It was pretty late when I called so you may not have heard it yet."

"I got it," Theresa said. "Crazy weather, don't you think? They're saying it's going to be a big one. The grocery store was packed this morning. People stocking up. You may want to do the same. Follow me."

The space was small, with two desks. Travel posters lined the walls. The usual suspects: Hawaii, the Caribbean, Pan Am. Blue leaned in to each one as if she was studying it through a microscope.

Theresa sat at one of the desks and began shuffling through paperwork. "Take a seat," she said. "You mentioned on the phone you're from the coast? Which coast is that?"

"East," I said.

She waited for me to say more. I didn't.

"What brings you to South Haven?"

"We needed a change," I said.

"Here we are. I have two properties I thought might interest you, a duplex apartment and a house. Both are within walking distance to town, and since it's the off-season, both are within the budget you indicated. Just so you know, after Memorial Day rents go up. The apartment will go week to week."

"We prefer the house," I said.

"Good choice. It's a lovely historic home just north of town, past the Dyckman Bridge, and it's fully furnished. I believe the location will suit your needs perfectly, across the street from Stanley Johnston Park, and two blocks to the beach and lighthouse. By the way, make sure you head down there. You won't believe the size of the frozen waves. Biggest I've ever seen. Folks are talking about sending pictures to *Guinness World Records*. I've marked the location of the house on this map. Here's the key."

"Can you give me directions to the grocery store?" I asked.

She pointed. "Just a block over on Eagle Street."

"Thank you," I said.

"No problem. If you need anything else, let me know. Welcome to South Haven."

Once outside, Blue said, "It's a wonder they don't just pipe that 'Welcome to South Haven' thing on the streets."

"They're just being friendly," I said.

"Look, the sun's coming up."

I peered into the distance. An orange glow was peeking through buildings. Soon daylight would spread through the sky and the large dense snowflakes, once night's only light, would paint a white-on-white landscape.

"It's glorious," I said. "I have a good feeling about this move."

"Are we going to stay for a while?" Blue asked.

"Maybe we'll even settle here," I said.

I knew that was a lie. I had a plan to carry out, a plan that required the help of a therapist named Dr. Henry Williams, a plan that on completion would require at least one more move.

"Yeah, right," Blue said.

"Conversation over."

Blue

I nearly said *Maize* when Sunshine asked me my name. Maize was my name in Erie, where we'd just come from. Both South Haven and Erie are located on Great Lakes, Lake Michigan and Lake Erie, respectively. There are five Great Lakes total, four of which—Superior, Michigan, Huron, and Erie—touch the state of Michigan. Only Lake Ontario doesn't. Together they make up the largest mass of freshwater lakes in the world. I learned that in school, not during my mother's lessons. Unless a subject is somehow connected to this book she has on art history, or the technical or creative aspects of paint, she doesn't teach it. She has been giving me lessons from as far back as I can remember because she believes "no one ever learned anything of value in school" and "school is a government conspiracy that is brainwashing our nation's children."

Maize was my favorite name, at least of the seven previous I can remember. I even liked the color itself, a kind of light caramel or butterscotch, my two favorite ice cream toppings. Prior to Maize, there was Sienna (short for Burnt Sienna), Orchid, Thistle, Rose (short for Brilliant Rose), Mulberry, Sky (short for Sky Blue), and Salmon. I was nine years old when my name was Salmon and fourteen when I was Maize. Doing the math, not counting Blue, I've had eight names in six years. I have no idea how many I had before that. I used to try to remember them all, but it hurts my stomach.

Remembering anything to do with moving, including moving itself, hurts my stomach.

"We need you to start eliminating food types from her diet," Dr. Joe had said. He came around our house for a while when my name was Thistle. And so I engaged in "not eating" certain foods for weeks at a time as a means to identify the cause of my stomachaches. The only foods I refused to *not* eat were variations of caramel and butterscotch, and so, since the stomachaches didn't stop, my mother (Dr. Joe and that town had been replaced by some other guy and town by then) decided caramel and butterscotch were the "culprits." For one whole year my mother wouldn't allow me to eat anything even remotely tinged with caramel or butterscotch. That year, my stomach not only continued to hurt; it hurt worse. On the anniversary of my caramel-and-butterscotch-elimination diet, I woke up irritated, walked to the grocery store, bought one bag each of Kraft caramels and Brach's butterscotch candies, and ate every single one. I still get stomachaches, but they never did have anything to do with what I eat or don't eat. My mother is forever saying I've changed, gotten less agreeable, more independent and opinionated. She blames it on my being a teenager. But I trace the new me to that morning I woke up and decided I'd had enough of no caramels and butterscotch, enough of moving, enough of crayon names, enough of buses, enough of being forbidden to play the piano, enough of the Rules. Not that any of it changed. But I figured at least my inner self had emerged, like a butterfly from a cocoon.

So now when my mother says, "You've changed," I say, "I've metamorphosed."

Speaking of caramels and butterscotch, I threw a bag of each in our cart when my mother wasn't looking. We are at the grocery store, walking up and down the aisles. My mother never makes a list. I make the lists. Her lack of attention to life's everyday requirements is infuriating. But since we just got off a bus and haven't even moved into our new house, making a list wasn't in the front of my mind. Just like Theresa said, the place is packed. Kids are crying or scream-ing or trying to crawl out of their cart seats. Moms are doing their best to shush and contain them. One woman just hit another's cart, which made the victim of the hit cart say, "You should watch where you're going. Don't you see my child is in this cart?" As if children can break so easily. The cart hitter doesn't engage, just keeps pushing her wheels forward, which I think is a good move.

"Only the essentials," my mother says. She says this every time we turn down a new aisle.

We've already collected eggs and milk and orange juice, bread and lunch meat, mayonnaise and mustard, hot cocoa and Lipton, canned fruit and vegetables, three Hershey chocolate bars, and six bottles of chardonnay. No salt ("makes you hold water") or granulated sugar ("bad for your teeth") or Coke ("full of sugar"). She sees the bags of caramels and butterscotch candies. Shoots me a look of disap-proval.

"You're getting chocolate," I say.

"Chocolate is different," she says. "You know that. The full moon is coming." *Full moon* is code for menstrual cycle. Ours has been in sync ever since mine started three years ago. She leaves me with the cart, runs down and out the aisle. Returns in a few minutes with a box of pads.

"What about wine?" I ask.

"What about it?" she says.

"Doesn't it have sugar?"

"Only from natural sources," she says.

I don't believe her, but decide to let it go. There is no arguing with people in denial. Or people who are addicted to something. Like her wine. Like my caramels and butterscotch drops.

The checkout line is long. "Should we cut in?" my mother asks, devilish look in her eyes.

"No," I say. Even though I secretly wish I were more like her. Less of a lace tatter. More of a dream weaver.

In addition to our backpacks, which now carry additional cargo, namely, six bottles of wine ("so they won't break"), we each carry a jam-packed grocery bag. Despite this, my mother skips and twirls along the slick sidewalk again, undaunted, as if everything that happened in between the night before—the restaurant, the bakery, the bus ride—and this morning didn't happen at all. Like always, I trail behind her. Also, like always, because she won't remember to, I memorize my surroundings. She used to be better about remembering. She used to be better about a lot of stuff. The street sign says we are back on Phoenix. We walk past empty parking spaces, vacant sidewalks, and paper-covered shop windows bearing handwritten signs that read, *SEE YOU IN APRIL*. We turn left at the light onto Broadway, then left on Dyckman Avenue, which leads to the drawbridge.

"Look, Blue," she says, my new name slipping off her tongue like marmalade. "The lighthouse. Isn't it magical?"

"Everything looks magical through snowflakes," I say.

She doesn't respond. She prances on, a puffy angel, over the rest of the bridge, past Stanley Johnston Park, and on toward our new house. All the time laughing with a kind of childish glee. That hasn't changed. She has always made sugar out of sand. She checks the map that Theresa gave us. "Here we are."

Even magic can't help what I see. I can't tell what color the house is. Is it the green that's peeling, or the yellow? The porch is leaning, screen door warped, mesh torn. A board is nailed over one of the windows. Gunshot? Burglars? Not to mention hanging from the eaves is a row of the meanest icicles I've ever seen. I peer at my mother's face. She doesn't look concerned, even though it's by far the most run-down house we've lived in.

"It looks like Humpty Dumpty crashed into it," I say.

"So maybe it could use a few repairs," my mother says.

"Or a bulldozer."

"Don't be disrespectful," she says. "Think of all the families she's kept safe and all the wisdom she's attained. *She's* a grande dame."

"*It* is anything but grand," I say.

My mother is forever assigning people pronouns to inanimate objects.

"If we didn't look so much alike, I'd swear the doctor gave me the wrong baby." (She says that a lot.) "I challenge you to say one nice thing."

"It's still standing?"

She puts the key in the lock, jiggles it a few times, opens the door. Sets her grocery bag on a table, drops the rucksack to the floor, stretches her neck and shoulders.

"I'm getting old," she says.

"Thirty-one isn't old."

The inside of the house isn't any better than the outside. First off, it's cold, and there's this awful smell. Mildew, stale cigarettes, and something dead. Mice? I shiver. The main room consists of a living area and kitchen*ette* somewhat divided by a lump of black metal I figure is a wood-burning stove. It doesn't look like it's burned anything in eons. The floor is dented and scarred, the varnish long since worn off. It feels wobbly, as if it could give way any minute. I imagine it swallowing me, splintered edges scraping my legs, torso, and armpits as I descend, the bones in my legs cracking in succession as they hit the ground of the crawl space below. A cat-clawed sofa and the aforementioned dining table with three mismatched chairs are the room's only furnishings, the table painted so many times it sheds rainbows. The remaining two rooms, a bedroom and bath, are in a similar state of disrepair. The tiles on the bathroom floor are loose and chipped. The shower faucet drips. A pair of pliers is duct-taped to one of the sink knobs. The toilet bowl is scratched and rusted. A spooled-pine bunk bed with crisscrossed metal platforms and stained blue-and-white mattresses barely fits in the bedroom. Window blinds bend every which way. Bare bulbs screw into ceiling sockets.

"We aren't really going to live here, are we?" I say. "We'll freeze to death or get eaten by rats while we sleep."

"You're being dramatic," my mother says. "A fresh coat of paint will do wonders." She starts opening drawers and cabinets. "Good, there are cleaning supplies. And a teakettle."

I open the fridge, start unpacking the groceries, while she starts the kettle. When finished, I fold the bags, put them under the sink, walk five steps, if that many, to what I'd guess you'd call the living room, and turn on the TV. A weatherman is warning about a major storm due to something called lake-effect snow.

"There's only three channels," I say. "And two of them are staticky."

"Good," my mother says while she pours the tea. "TV fries your brains."

She puts her tea and my cocoa on the coffee table and we sit together on the sofa and drink, and when our cups are dry, I lay my head on her lap and she runs her fingers through my hair. I love when she does this; it's one of my favorite things in the world. I wait for those little bumps that signal pleasure to rise on my skin, what my mother calls "goose bumps" because she says they resemble the skin of poultry after the feathers have been plucked. And while in so many ways I want to grow up, this experience is not one I want to move past. I want this part of "us" to last forever. Before long, I sleep.

A series of piercing chirps and claps wakes me. Nine in all. Why hadn't I noticed the cuckoo clock? And anyway, what do Swiss chalets and birds have to do with time? I wonder whose bright idea it was. My mother stands at a window. I join her. Outside, the snow falls and blows. Drifts over the sidewalk and porch.

"Pretty," I say.

My mother tries the front door. Caught by the wind, it slams into the wall.

"The TV weatherman said this was going to happen," I say. "He said we should be prepared to 'hunker down.' His exact words."

We stay inside for the next few days. Not by choice. Because within twenty-four hours the snow is nearly as tall as I. I have to stand on a chair to see over it. My mother insists being snowed in is "a blessing in disguise." She finds games in the cabinet under the kitchen sink, Scrabble and Clue. A deck of tarot cards. She reads our fortunes, tells ghost stories. We act out a scene from *Animal Farm*. She's Napoleon; I'm Snowball. "I decree there should be a full investigation into Snowball's activities," she says, and crawls through the house on all fours sniffing the floor for traces of my footsteps. While I play Bach and Mozart on my imaginary piano, she unpacks her brushes, mixes pigments, and because her canvases are yet to arrive, she paints on the wall, a little girl skipping along a hopscotch board. I stop playing, watch, and just like when she runs her fingers through my hair, the goose bumps come. They always come when I watch her paint. I feel a twinge of envy. I miss my real piano. She wears her white nightdress, rubs the brush across the wall, thick, gloppy strokes. "You have to be willing to waste paint," she always says. "Stingy with paint equals stingy with passion." My mother has never been stingy with passion. She lives big. Hard. Wide. Her body is so slight, so delicate, and yet the space she creates both in life and on her canvases is voluptuous. She dips her paintbrush into a mixture of yellow, paints the little girl's braids in such a way that they look like wings. In my imagination, I see my mother's arms stretch out, her body flying into the painting's sky, her white gown streaming behind her. And in that moment, I want no other mother, no other life.

That night, and the next two, I sleep like I did that first night, in my mother's arms.

On the fourth day, I wake to the sound of a large vehicle, run to the window. A snowplow is driving down our street scooping up snow, pushing it into mounds on the roadside. It goes up and down several times, until the street is smooth. Then some men in another truck start shoveling pathways through the high snow mounds, uncovering sidewalks. I see people outside their homes watching the activity with as much interest as I. This spectacle lasts for a few hours.

After they leave, I ask my mother if we can go outside. "We've been cooped up in here for days." We put long underwear on under our pants, wool sweaters, furry boots, and puffy winter coats. Outside, the air is so cold and dry it slaps our cheeks. "Where shall we go?" she asks.

"The pier," I say.

And so we crunch our way through sidewalks and snow mounds and snow-covered sand until we see the lighthouse. It is dripping with icicles, its surface barely visible beneath them, like that ice castle in *Doctor Zhivago* by Boris Pasternak. And I look back at my mother and she stares at it too, mesmerized, and for a moment, it is as if she too is frozen, and then she says my name, my new name, my Michigan name, and there is something about the way she says it, a certain lilt, a softness, like a kitten's purr, and I decide it is my new favorite name, even better than Maize, just as Maize was better than Sienna, and Sienna was better than Orchid, and perhaps blueberries are just as good as caramel and butterscotch, and while I contemplate blueberries and their natural, no-sugar sweetness, I hear my mother say, "Look at the icicles coming from the lake. They look like the spindly fingers of giant ice monsters, don't you think?" And though I don't say so, because I can't find my voice, I agree they do. They creep from the frozen water onto the pier and wind through the columns, and that's when I see those waves everybody is talking about. A line of massive frozen curls, like a never-ending row of question marks. And I wonder about the science behind such a thing. What caused them to freeze like that, mid-motion? And I imagine them rushing toward shore, swelling, rising, their high-pitched fury getting louder and louder, forming their final curl, their crescendo, their destiny within reach, but instead they are overcome by a force greater than they, caught, crystalized, and a feeling of profound sadness washes over me. And then anger, which I don't understand. I rush toward them, sliding and slipping until I stand inside one's arch, as tall and wide as half of a great tunnel. Something inside the ice catches my eye. A woman wearing only a thin white nightgown. Bare feet. Long, flowing hair. Hands bent into claws, the fingers bloody from trying to scratch their way out. I look at her face. Even though it's distorted, the mouth open in a scream, eyes fixed in terror, there's no mistaking it's my mother.

"I'm melting," I hear her say from somewhere behind me. She is spinning, her arms outstretched. She slows, falls to the ground, laughs. "See? I'm a snowflake."

Shaken and confused, I look back at the wave, see nothing inside it but dense striations of white and blue.

Henry

She was sitting in my waiting room the first time I saw her. She wore a puffy white coat that overwhelmed her slight frame, her blond hair sprinkled with snowflakes. Though it did not register then, her resemblance to my late wife, I felt an immediate familiarity, a feeling of arriving home after a long time away. It was the second week of January. South Haven had been having one of its characteristic blizzards, lake-effect snow.

"I'm Dr. Henry," I said. "You must be Scarlet."

"The sign outside your door says Dr. Williams," she said.

"My patients are more comfortable calling me by my first name," I said. "I'm pleasantly surprised you braved the storm. I've received a number of cancellations. And since this is your first appointment—"

I decided against finishing the explanation, because though she appeared attentive, her eyes were blank. As an analyst, I had encountered this before. I noted their color. Pale blue. Like the lake on a bright, sunny day. I couldn't say I had ever seen such pale eyes. They were striking. "Where are my manners? Come in. Come in."

As she removed her coat, her eyes darted between the leather sofa and leather chair that comprise the patient section of my office. She narrowed them in confusion.

"It's up to you," I said. "Some of my patients prefer to lie down, others to sit."

She chose the sofa, but did not lie down.

I sat on my chair, a leather cigar number, its quality and price superior to the patient seating. I had reasoned it embodied the relaxed yet scholarly image I wanted to portray, and its proration over my lifetime would equal mere pennies a day.

There was always an uncomfortable moment before the first session officially began. She was obviously nervous. She took time to get settled, scooting around on the sofa until she found a comfortable spot near its arm. She crossed her legs, began picking at the arm's grommets and shaking her foot. I could not help but stare at her. She looked to be in her twenties, but her posture and demeanor suggested a maturity beyond her years. Stick thin, but not at all gangly like the tall can sometimes be. She wore a red oiled-wool sweater, stretch pants, and tall fur-trimmed boots. Creamy white skin and rosy cheeks with nothing in the way of freckles or blemishes, indicating she had spent little time in the sun. Delicate features.

There it was again, the feeling. Lily, my wife, was not blond or blue-eyed, she was a brunette with brown eyes, but she exuded the same fragility. We met in college, in the dormitory cafeteria, my sophomore year, her freshman year. I was behind her in the food line, followed her to the soft-serve ice cream machine, watched her swirl the vanilla into a cup. When she turned, our trays collided, divine intervention, I thought, my chance to introduce myself. She briefly looked up, but our eyes did not meet. The moment was lost. I searched for her that evening at dinner, and the next day at breakfast, then lunch, then dinner again, to no avail. I was similarly disappointed the following morning. But at lunch I saw her sitting with a group of girls two tables away. She wore a sleeveless T-shirt and the same blue jean overalls she had in the food line. A friend who was a resident assistant saw me looking at her, said she lived on his floor, asked if I would like to meet her. I needed her to think I was cool. Had him invite her to watch me win at a game of table hockey being played on our floor that weekend. We made love a week later, married before either of us graduated, moved to South Haven to do my medical residency, had a child a year after I opened my practice, a boy we named Butch, after my father.

It was one of those less-than-memorable nights. Less-than-memorable until it was not. I had just finished my studies in psychoanalysis. Butch, three at the time, had gone to bed like any other night, but woke up crying with an earache. The doctor called in a prescription. I had worked late and was bone tired, so Lily suggested I stay with Butch while she went to pick it up. The police called to say there was an accident. I heard "drunk driver" and "ran a stop sign" and "she's been transported to Memorial."

She never came home.

I was a psychoanalyst. I helped my patients come to terms with all sorts of loss, physical and psychological. I told them there was life beyond death, that they would get through the pain, find happiness again. I said this because I wanted to believe it myself, but the truth was, I never got over Lily. I went through days, weeks even, keeping her in that safe place where I put her, but then, one day, I thought I saw her on the street, heard her laugh, smelled her perfume, or, like today, imagined it was her sitting in the waiting room of my office, wearing a puffy white coat.

But it was a woman named Scarlet, not Lily, who now sat before me.

She stopped fidgeting and looked directly into my eyes. There was something about her countenance, something I had missed on first assessment. Beneath her fragility there was a quiet confidence, a kind of breezy absence. It was almost as if while she was present, she was already gone.

"Why don't we begin with why you called," I said.

"I thought I needed an appointment."

"Yes, of course. Let me rephrase that. Why did you decide to seek analysis?"

"I'm not certain I actually am yet. I just wanted to try it out, to see if it might help."

"Help with what?" I asked.

"It's kind of a long story," she said. "I'm not really ready to tell it yet. Do you mind if we just talk for a while?"

"What would you like to talk about?"

"Have you ever helped someone escape?"

I found the question odd. "Do you mean metaphorically? I wouldn't say escape necessarily, but I do believe my job is to help people conquer their inner demons, and sometimes that can require a form of mental escape. A release of control. We tend to build our own prisons."

Her thumbnail picked at one of the sofa's upholstery tacks.

"Or perhaps you meant from a situation?" I asked. "A person?"

"No. Yes. I don't know. Maybe both."

"A particular person?"

"Yes," she said.

"I've helped clients leave abusive relationships. I've helped them leave jobs. Is that what you mean?"

"Kind of."

I knew I might be jumping ahead of myself by asking such a direct question, but I proceeded to do so regardless. "May I ask who this person is?"

"I'd rather not say. Do I have to?"

"You don't *have* to tell me anything."

"What do therapists do exactly? I mean, I know you're a head doctor. But how exactly does the therapy process work?"

"I'm a psychoanalyst," I said. "Not a therapist."

"What's the difference?"

"Education primarily. I have a medical degree and considered psychiatry, but was attracted to the teachings of Carl Jung. Jungian analysis explores a patient's inner world. Feelings, thoughts, behaviors, even dreams. You asked about the process. It's fluid depending on the individual and why they've chosen to seek analysis. Generally, patients come to me because they're in pain. Sometimes due to real-time issues. Other times they aren't certain what's causing it. My job is to ask questions that help them gain insight and to provide a safe environment where they can do the hard, and sometimes frightening, work of healing past wounds."

She cocked her head. "How long does that take?"

"It's different for everyone. It depends how hard you're willing to work and how strong you are. It gets worse before it gets better."

She looked away. "I understand that meetings between therapists, I mean analysts, and their clients are confidential. Is that true?"

"Yes, that's true."

"Anonymity is essential. I can't agree to this if there's any chance whatsoever that someone would find out."

Did I imagine she had stressed the word *someone*? "May I ask why you chose me, as opposed to another analyst? Did someone refer you?"

"I was just walking by and saw your sign. Do I need a referral? I just moved here."

"Where did you move from?"

"The East Coast."

"Northeast? Southeast?"

"Does it matter?"

"I suppose not." I wondered why she evaded the question. I opened the drawer of the end table beside my chair, pulled out an intake form.

"What's that?"

"Just a simple questionnaire."

"I would prefer there be nothing in writing."

"It's just your contact information and the like."

"Nothing in writing," she repeated.

"Are you okay with my taking notes during our sessions? It's standard for analysts to do so. I don't share them. They just help me track our progress."

"I read that case notes are subject to court order. Is that true?"

"In extreme circumstances, yes."

She grabbed a strand of hair, curled it around a finger, began shaking her leg. "I don't know."

"It's important you trust me. I understand that may not be easy at first, but our progress depends on mutual trust."

She did not appear convinced.

I looked at my clock, a nervous habit, one I had continually tried to correct.

"Is my time up?" she asked. "You said on the phone that initial meetings are twenty minutes."

"It's intended more as a kind of meet and greet," I said. "We have a few minutes. Have you given any thought to how often you'd like to come? If you decide to go forward, that is."

"Is there a norm?"

"Some of my clients come every other week, others once or twice a week. I even have a few that come every day. It's totally up to you."

"May I ask your fee?"

"I work on a sliding scale. Whatever you can afford. I believe everyone should be allowed to seek help when needed."

"Yes, but are there guidelines?"

"No guidelines."

"Once a week then."

I paged through my calendar. "I have this day and time available. Does that suit you?"

"That's fine." She stood. "Is that it then?"

"For now."

"Thank you."

She grabbed her coat and breezed out the door.

Through the small window in my office, I saw her exit the building below. I watched as she skipped across the street, down the block, and then the snow swallowed her.

I took a seat behind my desk and scribbled my first impressions so they wouldn't get lost. I considered these just as important to the psychoanalytic process as official case notes. In addition to my confession about Scarlet reminding me of Lily, and my description of her appearance, I recorded the following words: *raw, vulnerable, sad.* And one final word: *mysterious.*

Who was Scarlet Lake?

Scarlet

What an asshole. *Dr. Henry*. And all that blabber about the psycho-analytic process as if it were some precious religion and he was God. I came to South Haven to find him for one reason and one reason only: revenge.

He looked exactly as I had expected. Age hadn't changed him much. He dressed okay, doctor-like, tweed and whatnot, but he still wore those hideous glasses, large and black with bottle-thick lenses. Obviously, they weren't the exact same glasses. It had been several years. Which was worse, actually. You'd think by now someone would have helped him accessorize. I worried he might recognize me. Even though I was a child the last time he saw me, my eyes had always been distinctive. Large and unusually pale. I admit there was a small part of me that wanted him to remember me. Ego, I suppose. I wanted to see the recognition in his eyes, and the remorse that would follow. Guilt by association. I wanted him to drop to his weak, pathetic knees and kiss my feet.

How fortunate that he was an analyst. Made for easy cover. I was a pathetic woman with psychological issues. I was sad and broken. None of this was true, of course, but it would be fun to play the part. And he was a man after all. I learned the art of male manipulation early. Given my past, I didn't have a choice. Henry, however, wasn't easy fodder. While he wasn't the handsomest man in the world, he was what most women would consider a "good catch." He had a good job, nice house, and earned a decent income. I did my homework.

Those same women considered him an easy mark. After all, he'd lost his wife years ago and never remarried, so in their minds he had two penetrable walls. He was lonely and out of practice. But here was the problem with those women and their assessments: Henry was holding a big-time flame for his dead wife. Every woman believed that she alone could save a man, but where Henry was concerned, only one woman actually could. Me. Because I *knew* who Henry was. Our pasts were intertwined.

It had taken some time and soul-searching to commit to my murder plan. Though anyone in my shoes would have reached the same conclusion, and most likely much sooner, initially I wasn't sure it was the right thing to do. Not because of me—if it were just me, the decision would have been easy—but because I had a daughter to think about. Despite the challenges of our lifestyle, I wanted her to grow up as happy and healthy as possible. I didn't want her to experience the dark side of life. Like I had. But then I looked at it another way. As long as HE was out there, neither of us could have a happy, healthy life. Or, for that matter, a life at all. HE meant to kill us.

Actually, I was pretty proud of the way I handled the meeting. I was pitiful, what with that nervous leg shaking and hair winding. I saw a woman do that in a movie. The upholstery tacks on the sofa arm were a plus. Probably I should have picked harder. Broken a nail or something. It was funny how much of our discussion played out the way I'd imagined. Except that escape line. What did I say? Oh, yes. "Have you ever helped someone escape?" That just came to me. Sheer genius, I thought. And, oh, the look on his face. That was the highlight of the session.

I felt his eyes on me as I left his building and crossed the street, stole a glance at his second-floor window. A shadowy figure stood there, watching me.

Was he hooked? Not yet.

Curious? Definitely.

Blue

My mother left for a while this morning, to get some aspirin, she said. Only I didn't see her come back with any. Now she sleeps on the cat-clawed sofa. She sleeps a lot after we move. "I don't do well with change," she always says. I'm bored. I don't feel like reading, and there's nothing good on the staticky TV. I get bored a lot when we move. Because she sleeps so much, there's no one to do things with. I also get curious. About the Shadow Man. Because he's the reason why we move. I ask a lot of questions. Like, who is he? Why is he chasing us? Why don't we call the police? "You know we can't call the police," she says. "Why not?" I ask. It's always the same answer: "Conversation over."

It's her fault I'm so curious about the Shadow Man. Curious and scared. Sometimes I wonder if he's even human. It's like he's that devil in *Rosemary's Baby* by Ira Levin. When I got that book from the library, the librarian said it was an adult book and asked how old I was, which made me want to read it even more. I said it was for my mother. Though it was really good, and I couldn't put it down, I admit, given the Shadow Man, I probably should have listened to the librarian. I won't be reading it again—that's for sure.

She stirs. I wait a few moments, hoping she will wake because maybe then we can walk to town together, or back down to the beach to see those waves. Maybe if I walk from one end of the tiny, dilapidated house to the other, the noisy floorboards will wake her. I try that. Nothing. I cough a few times. Still nothing. Just then, the red bird comes out of the little Swiss house and shrieks. I jump. Look at my mother, still asleep. I grab the book I'm currently reading, bundle up, and head outside.

The streets and sidewalks are empty. The quiet is unsettling. I peek through tears in the paper-covered windows of clothing shops, gift stores, fudge shops and other confectioneries, pubs and restaurants. Some sort of country music emanates from a place called Cisco's. I try the door. Heat warms my toes. As if distrusting their luck, shivers scurry up my spine. The space is long and narrow. A bar runs the entire length of the left wall. Booths line the right. Behind them a pool table and pinball machine. A large stone fireplace with a steep chimney covers the back wall. The smell is a mixture of sour beer, burnt wood, and cigarette smoke. The source of the music is a ponytailed man playing a guitar on a small wooden stage. He wears a cowboy hat and intricate, inlaid boots. Brown and black and turquoise and red. I am the sole patron. I slide into one of the booths.

"Can I get you something?" The waitress's perfume, or maybe it's her shampoo, briefly cuts through the smells of wood and stale alcohol. Soft and clean like baby powder. She looks too young to serve alcohol. Her cropped hair is ginger. It is styled into thick fluffy curls, which flatter her round face and highlight her green eyes. Her outfit makes me cringe though: bright pink corduroy bell-bottoms, orange-and-blue Fair Isle sweater, red fake-suede vest with fringe that falls to her knees.

"Do you have hot cocoa?" I ask.

"Sure thing," she says and leaves.

Whiff of baby powder again when she returns with my cup and a plate of cookies. "I hope you like marshmallows."

"I do," I say while staring at the cookies. There are a reindeer and a Christmas tree and a stocking and two other roundish shapes I figure are ornaments. My mother and I made cookies one year, and we've gotten a tree before, but since we move so much, there hasn't been time or space or money to do a lot of things that normal not-moving people do like bake or decorate or collect reusable holiday heirlooms like stockings and ornaments. When we have gotten a tree, we've cut and painted circles and hearts and other shapes from my mother's canvas and tied them to the branches with string, and one time we made a garland from chewing gum wrappers that we added to over several moves, but it got too bulky and heavy to carry. My mother and I used to make things together a lot. I remember once the previous tenant of a room we were renting above a Sears and Roebuck store left behind some pink satin fabric. People leave stuff behind a lot. The landlord told us to throw it away, but my mother decided we should sew the material into fairy capes and cut and paste the cardboard inside toilet paper rolls into makeshift wands, and we spent an entire week turning people who passed beneath our third-floor window into princesses and frogs.

"They're left over from Christmas," the waitress says. "I kind of went crazy this year."

"What's he playing?" I indicate the guitarist.

"Willie Nelson," she says. "Billy says Willie Nelson's going to be a legend one day."

"Billy?"

"My, um, boss. I haven't seen you at school."

"We just moved," I say.

"Where from?"

"The East Coast."

"I've never been out of Michigan," she says. "Mind if I join you? I don't have anything better to do. Billy insists I come in even though most of the town is shut down. He's the nervous type." Without waiting for a response, she slides in opposite me. "So, what do you think of South Haven so far?"

"I really haven't seen much of it."

"In the old days we were a pretty important port town. Lumber mostly. It's because of where we're located."

"On the lake?"

"Lake Michigan *and* the mouth of the Black River." She holds up the back of her palm. "This is the Michigander's map. See? It's shaped like a mitten, just like the state. Over here on the thumb side is Lake Huron. We're here on the little finger side. It butts up to Lake Michigan. South Haven is down here, between the knuckles and the wrist."

"What about the Upper Peninsula?" I ask.

"Oh, yeah. That touches up here at the middle finger and reaches all the way to Canada on the east and Wisconsin on the west. By the way, my name's Hannah."

"Blue," I say.

"I can't say I've ever met anyone named Blue. Is it spelled like the color?"

"Yes." I almost tell her about the crayon box, but catch myself.

"Cool. What's that you're reading?"

"Hemingway's short stories," I say. I found it, and two of his other books, in our house (we don't bother to tell landlords about left-behind stuff anymore), along with F. Scott Fitzgerald's *The Great Gatsby*, which I've already read, and a ten-volume set of the Junior Classics, which I have no desire to read. Thankfully, there's a library in town.

"We studied him in Michigan history. He had a summerhouse here. On Walloon Lake up by Petoskey." She flashes the back of her hand again. "It's not where he killed himself though. That was in Idaho."

"He killed himself? That's awful."

"Yup. Shot himself in the head. How old are you anyway?"

"Fifteen."

"Me too."

"How can you work at a bar?"

"I'm the owner's daughter," she says. "I pretty much do everything around here. I'm not supposed to serve alcohol, but folks don't much care. Even Dan the cop is okay with it."

"Billy is your dad?"

"Yup."

"Why do you call him Billy and not Dad?"

"I don't really know. I just always did. It's just me and him."

"What happened to your mom?"

"She took off when I was a baby. You got a mom?"

"Yes, but not a dad."

"Did he take off?"

"I have no idea. I never knew him."

"That sucks."

"It doesn't really," I say. Which is true, but I admit to being curious about him. Whenever I ask my mother who my father is, she says, "Aren't I enough for you?" The truth is I've never missed having a dad. How can you miss something you've never had? In third grade, a lot of the dads helped kids do their science projects, so maybe that would have been a good time to have a dad, but my project turned out okay. Since my mother makes her own pigments from nature, and I usually help her, I just showed each step it takes to get yellow pigment from dandelions and blue pigment from berries. I got marked down for not doing red, because one of the judges said since I was doing yellow and blue, I should have done the other primary color, which wasn't too smart on his part because it seems to me a smart judge would know it's nearly impossible to make a pure red from nature.

"You'll go to South Haven High, right?" Hannah asks. "I'll show you around. Everyone will be so jealous I met you first."

I swallow my last drop of cocoa while thinking on that last question. My mother and I haven't discussed school here yet. We have discussed it before, ad nauseam. When we've lived in big cities, I didn't always go to school. City people don't care whether or not some faceless kid down the street is going to school, but small towns are different. They're "up in your business." The last thing my mother wants is for us to stand out.

"I don't know," I say.

"That's where everyone goes," Hannah says. "Do you want another hot cocoa?"

"No thanks. I should get going." I reach into my pocket, pull out one of the twenty-dollar bills I *borrowed* from my mother's stash. From as far back as I can remember, she's kept a roll of cash in a zippered compartment of the rucksack. She doesn't know I know about it.

"It's on me," Hannah says. "We should hang out sometime. Give me your phone number."

"I don't know it by heart yet," I say. "It just got hooked up."

"How about I give you mine then?" She writes it down on a napkin. "You'll call, won't you?"

"I will," I say. Which surprises me since I'm not really good at friends. "Do you know if that music store across the street is open?"

"Kline's? He closes down for a few months in the winter. Nobody knows where he goes. He's pretty secretive." She looks from side to side, lowers her voice. "They say he used to be a Russian spy, but he defected. That was a long time ago, before he played for the symphony.

He mostly gives piano lessons now, when he isn't running the store I mean."

"There's an orchestra here?"

"Not here. Chicago."

"Isn't that kind of far?"

"Two hours is all. We should take the train there sometime." She reaches out her hand to shake mine. "I just know we will be fast friends."

———————————

I decide to check out the stores on my way home. First stop, on the off chance it's open, is the music store. I peer through the window, but Hannah was right. It's dark inside. The only place that does appear to be open is the drugstore. It takes me less than ten minutes to walk through the rest of town, even with stopping and rubbernecking a bit. Still haunted by those frozen waves, I head down to the lake, and for whatever reason—lack of falling snow, lack of exhaustion from the long journey, or simply getting more used to things— they don't look as scary. I walk under their arches, peer through their ice walls, see nothing, not even a dead fish, but their massive size still makes me uncomfortable. And I find myself thinking about the time my mother took me to see *The Nutcracker*, the only ballet I've ever been to. We sat in one of the boxes in the farthest upper corner of the theater, a box owned by someone who bought one of her paintings, and I remember this feeling of profound awe and delight as I watched the prettiest girls and boys dancing across the stage, from my vantage point so small it seemed I could have flicked them with a finger, and yet so much larger than my own life that I couldn't even get my heart and mind around them. And I realize the same is true of these waves: While from a distance they are a series of pretty dancing shapes, up close they are so much bigger than me, and in that moment, I think I understand why we keep running from the Shadow Man instead of calling the police on him. Because, to her, he is so big she doesn't believe he could ever get small. And I hope this isn't true. I hope one day we can figure out how to shrink him, or disappear him altogether, so we don't have to run anymore.

It is dusk when I arrive at the dilapidated house. The lights are off. Hopefully my mother is still asleep. I was gone longer than I anticipated. The smell of turpentine permeates the space. She is crouched in a corner, knees to chin, rocking back and forth.

"Mama," I say. "Are you okay? Why are you sitting in the dark?"

She points at the wall. "Can you hear them?"

"Hear who?"

She covers her ears with her hands, shakes her head back and forth. "Please tell them to stop."

I switch on a light. What I see on the wall, her makeshift canvas, is jarring. The hopscotch board has bled into a lake. A boat is tied to the dock. The dimensions are somehow off, the boat much larger than the skipping girl or the dock, and it's distorted, as if it has grown out of control, a large yellow amoeba swallowing the room. When did she paint all this?

I hear her crying. She has never cried in front of me before. And I feel something I have never felt before, a fierce, all-consuming need to protect her. It is as if our roles have reversed. I am *her* mother and she is *my* child. And I go to her, wrap my arms tightly around her. "It'll be okay, Mama, it'll be okay," I say over and over as she sobs. But while I have always believed these words when she has said them to me, they ring thin and shallow as I say them now to her. After a while, she falls asleep in my arms. I carefully slip out from beneath her, grab a pillow and blanket from the bedroom, and sit back down beside her. Throughout the night, I watch her. When it gets light out, I go to the hardware store, buy white paint, and cover the wall. And when she finally wakes, she looks around the room, her expression confused.

"I decided to do what you said when we moved in," I say. "Give the place a fresh coat of paint."

"It looks nice," she says, back to her old self.

She seems to have no memory of the painting or being scared. And so I convince myself it was an isolated incident, that she is just scared and tired from seeing the Shadow Man and moving again, and that it *will* be okay.

And for a while, it is.

Scarlet

In the beginning, the voices didn't alarm me. They were infrequent and I could explain them away. I was twenty-one, living in New York, the first time I thought I heard someone talking to me. As a black Cadillac with tinted windows drove by the building where I shared space with other artists, a female voice whispered, "It's HIM." I remember looking around to see who said it, as I cowered and trembled, thinking perhaps I'd heard my own voice. After all, the voice had said exactly what I was thinking the moment I saw the car. It even sounded scared like me. My daughter was five at the time, and I feared more for her than me. I packed us up and headed to what would become our first town of many.

A few months passed before I heard a bodiless voice again, this one male. It was warm out that day. All the windows in our studio apartment were open. I was trying to relax by listening to a classical music station on the radio and slowly priming a new canvas—I've always found priming soothing—when I heard these words: "Paint a yellow boat." At first, I thought it had come from the radio announcer or someone outside, but then I heard it again, very distinctly, coming from the canvas. I startled, dropped my brush, stepped back, waited a few moments to see if I heard it again. Then relaxed. Laughed, actually laughed out loud, at myself. Obviously I'd drunk too much wine.

Weeks later, I heard the same male voice, uttering those same words, not once but three times. "Paint a yellow boat. Paint a yellow boat. Paint a yellow boat." Again, I pushed it from my mind. But the next morning when I went to inspect the previous night's progress, I saw a yellow boat sailing in a wide-open sea. I had no recollection of painting it.

Then, for two full years, I didn't hear them at all.

During that time, my daughter and I had run from the black Cadillac, from HIM, twice, from the studio apartment to a small guesthouse in an upscale neighborhood to a room above a Sears and Roebuck. We had spent the week pretending to be fairies. It was such a happy time. But of course HE ruined it. She was sleeping and I was painting when I saw the black Cadillac drive by. I felt the familiar dread and powerlessness. That's when I heard them, a faint chorus coming from my canvas. "Time to run," they sang. Then louder. "Time to run. Time to run. Time to run." The clipped insistence of their cadence resembling that of Figaro's aria, from Rossini's *Barber of Seville*.

I woke my daughter. We packed our bags, put on our pink capes, grabbed our wands, and twirled our way to the bus station.

From then on, the voices became a secret I could never share.

Then, one day, after it had been a while since I heard them, I slipped up. I was painting and my daughter (her name was Maize then) was attempting a Mozart sonata on the piano we'd found discarded in the wealthy part of town, a feeling of happiness washed over me, and I found myself considering what life might be like if we stopped running. I had never allowed myself to even think such a thing, but there was something about the moment and the music and the quiet in my head. A sense of fulfillment, a promise of life. "It's time," I heard someone say.

Without thinking, I responded, "Time for what?"

"Time for South Haven," the voice said. "Time for revenge."

My daughter stopped playing. "What do you mean?" she asked.

"Mean about what?" I asked.

"No," she said. "That's what you said. 'Time for what?'"

"I don't know why I said that. I was just lost in my painting."

But I could tell she didn't believe me. We were alone, the two of us, had been since she was very young. We knew each other better than we knew ourselves.

Later that very night, after seeing the reflection of the black Cadillac in the bakery window, after running home to pack yet again, after going to the bus station, instead of telling the ticket seller to send us wherever the next bus was headed, I said, "Two tickets to South Haven, Michigan, please."

Since our arrival in South Haven, the voices had become more insistent, and their chorus had evolved. No longer did they sing, "Paint a yellow boat," or, for that matter, sing at all. Instead they shouted, shouted so loud my ears hurt. "Kill him and put his body inside the yellow boat," they said over and over. They also suggested ways to do so. "Slice him open," or "cut off his head" or "his arms" or "his legs." All of which I dutifully painted, and truth be told, I actually enjoyed depicting him in these various states, imagining the blood seeping or squirting from his body. Because it was safe to relish, safe to fantasize.

Because he was just a blob of paint. Because he wasn't real.

But soon he would be.

Blue

It is the same old argument. Different words maybe, but same senti-ment. "My lessons are far superior and considerably less boring than what they teach in that brick box they call a school," my mother says. "Your brain will dry up. And what am I going to do all day?"

I want to say, *Paint.* That is what she will do anyway, whether or not I am home, but I've learned I can't win an argument with my mother unless I stay focused.

"It's a small town, remember?" I say. "Folks will notice if I don't go to school."

"They won't figure it out if you stay home during school hours. Re-member what it was like? When it was just the two of us? How we used to paint together and play games and talk for hours, how fun it was?"

I do remember. There is one memory in particular I keep close so no matter how irritated or angry I get with my mother, I'll be reminded who she is. It was the year we lived down the street from the toy store. I was nine. We'd walk by that toy store at least twice a day, when we left and when we returned from wherever we were going. Sometimes, even if we had nowhere to go, we'd walk by it. My mother was enamored with the window display, an ever-changing grouping of marionettes. One day we saw a sign in the window: *PUPPET SHOWS HERE.* My mother grabbed my hand, opened the door, and all but dragged me inside. The proprietor was putting the final touches on a theater structure he was making, which I later learned was called a castelet. My mother jumped with glee and immediately disappeared behind the castelet, climbed to the top platform, used the lever to pull open the red velvet curtain. "Is it okay she's doing that?" I asked him, my usual embarrassment over her lack of boundaries making me wish I could hide. "Definitely," he said. "Why don't you try it out?" She was already pulling Cinderella's strings. "You be the evil stepmother," she said. "But I don't want to be evil," I said. "Well then, make up your own fairy tale," she said. "Like how?" I asked. "Well . . ." She considered. "What if the stepmother isn't evil at all? What if she's just sad and all she needs is for someone to be nice to her." And then she made Cinderella hug the stepmother, and tell her how beautiful she was and how hard her life must have been and how grateful she was to have such a caring and smart woman watching out for her. Soon I was deftly pulling my puppet's strings and our impromptu theater took on a life of its own, and after a long while my mother said, "And Cinderella and her stepmother lived happily ever after." To our surprise we heard clapping and cheering and I peeked over the top of the castelet and saw that a group of families had gathered. My mother shot me a pouty face. "Just a little while longer?" she whined. "Okay," I said. And so we spent hours pulling the strings of the various marionettes and creating new stories with fresh endings instead of the old worn ones.

"It's still fun," I say to my mother and I hug her, and she hugs back with a fierceness that hurts my ribs, and when we finally stop, I say, "You know I have to go to school. But it'll be okay, I promise. I'll be cautious. And you'll still teach me, right?"

"Of course," she says.

This argument, like all school arguments, ends in a compromise. I won't start until after "we've settled in." Meaning *she's* settled in. The duration of the settle-in varies from town to town. I don't tell her this, but she's right about the lessons part of school being boring, though she doesn't teach all subjects better. Some she doesn't teach at all. But it isn't just about lessons. I feel an itch for something outside the silo that is our lives. For my mother, every year that goes by, every new school, every potential new friend, risks our closeness. That's why I have yet to tell her about Hannah.

Now Hannah stands in front of our school's red double doors wearing only a thin sweater. Always the same scent when I first see her. In my mind, I will never separate the physicality of Hannah from the smell of baby powder. It's the first week of March. A little over two months since my mother and I arrived in South Haven. One month since my mother went with me to enroll in school, using that same old excuse for our lack of paperwork. "It burned in the fire. That's why we moved here, because we lost everything and wanted a fresh start." And always a similar response and sad look from whoever ran the front desk, "Oh, how awful. Don't you worry. [Insert my current name] is welcome here."

"Why aren't you wearing a coat?" I ask Hannah. "It's cold out here."

"It's almost spring," she says.

"It's forty degrees."

"Yup," she says, as if forty degrees is a heat wave.

We head inside, go to our lockers, then homeroom.

Mr. Gordon, who is also the science teacher, tells us we are late. Why is it that adults always feel the need to state the obvious? I sneak a peek at the cute boy across the room. Wavy dark hair. Brown eyes. Our eyes meet. I look away. I always look away.

"Okay, everyone," Mr. Gordon says. "Quiet down and take your seats."

Like in a scene from an after-school special, note passing and whispering ensue. I brought my book of Hemingway short stories to read. I'm on "Big Two-Hearted River" I and II. Again. I've read every story three times by now. These two are my favorites. I read *A Farewell to Arms* (which was really sad) in between, but I didn't like it as much as the Nick stories, especially the fishing ones. I've never fished before, and in all honesty, I've not done much camping either, except in my mother's and my dilapidated house, but I decide that one day I will. That's another thing about books. They can make things I never would have considered doing seem doable. I wonder if the dark-haired, brown-eyed boy camps and fishes. Again, he catches me looking. Again, I look away.

Art class is next, which I enjoy, followed by math and science, which I don't. At lunch, Hannah and I sit with her friends Amy and Miriam and Colleen. They're nice enough, but I find groups overwhelming. The noise especially. Generally I just listen, but I've decided to try to enter their conversation. I've even rehearsed my opening line. But rehearsing and doing are two different things. I feel myself start to sweat, my breathing quickens, chest tightens. Colleen is talking about an article she read in *Seventeen* magazine about some boy named Davy Jones and monkeys. Hannah squeals, actually squeals, says, "Isn't he dreamy?" Everyone agrees. My knees start shaking. I take a deep breath and blurt.

"Have any of you fished in northern Michigan before?"

They stop giggling—my anxiety level immediately drops—and look at me, brows furled, mouths open.

"My family took a trip to Mackinac Island last summer," Miriam says. "It's so cool. They don't have cars there. We rented bikes and rode horse-drawn carriages. My dad says it's important to rough it sometimes. It builds character."

"Did you camp?" I ask her.

"You mean like in a tent? No. We stayed at the Grand Hotel. It's really expensive, but my mom wanted to stay there, and my dad gave in. She said everybody should stay there at least once in their lifetime."

"We went there once too," Amy says. "But we didn't stay at the Grand Hotel."

"What are you guys wearing to the winter dance?" Colleen asks. The conversation switches then to dresses and shoes and *nosegays*, whatever they are. Hannah had told me about the yearly event and said I should come, but I told her I don't dance. Which isn't necessarily true, but it's better than admitting my mother would never allow it.

I look for the cute, dark-haired boy again, but still don't see him. I never see him at lunch. There are two tracks, eleven thirty and twelve thirty. He must be in the first. I fantasize that he and I are having a meaningful conversation about trout fishing, which I am convinced, after reading Hemingway, is as much of an art form as playing the piano. It takes practice and nuance and the ability to listen. And quiet. My ears are hurting from the choir of high-pitched prattle surrounding me. I wish I were home. I wish the music store were open. I wish I still had my upright piano; I miss it so much. My mother once told me that daydreaming is a symptom of a creative mind. She'd gone into an oration on artistic temperament.

––––––––––––

"If you choose music, you need to understand that your life won't be normal," she'd said. "You may not see that now, but one day you will."

"That doesn't make sense," I said. "I already love music. How can I love it more?"

"It's not about love. In the beginning, yes, there is a passion, but it's the passion of the novice. Everything will be new and exciting. You'll experiment. Practice. Perhaps you'll lose some interest in other things, but you will still find pleasure in more than one experience. But the better you get, the more you hone your craft, the more focused you will become. Then, one day, your world will flip, and you will no longer have time or space for anything but your music. Days will turn into years. You will envy those who *live*. You will resent the very thing you once loved."

"If that happens, I'll stop playing," I said.

"You're not hearing me," she said. "What I'm telling you is that you won't be able to stop. It will become your master. Your only choice will be to surrender."

––––––––––––

I remember thinking she was wrong, that it wasn't music that posed a risk to my normalcy. It was her. The way we lived. I am irritated by the giddy laughter of Hannah and Amy and Miriam and Colleen, but in this moment, I promise myself I will try to understand it, because that's how I feel when I play the piano: giddy. I promise myself I will not close myself off to people and things that are different from me. Because one day I may change my mind. I may wish to visit worlds I don't understand at this moment. Worlds I have yet to even know exist. Like fishing.

Hannah decides to walk home from school with me instead of taking the bus. "My friends really like you," she says.

I know she's just saying it to make me feel good. The entire lunch conversation was awkward. *I'm* awkward.

"That's nice," I say. "I like them too."

"Do you want to hang for a while?" Hannah asks when we get to Cisco's. As I do every time I'm downtown, I glance at the music store across the street. Still closed.

"I can't," I say. "My mom expects me home. Tomorrow?"

"Sure," she says.

It's an excuse. I just can't do any more social today. I need to be alone with myself. To read Hemingway and play my imaginary piano. Maybe someday my mother and I will find another piano in a different alley. Maybe someday I won't have to pretend my fingers are dancing across smooth ivory keys. Maybe someday I won't have to imagine the roundness and richness of the sound.

Henry

While she was present, she was already gone.

It was as if Scarlet were a missed opportunity. Always just out of reach or slipping from my grasp. With the exception of her periodic signs of nervousness—the upholstery-tack picking or leg shaking or hair winding—rarely did she exhibit any emotion whatsoever. No anger. No tears. If she did not like one of my questions, she might say, "I prefer not to answer that" or "I prefer we talk about something else." She received everything I asked or said, no matter how direct or unpleasant, with a kind of cool curiosity, like a student who trusts her teacher implicitly. The kind of student every teacher wanted in his or her classroom. The kind of student who made a teacher feel knowledgeable and necessary, who restored faith in their chosen profession. Replace the word *teacher* with *analyst*, and it was understandable I looked forward to our sessions.

Scarlet and I had been meeting for nearly three months when I noted a small shift in her behavior, a slight show of agitation. The session had begun politely enough. She took her usual seat on the leather sofa. I asked her how her week had gone.

"Fine," she said.

I waited for her to elaborate. A full minute went by. She just sat there looking around the room, now and then shaking her leg. Finally I asked, "Is there anything you'd like to talk about?"

Her response was immediate. "Psychoanalysis."

"What about psychoanalysis?"

"Is it true that prior to the eighteenth century, people diagnosed with a mental illness were punished or confined?"

"Yes, before Sigmund Freud and psychotherapy, what he called the 'talking cure,' mental illness was often misunderstood."

"The penis-envy guy," she said.

I tried not to smile. "Why do you ask?"

"I was just wondering how often someone was misdiagnosed because they were merely different, eccentric, or artistic. Though slips into madness aren't that unusual for highly creative people. Take Van Gogh, for instance. We all know what happened to him."

"I suppose it depended on the level of madness exhibited. I imagine eccentricity or minor displays of nonconformist behavior may have passed for normal."

"How about now?" she asked.

"What do you mean?"

"Is eccentricity or minor madness considered normal for artists?"

"I didn't say minor madness. I said minor displays of nonconformist behavior. Why do you ask? Do you think it should be considered normal?"

"What do I think?" Scarlet asked. "I think you mean *men* who exhibited artistic genius. I doubt women got a pass back then and I'm betting they still don't. I read that sometimes merely because a woman was infertile or only had daughters, her husband would commit her. Postpartum depression could cause a similar fate." She sounded angry. Foot shaking, hair winding, flushed cheeks.

"I've read similar accounts," I said.

"You told me in our first meeting that you are a Jungian analyst. Why not Freud?"

"Freud believed that disorders stem from human behavior and repressed emotions about such things as sex and aggression. Carl Jung was one of his students, and initially built on these ideas. Later he developed his own theories, concentrating more on the collective unconscious. Instead of sex and aggression, Jung felt who we are is influenced by our lived experience. He was also more holistic in his approach, employing philosophy, mythology, and dream interpretation in his work. Interestingly enough, sex was the reason the two parted ways. Jung developed a crush on Freud and feared he was harboring displaced homosexual feelings." I was explaining Jung's ultimate repulsive feelings toward Freud, and Freud's insistence that Jung harbored death wishes toward him, when I heard Scarlet thank me.

"For what?" I asked.

"For agreeing to work with me. I feel certain you'll be able to help me."

"Why is that?"

"It's obvious to me that you're competent. And I'm always right."

"What did you mean by escape?"

"Sorry?"

"In our first session, you said you needed someone to help you escape."

"I prefer we get to know each other a little better before we discuss that." Coy smile.

I straightened, looked at my clock.

"You look at the clock when you're at a loss, don't you?" she asked.

Why did she make me so uncomfortable?

"I was simply checking the time."

She rolled her eyes.

I recognized the emotion rising inside me: anger. Pushed it back. My need to control was a shadow. It stemmed from a childhood in which I'd lacked any semblance of control over my environment.

"Is there something you'd rather discuss?"

"My running," she said.

"So you jog? I've heard that's a great way to keep in shape."

"I don't mean running in that sense. I mean running away. From places, towns."

"Does that happen a lot?"

"More than I'd like."

"Then why do you do it?"

"I don't have a choice."

I noted the response on my legal pad; she had relaxed her request for nothing in writing. Primarily because at the end of every session I crumpled up the paper and tossed it as she watched, though I retrieved and smoothed it after she left, to my mind a minor breach of trust as compared to my larger responsibility: helping her. I always took in-session notes on a legal pad. I felt it appeared more casual and thus less intimidating. Later I organized the data I had collected and added it to my case journal. Yet although my case journals served as my official documentation, I did not discard the session notes. On more than one occasion, I found useful information in them, information I had not considered significant enough to transfer at the time.

"We always have a choice," I said. "Sometimes we just choose not to choose."

"Why would we do that?" she asked.

"Any number of reasons," I said. "Obligation, worry what others may think, fear."

"I disagree." The affect had been flat, as if she were commenting on the weather.

"With what do you disagree?"

"I don't believe we always have a choice. I'm a secondary player in the situation." She looked away. "Do you ever feel that you aren't living the life you were meant to live?"

"Now and then I wonder whether I should have followed a different path," I said. "Made different choices. Is that what you mean?"

"Kind of."

She retreated into the sofa, appearing smaller, pensive.

"What are you thinking about?" I asked.

"Rapunzel."

"The fairy tale?"

"Yes," she said. "And the girl."

"What made you think of her?"

"I feel like her sometimes. Like I'm trapped in a tall tower that is sparsely furnished, and there's a cold concrete floor and very high ceiling, so high I can't actually see it. But then I remember the window. It looks out to a beautiful garden, but the garden, like the ceiling, is out of reach."

"Out of reach how?"

"It's several stories below me."

"Do you ever consider jumping?"

"All the time. But then I get scared because if I jump, I might die, and I'm not sure I want to."

"You're not sure? Do you mean sometimes you do want to?"

"It's not like that. What I mean is that for the most part I'm fine with my room. I'm used to it. It feels safe. But the garden doesn't feel safe. It feels like a trap. Sometimes I try not to look out the window because it confuses me, makes me question the limitations of the room. Other times I think the garden isn't a trap at all. It's the life I was supposed to have, could still have, and the room is the place that isn't safe. That's how it is with the running. Every new place is the room, and just when I start feeling brave enough to jump, I have to run again and there's a new room, and the whole thing starts all over again."

"Can you tell me more about the running?" I asked.

"What about it?"

"Why do you feel it's the only option? Could there be others?"

"Such as?"

"Let's get back to your Rapunzel analogy. How do you know that there's only the one room in the tower? What if there's a room below it or above it? What if every room has a window?"

"I don't understand."

"Maybe you can have both. You can live in the tower *and* have the garden."

"You aren't listening. There aren't any other rooms, and there's no way to get to the garden unless you jump."

"Who says?"

"The Brothers Grimm."

"We are the authors of our own stories," I said. "You can write your way out of the room. I'm not saying that will be easy, but we can work on it together."

She looked into my eyes. There were tears in hers. I felt a stirring and crossed my legs. What on earth was wrong with me? I had never in all my years of practice been attracted to a patient. And then Lily came to mind again. Lily and how we met, our trays colliding, our marriage, Butch's birth, Butch's earache, Lily going to pick up the medicine, the accident, her funeral, and then I was back where I needed to be, loving Lily, loving only Lily for the rest of my life.

"You're wrong," she said. "I'm not in charge of my story. Someone else is writing it." There was her anger again.

"Who?" I asked.

"I don't want to talk about this anymore." She rose.

"There's still time on the clock," I said. "We can talk about something else."

"That's okay. I need to think."

"See you next week?"

"Yes. Next week."

That night, like most nights, I sat at home facing overfull, wall-to-wall bookcases, always a warm and comforting view. I was performing my normal nightly routine: reviewing the day's legal pad notes and transferring pertinent information to my official session notes. One of the pitfalls of a small, private practice was lack of staff. My caseload, while not at capacity, was heavy, and given my dedication, and tendency toward overachievement, I spent most evenings and at least one weekend day doing follow-up work. There was a time I had enjoyed playing golf or shooting hoops at the gym, but after Lily died, I retreated from social activities. I took up escapism instead, reading light fiction like crime novels, generally the cheap drugstore variety, but now and again a classic, cozy, or new mainstream. I excused this passion as research, even going as far as to write off the purchases on my taxes, because as far as I was concerned, what else was a psychoanalyst if not a detective of the mind?

Butch was not home. He was at a basketball game with his buddies. He was not a huge basketball fan, but South Haven was in the playoffs this year. Butch preferred outdoor activities, especially fishing. He had won several fishing trophies. I was so proud of his achievements, and continually told him so.

I put down my notes, went to the liquor cabinet, poured myself three fingers of Old Forester.

The house's interior was somewhat on the cold side. In a previous life, it was an abandoned grade school gymnasium. Lillian and I had purchased the building for a song soon after moving to South Haven. She had insisted on living by the water, but our income and the price of lakefront homes didn't mesh. She was the one who saw the place's potential. She was like that, always finding the best in everything and everyone. We kept the exterior true to its WPA roots—red brick, double metal doors, high windows. Over time, we were able to renovate the interior to resemble a modern loft, with open floor plan, high ceilings, industrial kitchen appliances, a large dining area, two spacious living areas, and a bath with a good-size tub, for the Newfoundland we planned to have one day. A second floor was added to the back half of the space featuring a master suite, two additional bedrooms, and a third bathroom. It was my idea to preserve the original concrete floor, complete with the court outlines, basketball nets, drop lighting, and ceiling fans. Nice design, but not the warmest environment. With the exception of books or kitchen gadgets here and there, I'd neither purchased nor added anything to the space since Lily died. I also never got the Newfoundland.

I settled back into my easy chair and picked up where I'd left off. I was clicking along when I got to Scarlet. Questions cluttered my mind. When would she fill out my intake form? *Would* she fill out my intake form? Why did she run from town to town? From whom or what was she running? Why had she chosen South Haven?

I liked to think that if I were a fictional detective, I would be the one who dogged a case relentlessly. Like Philip Marlowe or Sam Spade, I might get stumped, but then I would have an epiphany or wake from a bender and *know*. But that was not how the therapeutic process worked. An analyst could not "solve" a patient's psyche. The best he or she could do was expose it.

I looked back on my notes and asked the same question I did that first time we met: Who was Scarlet Lake? Sometimes I was certain she was playing me. Other times she exhibited acute vulnerability. Both of these behaviors indicated childhood trauma.

A vision of Scarlet as a child popped into my mind. She was in a swing, long blond braids flying behind her. Her eyes met mine. They were pleading. She looked frightened, vulnerable, as if she needed my help, but I couldn't move, couldn't help. It was as if my feet were glued to the ground.

Where had the vision come from? I shook my head to get rid of it. Checked to make sure my feet and legs could move. Then I sat back, took a sip of bourbon, and added the vision to Scarlet's case notes.

Scarlet

I had been listening to him rattle on about Freud and Jung for twenty minutes. I know I initiated the conversation, but I didn't expect a keynote address. I only asked him about psychoanalysis because I was trying to butter him up, make him feel smart and powerful. I already knew all that shit about Freud and Jung and psychotherapy and psychoanalysis. I'd gone to the library and looked it all up so I'd be prepared when it was time to meet Henry and carry out my plan.

"Thank you," I said. I didn't know how else to get him to shut up.

Henry asked why I'd thanked him. I had to think about that. Lies weren't always easy to find. "For agreeing to work with me," I finally said, adding I knew he'd be able to help me or some such, more empty flattery, but he totally bought it. He sat up, pushed his chest out all peacock-like, and then brought up that escape line I used way back in our first session. It was time to toss a wrench.

"You look at the clock when you're at a loss, don't you?" I asked.

"I was simply checking the time," he said.

Bullshit.

He looked angry. He didn't like being challenged. What man did? They liked us inside their little boxes.

He straightened and, in a voice that he thought sounded non-wounded, asked me what I'd like to talk about. *Again.* It was his go-to line. I wanted to say something like *Why do you keep asking that?* but I needed to appear weak and pathetic, so I said, "My running." He thought I meant for exercise. Fool. He began writing on that goddamn legal pad, which I'd decided to let him do, to create the illusion that he was in control.

"We always have a choice," he said.

Now, I'd been doing pretty well at putting up with Henry's condescension. I'd been complimenting him continuously. I'd been acting needy. I didn't argue with him (too often). I figured thanking him and telling him he was a good analyst would buy me some mileage. I should have known better (who was it who said between flattery and admiration there often flows a river of contempt?) because he went all therapist on me, and while he rattled on, I felt my chest and throat tighten. But then I pulled off this most unbelievable save! I said I felt like Rapunzel. *Rapunzel?* I rode the analogy all the way to the end of our session. I even got tears in my eyes, which was confusing and disorienting, and I felt myself beginning to sweat, and the words scampered out of my mouth like mice running from the rain.

"I don't want to talk about this anymore."

He ripped the page from his legal pad, crumpled it up, stood, and tossed it in his wastebasket.

Did he think I was stupid? That I didn't know he took the paper out as soon as I left?

But at that moment I didn't care about Henry. My mind was on someone else. The owner of my gallery was driving down from New York with a roll of canvas and stretcher bars.

"Hello, love," he'd say in his British accent.

We'd open a bottle of wine and set to work assembling the wooden bars and stretching canvas over them. Then we would prime. After he left, I'd paint until dawn. It had been weeks since my paint-dipped brush met the tacky surface of a gesso-prepared canvas, and as always, after a dry spell, that initial moment would be the most fulfilling ever, better than the first taste of a glass of fine wine, or the first sip of hot tea in the morning, or the dip of a toe in warm bathwater. Most certainly better than the hollow feel of a brush meeting a flat, smooth wall.

Blue

The first thing I notice when I get home from school is the smell, fresh and airy, not the normal stuffy and musty smell to which I've become accustomed. It's the windows. They're all open. I see her canvases have finally arrived, a bunch of them of all different sizes. My mother is painting, her back to me, neither of which is unusual, but what is unusual, more than unusual, *abnormal*, is that she is naked. Except for her painter's apron. Before I even have time to make sense of this, she says, "How was school?"

"Boring," I say. I *hear* her smile. "Why are you naked?"

She turns, the roundness of her breasts spilling out the sides of her apron. I'd seen them before, completely uncovered, but somehow this partial exposure makes me feel like a voyeur. I blush.

"It's warm out," she says. Which is true. Everyone is calling it a heat wave. "Clothes are so restrictive. How about we head up to the drug-store and get a malted? I feel like celebrating."

"Why?"

"I sold a painting."

"Okay."

"Good. I'll get dressed."

While she is gone, I study the painting on her easel. A portrait of a young woman in a sleeveless blue evening gown that matches her eye color. She sits on a maroon-colored chair staring boldly, almost defiantly, at me, her viewer. I can't tell how old she is, young yet mature, twenty perhaps? The style of the painting doesn't look at all contemporary. Nineteenth century? Why is my mother painting a nineteenth-century portrait? In almost every way, the painting is a departure for her. She's employed short, tight brushstrokes, like Impressionist painters of the time. Monet, Degas, Van Gogh. Even the palette is different, vibrant except for the reds. She continually struggles with the reds.

"Her name is Madame Léon Clapisson." My mother has walked into the living room. "She will be the subject of our next lesson. I'm calling it Renoir's True Colors." She titles all her lessons. Last week's lessons were called Flowers and Skulls. They centered on the paintings and life of Georgia O'Keeffe, whose paintings I really like, and whom I've come to really admire.

"What's it a lesson on?" I ask.

"Fugitive pigment," she says.

"What's that?"

"You'll see. Are you ready?"

Town is busy, but not packed. Tourist season hasn't begun yet. The tables at South Haven Drug are all occupied. My mother and I sit at the soda fountain where we sat that first morning we arrived. Sunshine comes over to take our order.

"I haven't seen you since the two of you first arrived," she says to my mother. "I see Blue pretty regularly. How are you settling in?"

"Just fine," my mother says.

"Happy to hear it," Sunshine says. "And the universe finally brought you some nice weather. Best take advantage of it now because it won't last. March weather is very unpredictable in these parts. I've lived here coming on forty years now, and it's never the same. What can I get you?"

"Two blueberry malteds," my mother says.

I hear someone say, "Hey, Blue." It's Hannah. I scan the room, see Amy and Miriam and Colleen sitting at a table in the far corner. "Is this your mom? Hi, Mrs. Lake. I'm Hannah. I'm a friend of Blue's. We're in the same class at school."

My mother looks overwhelmed by Hannah's straightforwardness, but responds, "It's Miss, not Mrs., and please call me Scarlet."

"Oh my, sorry," Hannah says. "I knew that. Blue told me. Habit, I guess. My dad is my only parent too, but you can't get that wrong since Mr. is the same whether a man is married or not. Well, I better get going. My dad expects me at Cisco's. It was so nice to meet you, Miss, um, I mean Scarlet." Then, to me, "See you at school tomorrow?"

"Yes, tomorrow." I realize it's the first thing I've said.

After Hannah leaves, my mother asks, *Friend?* Since when do you have friends?"

"Just Hannah," I say. "She's nice. You'd like her."

We drink the rest of our malteds in silence. Once finished, my mother suggests we walk along the beach. *Good*, I think. *She's forgotten about Hannah.*

We head down to the lake. The beach is empty. The moon is full. No snow covers the sand. There is an eerie quiet to the night, a sense of anticipation. I hear the crackling first, thin and sharp like ice under footsteps. It gets louder, more insistent, and then I realize what it is. The waves. Over the last couple of weeks, as temperatures rose above freezing, their tacky surfaces softened, jagged edges smoothed, height spread, bulk thinned. Every day, I walk by them, hold them with my eyes, fearing their loss, fearing the pang of sadness I experienced once before, when my doll fell out the window of one of our many buses. A doll I never replaced for fear I might lose it too and feel that sting all over again. Sometimes I wish I had at least taken a picture of her because now I can't remember what she looked like. Did she have blond hair? Brown? Were her eyes blue? Green? Then it happens. In a matter of moments, the waves collapse upon themselves. And instead of sadness, I feel relief and joy, and I realize unlike my doll, the waves don't require a camera. Because their majesty and their melt are etched in my senses. And I know I will never forget the music of it. The crackle and crash. The plop. The swish. And just like that, they are rolling again.

FEBRUARY 12, 2014

Chicago, Illinois

46 Years After the Murder

The Pianist

I remember the day the waves melted as if it were yesterday. The music of it still plays in my mind. Frozen or melted, the waves are the only clean memory I have of that year. All others remain cluttered. That is not to say that everything about the waves left me with fuzzy feelings. Quite the contrary. I remain haunted by that fleeting image of my mother floating inside one, her hair and gown streaming behind her, her mouth open in a scream, her fingernails bloody from trying to scratch her way out.

Now here I sit on a smooth wooden bench inside the Impressionist wing of the Chicago Art Institute staring at twin portraits of Pierre-Auguste Renoir's *Madame Léon Clapisson*.

What was it about *this portrait* that had so fascinated my mother? Her fixation on *Madame* has continued to elude me. She must have painted and repainted it twenty times that year in South Haven. Not only that, she copied it down to the minutest detail. She'd never copied a painting by an artist we studied. Sometimes she borrowed fragments of their imagery—a Salvador Dalí clock or a René Magritte bowler hat, for instance—but only to "pay tribute" to the artist. I remember asking her why she was copying this one, going so far as to accuse her of cheating, and then, when that didn't raise her ire, suggesting she was lowering herself to the level of a paint-by-number artist, an accusation that would have, under any other circumstance, offended her purist sensibilities. But all she would say about her fixation on Renoir's *Madame* was, "I need to get it right."

The painting on the left is the original, painted by Renoir in 1883. Its palette is much less vibrant than that of its sister to the right. The woman herself is lovely in both. Round and fleshy like well-kept women of the time. Flawless creamy-white skin. Large blue eyes. Full pink lips. Wispy brown curls falling about her forehead. Hair pulled back from her face. Sleeveless, dark blue evening gown with a revealing neckline. Yellow elbow-length gloves. In her hands, and atop her head, plumes of white feathers.

On first assessment, three things about the painting strike me.

The first is her youth. I was fifteen years old when my mother was painting her, the same age Madame is in the painting, but to me, back then, she'd appeared older. Now I can recognize her youthfulness.

Second is coincidence. Why had both my mother and the curator of this exhibit chosen this particular painting to illustrate fugitive pigment, a heretofore little-understood reaction caused by the exposure of artists' pigments to air and light? Pigment fading over time was not isolated to the works of Renoir or even Impressionism. It is important to note that most of my lessons had centered on what my mother called the "cultured arts," and my primary text was *The History of Impressionism*. She relied on the book for other subject lessons as well. The juxtaposition of random page numbers created math problems. History was learned through art periods. English, through its words and sentences. Science, through paint mixing and thinning. Every lesson, everything in life, came down to art.

There is a sign on the wall with a good amount of type. I reach into my purse and pull out my reading glasses, lean forward, squint (as has become my practice of late), and read:

> *This digitized reproduction of the original painting illustrates the effects of chemistry and circumstance on paintings of the era. Scientists call this change in coloration* fugitive pigment *because the paint has not only faded; it has fled.*

Fled. My mother had used the same word. A word I reminded her perfectly described our lifestyle.

And the third thing? The reds obviously. The difference between the now faded original and the facsimile is striking.

"Once upon a time, there was no such thing as permanent dyes," she'd said. "Roots and resins were ground into fine powder to make yellows, greens, and blues. Snails were crushed to make purple. But vibrant reds were elusive until the discovery of a miniature insect called the cochineal, which yielded the brightest and most saturated red anyone had seen."

"Were they red?"

"*Are* red. Cochineals remain a source of red pigment, though when synthetic dyes became available in the late nineteenth century they became harder to come by. Cochineals live on cacti in places like Peru and Mexico. To protect themselves from predators, pregnant females produce a substance called carminic acid, or carmine, which makes their bodies red."

"But how does that make red paint?"

"Farmers scrape them off the cacti, and much like those other color sources I mentioned, boil and crush them into a fine powder, which they then mix with aluminum or calcium salts to set the dye. Renoir was obsessed with finding the perfect red and bought a large amount of the pigment, some of which he used for *Madame Léon Clapisson.* Unfortunately, it wasn't lightfast. So over time the reds faded."

"The reds in this painting look pretty bright to me."

"In the book, yes. The colors have been enhanced to more closely resemble the original painting. If you were to come across the actual painting, you'd see the loss of pigmentation, especially in the reds. It's like they disappeared into thin air."

"Is that why the reds in your paintings are dull?"

"I am yet to find a source from nature that yields a saturated red."

"You could just use paint from a tube like everybody else. It's not like we don't have any." Piled in a box under the rainbow table at that very moment were tubes of every single color that Winsor & Newton made, tubes she used for lessons and color matching only. Tubes that had accompanied our moves as far back as I could remember.

"And release all those toxins into the air? No thank you."

I wanted to correct her. Winsor & Newton insisted their paint wasn't toxic, not to mention she used turpentine and other solvents with labels warning *DANGER: FATAL IF SWALLOWED*, but there wasn't any arguing with my mother.

If you were to come across the actual painting . . .

And as happenstance would have it, here I sit.

At the time, I thought she was exaggerating about the reds, and making up that bug stuff. But now, with the twins no more than five feet in front of me, I can't deny the difference in the reds. Madame's flushed cheeks have paled. The chair she sits on appears more like dull cotton than the original luscious velvet. But the largest contrast is in the background. Its deep saturation has seemingly bled, leaving behind a festering wound of greens and grays.

"Madam," someone behind me says. At first, I think he is addressing the woman in the painting. He says it again, adding, "If I may be so bold."

An older gentleman wearing a fedora and pinstripe suit. He doesn't look like a security guard.

"Yes?" I say.

"I don't mean to interrupt, but I noticed your interest in these two paintings. There is a detailed explanation of them in the exhibit catalogue. I have an extra. Would you like it?"

Is he lonely and wanting to strike up a conversation, a friendship? If that's the case, he'll be disappointed. I don't do friendship. Not anymore.

"No catch," he says and smiles. Remarkably white teeth for his advanced years. "You're welcome to it if you'd like."

"Thank you," I say. "That's very kind of you."

"Enjoy the exhibit." He walks away.

I look at the cover. The twins stare back at me. I feel warm, start sweating. My heartbeat picks up. Do I really want to stay here, continuing down memory lane?

I decide to return the catalogue, turn, but don't see the older gentleman. He isn't behind me. He isn't anywhere. *Where did he go?* Surely he can't have exited the exhibit that quickly.

It is as if, like my mother said about fugitive pigment and the reds, he has disappeared into thin air.

I look back at the paintings, my heart now beating wildly, and start packing up my belongings. Coming inside the museum was a mistake. I rise, put on my coat. A young woman carrying a backpack that looks nearly as big as she approaches me.

"Are you leaving?" she asks. "I mean I don't want to rush you, it's just that I've been waiting on a bench for a while, and if you are, well, if you wouldn't mind, can I put my backpack on it while you gather your things? I'm writing a thesis on the French Impressionists for school, and it's hard to take notes while standing."

And I can't exactly say why—perhaps I've gotten attached to this bench, or it's my competitive nature, or my curiosity has gotten the better of me—but in that moment, I decide to stay.

"Sorry, dear," I say. "I was just stretching my legs."

SIX MONTHS BEFORE THE MURDER

RED: A primary color, or any of a spread of colors at the lower end of the visible spectrum, varying in hue from that of blood to pale rose or pink; a pigment producing this color.

Blue

In Michigan, the transition from winter to spring is a study in pitch. *Forte* and *piano*. Harsh and mild. Despair and desire. After the waves melt, the temperature stays close to seventy degrees for a week. Everyone hopes we've said goodbye to the cold weather and gray skies. Some even consider putting their boats back in the water. But then, as if it is a cruel April Fools' joke, the temperatures drop to freezing again and it snows off and on for three days straight.

Today the sun has finally found its way out. Hannah and I are walking to Cisco's after school. It's like an obstacle course. I've decided that what Michiganders call spring is in fact nothing more than winter's sweat. Snow may not be dropping from the sky, at least at this minute, but it still lines the streets. Dirty banks of frozen slush teasing their yearly melt. My steps cracking the thin sheet of ice on the roadway. When we turn onto Phoenix, I see that the lights are on in Kline's Music Store.

"I'll catch up in a few," I say.

I cross the street, cup my eyes in my hands, peer through the window. A face meets mine, shaggy white hair, soulful brown eyes, ruddy complexion. He smiles, motions me inside.

"I've seen you peering through my window," he says, with a heavy accent.

"I didn't know you were in here."

"I go visit my sister in Schenectady for a couple of months in the winter," he says. "Slow season. But I've been back for a while now. I live above the store. Just catching up on busywork. Inventory and taxes and the like. I'll bet someone told you I go to Russia. And that I used to be a Russian spy. All poppycock."

"Poppycock?"

"Foolishness," he says. "I'm Boris Kline. Most folks around here call me Old Man Kline, because of the white hair, I guess, but I'm really not that old. Just seventy-eight. Who might you be?"

"Blue Lake."

"Sounds like a song. How can I help you, Miss Lake?"

I try to respond, but the words won't come. I am mesmerized. The shop is full of pianos, uprights and grands. I want so bad to touch one, play one.

"Do you play?" he asks.

"A little."

"Sit," he says, indicating one of the piano benches.

"Really?"

He nods.

I slide on, cautiously.

"This here's a Bösendorfer, named for the company's founder Ignaz Bösendorfer. He started the company in the early nineteenth century in Vienna. It's an exquisite instrument."

"It's beautiful." I touch one of the keys.

"Do you need sheet music? We have just about anything."

I begin playing Beethoven's *Moonlight* Sonata, one of my favorites, and it is as if I've come home after a long journey, and I marvel at the smooth feel of the ivory keys, the sensitivity of their touch, the quality of the sound, and I imagine I am playing in a vast auditorium and that I have hypnotized each and every member of the audience, put them deep inside a musical trance that I alone can release. My fingers slide back and forth and back and forth, and I leave the auditorium just long enough to remember where I am. I take my fingers off the keys. "I'm so sorry. I didn't mean to play so long."

"Don't you worry," Mr. Kline says. "Pianos are made to indulge the passion of their players. Where did you learn to play like that?"

"A couple of teachers taught me a little."

"What teachers are those? I didn't know there were other music teachers in town."

"Not this town. We only moved here in January. And not like music teachers. Just schoolteachers."

"Ah, I see. I'd be honored to offer my services. Although I'm betting it won't be long before you surpass them."

"I'm not sure my mom will let me," I say, before I think. Then add, "It's just her and me. We don't have a lot of money." *Half-truth.* Her not letting me take lessons has little to do with money. She doesn't want us to stand out.

"No charge at all," he says.

"I don't understand."

"Well, young lady, it's not every day I come across a natural talent such as yours. Do you have a piano at home?"

"No, sir."

"If your mother approves, we can begin this Saturday. Say, ten A.M.? And you are welcome to play here whenever you please."

"Thank you," I say. While my voice may sound measured, inside I'm giddy.

"You on your way to get one of South Haven Drug's famous blueberry malteds?" he asks.

"Cisco's," I say. "I'm meeting my, um, a girl I go to school with."

"Well then, I'll see you Saturday."

––––––––

Hannah is sitting at what has become our regular booth when I arrive, steaming mugs at our spots. I'm beginning to understand there is comfort in routine. "Two hot cocoas with marshmallows," she says.

I think about what I said to Mr. Kline about Hannah being a girl I go to school with. From the outside, folks may say we are "friends" since we are always together, but though I like Hannah and all—she's easy to be around and doesn't ask a lot of personal questions—I'm still reticent to use that term to describe us. Not because of Hannah. She gets friendship. Because of me. I don't get friendship. Both because I have nothing to compare it to, and because it feels like a big word to me. Something that requires time and trust, two things I've never had much of. And in all honesty, I don't understand why she even likes me. Compared to Amy and Miriam and Colleen, I'm not that fun. Or talkative.

I slip into the booth.

"You were there a long time," she says. "Did you see Old Man Kline?"

I tell her about playing one of his pianos and about him offering to give me lessons for free.

"Wow," she says. "That's amazing."

"Isn't it?"

"What's he like?"

"Nice."

"He doesn't look very nice," she says. "What with those bushy white eyebrows. I can't believe he actually talked to you. He never talks to anyone. He's always shooing us out of the store. No one can understand a thing he says. Did he speak English?"

"Yes."

"Maybe he only yells in Russian. Did he say where he goes every winter?"

"I didn't ask." *Half-lie.*

The bar is empty, the faraway sound and comforting smell of the crackling fireplace the only diversion. Soon the regulars start filing in—Bobby the barber, Big Al the plumber, Joe Hillier the hardware store owner, Dr. Nichols the local dentist, and so on—and claim their seats at the bar, and before long cigarette smoke fills the room, and it gets hard to hear Hannah over the clanging of beer mugs, clacking of billiard balls, and blasting of country-western tunes from the jukebox.

"I hate that smoke smell," Hannah says. "It gets in my hair. I'm forever washing it and my clothes."

"I should get going," I say.

"What about *Dark Shadows?*" she asks.

"I forgot," I said.

And so we go up upstairs to her and her dad's apartment above the bar, and watch, and afterward I head home.

My mother stands before her easel, her back to me. While I don't like lying to her, I haven't yet figured out how to tell her about Mr. Kline and the piano lessons. I know she will get mad. So I head to the bathroom, wash my face, and brush my teeth, all the while considering my options, then I return to the living room and plop down on the sofa. I like everything about watching her paint, its silence, its mystery, her slow but purposeful sway, a tableau vivant. The goose bumps are gathering. Now it is merely an outline in shades of gray, an underpainting, also called *abbozzo.* It's how she lays out the general composition. She takes her time, applies just a hint of pigment. She is searching for form.

"Did you stop at the grocery store?" She doesn't turn around.

"I forgot," I say. "I'm sorry. I can head back out."

"You smell like smoke. Where were you?"

"I was visiting Hannah at Cisco's." I hadn't meant to mention Hannah. It just slipped out. It's hard to keep a secret from my mother. "Her dad owns it. A block down from South Haven Drug?"

"I know where it is," she says. "What do the two of you talk about?"

I ignore her disapproving tone. "Just stuff."

"What kind of stuff?"

"TV shows mostly." *Half-truth.* "Like this one called *Dark Shadows.* It's about this vampire that owns this big scary house on a cliff that overlooks the ocean. It's been in his family for centuries. He's been a vampire for forever, you see, and he's tragically in love with this dead woman named Josette. It's dumb actually."

"Why do you watch it if it's dumb?"

"It's kind of addicting."

"Why don't we watch it together?" she asks. *Code for "You have me, so you don't need Hannah."*

"That channel's kind of staticky." *Full truth.* I see no reason to tell her I do watch it and other TV shows here sometimes, but she wouldn't know that because she's sleeping. Her afternoon naps have been getting longer. "Maybe we could get a TV repairman to come."

"To come here?" my mother asks. "What do the Rules say?"

"No unnecessary visitors." I want to add that TV repair is necessary, but know she won't agree.

"Why did you brush your teeth?"

"What?"

"Just now, when you came home, you went right into the bathroom and brushed your teeth. You brush your teeth whenever you're anxious or thinking through something."

"I do not."

"Yes, you do. Why did you?"

I tell her about Mr. Kline and the piano lessons. Brace myself for her anger.

"Why would he just offer to give you free lessons?"

"He called me a natural talent." I smile proudly.

"We don't take things from people. You know that. What is going on with you? This is exactly what I meant about school. I let you go and you forget everything."

I feel the disappointment coming on. Of course she wouldn't let me take lessons. Why do I keep thinking things might change, that she might change?

My mother takes a deep, heavy breath, backs away from the canvas, puts her brush in the turpentine jar, swishes it around, wipes it with a cloth, swishes it again, repeats this ritual two more times. It's effective. She sets the brush on the table. Sits in one of the chairs at the rainbow table, her self-critique chair.

"Do you remember our lesson on pentimento?" she asks.

"It was just last week."

"Tell me about it?"

"It's when paint from a previous painting, one buried beneath the current one, shows through."

"I want you to think of your music that way."

"What way?"

"That it will always be inside you," she says. "But now it may need to be covered by another painting. A painting that *can* be shown to the world."

I am dumbfounded. Surely she doesn't mean what I think. "Are you saying I need to give up the piano? You didn't seem to mind when we found the other piano."

"That was different. We were far enough away. It won't be forever. Just until—" She stops mid-sentence.

"Until what?" I ask. "And what do you mean, we were far enough away?"

"Forget it."

I feel sick, nauseated. My stomach hurts. It's not fair. I just got a piano teacher, who praised my talent, who said I could play one of the pianos in his store whenever I want to. All I've ever wanted, all I've ever asked for, was to play the piano. How can she take this opportunity away from me? I hate her Rules. In this moment I hate her. "No," I say, surprising myself.

"What did you say?"

"You, of all people, should understand. What if somebody told you to give up painting?"

"No one here sees my paintings," she says. "And it's not as if I'm strutting through town meeting strange girls and taking lessons from someone we don't know. What if they get curious about us? What if people hear you play? Not just this Mr. Kline. Once they hear you play, there is no way they will forget you. How could anyone not remember the young girl who makes such beautiful music? Besides, my paintings pay the rent."

"For this dilapidated house?" I ask. "Why don't I just get a job? I see signs looking for help all over the place. I'll pay the rent and you give up painting." I'm choking back tears. "Besides, I go to school with Hannah and other kids. Am I supposed to bury all of them too?"

"This is exactly why school is a problem," she says. "You should have known better than to make friends. Remember who you are."

"Who am I? Don't you mean who do *you* want me to be? Does what I feel, what I want, even matter to you?"

"That's not the point and you know it."

"It's *him*, right?" I don't say the Shadow Man. I don't want her to know I call him that. She thinks anything other than a pronoun gives him value. "Why should I follow all these Rules when you don't even tell me who he is or why we're running from him? It's not fair." The tears are running down my cheeks.

"It's fair if I say it is. I'm your mother."

"Some mother." I regret the words as soon as they leave my mouth.

"What did you say?"

"I'm sorry. I didn't mean that. But please. It'll only be Hannah and Mr. Kline. I promise. And I'll tell Mr. Kline I'm shy and don't want to play in front of other people."

I wait for those two words, the words that mean there will be no more discussion on the matter, the words that ensure *I* will be painted over, buried beneath a me without music, a false me, a me who will suffocate unless, and this is a big unless, I am somehow able to escape all those layers. But the two words don't come. My mother leans her head back in a show of defeat. In that moment she looks very tired. When her head straightens again, she doesn't look at me, doesn't attempt to hug me, doesn't mention my tears. As always, it is her painting that draws her interest.

"Do you think it looks like a Renoir?" She continually tells me that the critics compare her use of color to that of the artist Auguste Renoir.

"Renoir's paint isn't runny."

"My paint isn't runny. They're washes. I'm building layers."

"The critics say it is."

"Who told you that?"

"You did."

"Not all critics," she says. "Just that one. That asshole Morris Abernathy."

I want to say more, that artists *are* their art, and vice versa, that her paint runs because she does. I want to ask her when was the last time we stayed anywhere for more than nine months. I want to remind her that I am not a little girl anymore. That she isn't my whole world. That though school is boring, I like parts of it. A lot. Like that dark-haired boy, like Hannah, and sometimes even Hannah's friends. That she's suffocating me. I need to find my own way. But I don't say any of this because she is no longer present. She is lost inside her painting again. I watch her watch it. I know what she is feeling in this moment, that escape into one's art, whether it be painting or music or carpentry or gardening or hiking or heart surgery, that symbiosis of body and mind, that intimacy with one's true self. And I wonder if that is why she hasn't said those dreaded words, *Conversation over.* She picks up her brush, dips it in a glob of brownish paint that resembles a mixture of burnt umber and yellow ochre, applies it to the canvas. I wonder what elements of nature contributed to the pigment. Flowers? Leaves? Bugs? She dries them. Grinds them down to powder. Mixes the powders with oil. It's a long and tedious process. Those goose bumps return, scamper across my back, my neck, my arms. I shiver. And I realize now even my tears are gone. I could watch her all day, but we're out of milk and bread and tea, and pretty much everything else. The only thing we seem to never run out of is wine.

As I pass by her, she asks, "Have we studied chiaroscuro yet?"

"No."

"Next week then."

———————————

And when I return from the grocery, what was merely form when I left is now a yellow boat.

Henry

The next two weeks with Scarlet were so amicable they bordered on mundane. For instance, we spent one entire session talking about the TV program *Dark Shadows*, which I had never seen. Pleasantries often bespoke a lack of trust. I could not help her unless she let me in. Yet I also could not push too hard. There was a fine balance between asking too many questions and not asking enough. Then, in the third week, seemingly unprovoked, her antagonism resurfaced.

"Do you know the term *chiaroscuro*?" She pronounced the word slowly: *kee-ar-uh-SKYOOR-o.*

"It has to do with the juxtaposition of lights and darks, right?"

She looked surprised. "Yes. The term comes from the Italian *chiaro* for light and *oscuro* for dark. The artist Caravaggio used it. Rembrandt also. By creating strong contrasts of light and dark in their paintings, they could manipulate viewers into perceiving depth and form on a flat canvas. I think that's what analysts do." Her smile was smug.

"What do analysts do?" I asked.

"They insert carefully considered moments of light into long periods of darkness. You could say they manipulate their patients, that patients see and believe only what their therapists paint. What do you think?"

"I have never thought about it that way," I said. "But it's an interesting concept."

"Why interesting?" She narrowed her eyes.

"I'm intrigued by the comparison to painting," I said. "I suppose you could say there's a similarity of purpose between the two, but manipulation implies doing something for self-gain. I believe analysts do this work because we want to help our patients, and sometimes that requires managing what you call the amount of darkness we allow them to experience. Analysis is hard work. Patients need to gain access to deep-seated fears at their own pace."

"So, you believe I have deep-seated fears?"

"I believe we all do."

"Why did you decide to become a head doctor?"

"I took a psychology course in medical school and it fascinated me."

"That's it?"

"You don't think that's reason enough?"

"I read somewhere that some people choose to be therapists because they themselves had traumatic childhoods," she said.

"My childhood is not relevant to our work here."

"I disagree," she countered.

"Why is that?"

"I think fucked-up people are more likely to understand other fucked-up people. It gives them perspective. Let's take you, for instance. Your father beat you, didn't he?"

The statement hit a nerve. She could not possibly know about my stepfather's abuse, could she? "What did you mean by that?"

"I was just messing with you," she said. "Do you like cookies?" She unzipped her purse, removed a white paper bag. "Ginger molasses. I got them at Golden Brown Bakery."

I was taken aback. Ginger molasses cookies were my favorite.

"Oh, don't look so worried," she said. "I can't read your mind. I asked the girl behind the counter what you liked."

"You weren't concerned about revealing you're in analysis?"

"I didn't tell her that. I said we were dating and I wanted to surprise you."

Before I had a chance to respond, she added, "I'm kidding, of course. I didn't say we were dating. I didn't tell her anything. It's none of her business. Besides, what's wrong with therapy? Doesn't everybody do it now?"

I had no idea where to begin. Her response raised many questions, not the least of which was, what had happened to her privacy concerns?

"Geez," she said. "You need to lighten up. It's just two cookies. I was only trying to be nice. And I'm sorry for saying your father beat you. He beat me too, you know."

"Who beat you?" I asked.

"Were you a kiss-up when you were a child?" She'd changed the topic. "I imagine you being that kid who always obeyed and did as he was told. I bet you were a teacher's pet."

I ignored the statement. "What were you like as a child?"

"What was I like? I was a pain in the ass. I didn't listen to or do anything anyone told me. I thought everyone was full of shit and I was right. People are out for themselves. They don't want to get involved. They see a withdrawn child with bruises on her body, and they don't say or do anything about it."

"Bruises? Bruises from what?"

"I was joking."

Kidding and joking. Flippancy. Another way to keep people at a distance.

"You're safe here," I said. "Would you like to talk about it?"

"Our time is up," she said while grabbing her bag.

I looked at the clock.

"My next patient isn't due until one. I think we need to talk for a few more minutes. To make certain you are okay."

"I'd rather not. You said fifty minutes, so that's what I plan for."

"Next week then?"

She left without responding.

As always, I watched her through my office window. She waited for a car to go by, sprinted across the street and out of sight, and all the while I was processing our conversation. Her needling and challenging. Her contrariness. But I knew that while Scarlet had directed her anger at me, I was not its target. She was projecting her negative feelings about someone else, usually a primary childhood relationship, onto me. In the analytic process, this is called *transference*. We had passed a milestone. The question was, with whom was she really angry?

While reviewing my session notes that night, I came across Scarlet's statement about my father beating me and again I wondered why she'd said it. Given the tenor of the session, probably she just wanted to rile me and had no idea she hit a nerve. The truth was, my *step*father (a term I use loosely because the two of us never shared one iota of a father/son relationship) *did* beat me when I was a child. He also beat my mother. I did my best to shield her. One time, however, my attempt at heroism resulted not only in a broken jaw and arm, but also enrollment in an all-boys boarding school several hours from home, where I could no longer protect her.

"The boy is too unruly and rambunctious for his sickly mother," my stepfather told the provost.

It was a lie. My mother was weak, but not sickly. Marriage to an abusive man had depleted her energy and self-esteem.

I was at Andrews Academy, my boarding school, the day she died. I was called out of math class by Mrs. Blankenship, the school secretary, and told to follow her to the library. A man in a three-piece suit sat beside the provost.

"Henry," the provost said. "This is Mr. Pierce, your father's attorney. Why don't you take a seat? I'm afraid he has some bad news."

Mr. Pierce wasted no time. "I'm sorry to tell you that your mother has passed away. She took a fall down the stairs and broke her neck."

Took a fall down the stairs and broke her neck. As if that sort of thing happened every day.

"She didn't fall," I said. "*He* pushed her." I choked back tears.

"Who pushed her, son?" the provost asked.

"My *step*father."

"Now, I know you're upset, young man," Mr. Pierce said. "And sometimes when we're upset, we look for someone to blame, but I assure you it was an accident. Your father wasn't home at the time."

"He's not my father," I said. My father had died of an aneurysm when I was eleven.

Mr. Pierce continued. "It appears she was carrying a laundry basket and lost her footing." He cleared his throat. "Your father wanted me to tell you that this situation doesn't affect your studies here at Andrews Academy. He will continue to pay your tuition and living expenses, and if you'd like to return to the estate now and again, on holidays and the like, you're welcome to. With prior approval."

"I told you he's not my father." I hit my fist on the table. "That property has been in my mother's family for generations. He has no right to it."

The provost put his hand on my shoulder. "I understand you're upset, son, but you need to calm down. I'm certain Mr. Pierce here is handling matters."

I ignored the statement. I knew who my stepfather was; they didn't. "What about her funeral?"

Mr. Pierce and the provost shared a guilty look. "Again, I'm sorry," Mr. Pierce said. "It was her preference not to have a funeral, nor to be buried in the ground. She was cremated."

"When?" I asked.

"Over a week ago, I'm afraid."

I wanted to say, *Don't you see what he's doing? Why else would he have waited to tell me?* But I did not. I said nothing more. My *step*father was charming and manipulative, one of those guys who knows just how to play people. Even as a child, I knew who and what he was the moment my mother brought him home for dinner, though I didn't know the psychological term for it then, a *narcissistic sociopath*. I warned her about him, but she said I would not like any man she brought home. That no one could replace my father. That part was true. My *step*father preyed upon her, a young widow with a nice house and money, constantly told her how beautiful she was, made her meals, bought her gifts. She was lonely, flattered. She married him only two months after that first dinner. After that, things changed. He requested she add his name to her bank account. When she resisted, his temper flared, so she gave in. He stopped telling her how beautiful she was. He called her ugly and stupid. She cried. He got angrier. Then he started hitting her. And, before long, me.

When that meeting with the provost and attorney ended, I returned to class and went about my day. But that night, I turned on my side, put my pillow over my head, and silently, so my roommate would not hear, cried myself to sleep. I never saw my *step*father again, the invitation to visit the only home I had ever known was yet another lie, an act to fool the two of them into believing he cared, and one day Mr. Pierce called to tell me my *step*father (the man who had married into my mother's money, who prior to their marriage had no property or savings of his own, who stole what should have been my rightful inheritance) had chosen to alter his financial arrangement with me. Mr. Pierce's exact words were, "Your stepfather has chosen to discontinue his support." He provided reasons. He had never legally adopted me. He now managed the family estate, so how money was spent was his choice. He had been more than generous by sending me to such a fine school. He would provide a check to Andrews that covered only my remaining tuition, and room and board. There would be no allowance for clothing or personal needs, and once I graduated I would be completely on my own.

My anger propelled me forward. I studied hard, got scholarships to college, and saved for medical school. When I turned twenty-one, I received a letter from a different attorney, a Mr. Jeffrey Corrigan, Esquire, a friend of my late father's, who informed me that three months after my mother married my *step*father, she had transferred a large portion of her estate into a separate account and established a trust fund for me. I quickly did the math: That would have been right around the time he started hitting her. Even better, though my *step*father was allowed to live in our family house, he had no claim to the property beneath and surrounding it, and upon his death the house would revert back to me. I felt lighter than I had in years. The fact that my mother had not only realized who he was (why else would she have transferred the money?) but had taken steps to protect our family's legacy, and me, her son, told me she had reclaimed her power. I felt connected to her in a way I hadn't in a long time.

After that, whenever I imagined my *step*father's reaction to that news, I felt a smug satisfaction. My only regret was that I was not there to see the look on his face when he read Mr. Corrigan's letter. How had he felt when he realized my mother had outsmarted him? That his whole sordid scheme had backfired? Though I knew, since Corrigan hadn't told me otherwise, that he was still alive, I looked forward to the day the bastard died. And I hoped whatever killed him hurt like hell.

Scarlet

It was Week 15, which, according to my graph, was when I was to introduce Anger into my interactions with Henry. I began creating the graph when I found out about Henry. Over time I refined it, but I stuck to the general timeline. I'd been looking so forward to this day. Henry had been engaging in the same boring song and dance for weeks. I'd been filling time. Talking about whatever I could think of. Blue loved that stupid *Dark Shadows* show. Who knew you could talk about vampires for fifty minutes straight? I get most of my material from Blue. With the exception of the days I met with Henry, which was also when I restocked my wine and purchased other essentials, I didn't get out of the house, and I couldn't risk talking about myself for fear I'd slip and he'd figure out who I was.

The problem was, I didn't anticipate *actually* getting angry.

It started with the cookies and that surprised look he got on his face, like he was more worried about what people might say than he was about me. "He beat me too, you know," I said. I wanted to shock him. And then I immediately wished I hadn't said it because it wasn't time yet and I didn't want Henry asking me about it, so I deflected by pouncing on him. I called him a teacher's pet and a bad analyst and god knows what else. I hardly remember what I said. I'd never been good with anger.

Then he asked what I was like as a child, and I said I was a pain in the ass, but I wasn't. I couldn't be. The man who raised me, not my father, did beat me. He hurt me in ways a little girl should never be hurt. I was five years old when he took me. In the beginning, he kept me locked in a pink room. Pink walls, pink carpeting, pink bureau and vanity, pink bedspread, pink teddy bear. Later, after I'd "acclimated" (his word)—I'd call it "surrendered"—I was allowed more freedom, but he kept me within his sight. He was a traveling salesman, sold encyclopedias. When he wasn't traveling, he worked out of the house. When he was, he brought me along, paraded me around to various colleagues, told potential buyers that his wife had died so they'd feel sorry for him, called me "Daddy's pretty little girl." More pink. Dresses and coats and socks and sweaters and ribbons.

I didn't like thinking about the past, I definitely wasn't ready to talk about it yet, both because, per my graph, my well-considered graph, the timing wasn't right, and because I had to be there for Blue. I couldn't fall apart. I couldn't simply (as Henry had said during our first appointment) "overcome what was stopping me from becoming my best self." Did he even know what he was talking about when he said that? How arrogant that statement was? He had no clue what was "stopping me," and yet he just threw out those words like I had the flu or something, like aspirin would cure me.

Believe me, I wished all I needed was aspirin. I wished I could just vomit all those years on Henry's shoes.

Pink walls, pink carpeting, pink bureau and vanity, pink bedspread, pink clothes. And a fucking pink teddy bear that I despised.

I came to South Haven to find Henry because the voices told me it was time, but sooner or later, I would have come regardless. (After all, *I* created the graph.) They had just given me a little push.

Blue

My mother no longer fights my piano lessons. She rarely argues with me about anything. We don't do our elaborate breakfasts, nor have we fallen asleep in each other's arms. All she does is paint. I have to make her eat and take baths. She sleeps more too. What's scary is that she'll be painting, then run to the sofa and immediately fall asleep, leaving me to cover her mixed pigments with cellophane and clean her brushes. Then there's those voices. She tries to pretend there aren't any, but I catch her covering her ears and shaking her head. It's like the old her is disappearing, just like that paint we studied, that fugitive pigment.

It's easy for me to put all of this out of my mind though, because of school and my piano lessons, which Mr. Kline keeps increasing. By now, once a week on Saturday has turned into two additional afternoons after school. "Three times a week is the difference between great and exceptional," he says. I wonder how many days a week is the difference between exceptional and brilliant.

"Let us tiptoe through the composers," Mr. Kline had said during my first lesson. "We will attempt each piece three times, while studying the composer's homeland and childhood, what prompted their love of music, and stylistic considerations, and then we will start anew, perhaps homing in on some pieces over others, and over time you will see how you've improved." This translated to the sonatas of Chopin, Bach, and Scarlatti, then on to Beethoven's *Waldstein*, Debussy's *Clair de Lune*, Ravel's *Jeux d'eau*, Scriabin's Etude in C-Sharp Minor, and, finally, Mussorgsky's *Pictures at an Exhibition*. But it was that last piece, the Mussorgsky, that both broke and delivered me. "It is a musical tribute to Mussorgsky's good friend, the Russian artist Viktor Hartmann, who died when he was thirty-nine," Mr. Kline had said the first time I attempted the piece. That was eight lessons ago. He added, "The piece is meant to capture the experience of viewing the 1874 exhibition arranged in Hartmann's honor at the Academy of Fine Arts in St. Petersburg. I want you to play not as if you see each drawing, each watercolor, but as if they are a part of you. As if every curve of the pen, every stroke of the brush, is inside you. Sometimes reading the music isn't enough. You must *know* it." I was perplexed, asked him how I was supposed to do that. "Knowing Hartmann's art might be a start," he responded. "You mean the drawings and paintings? But aren't they in Russia?" I asked. "That's what books are for," he said. And so I asked the library to order a book for me, and I studied "every curve of the pen, every stroke of the brush." Confident my heart and fingers *knew* the pictures, I told Mr. Kline I was ready to attempt the piece again. Deafening silence. Then these six words: "Confidence is vanity. Art requires humility."

For a long while his words weighed on my attempts at the Mussorgsky, but today on my walk to town I feel a lightness I haven't before. Immediately upon sitting on the piano bench, before Mr. Kline even greets me, I begin the Mussorgsky again. And this time, as my fingers glide, I hear and feel nothing but music. I am less than humble. I am no one. I am a fragment of Viktor Hartmann's pencil. I press the keys, create fluid lines of color and energy.

"Perfection," I hear Mr. Kline say from somewhere far away.

Once outside, it takes several minutes for me to find my way back to the world, and even then, I am only part of me. I take extra care crossing the street. I am all the way in front of South Haven Drug when the brightness registers. The sun is shining, the sky a clear, whitewashed blue. Hannah sits at a window table sipping a malted.

"I already ordered yours," she says. "How was practice?"

"Good." I always say good, mostly because I don't know how to explain the combined feeling of peace and exhilaration. One time I tried, but Hannah's eyes glazed over.

"Isn't this weather divine?" she asks. Hannah uses the word *divine* a lot (along with a periodic *fab*, *groovy*, or *dreamy*). She says all the hippies are using these words. I envy Hannah's knowledge of popular culture because it seems to be a normal teenager thing.

Just then, my mother walks by. Since when does she leave the house? She crosses the street. Enters a door sandwiched between a ladies' clothing store and a beachy gift shop. Minutes pass, fifteen, thirty. I hear Hannah's voice, snippets of sentences—math test, cheerleading tryouts, *Dark Shadows*—that merely require periodic nods. I look at the clock behind the counter—an entire hour has gone by—then back at the building. A door opening. My mother exits, walks straight toward us.

"Duck," I say to Hannah.

"Why?"

"Just do it."

I count to sixty—*one a penny, two a penny, three a penny*—raise my head. "Coast clear," I say.

"Why were we hiding?" Hannah asks.

I tell her about seeing my mother.

Hannah has only met my mother that one time at South Haven Drug, the night we went out to celebrate her selling a painting, the same night the waves melted. I've told Hannah some things about my mother, like that she is a painter and doesn't like being interrupted, so she'll understand why I never ask her over to our house. *Half-truth.* But I probably didn't need to worry. As I've come to know Hannah, I've realized she isn't that curious. She's one of those people whose brain jumps around. Sometimes it's hard to keep up with her.

"What's the big deal if she sees us?"

"I just didn't want her to. She came from that door across the street. Let's go see where it goes."

We pay our bill, dart across the street. The glass-fronted door leads only to a narrow staircase. I check the name on the gold plaque beside it: *Dr. Henry Williams.*

"There sure are a lot of letters behind his name," Hannah says. "You know what? I think that's Butch's dad."

"Who?"

"You know, Butch? From homeroom? Dark hair, dreamy eyes?"

I hunch my shoulders as if I have no idea who she's talking about. I'm hoping that bouncing brain of hers hasn't noticed me staring at him in homeroom.

She rolls her eyes. "I could introduce you to him."

"I don't think so," I say.

"Oh, come on," she says. "It'll be fab. And besides, you can ask him if he knows why your mom went to see his dad."

After much prodding from Hannah, and promises she will be sitting right next to me the whole time, I agree to meet with Butch Williams. The night before, my stomach churns. The spaghetti I'm making doesn't smell or taste good. I sleep in fits and starts. The following morning, I try on everything I own, which isn't a whole lot. Not one piece of clothing adds curves to my scrawny body. At practice, Mozart fails to suck me into his vortex. Twice I trip on uneven sidewalks on the way to South Haven Drug. The bell on the door sounds unusually loud.

Butch is sitting at a window table talking and laughing with Hannah. His voice is deeper than I imagined, round and rich like a well-tuned piano. I force myself to overlook his wavy dark hair and, yes, *dreamy* brown eyes as I float toward them.

Hannah rises. Hugs me. "Butch, this is Blue."

He smiles.

I think I may die right there and then.

"Well, I need to get going," Hannah says. "See you both later." She hops up from the table.

"What?" I say. "Where are you going?"

"I've got that thing." She winks. "Remember?"

I glare at her. Sunshine appears, giving me no time to argue with Hannah, who is heading briskly toward the door. "Hey, Blue." She raises an eyebrow, addresses Butch. "Mind your ways. This one's special. Old Man Kline says she's the next Beethoven." Then, to me: "Blueberry malted?"

"Sure," I say. As if I don't order the exact same thing every single time.

"Two blueberries coming right up," Sunshine says and leaves.

"Sorry," I say to Butch. "That was awkward."

"What's there to be sorry about?" Butch asks. "She likes you. And that's saying something. Sunshine doesn't like most people."

Hannah's abrupt exit is what I meant, but I decide to go with his comment. "Really?" I ask, though everyone knows that about Sunshine. She "detests a-holes" (her words), "abhors" uppity types and bad tippers, and "tolerates" tourists. But if she likes you, she's as loyal as they come.

"Oh, come on," Butch says. "Surely you know that. And the fact that she likes you means you aren't a bullshitter."

"You're right," I say. "I do know that, but I was trying to sound modest."

"Why?"

"Because I've heard that's what boys like." *Half-truth.*

"I'm not most guys. I'm an open book. Hannah says you just moved here. From where?"

"The East Coast."

"Whereabouts?"

Sunshine returns with our malteds. While taking a sip, I weigh the consequences of my answer.

"Pennsylvania."

"I've seen you in school. I was happy Hannah suggested we meet today."

"Why?"

"I don't know. I guess because I think about you sometimes."

He thinks about me? Keep calm. "Why would you think about me?" I ask, my speaking voice finally shifting into gear over the panicky little voice inside me, though rather than excited, the words sound flippant.

"Honestly? There's just something about you. You know how it is."

"I don't really." *Total truth.*

"You're trying to figure out if I think you're pretty. If I want to hang out with you. I'll make it easy for you. The answer is yes to both. That's why you asked to meet me, isn't it? Because you feel the same way?"

Responses to his questions skip through my mind: *Yes. Yes. Okay. Wow. I didn't ask, I agreed. He likes me?*

I've heard Hannah and Amy and Miriam and Colleen talk about butterflies, which I understood in theory but not practice. My belly gets tight, spine tingles, breath catches. I search for my voice, which is hiding, find it. "Actually that isn't why I asked you to meet me." *Half-lie.* There is no mistaking his confusion.

"Then why?"

"Hannah says that doctor across the street is your dad. I saw my mom walk in there yesterday and was wondering if you might know anything about why she was there."

He laughs, which surprises me.

"I don't know anything," he says. "And if I ask, he won't tell me. Doctor-patient confidentiality."

"You think she's his patient?"

"Why else would she go to see him? But I wouldn't be too worried. The designation *MD* is misleading. He's a psychoanalyst."

"You mean like therapy?" I admit I was somewhat relieved, but now I was *really* curious. "That doesn't seem like something she'd do."

"Why not?"

"She's not the share-her-feelings type." *Translation: Her whole life is a secret.*

"Sometimes people surprise us," he says. "You could ask her."

"Ask her what?"

"Why she went to see him."

"She won't tell me."

"How do you know that?"

"I just do."

And then I do something I've never done before. I *tell* him things. Things he hasn't even asked about. That my mother and I move a lot. That she's an artist. That she's *eccentric*. That she doesn't like to be alone. That I'm studying with Mr. Kline. That I want to be a concert pianist one day. That I love to read. That I've been reading Hemingway and want to know what fishing feels like. (That last thing is actually me fishing to see if he fishes.)

"Who's your favorite composer?" he asks.

"That's a really hard question. I like whomever I'm learning at the time. Right now that's Bach. I'm working on his *Goldberg Variations.*"

"I'm not familiar with that. Though my mother loved Bach. She took piano lessons from Mr. Kline too."

"She doesn't play anymore?" I ask.

"She died in a car accident when I was three."

"I'm so sorry."

"It's okay," he says. "I barely remember her. It happened a long time ago. My dad told me about her favorite composers. We still have her piano, a Bösendorfer."

"Wow, you own a Bösendorfer? I've played one in Mr. Kline's shop. The sound quality is amazing."

"Have you ever thought about finding out what it feels like?" he asks.

"What *what* feels like?"

"Fishing."

"Yes. But I wouldn't even know where to begin."

And so we talk about fishing, about how much he likes it, about how it makes him feel as if he is inside something bigger than him, which is the same way playing the piano makes me feel. And he tells me about the largest fish he ever caught and how he won a prize for it. And then he says how much he likes the outdoors and animals, and that he wants to be a veterinarian one day. And I realize though I want to hear everything about him, the moment for him asking me to go fishing with him has passed, and I hope that maybe he'll like me enough to ask another time. After one more malted each and two cups of peppermint tea, Butch and I leave South Haven Drug. Like the day I played *Pictures at an Exhibition*, it takes several minutes for me to find my way back to the world, but it has nothing to do with Mussorgsky or Viktor Hartmann's drawings. This time, it is because I am drunk to a different kind of music. As Hannah would say, a *divine* music.

Henry

It was the middle of May by the time I heard the insistent squawks of the gulls. With the exception of those few warmer days in March, it had been a long, unrelenting winter. The arrival of spring, the real one, not the calendar one, had boosted everyone's spirits. Especially Scarlet's. I noticed it immediately upon opening the door to my waiting room. She appeared lighter, more confident, her posture and facial muscles relaxed. Since the session when transference occurred, her anger hadn't returned. Her smile was wide.

"It's a lovely day, don't you think?" she asked. "I feel as if I could conquer the world. Do you know that feeling?"

"I believe it's called happiness," I said.

"I don't believe in happiness."

"Then how would you characterize it?"

She cocked her head to the left, her considering posture. "Power."

"The sun can do that for us," I said. "Michigan has such harsh and dreary winters."

"It's not just the weather. It's my painting. It's going so well it's as if I can do no wrong. My paint mixtures are perfect, the brushstrokes spot-on, and I'm so inside of myself. There's this symbiosis, this oneness. I am my canvas. I didn't even want to come here today. I could barely pull myself away."

"I didn't realize you were a painter." I briefly wondered why she had not mentioned it before, but then dismissed the thought. Peeling away Scarlet's layers had become a norm.

"I've been painting since I was a child. It started with sidewalks. My nanny brought me back a large box of bright-colored chalks when she went on vacation one time. I covered the driveway and every walkway, and even the walls in my bedroom." She paused, laughed. "That's when my mother bought me acrylic paints and an easel. I use oils now. I make my own pigments, from nature."

I was pleased she had shared this memory with me, that she was letting me into her life. Sharing aspects of her childhood, her love of "bright-colored chalks," and her painting was a sign she was starting to trust me.

"Do you sell your work, or is it a hobby?"

"Hobby? Art is never a hobby. It's a calling."

"I do apologize. Are you represented by a gallery near here?" It had been a while since I frequented the galleries in Saugatuck, a quaint town up the Lake Michigan coast with several galleries and arts venues that drew artistic elites from Detroit and Chicago and other large cities in and outside the region.

"Yes. In Tribeca."

I had not expected that response. "Your gallery is in Manhattan?"

"Just down the street from my studio."

"Your studio is in Manhattan?"

"Where else would it be?"

It was not out of the question she might have a gallery in New York. I knew of an artist in Saugatuck who also exhibited in New York. But a studio there? I studied her face. No sly smile.

"I thought you meant closer to home," I said. "A gallery in New York is quite an accomplishment."

She appeared confused, began shaking her foot and looking at her surroundings as if she did not recognize them.

Inch forward, I told myself.

"I'd love to see your work some time. Carl Jung painted as a kind of therapy. He believed his canvases were extensions of his soul."

"I think that's true," she said. "Perhaps I'll bring in my portfolio.

I don't want to brag or anything, but the critics say I'm one of the greatest colorists of my time. My paintings have been compared to Renoir's. Do you know him?"

"I do, but not well."

"He was one of the leaders of the Impressionist style of painting, and a celebrator of beauty. He believed a painting should be joyous and pretty because life is unpleasant enough."

"Do your paintings celebrate beauty?" I asked.

"All artists celebrate their own idea of beauty," she said, her foot still shaking. "No, it's more my style. The use of vibrant light and saturated color. And the subject matter. I strive to capture people in intimate settings, almost as if they've been caught unawares by a camera." She paused.

By now, I was pretty certain that Scarlet was, in fact, a painter. She obviously knew the terminology, and she lit up when she talked about it. But just because she liked to paint didn't mean she was famous or exhibited in New York. How much of what she was telling me was true? How much was she fabricating? And why? Was she purposefully lying? Or did she believe what she was saying? If the latter, I needed to proceed with caution. It was best if I acted as if I believed her. I did not want to destroy the trust we had built.

Before I had formulated a question, she cocked her head and added, "I've lived in New York my entire life, you know. I was born here. Grew up just a block off Central Park. Back when it was still pretty safe to play there. My mother took me to the park every day. I met some of my best friends in the sandbox." She laughed. "We all say that. Or that we met in our strollers. I studied painting here too. At NYU. That's where I met my studio mates."

"And South Haven?"

Confused look again. Tack picking, hair winding.

"What about it?" she asked.

"Do you have a second home here? Or a beach house you rent? I just wondered since you've been living here for over four months now, right?"

"Beach house. Yes, that's right. Near Montauk. I just forgot the name of the town for a moment. It's lovely here."

I sat back in my chair. My head was spinning. How could I have missed this? These types of fantastical imaginings do not just pop up overnight. Generally someone has been living with them for a while, though it was not unusual for them to go unnoticed, or for the fantasies to come and go. It was amazing how well the unbalanced mind could adapt to the outside world. Often patients were able to hide their mental state from even their families, especially if they exhibited eccentric or artistic qualities. I was reminded of the conversation I had with Scarlet earlier, about Jung and Freud. She said she had done some research into psychosocial behaviorism. Why?

"Scarlet, do you know who I am?" I asked.

"Don't be silly. Of course I know who you are. Why would you ask such a thing? You're Dr. Henry. My analyst."

After that, the conversation seemed to get back on track. We discussed more about her painting and her gallery. She referred to New York as "there" instead of "here."

Before I dismissed her, I said, "You seemed a little scattered today. Are you okay to walk home?"

"Of course," she said. She flashed a disingenuous smile, and left.

That night while reviewing my notes, I saw I had recorded only seven words during my session with Scarlet: *Patient believes she lives in New York.*

Scarlet

Poor Henry. He was all over the place today. I finally told him I was a painter. I didn't want to tell him earlier because it might help him identify me, and besides, my painting was the one thing that belonged to me only. Against my better judgment, I heard myself telling him a *true* story about when my nanny bought me chalk and I drew on everything, which prompted my mother to buy me paints. But he didn't seem to care about origin stories; instead he asked if I sold my work or if painting was a hobby. A hobby? What an ass. I tried to explain art was a calling, but he stuck to the monetary stuff and asked me if I was represented by a gallery. I said, "Yes, in Tribeca." And his face—wow—he wasn't one to hide his emotions. It was obvious he didn't believe me. As if he thought I was some sort of Sunday painter. And then, no surprise, he brought Carl Jung into the conversation—he was obsessed with Carl Jung—and went off on some tangent about him being a painter. Seriously? Carl Jung wasn't even in my league. There was no way I was going to sit there and listen to Henry's total ignorance on the subject of art.

So, I zoned out.

After a while I heard him ask, "Scarlet, do you know who I am?"

Did I know who he was? I said yes, or some such, but sometimes I thought he was the one who needed therapy.

He started writing on that ridiculous legal pad of his, and while he did, I looked at the clock and saw that our time was almost up and I realized it was either the shortest session there ever was or he'd tricked me. He'd done something to the clock so I would wonder what happened to the time, and then I'd start freaking out and wondering if I was going crazy, because that was just it, wasn't it? He wanted me crazy. Because if I was crazy, it justified his existence. Because if I was crazy, he could save me. I do not need saving. Who's running this show anyway?

When I was certain his attention was focused on his note taking and scratching away with that cheap pen of his, otherwise totally clueless to my wily ways, I peeked over at the pad, and even though Henry was sitting six feet from me, I could see right through his legal pad. It was as if my eyes had turned into magic magnifying glasses, which was actually fascinating and I would have loved to test their power on other things in his office, like the individual carpet threads and those holes in his dropped ceiling, but then I saw what that asshole was writing.

She's crazy.

She's crazy not.

She's crazy.

She's crazy not.

She's crazy.

She's crazy not.

All the way down the page, and the next and the next and the next, like he was pulling petals off daisies or something.

But if he thought messing with the clock and writing the word *crazy* on his notepad a million times was going to upset me and thwart my plan, he was wrong. He had no idea whom he was dealing with.

But the truth was, as much as Henry and his boring sessions irritated me, I needed him. I couldn't do it alone. And he was the only person in the world who stood to gain as much as I did. So I adopted my most pleasant manner and said to him, "Don't be silly. Of course I know who you are. Why would you ask such a thing? You're Dr. Henry. My analyst."

My sweetness did the trick. He stopped writing. Flashed me a look of pure and utter fondness.

But of course he couldn't leave it at that. He had the nerve to say *I'd* seemed a little scattered. Now, I could have gotten angry and told him to fuck off or stomped out of his office or some such, but that wouldn't have been smart. So instead I flashed him a big fake smile, and right before I left, I snuck another look at his legal pad. Oddly all the crazies and crazy-nots were gone.

Blue

I have turned into one of those giddy girls. It has only been two weeks since I met Butch at South Haven Drug, but it feels much longer. In a good way. We hang at school, meet at my locker every morning, and he carries my books from class to class. This morning he's already at my locker when I get there. He's pacing back and forth as if he's nervous, stops when he sees me. His entire face smiles.

"I have something for you," he says, and hands me a long chain with two flat metal pieces attached to it.

I stare at them, not sure what they are, but thank him.

He laughs. "They wear them in the army. See, they have my name stamped on one and yours on the other. There's an engraving machine at the hardware store. It's kind of a thing now, guys giving their girlfriends dog tags. But usually both tags have the guy's name on them, but I didn't think that made sense." He pulls something out of the neck of his shirt. A duplicate chain and tags. "See, here's my name and here's yours."

I wonder if I heard him right, not about the dog tags. About that one all-important word. "I'm your girlfriend?" I ask.

"If you want to be." *He has the cutest dimples in the entire world.*

"Okay."

"Here, let me help you put it on." He lifts the chain over my head, positions it around my neck.

"It's beautiful," I say.

Out of the corner of my eye, I see Amy, Miriam, and Colleen whispering behind Amy's locker door. They always whisper when they see me with Butch. They think I don't notice? Hannah says that Amy has had a crush on Butch since fourth grade.

The bell for last period rings. Butch's class is in the opposite direction from mine. I walk by Amy, Miriam, and Colleen. They stop whispering.

"Hi, Blue," Colleen says. "I really like your blouse." Colleen is always complimenting my clothes even though they're from Goodwill. I like Colleen the best of the three. She's quiet, sweet, and though she's really pretty (long dark hair and big blue eyes), she doesn't seem to know it. Sometimes I think if Colleen weren't so tight with Miriam and Amy (whom everyone calls bitchy Amy behind her back), she and I might have been friends. We have three classes together, the smart math and science classes, and art. We also have physical education, but that isn't really a class since it only meets once a week and all the girls from every grade are in it.

"Thank you," I say. "Yours is nice too." (An expensive-looking pink-striped seersucker—my mother never lets me buy anything pink.) The comment sounds awkward. I'm not especially good with compliments, either given or received. "Hi, Amy. Hi, Miriam."

They say hi back, all smiles.

I walk past them and head to class.

Now, like most days, I sit with Hannah at South Haven Drug. She is holding the dog tags in her hands admiring them. "They're really groovy," she says. "Donny Raymond gave some to Kelley Kolar a couple of weeks ago, but he already asked for them back."

"Why?" I asked.

"He likes Beth Zimmerman now," Hannah says. "Oh, don't look so worried. If Butch was going to like Amy, he would've by now. I'm pretty certain he isn't going to like anybody but you ever."

"I wasn't worried." *Half-truth.*

She rolls her eyes. "Where is he by the way?"

"At fishing club," I say.

"That's right," she says. "I forgot it started in May. Has he asked you to go fishing with him yet?"

"No," I say. "Maybe he doesn't like to fish with girls." I try to sound nonchalant, but actually I'm disappointed.

"He will," Hannah says. "Trust me. During fishing club there's not really time to fish with anyone other than your partner. He and Curly do pretty much everything fishing-related together."

"Curly?" I ask.

"Dave Curly? You know, red hair, wire-rim glasses? He's in our homeroom. By the way, have you asked your mom why she's meeting with Dr. Williams?"

"Not yet."

"Why not?"

"She's always busy painting."

"You should. You'll feel better if you know." She sucks up the last bit of malted.

Sunshine, who continuously reminds everyone that she "can hear someone slurping up the last bit of a drink all the way from the next room," walks over and asks if we want another round.

"I need to get home," I say. *Total truth.*

My mother has been acting even less normal than usual. She's painted naked almost every day this week, and yesterday, after I got home from piano practice, I caught her pointing and yelling at the yellow-boat painting she's currently working on. "Get back inside," she was saying, and "Stop walking across the wet paint, you'll smear it." When I asked who she was talking to, she said no one. I told her I was worried about her, which I am, but she told me not to be, that it was a fly she was talking to. I didn't see any fly.

"Okay, see you tomorrow," Hannah says.

───────────

On my way home, I practice asking my mother about Butch's dad. Run several scenarios through my mind. Decide I should come right out with it, but I should sound *casual*. As if it's no big deal.

Like always, she's painting when I arrive. I can't tell if it's the same yellow boat she was working on yesterday or a new one. I set down my backpack and sit on the cat-clawed sofa. There's not one but two

Renoir *Madame* paintings propped against the wall behind her. They're actually pretty good, detailed, better than the boats and hopscotch paintings. The brushstrokes in those are looser, haphazard. They seem to be getting more and more so. I keep working up my nerve to ask about Dr. Williams. Given her laser-focused concentration on the canvas, it is 99 percent possible she won't hear me anyway. Which is actually preferable. I can at least tell myself I tried. I decide to start with something less abrupt.

"We don't have as many lessons as we used to," I ask. "Why not?"

No answer.

"I miss our talks, do you?"

"What?" she says absently.

"Our talks," I repeat. "I miss them."

To my surprise, she looks at me, a hazy film covering her eyes. She sets down her brush but doesn't clean it, and sits on her self-critique chair. "What do you want to talk about?"

I blurt out the question. "Why are you meeting with a therapist?"

"How do you know I'm seeing a therapist?"

"I saw you," I say.

"I thought I should talk to someone," she says. "And Henry's a psychoanalyst actually. Not a therapist. He gets rather persnickety when the terms are mixed."

Henry? My mind is overfull with questions, not the least of which is, *Does she know she isn't normal?* The thought that she might actually eases my mind. If someone knows she isn't normal and is going to therapy, it stands to reason that she's working on getting normal.

She notes my surprise. "Ask me anything you want."

"When did you start going?"

"Soon after we moved here."

"Why?"

"Do you mean why did I decide to seek analysis?"

"Yes."

"I really don't know. Just an impulse."

"What do the two of you talk about?"

"That's between Henry and me."

"You call him Henry?"

"What else would I call him?"

I want to ask so many more questions, like, *Do you talk about your childhood, the childhood you never discuss with me? Have you told him how often we move? Does he know your real name, the name I don't even know?* And as I often do, when I allow my mind to wander into the land of unanswered questions, I begin to worry about something bad happening, about her not being in my life, about what would happen to me, but then I push these thoughts away and concentrate on the opportunity, however small, before me because I know that soon she will end our conversation. That I may get responses to one, maybe two more questions. I choose carefully.

"Have you told Henry about HIM?"

"No."

"Why not?"

"It's not time yet."

"I don't understand."

"Someday you will," she says. "Who is Butch?"

"What?"

"You said that Butch said you should just ask me."

I don't remember mentioning Butch.

"A boy I go to school with." I don't think it's wise to tell her he's Dr. Williams's son.

"Tell me about him." She says this without the least bit of concern, as if she's checking his references for a job.

"He's cute."

"And?"

"Nice."

"Do you like him?"

"I think so. I don't know yet." *Half-truth.* I do like him, but I don't want my mother to know that because she may say I need to give him up like she did Hannah and playing the piano. And in all honesty, I also don't yet know what liking a boy should feel like. Sometimes it feels good, but sometimes it feels scary. I don't like when it feels scary. My stomach hurts a different way, not an anxious or fearful way, a nervous way. I wish I could talk to my mother about this, but we've never had those kinds of conversations, *feelings* conversations.

"You know to be careful, right?" she says.

Most mothers who ask that question would be referring to something entirely different. She means careful with how much I tell him. "Of course."

She leans back. "What do you think of my painting?"

Good, I can get to the bottom of these boats. "It's okay, I guess. I mean it's good and all"—*half-truth*—"but it's like the fourth yellow boat you've painted this week alone. Are you taking a break from that woman you were painting?"

"*Madame?* She's in one of those stacks somewhere." The stacks are everywhere. In the hallway. Between the bunk bed and the wall. Behind the sofa. "I need to repaint her. She isn't right yet."

"When I was at the library yesterday, I looked up that art term you taught me about, *fugitive pigment*," I said. "I couldn't find anything about it anywhere. I even asked the librarians about it, and they'd never heard of it either."

"Science," she says.

"What?"

"It was a science lesson. So, it's a science term, and you know how people are with science."

"How are they?"

"It's dry and requires a modicum of intelligence, so they avoid it."

"Well, I couldn't find anything about it. And besides, I've been thinking about what you said about the reds just disappearing. Real fugitives leave parts of themselves behind no matter how much they try not to." *Like us*, I want to say. My mother believes we leave nothing in the towns where we've lived, but I hope that isn't true. I have to believe that we touch people, that someone somewhere remembers us. Maybe the women who helped me play the piano better, like Mrs. Lord and Mrs. Dunlap, and, though he's not a person, Mrs. Dunlap's dog, Turnup (so named because when he was a pup he turned up his nose at whatever she fed him), who was definitely my friend, and even Mrs. Stewart, who worked the grocery checkout. I get to know a lot of the checkout ladies. Surely they remember me. I have to believe they do. I have to believe that now and then they think of me or wonder about me, about where I went, about why I just disappeared. I have to believe I left something of myself behind. Because the alternative means *I* am nothing.

"You are my doubting Jane." She rises, picks up her brush, continues painting.

I watch her, grateful for her momentary clarity, and for everything I learned. And after a while, I say, "I'm going to make dinner."

She doesn't respond. She is lost in painting land. My mother has taught me that the creative act is like a sleep cycle. The artist can be fully immersed, but now and then may surface just enough to hear a siren in the distance, a buckle in the ceiling or wall, the tick of a clock (or in our case the chirp of that obnoxious bird). In those brief moments, she may register the interruption, even pause. That's what happened when I asked her about Dr. Williams. That's also why she was more willing to honestly engage with me, because she was only half present. But there is a risk to the creative pause. If the artist stays awake to the real world for too long, she may have difficulty finding her way back into the creative one. Or vice versa. If she stays inside the creative world for too long, she risks not finding her way back to the real one. Perhaps that is why highly creative people have been known to go insane.

I head to the kitchenette, look in the refrigerator. Bare except for milk, three slices of American cheese, and a half stick of butter. I open the milk carton. Sour. Pour it down the sink. Put the cheese and butter on the counter. Check the bread. Moldy. Open a cabinet. Two cans of tomato soup and a box of macaroni and cheese. And as I wait for the soup to boil, I pull the dog tags out of the neck of my blouse and run my finger over Butch's name. *Yes*, I think, *I do like Butch*. In fact, I more than like him.

Scarlet

Week 20.

This is what I wrote in my graph several years ago, plus some notes I added when I reviewed it yesterday:

1. Tell Henry about the wallpaper. (Note: Be sure you linger over the roses, candlelight, and fragrance. Henry is a romantic.)

2. Ever so subtly mention HIM. Gauge his reaction.

3. Bring up the funeral out of the blue. (Note: Better if it isn't connected to other thoughts. Disjointed memories will intrigue the head doctor in him.)

4. If he asks questions, answer some but not others. (Note: Keep him on his toes.)

5. Casually mention the fires. BREVITY. (Note: Say only enough to pique his interest. Delivery is everything.)

6. If at any point you feel yourself getting emotional, DEFLECT. (Note: A show of strength at this point will do more to emphasize vulnerability than fragility.)

7. BE MYSTERIOUS. (Note: That drives him crazy.)

Note: In summary, if you feel you've come up short anywhere, add to what you've said. It doesn't matter where or when. Remember, as mentioned in number 3, disjointed thoughts will only enhance his interest, not to mention you excel at impromptu theater.

Henry

The patient whose appointment preceded Scarlet's was Joanne Burns (she preferred I call her Mrs. Burns). We had been meeting for nearly six months. She came to analysis to discuss her daughter-in-law, who she was convinced was trying to steal her son. Much of what she shared was attributable to the shifting priorities of her son: distance (he lived in California), a demanding job, and a new primary female relationship. Fear and pride were clouding Mrs. Burns's perception of the situation. Rather than, in her words, "confront" him and risk losing him altogether, it was easier and safer to make her daughter-in-law the scapegoat. My work with Mrs. Burns centered on helping her come to terms with this new dynamic between her and her son and find the strength to honestly share with him her feelings of loss and abandonment. Honest words, I have learned, are often the most difficult to share.

In between appointments, I reviewed my notes from my last few appointments with Scarlet. Last week, there had been no mention of New York, leading me to hope her previous behavior had been an isolated incident, perhaps brought on by stress. Still, my focus on her behavior had sharpened. As always, she arrived right on time and took her normal seat on the leather sofa. We exchanged our normal pleasantries, but rather than taking her time to settle in, generally somewhat of a choreographed ritual, or waiting for me to ask her a question, she launched right in.

"I'd like to tell you about a memory I have." She gave me no time to respond. "I'm in a store with my father. It is filled with fabrics and books of wallpaper samples, and he tells me I can choose any wallpaper I wish. I page through the books, run my palm over each page, and then, like magic, it finds me. Small pink roses on a white ground. So pretty. That afternoon he allows me to help him dip the roses into a pan of water and roll them onto the wall. The very next weekend I move into my rose garden."

"Do you know how old you are in the memory?" I asked.

"I'd just turned five."

"What else do you remember?"

"The candlelight and the roses, dozens of them, and the fragrance." She stopped, bit her bottom lip, twirled a lock of hair.

"Are you okay? Do you need some time?"

"No, I'm fine. It's just that I remembered another time, a different rose. I pricked my finger on one of the thorns, got blood on the comforter. I tried to hide it, but he saw. He got angry."

"Angry how?"

"He slapped me with the back of his hand. I hit my head on the bedpost. He took me to the hospital. I had to get stitches. He told them I was his niece." She pointed to a scar on her forehead I hadn't noticed before.

"Why do you think your father told them you were his niece?"

"My father?"

"You said you were in the store with your father."

"I was." She paused. "But that was before."

"Before what?" I asked.

"Shouldn't there have been a funeral? If he was my uncle, shouldn't he have taken me to their funeral? But he didn't, so obviously he wasn't my uncle."

"Whose funeral?"

"I don't want to talk about this anymore," she said. Leg shaking.

"Are you sure?" The information she'd just shared was concerning, and I felt we needed to continue, but pushing her could result in her shutting down completely.

"Can we just not talk at all for a while? I need to think." She sat back on the sofa and closed her eyes.

While I waited, I jotted down a few questions. *Who is the man in her memory? Her father? Her uncle?* Beneath that I wrote *PA?* and *SA?* for physical and sexual abuse. Her skittish demeanor and hunched posture could suggest one or the other, or both. Beneath *PA*, I added, *Mirroring?* (This in reference to me.) I wanted to be certain my judgment was not clouded by my own past, though I had done a lot of work, through my own analysis, around ensuring otherwise. When Butch's picture made the newspaper for catching the biggest fish at a festival in town, I praised the achievement even though memories of my stepfather belittling my lack of accomplishments had surfaced. He had also belittled my mother. This duality was the root of my savior complex. I invariably believed women's stories of abuse over men's denials, and often spoke on their behalf in front of lawyers and judges. But though my past could have biased me, I was careful to remain impartial. My sole goal was to help people who had experienced the kind of mental pain that left them powerless, the kind I had experienced. What was it Scarlet had said about people who had suffered abuse being better equipped to help other abused people?

I heard Scarlet say something.

"Excuse me?" I asked.

"You were off someplace."

"I do apologize," I said, while internally berating myself.

"No worries. My daughter says I do that all the time, when I'm painting especially."

"I didn't know you had a daughter. You haven't mentioned her before."

"Yes, I have, remember? When we were talking about that TV

show *Dark Shadows.* I said it was her favorite show, so that's why I watched it."

I would have remembered if she told me that.

"You look skeptical," she said. "Why don't you check your notes, the ones you crumple up and throw away? I know you keep them."

Rather than argue with her, I asked, "How old is your daughter?"

"Fifteen."

I almost said I had a son the same age but caught myself. Discussing my life with a patient was not appropriate.

"You mentioned a funeral. Whose funeral were you referring to?"

"There was a fire," she said. "At our house in Traverse City. My parents died. Someone set it."

"Arson? I'm so sorry."

"It was a long time ago. Shortly after my father wallpapered my room."

"Do you remember them?"

"Not totally. Not what they looked like, but sometimes, if I concentrate, I can feel them, their essence. My mother dancing, she loved to dance, holding my hands and twirling me around. My father playing the piano. His parties. He loved parties. Caterers bustling about as if part of a choreographed ballet. People gathering around the piano singing. I don't remember the two of them ever arguing or fighting. They were always hugging and kissing." Her eyes open. "There was a party that night."

"The night they died?"

"Yes. The police had two theories. Someone taking revenge on my father—he was the district attorney, and he'd put a lot of bad people in jail—or some local kids playing with matches."

"Did they find out which?"

"No. The case was never solved."

"Were you home?"

"I escaped."

"Escaped to where?"

"The orphanage."

"When was this?"

"I don't remember."

"What was the name of the orphanage?"

"I said I don't remember."

"You don't remember anything?"

"Only the fire."

"The fire at your parents' house?"

"No," she said. "At the orphanage."

My initial reaction to her response was confusion. "Are you saying both your family home and an orphanage burned down?"

"Yes," she said in a childlike voice.

Then worry overcame me, because if I had any doubts regarding my assessment of Scarlet's earlier comments about living in New York, what happened next quelled them. She rose, walked around my desk, and crawled under it.

I followed her, bent down on all fours. She sat with her knees drawn to her chin, her arms around them, rocking back and forth.

"It's okay, Scarlet. Here, let me help you out of there." I took her hands in mine. The gesture woke her, and a look of embarrassment crossed her face. "How did I get here?"

"You walked here," I said. "Do you want to talk about why?"

She shook her head no.

"Why don't you sit for minute?"

"I need to go. We're over our time limit anyway. You should be proud of yourself. I stayed five whole minutes extra."

I checked the clock. She was right. We had gone over.

She smiled, rose. "See you next week?"

"Yes, next week," I said.

PTSD? I remembered asking myself that in those minutes immediately following her session. It was obvious something traumatic had happened to Scarlet in the past, and because the memory of it had been too difficult to face, she had buried it. Little by little it was resurfacing.

But that night, I questioned the diagnosis, at least in isolation.

Prior to Scarlet, the most serious issues I had encountered in my practice were grief and depression, and although I found all my work rewarding, I welcomed the prospect of solving a more intricate and layered puzzle. I opened the *DSM*, skimmed through disorders that might fit what I had witnessed: mood, anxiety, bipolar, dissociative, delirium, dementia, substance abuse. But it was the section on schizophrenia that gave me pause. Schizophrenia fell into three categories: positive, negative, and cognitive. Positive presenting the most extreme symptoms—hallucinations, delusions (sometimes accompanied by paranoia), thought and movement disorders. Hallucinations and delusions could explain her belief that she lived in New York. Paranoia could explain *him*, the non-uncle, the man from her past who might or might not exist. She also exhibited some of the negative symptoms, flat affect and difficulty beginning and sustaining activities (her continual moving from one town to another), and cognitive symptoms, namely, trouble focusing, paying attention, or remembering. Like believing she had told me she had a daughter when she had not.

I put down the book and closed my eyes. It had been a long day.

"You okay, Dad?" I heard Butch ask. I must have dozed off.

"I'm fine," I said. "Just taking a catnap. Are you just getting home from fishing club?"

"I stopped off at South Haven Drug for a malted."

"You've been going there a lot lately. Were you with Curly?" Butch and Curly were in fishing club together. I was happy Butch was socializing more. He was a loner by nature. Although he spent time with others, Curly was perhaps his closest friend. His response to any concern I might have expressed was that he preferred one or two "genuine friendships" to a collection of "shallow" ones. Butch had always been wise beyond his years. His mother would have been so proud of him.

"No," he said. "Some other friends."

I found the statement somewhat curious. Generally he volunteered names and details. We were close. Since Lily died, it had always been just the two of us.

"There's some fried perch on the counter that you can warm up. I stopped off at Clementine's on the way home."

"Thanks, Dad," he said.

I went back to my reading, and as I became engrossed in the lives of my patients, the sounds and smells from the kitchen faded away.

Blue

It's June when it happens. The last two weeks of school. There are field trips and end-of-year parties planned, not to mention exams, but I'm unable to take part in any of these activities. Because one morning, as if she's flipped a switch, my mother wakes up believing she lives in New York. Her mind has created a full-blown and elaborate fantasy world. There is no South Haven. There is no me. She doesn't have a daughter.

The first thing I do after I've sorted through the potential risks of the situation is call the school (pretending I'm my mother) and say this: "This is Mrs. Lake." (I think saying *Mrs.* instead of *Miss* makes it seem more credible.) "I'm calling to say that my daughter, Blue, has a fever and strep throat. The doctor says she's highly contagious and needs to stay home until all symptoms subside."

"I am so sorry," Mrs. Stevens, the woman who works the front desk, says. "That seems to be going around. I hope Blue feels better." I find the "seems to being going around" part reassuring. Either I have partners in crime, or there are enough other sick people to make my lie more believable.

After that, I call Mr. Kline and Hannah and Butch, and, trying to sound as sick as I can, tell each of them the same thing, emphasizing the very-contagious part. All three ask if there's anything they can do for me, and I say no, that my mom is taking care of me, but thank you. I add that I will call them as soon as I'm feeling better.

Then I monitor the situation.

When I say my mother believes she lives in New York, I mean she imagines activities that happen both wherever it is she thinks she lives, in a home or apartment or wherever (she isn't too clear on that front), and in places around the city. For instance, she and I (whoever I'm supposed to be at any given moment) go to the Metropolitan Museum of Art and the Museum of Modern Art. We go to the Frick, the Guggenheim, and the Whitney. We see exhibits by Matisse and Renoir and Jackson Pollock. We go to the theater and the opera and the symphony. We see *Hair. West Side Story. Madame Butterfly.* When we aren't home or traipsing through cultural events, we "hang" at her studio in Tribeca. There she introduces me to the other artists with whom she shares space. A British painter named Jeremy. A French sculptor named Juliette. An American mixed-media artist named Rachel. I am surprised by their detailed histories and backgrounds. Jeremy is handsome, six feet tall with dark wavy hair, and gay. He's partial to hats, dresses flamboyantly. His current boyfriend's name is Sebastian. Jeremy is a talker and drinks too much, wine mostly, like my mother. Juliette is a quiet and thoughtful brunette with aquiline features. Her English is broken. Her sculptures consist primarily of old clock innards she had shipped directly from a vineyard in the historic province of Champagne in the northeast of France where she grew up. She drinks Perrier or fine champagne. Rachel is married to a musician named Otto. She has green hair at this moment, but changes the color often. They moved to New York from Tacoma, Washington, where Otto played a few times with a garage rock band called the Sonics, his claim to fame. She adds broken plates, hot rollers, and old album covers, among other found objects, to her plywood canvases. Otto hangs out with her sometimes. They don't drink. They smoke pot.

None of these people exist, not Jeremy, not Juliette, not Rachel or Otto. Nor do the places where we apparently spend time. There isn't a studio building with a flower shop on the street below. There are no museums or theaters or opera houses or symphony halls. There is only our little dilapidated house. My mother walks around talking to people who aren't there. She comments on architecture and artworks that don't exist. Critiques plays and exhibits and performances that don't happen. Sits on the sofa laughing with nameless invisible friends (sometimes laughing so hard she pees her pants, like when we found that piano in the alley). Dances without partners. And one time even plays Twister with a ghost.

She spends most of her fantasy time with non-Jeremy and refers to him as her best friend. They drink wine together, bottle after bottle, while sharing what sounds like memories of their art-school days and lamenting their individual love lives. Sometimes my mother asks whoever I am supposed to be to get them another bottle, and she proceeds to drink it, get sloppy drunk (the entire time engaging in slurred conversation with non-Jeremy), and pass out. This, or a similar scenario, happens every night.

After one of these episodes, I make sure her head is safely on a pillow and her body covered by a blanket. Then I clean up. And watch her. I don't sleep; sometimes I try to, but the sleep won't come. I worry if I do, something bad will happen. She'll wander outside the house or hurt herself. I imagine her falling and hitting her head. I imagine her gouging herself with her dull palette knife, inadvertently or on purpose. I've hidden all the sharp knives, tossed cleaning agents and aerosol sprays, shoved her turpentine and linseed oil under the far corner of the bottom bunk, moved furniture up against walls. She doesn't eat, even though I continually try to get her to. If I get hungry, which is rare since my stomach is acting up, I eat whatever there is, canned food or crackers or noodles. I drink water or Lipton.

On the night that becomes the last night of my mother's fantasy, she and her studio mates have an exhibition of their work. She spends several hours dressing in her "most alluring black dress" (she owns only one), which amounts to her trying on the same dress over and over, and moving her paintings from one place to another. According to her, everyone who's anyone in the art world is in attendance. Her paintings sell out.

Then, without ceremony, my mother returns to South Haven. According to the calendar two weeks have passed. It doesn't happen suddenly, the way it began. There is a day of in-between, where she lives in both worlds, fantasy and reality. Whereas I am exhausted, she wakes that first morning chipper and relaxed, recognizes me as her daughter, and asks me about my plans for the day. I overhear her call Dr. Henry, rave about her trip to New York and her exhibit, and make an appointment to meet with him. She doesn't engage with invisible studio mates, nor does she attend nonexistent functions, though she does talk about both in the past tense, saying such things as "Wasn't our trip fun?" and "Didn't you just adore the Renoir exhibit?" And comments on my appearance: "You look tired, sweetie. You should get some rest." And then, one sleep cycle later, the entire fantasy, and her memory of it, disappears into our floorboards. My memory, on the other hand, is intact, though I wish it weren't. Living so intimately inside her crazies has caused me to question reality. Maybe I did live in New York. Maybe I did go to all those cultural events. Maybe there is a Jeremy and a Juliette and a Rachel and an Otto. Later that night, while she prepares to paint, she asks, "Do you have any idea what happened to my turpentine?"

And while I watch her paint, my eyes become heavy, then heavier still, and I sleep for nineteen hours straight.

Henry

After the day that Scarlet hid under my desk, she failed to show for her next three appointments. I chastised myself for not insisting she fill out her intake form, which included a space for her phone number.

When she missed her first appointment, I blamed myself. Had I pushed too hard? Did I not take her behavior that day seriously enough? Then I reminded myself that it was not unusual for clients to skip an appointment here and there without calling. Walter Gardner came to mind. Over the year since we had been meeting, he had failed to show for four appointments, providing excuses after the fact for three of them, and calling halfway through the fourth to say he'd "spaced it." Prolonged periods of self-reflection could breed forgetfulness.

When Scarlet missed her second appointment, despite my best efforts I became irritated. She could at least have called, I told myself. Was she being passive-aggressive? Had her behavior during our last session unnerved her? Was she trying to regain control of me and our sessions?

On the occasion of Scarlet's third missed appointment, worry crept in. I was just considering whether I should report her absence to the local authorities when the phone rang.

"Dr. Henry. It's Scarlet."

"Scarlet. Is everything okay? Are you okay?"

"I'm fine. I'm so sorry. It's just that I left in such a hurry I forgot to call. I just got back today."

"Left?"

"Yes, for New York. I told you I was going, remember? I meant to call to remind you . . ." Her voice trailed off.

New York again. I began searching my memory for any discussion we might have had about an impending trip, but then stopped myself. I had revisited my session notes many times since her absence; there had been no mention of a trip.

"Of course," I lied. "How did it go?"

"It was perfect," she said. "My studio mates and I had an exhibit. I sold every single painting. Isn't that amazing? The *Times* was there. Did you see the review? It was so flattering. Morris Abernathy, do you believe it? He called me the next Renoir. I mean, he's compared my work to Renoir's before, but this time he compared my entire career to his. Jeremy says I'll surely be in the history books, and that MoMA will be giving me a one-woman show. I can't wait to see you to tell you all about it."

"Jeremy?" I asked.

"One of my studio mates."

"Did your daughter go with you?"

"Daughter? I don't have a daughter."

At that moment, I was happy we were talking on the phone. If she had been sitting across from me, she would have seen the look of incredulity on my face.

"Will you be here next week?" I asked.

"It's on my calendar," she said.

She greeted me with a wide smile. Childlike in her enthusiasm, she all but skipped from my waiting room into my office, humming a tune I could not identify as she hung up her coat, extending her arms and twirling before she fell into her normal seat on one end of the leather sofa.

"It's a beautiful day, don't you think?" she asked. "And the sidewalks are packed."

She was correct. Downtown was lively. The tourist season in

South Haven ran from Memorial Day to Labor Day. It was now one week before the first official day of summer. Tourists filled the shops. Restaurants held waiting lists. Parking was at a premium. Colorful umbrellas and brightly striped towels covered every inch of the beaches. Boats of all sizes filed down the Black River on their way to the open lake, causing the drawbridge to open and close. Familiar smells and sounds sifted through the air. Barbecuing and bonfires and people reeking of suntan lotion. The laughter of children and cackle of low-flying gulls.

"Yes, it is," I said. "What was that you were humming?"

"'Summer Wind,' or my off-key version of it. I was listening to Frank Sinatra on the radio right before I left the house. Do you like him?"

"I do."

"Me too. Blue doesn't. She calls it old-people music."

"Blue?"

"My daughter. I thought I'd mentioned her before."

My head was spinning. I was confused, trying to make sense of her earlier denial. Should I say she told me when we talked on the phone that she had no daughter?

Again, I decided it was best not to question the assertion. It was more important to let the conversation go, to see if perhaps she'd merely forgotten what she said. However, I was not convinced. "You did," I said. "But I don't believe you mentioned her name. What would you like to talk about today? Your trip to New York?'

"What trip to New York?"

"You said on the phone that you'd been to New York."

"When did we talk on the phone? You must be mixing me up with another patient."

"Are you certain you weren't away?"

"How could I be? I just saw you last week."

"Last week?" I repeated.

"Remember? We talked about the fires? Are you feeling okay?"

I studied her face. She appeared genuinely perplexed. She seemed to have no memory of missing the appointments, calling me, or tell-ing me she did not have a daughter.

"We share a common enemy, you know," she said.

"Who is that?" I asked, trying to keep my voice neutral.

"Him."

"I don't understand."

"You know. The man I've mentioned?"

"Are you saying I know this man?"

Her leg began shaking.

"I was just doing that 'we' thing you always do," she said. "You share him through me. He's evil."

"Evil how?"

"He hurts little girls."

"Did he hurt you?"

"You're being obtuse."

"I don't intend to be."

"You think if you tiptoe around the subject of him, I might break. Tell you all. But I won't. Not yet anyway." She paused. "We lived up north."

"Who lived up north?"

"The man and me."

"The man you're trying to escape?"

"Yes."

"Where up north?"

"Does it matter? It wasn't Traverse City, that's for sure." She looked up, focused her eyes on the ceiling, shivered, as if she saw a spider. Her fingers began picking at the sofa grommets. She had not touched them since she arrived. Something I said obviously had un-settled her. Her eyes bored into mine. She added, "In order to escape, sometimes you need to destroy."

"Destroy?"

"I hate it when you do that."

"Do what?"

"There you go again." For a moment, I felt her pulling away, but then she surprised me. "At first, I thought it was just him and me, but then, one day, a woman appeared with luggage, like she'd been on a trip. 'This is my wife,' he said. Stuff changed after that, though it didn't last."

"How so?"

"She despised me."

"Why do you think she despised you?"

"Because she knew why I was there."

"Why was that?"

"Why do you think?"

"I don't know. Would you like to tell me?"

Leg shaking. "She left and never came back. Which was too bad, actually. He didn't touch me while she was there."

"What do you mean, touch you?"

"Jesus," she said. "Really? Why do you keep repeating everything I say? I tell you there was a fire, that my parents died, that a man took me, a man that said he was my uncle but wasn't. Just some pervert that happened upon a five-year-old girl playing hopscotch and decided to make her his sex toy. Don't you see? He just *took* me." Her anger and fear were palpable.

A man took her? I flipped through my legal pad, a ploy, while trying to digest the impact of what she'd said. A child being taken and sexually abused, even after all these years, could be considered a matter for the police. *If she was telling the truth.*

"Don't even think about contacting the police," she said, as if she read my mind. "I'll deny it. Besides, I was lying."

"About what?"

"About everything. There is no man." She rose and, without even looking in my direction, walked out of the room.

Blue

I see Butch through the windows of the red double doors. I've just finished taking my last makeup exam from the days of school I missed. He is in the parking lot kicking stones around. I haven't seen him since my mother's fantasy trip to New York. What if he asks about my strep throat? This is always how it starts: the lying. Someone lives next door or works at the local grocery or frequents somewhere my mother and I do and strikes up a conversation about something innocent like the weather or where we're from, and my mother lies. Then, paranoid that person may tell HIM they've seen us, my mother avoids the person. I avoid the person too, but for different reasons. It's hard to look someone you've lied to in the eye, and I know from experience that one lie leads to another and another and so on. And before long the person stops greeting us and goes about their life without us in it. I don't want this to happen with Butch.

I push the red doors open. Butch sees me, rushes toward me. "I missed you," he says. "How are you?"

"I'm fine," I say.

"Are you sure?" he asks. He cocks his head, looks at me with compassion. "You don't seem fine."

And maybe because I'm not used to people responding to a mean-ingless response like "I'm fine" with kindness, or because I'm tired of longing and lying, tired of being so self-sufficient, tired of sadness and loneliness, I start crying.

He puts his arms around me, strokes my hair, says, "Let's find some-where to talk, okay?"

And so we walk down to the beach, find a bench in the park area overlooking the water, and I tell Butch my entire life, not just some of it like I did that first time I met him at South Haven Drug. I tell him about my mother's crazies and what really happened during those two previous weeks and the Shadow Man and how my mother and I have been running from him for as long as I can remember and how I'm no longer certain he really exists. And I realize that it's the first time I've ever confessed this, not just to someone else but to myself, and I swear that in that moment the water gets bluer and the sky gets brighter and the world seems bigger. And I lay my head on Butch's lap and he runs his fingers through my hair like my mother sometimes does, but it feels entirely different. It is a safe and comforting feeling, a "the world's arms are around me" feeling, a "this is where I belong" feeling. And we stay like that without talking, just being, listening to the waves rol-ling ever so softly to shore, and when the sun begins its journey into the lake and darkness begins to set in, Butch walks me home.

And there, on the crooked front porch of the dilapidated house, he kisses me and the taste of his lips awakens something inside me, something both new and primal, and afterward he smiles, tells me goodbye, and that he'll call me in the morning, and as he begins to walk away, as if he just remembered something, he turns, says, "Do you want to go fishing with me this weekend?"

And I don't even try to hide my excitement. I smile wide and say, "Yes!"

Scarlet

I was losing track of time again. I could hear it. A crackling. Like radio static. Maybe it wasn't me. Maybe HE had found out about my plan and it was part of some huge conspiracy to undermine it. He knew people. People in high places. The FBI. The CIA. The South Haven Police. The Vatican. But how did he do it? How was he able to turn back *all* the clocks? To steal entire chunks of time?

I wanted to tell Henry about losing time when I was last there. But I couldn't. What if he didn't believe me? Or what if he already knew? Oh my god, what if he was in on it? He said we'd talked on the phone. We hadn't. He said I told him I'd been to New York. Why would I tell him that? Was he trying to confuse me?

Then there was Blue. She knew someone had stolen those two weeks from us. She looked about before she mentioned it, lowered her voice. She knew *they* were listening.

"Did you notice the date on the calendar?" she asked.

"What about it?" I whispered.

"It's the middle of June."

"I think they're in the clock."

"Who's in the clock?" She climbed atop a chair and looked inside it. "There's no one in here," she said. "Just the bird." She jumped down. "Mama, do you remember New York?"

"New York?" Why was everybody talking about New York?

"You lost some time," she said.

It dawned on me I might be scaring her. What was happening to me? "I think I'm just tired."

"Do I need to stay? I'm supposed to meet Butch at the pier to go fishing, but I can call and ask for a rain check."

"No, don't do that," I say. "Go have fun. I'll be fine."

I started to paint then. After a while, a long while, I looked behind me. She was gone.

The truth was, I was worried. The crackling sound wouldn't stop. I shouldn't have told Blue about the clock. I didn't want to worry her. How did a mother tell her child something might be very wrong with her? How did a mother tell her child she might be losing her mind?

I sat on the floor, brought my knees to my chin, put my hands over my ears, rocked back and forth. I felt so alone. I'd always felt so alone. In my mind, I was a little girl again, waiting for my father to find me and take me home, waiting for my mother's smile when she saw me, her bear hug, her happy tears, waiting for her to take my hand and twirl me around. Waiting.

But no one came.

Blue

Butch meets me at the pier, which is already lined with fishermen and -women in rolled-up trousers, their feet dangling over the edge, their rods, like notes on a music score a succession of angled marks against the solid blue morning sky. We find an opening about halfway down. He opens the tackle box he's brought along, then a small Tupperware container. Inside is a mound of worms crawling in and out and through one another. I feel a twinge of nausea.

"Basically you need six things to fish," he says. "A rod, a reel, fishing line, a hook, a bobber, and bait. A tackle box for your gear and a bucket to put the fish you catch in are good ideas too. I've already prepared your rod. You just need to do the bait." He points at the worms. "Are you okay to do that, or would you prefer I do it?"

I'm not okay with it, but of course, since he asked, I can't say that. "No. I'll do it."

"Watch me," he says.

He reaches into the bucket of worms, pulls one out, and ties it to his hook. "Okay. Now you do it. Be careful not to pinch the worm too hard or it'll squirt all over you." A teasing smile.

I hesitate.

"They won't hurt you."

I zero in on the closest worm with my thumb and index finger, lightly squeeze. The thing squirms and flails.

"You got it. Don't let it go. Here. Slip it through."

I put it through the opening of the knot Butch made. He tightens it around the worm.

"You can let go now. Good job. Now you have to cast."

I mimic his actions. With less precision.

"Not bad for a first time," he says. "You need to take up some slack in your line. Here, let me show you."

I do what he did.

"Okay, good."

"Now what?" I ask.

"We wait," he says.

The silence within this linear crowd reminds me of a music score. Notes of all different heights and widths, mute scratches waiting for the pianist, the artist, to give them voice. Periodically I hear the music of fishing, a splash in the water, the winding of a reel, the flapping of a fish, the opening of a container.

My line tugs.

"You caught one!" Butch exclaims. "Bring up your rod. Keep the line tight. Yup, like that. Now reel it in."

And I see *my* fish and I feel such joy, a sense of accomplishment, a pride, and I hear clapping and cheering and look to see the row of fishermen and -women smiling widely.

"Your first?" a man with a long beard asks.

"Yes," I say with more exuberance than I intend.

"May there be many more," he says.

Butch helps me unhook the fish. "Do you want to keep it or throw it back in?"

There is no way I'm throwing it back in. "Keep. What is it?"

"Lake trout. A nice-size one too. Good job."

We stay on the dock a while longer. Catch four more fish between us. And then we gather the tools of our art and head to the edge of the pier.

"Want to go again tomorrow?" he asks. "We need more before we can fry them up for dinner."

"Okay," I say.

———————

On the way home, I relive the euphoria I felt when I caught my first fish. The only other time I've ever felt that sense of elation is when I am lost inside a sonata or a waltz or a nocturne. Music is lonely, a good lonely. Fishing isn't. And not just because I shared it with Butch and other anglers; because even if I'd gone by myself, I wouldn't have been alone. I'd have been surrounded by life. In the vast landscape where everything is larger than me. Where everything and everyone is connected. And right then I decide that music and fishing together are perfection.

My mother is asleep on the sofa when I get home, a paintbrush perched precariously on her stomach. She painted into the night again. This isn't new; it is just happening more often. I asked her once how she could see. "I create my own light," she said. "Like a firefly." I return the brush to the turpentine jar, douse it a few times, and wipe it clean with a cloth, all the while assessing the painting she's been working on. Yet another yellow boat floats in the middle of a vast lake. The sky is dark. The water choppy. The boat threatens to capsize. Inside the boat is a suit-clad man. He lies splayed across one of the seats, his white shirt and jacket soaked in the dull-colored paste she made from crushing ladybugs, the most saturated red she's been able to find in nature. The brownish liquid drips onto the boat's deck. The man's mouth and eyes are open as if caught by surprise. The painting is disturbing. It's not just the bloody dead man; it's the inevitability of the circumstances: the brewing storm, the sinister sky, the angry water of the vast lake threatening to swallow the lonely boat as if it means to bury the evidence of the man's murder. The entire scene is fated. The man will always be murdered. The lake will always consume the boat. The crime will never be discovered. Nothing will ever be solved. In that moment, I think about her seeing Butch's dad, hope their meetings are helping her, wish I could ask him, wonder how strict doctor-patient confidentiality is.

Why is she painting a dead man? Is this the only time she's done so?

I remember our lesson on pentimento.

I grab the cloth, dunk it in the turpentine, flip through the stacks of paintings until I find another yellow boat, touch the paint that covers its deck—it isn't as dry as the rest of the canvas—carefully rub the wet cloth over it, its strong odor causing my eyes to water and throat to burn. There, a layer beneath, is the same suit-clad man, this one headless. I steep the cloth again and again until I've wiped away the top layer of every boat, and just as I feared, each one is a tomb for the same dead man in various states of carnage. In some he is headless, some armless, some legless. Some quartered as if they are slabs of meat. Some completely contained in the boat. Some with body parts and entrails spilling over the edge into the water.

My mother stirs. I freeze. I need to fix the paintings. I don't want her to know I've been sneaking around in them. I wait for the sound of her rhythmic breathing and then grab a brush. I am confident I can mimic her style. She taught me how to in one of our lessons. Interestingly it was on Vincent van Gogh.

———————————

"Why did he paint so many prostitutes?" I'd asked her.

"He was trying to work through something," my mother said. "That's what artists, what writers, what musicians, do. They use their art to work through something that plagues them. For Van Gogh it was love."

"I don't understand."

"He was attracted to those that society looked down upon. He related to their suffering. He had relationships with prostitutes and fell in love with a heavily pregnant one named Sien. She came to live with him and was his muse for a time, but after her child was born, she left him. He was lonely and unlucky in love. That's how he lost his ear. He got in a fight with Gauguin, and in a fit of madness cut it off and gave it to another prostitute as a sign of his love. He almost died from the wound."

"Was he already crazy and that's why he was unlucky in love?" I asked. "Or did love make him crazy?"

"That is the age-old question, isn't it? Which came first, the artist or their art?"

"I wish I could paint like him."

"You can paint better," she said.

"How do I do that?"

"Close your eyes," she said. "Imagine yourself standing with Van Gogh as he paints. Do you see him? Now imagine you both as pure energy, mere ghosts of your former selves, and merge. Then open your eyes and paint."

That day, I tried to step inside Van Gogh many times. Over and over I closed my eyes and imagined my body merging with his, without success. "No," my mother finally said. "You are doing it wrong. It isn't about you entering him. It is about him entering you. Don't you see? *You* are the artist. Throughout time, artists have borrowed from those whose work they admire, but they haven't stolen it, they've simply made it their own."

————————

Now I think about the similarities between that lesson and what Mr. Kline said about Mussorgsky: "I want you to play not as if you see each drawing, each watercolor, but as if they are part of you. As if every curve of the pen, every stroke of the brush, is inside you." And it is as if I've grasped something profound. I am both me and all who came before me.

And so I do what I did with the Mussorgsky. I close my eyes and imagine my mother entering me. Then I pick up her wooden palette, sift through the mess of tubes under the table ("sacrilege," she would say), squeeze and mix until I match the colors of the black leather seats, gray speckled decks, shiny yellow hulls. And then, so she won't know I've discovered her secrets, I do what she did. I paint over all the dead men.

FEBRUARY 12, 2014

Chicago, Illinois

46 YEARS AFTER THE MURDER

The Pianist

I remember feeling scared and worried. I remember wondering why she was painting suit-clad men in various states of carnage and then covering them up. I remember trying to convince myself that all of it—those two crazy weeks, the voices, the times I found her painting naked—were just the products of a highly creative mind. I remember hoping that Butch's dad was helping, wondering if I should try to contact him. Should I have?

It was mere weeks after the murder when Dr. Henry told me about schizophrenia.

"Ten to fifteen percent of children with a schizophrenic parent inherit the disease," he'd said. "But you shouldn't let it worry you."

I shouldn't let it worry me? How was that possible?

"How will I know?" I asked. "Will there be warning signs?"

"Some say they experienced depression, insomnia, and irritability, but in general, by the time you experience actual symptoms, the disease will already have set in. It is much like the common cold. One day you're fine, or at least you think you are, and the next you wake up with a sore throat."

As if schizophrenia and a sore throat were equally bothersome. Dr. Henry never did have much of a bedside manner.

He went on, "The good news is that symptoms usually start between the ages of sixteen and thirty. Rarely do they occur past the age of forty-five."

"So you're saying I only have to live in fear for the next thirty years?"

"The next fifteen is more likely."

"My mother was thirty-two."

"We *discovered* it when your mother was thirty-two. Given what you've shared with me about your life together, the constant moves, her erratic behavior, her hallucinations and delusions, her paranoia, I believe the disease set in years earlier."

"What about after the age of forty-five?"

"As I've said, it's rare."

"What percentage?"

"Less than one percent."

"But it happens?"

"Yes, it happens."

And so every time I experience bouts of depression or have trouble sleeping, which then makes me irritable, or I get paranoid or think I'm imagining something or someone, like the man wearing the fedora and pinstripe suit who gave me the catalogue, I am absolutely certain this is the moment. Within weeks I'll be hearing voices and walking around naked.

On the cover of the catalogue given me by said fedora-wearing man, the twins stare back at me. It is as if we are in some sort of standoff. Whoever blinks first loses. Two sets of blue eyes, two sets of sweaty curls tickling two foreheads, two blue dresses, two pairs of yellow gloves, two faces, two necks, four arms. Two pinkish chairs, one slightly less pink than the other. One red background. One fugitive background.

There is something about duplicates, an implied order, a promise of more to come, even if one of the two is more faded than the other. I went to Juilliard with two sets of twins. In both cases, one stood out. One's personality more vibrant, one's gait more confident, one's smile warmer.

Like the replica of *Madame.*

Who was she?

"She was the wife of one of Renoir's wealthiest patrons, a stockbroker named Léon Clapisson," my mother had said. "Not much is known of her beyond her maiden name, Marie Henriette Valentine Billet. Some accounts refer to her as socially ambitious, while others emphasize her youth." It was one of the things about my mother's lessons I enjoyed most. Learning not just about art, but also about the painters themselves, their motivations, their subjects.

"How old was she?" I asked.

"When she married? Your age. Just fifteen."

"Married?" I couldn't imagine being married.

"The portrait was Renoir's second attempt. The first was set outdoors, but neither the artist nor Monsieur Clapisson approved of it. Renoir was so proud of the second that he chose to enter it alone in the 1883 Art Salon of Paris, the most influential exhibit of the time."

"What's so special about it?"

"He felt he had mastered the background. Remember I told you about cochineals? Well, the pigment they produce is known as a *lac,* or lake, because it combines an organic substance with an inorganic substance. Even back then artists knew that lake pigments would separate and ultimately break down when exposed to light—they've found color recipe journals made by artists of the period that show how certain mixtures faded over time—so it's a mystery why Renoir chose to use it. Some accounts say he was so intent on using the most luscious of reds, he chose to sacrifice longevity for immediate gratification. Renoir painted Madame as a child who had just transitioned to womanhood. Her flushed cheeks are those of youth. Note that the background he was so proud of nearly consumes the woman. Red is the color of passion as well as the color of blood. Here both are at play. In those days it was not unusual for a man to marry a young girl. Often the marriage was arranged."

I wasn't convinced about all that symbolism stuff, so I paged through the Impressionist book, using my finger to underline each line as I read.

"I don't see anything about any of that in this book," I said. "Did you read it somewhere else?"

"I didn't need to read it," she responded. "It's obvious. Can't you see? *Everything* has been taken from her, her life, her parents, her home, even her name. Stolen by a man. A stranger."

Taken and *stolen*. Those are the words she'd used.

Now, as I sit on my smooth wooden bench staring at twin portraits of *Madame*, the original and its facsimile, I find myself contemplating the truth behind Renoir's pride. Is it, as history says, because of the painting's background? Or is it, as my mother said, that he believed he'd perfectly captured a young girl's passage to womanhood? Or perhaps it's simpler than either of those explanations. Perhaps the "celebrator of beauty" simply admired his model's beauty. After all, he was known as a womanizer.

I take a deep breath, open the catalogue, flip past the cover page and dedication to a page entitled "A Brief History of Pierre-Auguste Renoir." He was French, born 1841, died 1919. Along with the artists Edgar Degas and Camille Pissarro, he mounted the first exhibit of a new style of painting known as Impressionism. But the catalogue contains little information on the painting of *Madame* itself, with the exception of when it was painted, 1883. Instead, the text centers on the investigative process scientists went through "to solve the mystery of the missing pigment." As part of an effort to create a digital catalogue of the museum's collection, *Madame* and other Impressionist paintings were removed from their frames, which led to a surprising discovery. The colors hidden beneath the frames were more vibrant. To accurately portray *Madame*, they needed to identify the red pigment Renoir had initially used: carmine lake. Exhaustive information on cochineal bugs and the extraction process follows.

"I refuse to hear any more about this," I'd said.

"You need to learn it," my mother said.

"I won't."

"If you were learning this in school right now, you'd get an F."

"Well, I'm not learning this in school, am I? Besides, who wants to know the gory details of boiling a bunch of bugs in a vat and crushing them? They probably screamed."

"I'm sure they didn't scream."

"How do you know that? Lobsters scream."

"Conversation over."

All these years later and the thought of boiling those poor helpless, not to mention *pregnant*, bugs alive still hurts my heart.

The catalogue says *cochineal* comes from the Latin *coccinus*, meaning scarlet-colored. It goes on to verify what my mother had told me years earlier, that the unusually high level of saturation is a result of carminic acid, which the bugs produce naturally to deter predators.

It's a shame that something Mother Nature gives you to survive ends up being the very thing you're killed for.

I look at the paintings.

The pinks and reds of the reproduction do indeed rival the intensity of today's permanent pigments: alizarin crimson, cadmium red, permanent rose, permanent carmine, scarlet lake.

Scarlet lake? So stunned am I that I nearly say the words out loud.

Surely I had checked the crayon my mother pulled. Or did I? Her selection of that particular name couldn't have been random. She knew exactly what she was going to do. And yet, afterward, she had insisted the murder wasn't planned, that she didn't call him, didn't wave him down when he drove along our street searching for the address of the dilapidated house, didn't invite him inside. Didn't, as the district attorney said, "lure him." She said she didn't even remember killing him, that she must have been inside one of her episodes. Was all of it lies?

I take out my phone and google the names of the crayons in a box of sixty-four. No scarlet lake.

I am such a fool. All these years I have believed, *wanted to believe*, that scarlet lake was the crayon she had selected before we boarded that final bus to South Haven, the murder was self-defense gone wrong, and she had no memory of performing the act itself. No memory of putting a sedative into a man's wineglass, waiting for him to lose consciousness, and slitting his throat.

How long had she known what she was going to do? For how many towns?

SUMMER 1968

South Haven, Michigan

THREE MONTHS BEFORE THE MURDER

SCARLET: A very bright red with a slight orange tint; one of the varying hues of the primary color red, most closely associated with the color of blood.

Blue

I exit our house to a plenty of color. Yellow sunflowers and pink dahlias, green lawns and pastel houses. Black squirrels scurry up tall-trunked trees. Birds perch on telephone wires. Children run through sprinklers. As I pass Mrs. Proffitt's house, Peaches, her poodle, runs to the fence and yaps. Brutus and Barney, Mr. Frank's Labs, respond in kind, and for a moment, the entire street's canine population becomes a barking band. I cross the street. Mrs. Quagmire's calico cat sees me coming, saunters over, rubs against my leg.

"Hello, Maggie," I say. "Isn't it just a divine day?"

Mr. and Mrs. Mulligan sit on their front porch, which overlooks the beach. "Well, good morning, Blue," says Mr. Mulligan. "Fine day for bikinis." He raises his binoculars to his eyes in jest. Mrs. Mulligan slaps his wrist.

Down by the water, bold umbrellas march in formation against a clear blue sky. A fusion of sounds: laughing and splashing and shrieking of gulls. I head to the Coke stand and order a strawberry slush. While I wait, I overhear a girl not much older than me ask her boyfriend to slather baby oil on her back. She rolls over, unties the top of her white bikini. I wonder if my scrawny body would look as good in a bikini.

"Here you go, Blue," Jeffrey, the stand's owner, says. "God sure gave us a pretty one today."

"Sure did." I suck on the straw, kick off my sneakers, grab them, and rush to the lake, the sand burning the bottoms of my feet. I stand at the water's edge longer than I should, wade in the wetness, bathe in the heat. A feeling of pure happiness washes over me. I want to stay forever. Here, on this shore. Here, in this town. I run to the community spigot, rinse off my sand-caked feet, slip back into my sneakers.

In town, the buzz of crowds, hum of auto engines, swish of bicycle wheels. Clementine's staticky loudspeaker announces, "Goldwater, table for two" and "Mills, party of eight."

Mr. Kline sits on a green-and-white lawn chair under his shop's awning, a straw hat atop his head. "It's a scorcher today," he says. "You're late. By the looks of that sand stuck to your legs, I'm guessing you stopped by the beach."

"Sorry."

"Next time," he says, "let me know and I'll meet you there."

Inside, the ceiling fans wobble and purr. He shuts the glass door behind us, pulls down its shade, removes his hat. "I know it's muggy in here, but the street noise will distract us. Have you made that list?"

"Yes," I said. He had asked me to choose three sonatas each by Beethoven and Chopin that I would like to perfect.

"Go ahead."

"Beethoven's *Waldstein, Hammerklavier,* and *Moonlight.*" I'd played the *Moonlight* for him that first time I entered his store. "And Chopin's *Sonata no. 2, Military* Polonaise, and *Fantaisie-Impromptu.*"

"What about the *Andante?*"

He's testing me. He knows that while the *Andante Spianato et Grande Polonaise Brillante* is my all-time favorite, I also fear its technical demands.

"You said to choose only three," I tease.

He points at Old Reliable Bessie, the piano in his shop I play the most, and says, "Sit."

I shake my shoulders. Stretch my arms, close my eyes for a moment, then open them and play. My fingers stretch across the entire keyboard as they attempt fast arpeggios and quick scales.

"Chopin's father was French, his mother Polish," Mr. Kline is saying. "He began working on the *Andante* around 1830. It was originally composed for piano and orchestra. He added the piano solo in 1834, then joined the two pieces, completing the entire work in 1836. Can you imagine? Six years? But it is perfection."

I've played the piece so often that I know it and these words by heart.

"Again," he says after I finish.

I used to fight his "agains." Not verbally. Internally. There are days we work on only sixteen measures or so of a piece, playing them over and over. I pretty much fight anything I don't decide for myself. But I've learned to let go, to give in to discipline. To, as he says, respect the music more than my ego.

I straighten my back, roll my neck, caress my aching wrists and hands. He flashes me a knowing smile. "You must be meeting that young man of yours this afternoon."

"Why do you say that?" I've never mentioned Butch. It's true what Sunshine says. *Small towns have eyes.* Everybody in this town knows everything about everybody else.

"Your heart is somewhere else. Just so you know, I like that boy. Good people, he and his father both."

"What is his father like?" I try to sound casual, as if my curiosity has nothing to do with Butch's dad treating my mother.

"Smart girl," he says. "If you know the father, you'll know the son. He is an honorable man. I knew his wife. She died years back. He was devoted to her. I can't imagine he'll ever remarry. Raised that boy by himself and did a right good job of it."

"How is he as a doctor?" A little more direct, but he doesn't seem to notice.

"Well, I don't really know," he says. "Not personally anyway. But I've heard folks praise him to others when they don't think they're being overheard. Me? I can hear a pin drop two rooms away. Bet you can too. That's the pianist's gift, exceptional hearing. Else how could we discern the nuances in the music?"

I think about how I can hear my mother's breath from rooms away. "But wasn't Beethoven deaf?"

"Not always," he says. "He didn't start losing his hearing until his late twenties. And hearing comes in many forms. Beethoven *felt* sound through his feet. We have time for one more piece. How about we play a little waltz between Chopin and Beethoven. A re-freshing interlude, and waltzes are about love."

I want to argue both suggestions, that exceptional hearing and deaf-ness are somehow similar, and that Butch and I are in love (what we are is between Butch and me), but don't. The only person I ever ar-gue with is my mother.

After the *Lieblingswalzer* and a brief summary of Mozart's life ("He wrote his first minuet when he was five years old. He was an accom-plished dancer himself. His family hosted dancing parties in their home in Salzburg.") he switches the sheet music to Beethoven's *Hammerklavier*, my second favorite sonata, and as challenging as, if not more challenging than, the *Andante*. The piece, which literally means "hammer keyboard," is known for its technical requirements and emotional complexity, ranging from the uplifting opening chords to the shadowy menace of the second movement to the sorrow of the third. But it is its length that is most demanding. While sonatas gen-erally take between twenty and twenty-five minutes to play, the *Ham-merklavier* takes forty-five to fifty minutes. It requires immense focus to maintain such high intensity for such a long period of time. I have yet to play the entire piece all at once.

"Why don't we work on the Allegro today?" Mr. Kline asks.

Nine minutes, I think. I can sustain my concentration for that long. As I play, he tells me about Beethoven. About his birthplace, Bonn, Germany, how he was initially taught by his father and later by the composer and conductor Christian Gottlob Neefe, the publication of his first work at the age of thirteen, the dysfunction of his child-hood, and the relief he found in the home of Helene von Breuning, whose children he taught and who educated and introduced him to Bonn society.

He says more, but I don't hear him. Yes, he's talking and I'm playing, but my mind is on meeting Butch and Hannah at the beach. Hannah is bringing folding chairs. Butch, rubber rafts. He said he'd have them blown up and ready by the time I am through with practice. We will spend the afternoon floating and swimming and, like those older teenagers by the Coke stand, slathering ourselves with baby oil, only ours will be laced with iodine because Hannah says it will make us tan faster. Hannah, who only burns. I'll be wearing my same old dark green one-piece swimsuit. And for a time, I won't think about my sore hands or Beethoven's feet or the competition. This afternoon, for a few glorious hours, I won't think at all.

Scarlet

Jeremy went with me to the grocery store to get the ingredients for Blue's favorite meal: lasagna. It had been a long while since I made lasagna, or had done much cooking at all, but I thought I could pull it off. All I had to do was follow the recipe on the back of the noodle box.

Lately my hold on Blue had felt as precarious as a kite caught by the wind. It was more than teenage obstinance. She used to mind the Rules at least most of the time. Now she challenged them, and sometimes outright broke them. Did she think I didn't know this? She had yet to understand the biological connection between mother and child. Even when I was lost in my painting and she was lost in her music, even when she was at school or piano practice or off with Hannah or the new boy, Butch, even then I felt her inside that energy field that connects the two of us, that shrinks with closeness and expands with distance.

The lasagna dinner had been Jeremy's idea. "You, of all people, should know what imprisonment feels like, love. You need to let up on her."

"How do I do that?" I asked.

"You should invite her friend Hannah over for dinner."

"I don't think that's a good idea."

"It's a splendid idea," he said. "If you want to be part of her life, you need to embrace her world."

Jeremy could be so irritating, but in this situation, at least, he was right. Blue was no longer a child I could make do what I said. She had to want to be home, want to spend time with me. He was also right that I, of all people, knew what forced confinement felt like.

It was a balance. My world, our world, her world. Up until now, her world had been missing from the equation.

Even though I felt a panic attack coming on, I had agreed to the dinner idea. In addition to the lasagna ingredients, we bought salad fixings, a baguette, a six-pack of Coke, and two bottles of chianti.

"Remember," Jeremy said. "You did the shopping. I wasn't even here." He kissed my cheek and left.

"Who were you talking to just now?" I heard Blue ask. She had just emerged from the bedroom.

"Good morning, sleepyhead," I said. "I had the TV on for a bit."

"It's not on now."

"I turned it off when I heard you getting up."

She walked past me, went to the kitchen, and stared at all the groceries on the counter. It appeared as if she were trying to make sense of the situation. "What is all this?" she asked.

"Lasagna," I said. "That's still your favorite, right?"

"*You* went to the store."

"I did," I said. "I was wondering if you'd like to invite your friend Hannah over for dinner tomorrow night."

She looked at me, eyes narrowed.

"Cat got your tongue?" I asked.

"Um, well, I mean, it's just that—"

"Just that what?"

"You've never let me bring someone over before. And dinner. It just seems so *normal*."

I laughed and then we were both laughing, full and hard—it was a wonderful moment—and when we stopped she asked if Butch could come too.

I paused to reassess. There was obviously enough food, but was there enough me? I wasn't sure I could handle not one but two of

Blue's friends, one of them a boyfriend. I didn't do well with brand-new. I didn't do well with small talk.

"Don't worry," Blue said.

"About what?"

"I'll help cook and manage things. You'll see, you'll like them. What time should I tell them?"

"Around six?"

"Okay."

Blue ran to me then, hugged me tighter than she had in months, since before South Haven, and I hugged her back.

"I love you, my sweet Grace," I said.

"I love you too, Mama. Who is Grace?"

"Grace?"

"You just said, 'I love you, my sweet Grace.'"

"Oh, you know, some people say 'my sweet angel.' I always think of you as my sweet grace. Where are you off to?"

"Practice, and then we're heading to the beach, well, probably the lighthouse, since Hannah got burned yesterday. By the way, can I get a bikini?"

"A bikini? What's wrong with your green swimsuit?"

"All the girls wear bikinis."

I told her I'd think about it, but I doubted I would approve, at least not until she was older. Technically she was still a child.

I waited for her to argue, but she didn't.

After she left, I started painting, but couldn't concentrate. I got out paper and a pen and copied down the lasagna recipe from the noodle box. Twice. I used to be better about reading and remembering. Writing things out helped. I wanted tomorrow to be perfect. I wanted Blue's friends to like me. I started copying the recipe again. I had to get it right. More than anything, I wanted Blue to be proud of me.

Blue

Everyone calls them the summer people, but Butch, Hannah, and I have our own name for them: the pigeons. Because of how they arrive, in clusters, and because they gather in our streets and shops and restaurants and beaches like flocks of fluttering and frolicking birds. They hail from nearby urban areas—Chicago, Indianapolis, Michigan City, Detroit, Ann Arbor—so they are accustomed to crowding and noisiness and pushiness. The townspeople are divided. Some see them as bossy, wealthy, disrespectful intruders. Others welcome their impact on the local economy. Still others enjoy the flurry of excitement and unpredictability they infuse in our methodical, sleepy lives. For my mother, they are a lifeline. She has changed for the better this summer. She develops a routine. She wakes early, showers, sometimes makes breakfast like she used to, and walks me to piano practice. I know she paints some, I've mapped her progress, but nothing like she did this past winter or spring. It is as if she has chosen to inhabit the canvas of the real world instead of her imagined one, and, as she does so, youth and beauty find her again. The art of living brings color to her cheeks and lips. The sun browns her skin and pales her hair. She walks with an air of confidence. Smiles openly and freely. And I find myself hoping those two weeks in New York were just some sort of nervous breakdown like I read about at the library. It's where an inability to handle life's hardships can cause someone so much stress and pain that their emotions reach a breaking point. It can be cured with calm and lots of rest.

Then this happens.

I hear her talking to someone as I brush my teeth one morning. Not sure what to think, I head out to the living room. By now the voices are an unacknowledged reality. She doesn't want me to know she hears them, and I don't want her to know I hear her talking to the air, so we both play this confusing game of pretend that somehow makes sense to each of us. While the cause of the game is, by normal standards, abnormal, I've decided that it's not that different from what's going on with Amy's parents. Her mother wants to stay married to her father even though he has serial affairs (Hannah told me this, but apparently pretty much the whole town knows it), so she pretends she doesn't know he has affairs, and he pretends he isn't having them. That way they can still live together and keep the peace. That's what I do this morning. I decide not to tell my mother I only heard *her* voice. Just then, I notice the kitchen counter is full of groceries, ingredients for lasagna (my favorite), and since she hasn't cooked anything but a periodic breakfast in years, I am curious, to say the least, so, without thinking, I ask, "You went to the store?"

"I did," she says. "I was wondering if you'd like to invite your friend Hannah over for dinner tomorrow night." And I swear I've fallen into Wonderland, where everything is upside down. And I just stand there staring at her, probably with my mouth open, a side effect of befuddlement and other states of dismay, and she adds, "Cat got your tongue?"

I hate it when she says that. Like I'm five or something.

And I forget to pretend, and I say something about the dinner invitation seeming so normal, and she starts laughing as if it's the most hilarious thing she's ever heard, and then I catch her laughter, and neither of us can stop, and when we finally do, our eyes are left with tears and our faces with that weird smile you can't get rid of after uncontrollable laughter. And then, since she is in such a good mood and it may be my only opportunity, I ask if Butch can come too.

The old her, the one from before this morning, returns for a minute. She starts biting her lower lip and winding a strand of hair around her finger.

I swoop in before too much considering time goes by, tell her not to worry, and I run and hug her, tight. It feels really good—we haven't hugged in forever. Then she calls me her sweet Grace. *Grace?* When I ask why, she says it is the same thing as calling someone an angel, but I think that's a lie. But since it seems to be raining miracles, I decide to try one more thing. "Can I get a bikini?" She says she'll think about it, which means no, and then she picks up her brush, so I leave.

Now, as has become our customary summer routine, I meet Butch and Hannah after practice. (I admit I was hoping maybe this time it could be just Butch and me, but since this routine is established, we'd have to disinvite Hannah, which would hurt her feelings and our friendship. I did ask her once, selfishly, why she never hangs out with Amy and Miriam and Colleen anymore, and she said, "I'm tired of everything always being about Amy. She's not all that.") Usually we go to the beach, but today, since Hannah's skin is blistered and salved with chalky green stuff, a pretty common occurrence since she refuses to acknowledge that her skin is too pale to tan, Butch suggests we sneak to the top of the old lighthouse that is no longer in use. He picks the padlock on the door. We climb the stairs, head out onto the narrow circular balcony, and look out over the lake. Hannah has brought along a joint she stole from her dad's stash. I'm not sure I want to partake, but Hannah, who has "researched the positive effects of the cannabis plant," insists it is good for us, and her skin.

"It originated in the Himalayas," she says while I puff.

I cough.

"Don't inhale so deeply." She passes me her Coke. "Anyway, it's long been used for medicinal purposes. My dad says that's why he smokes it."

"What's wrong with him?" Butch says and takes the joint from me.

"He has arthritis in one of his hips from too much snow- and water-skiing when he was younger. He says he was a hot dog."

"Hot dog?" I ask.

"Like a show-off," Hannah says.

Butch breathes in slowly, holds his breath for a moment, and lets the smoke out through his nose. He doesn't cough.

"Wow," Hannah says. "It's like you've done this before."

Butch's smile is cocky as he passes her the joint. She shakes her head, mutters the word "boys" under her breath, and inhales.

Butch points toward the water. "Look at that guy."

"What guy?" Hannah asks.

"That parasailer."

"How's he doing that?" I ask.

"That boat is pulling him," he says. "Geez, that looks fun."

"To you maybe," Hannah says, and hands me the joint.

This time I don't cough. I feel proud. But nobody comments. Butch and Hannah are staring at the parasailer with a kind of awe, their mouths open, their eyes wide. This lasts for what seems like forever.

Butch waxes on about the beauty of the sky.

Hannah lies on her back and closes her eyes. "I can see colors behind my eyelids."

"Does anyone want this joint?" I ask.

"There's like a hundred shades of blue," Butch says.

"Where?" Hannah asks.

"In the sky," Butch says.

"What about the parasail?" she asks.

"White," Butch says.

"I'm pretty sure it's blue. What do you think, Blue?" She laughs. "That's funny. I'm asking someone named Blue about the color blue."

I wonder what's funny about that. "I don't know." I'm having trouble thinking. "Hey, do you guys want to come to dinner at my house tomorrow?" I hold the joint up in the air.

Butch takes it from me and says, "Sure, what time?" I figured he would ask more questions than that. "I don't want any more. You guys?"

Hannah and I shake our heads no.

"Six," I say. "Hannah?"

"What?" she asks.

"Do you want to come to dinner at my house tomorrow night? My mom's making lasagna." I wonder if the words sound boastful, being that's how I'm feeling.

"I must be really high," she says. "I thought you just said your mom's making lasagna and she asked Butch and me to come over for dinner."

"That's what I said."

"Wow," she says.

"Do you want to come or not?" I ask.

"Sounds fab," Hannah says, her new word replacing *divine*.

Butch pushes the butt gently into the metal floor. Then we all lie back and close our eyes, and soon we sleep, there on the balcony, shaded from the sun.

Scarlet

I helped Blue make the lasagna. Even though I'd read and written out the recipe, it still overwhelmed me. There was a time when Blue was the one helping me cook, but even before cooking got hard, I preferred sautéing over baking. Throwing stuff in a pan until it tasted good was so much more painterly. Baking, on the other hand, required work up front, like chopping and mixing and distributing, then heating for a designated period of time, a practice that seemed more like what a ceramist might enjoy. Cookies were the exception. Many a Christmas we rolled out the dough, created holiday shapes, and spent hours decorating them with colored frosting and sprinkles. I was reminded of those times now, of that comfort of shared domesticity, as I watched Blue chop and mix with an impressive deftness. But there was also something fleeting about it, a sadness born of fear. Fear of an elusive future, a future that was slowly fading away. But I tried not to think about that. I tried to stay in the moment, to watch Blue as she layered the noodles and tossed the salad, to feel my hands as they sliced and buttered the baguette.

"How much garlic powder should I use?" I asked.

"Just cover them totally," she said.

Butch and Hannah arrived just as the oven buzzer went off.

Blue answered the door. "Mama, you remember Hannah, from South Haven Drug? And this is Butch." He was cute, just like Blue had said. Dark hair and eyes. Friendly smile. Dimples.

"Nice to see you again, Hannah," I said. "And Butch, nice to finally meet you." I'd practiced those lines with Jeremy.

"Hi, Mrs. Lake," Hannah said. "Butch and I brought a cheesecake. We stopped off at Golden Brown Bakery. They make amazing cheesecakes."

"How thoughtful," I said.

Blue got Butch and Hannah Cokes and refilled my wineglass. I was on my third. I set the table while Blue took everything out of the oven.

"Dinner is served," Blue said. "Grab a plate and help yourself."

The table conversation was polite. Blue had coached me beforehand not to ask about either of their parents. She said doing so could lead them to ask about our family. I agreed, pleased that Blue was doing her best to maintain the Rules. Hannah was as chatty as I remembered. On several occasions she invited me into the conversation with insipid questions like was I liking South Haven and when did I start painting and wasn't it fab that I did. *Fab* was not a word Blue and I used. Butch was quiet until I asked about his fishing. His face lit up as he talked about it. He also mentioned how good Blue was getting, that before long she'd be "an expert angler." I felt envious as I listened to the three of them talk.

Blue and Hannah washed the dishes, and Butch dried. They left soon after.

"What did you think?" Blue asked.

I knew what she meant. "He was like you said. Nice and cute."

"But did you like him?"

"From the little I saw of him, yes."

She talked on for a bit about how much she loved South Haven and her new friends, that she wanted to stay forever, maybe get a dog, and other impossible things, but I let her dream. I let her have her happiness because I knew it would be short-lived. We wouldn't be here too much longer. Somewhere during the conversation, I found my way to my easel, and my newest painting of *Madame*. I was stressed from cooking, overstimulated from socializing. I zeroed in on the reds, told myself they were getting more "sonorous" (Renoir's word), but they weren't. I had yet to find the magic recipe that would produce the richness of pigment, vibrancy of color, that Renoir had fleetingly mastered.

Only for it to fade.

Blue

Summer stretches on. The initial gratefulness for warm temperatures turns into complaints over record-breaking heat. Ninety-degree days test patience and endurance. Window fans work overtime. Screen doors clap. Mr. and Mrs. Mulligan, and other townsfolk, fan themselves with accordion-folded pages torn from *Reader's Digest* magazines as they rock on their front porches. Beach umbrellas triple in number. An ever-changing crop of tourists splashes and screams or drinks and hollers. Locals clean their weekly rentals, clear their trash, plunge their toilets, change their sheets. Tensions rise.

We are at Hannah's house above Cisco's trying to figure out what to do. We've listened to her entire record collection. Danced to the Beatles and Monkees (bugs and primates) and Tommy James and the Shondells, who Hannah says are from Michigan.

"It's like this every summer," Butch says. "People act like jerks."

"Pigeons or locals?" I ask.

"Both," Hannah says. "The hotter it gets, the more the pigeons strut around like they own the place. We let them know they don't. They get uppity. We get offended. And before you know it, fights break out."

"Fistfights?" I ask.

"Verbal mostly," Butch says.

"Three years ago, there was a fistfight at Cisco's," Hannah says. "My dad had to call the police."

"That wasn't between pigeons and locals," Butch says.

"I know that," Hannah says. "When Blue asked about fistfights, it just reminded me."

"Who was it between?" I asked.

"Some college kid from Michigan got into it with one from Ohio State," she said. "They're rivals."

"Rivals?" Butch says. "They hate each other."

"Was it hot that year too?" I ask.

"Hotter," Hannah says. "It hit nearly a hundred."

"One hundred degrees?" I ask.

"She's exaggerating," Butch says.

"I am not," Hannah says.

The two of them have been sparring all morning. Again I wish it were just Butch and me. I like it when he holds my hand and rubs my neck or back for no reason, but Hannah gets agitated. (He's never kissed me in front of her.) Sometimes she's so disapproving she feels like our chaperone.

"What should we do now?" Butch asks.

Our options are somewhat limited. We are still too young to drive. We don't hang with the pigeons; we're too proud. There are only so many records we can listen to, so many hours we can spend roasting our skin, so many joints Hannah can steal from her dad.

And then, as if it's the most natural idea ever, Hannah says, "How about a scavenger hunt?"

Butch comes up with the rules. We can each suggest three objects, bringing the number of collectibles to nine. The initial list is pretty mundane. Butch: roll of toilet paper, baseball, turtle in a jar. Hannah: candle, book on South Haven history, cookie recipe. Me: Halloween card (which isn't as difficult to find in the summertime as one might expect), piece of sheet music, seashell that whistles. We have one hour to complete the hunt. The first person to collect all the objects is the winner. The most difficult object proves to be the whistling seashell, which no one scores.

After two more games of no winners, Hannah suggests we relax the rules. We keep the one-hour time frame, but add three caveats. The winner can be the person who collects the *most* objects. There can be more than one winner. In the event there is a clear winner, meaning someone does collect all the objects, that person can subject a loser of their choice to a dare.

It's dusk when Butch becomes a clear winner and chooses me as the recipient of his dare. We head to the pier while he thinks of a dare, and after a while, he says, "Adelaide."

"Yup," Hannah says. "Adelaide is perfect."

"Who is Adelaide?" I ask.

"Not who, what," Hannah says. "Adelaide is a tree."

"I dare you to climb Adelaide," Butch says. "Unless you're afraid of heights or something like that. Then I could think of something easier, I guess."

"No," I say. "Adelaide is good." As if I'm going to admit I've never climbed a tree before. Besides, how hard can it be?

"Tell her the story first," Hannah says.

"So way back when," Butch begins, "there used to be a lot of ship-wrecks up and down the Lake Michigan coast. One such wreck in-volved a propeller steamer called the *Chicora* that docked in St. Joseph, and carried produce and passengers to Milwaukee and Chicago."

"What's a propeller steamer?" I ask.

"Basically a ship with a wood and iron hull that can ram through thick winter ice." He continues. "Three years after *Chicora*'s first voyage, it was called to make a run of flour to Milwaukee. Every-thing was going along fine until a big storm approached. No one knows for sure what happened, but the next morning, wreckage was strewn over the lake from South Haven to Saugatuck. There was only one survivor, a dog named Adelaide."

"So Adelaide got adopted by a family that lived on North Beach," Hannah interjects. "They took her to an animal doctor, who said she was just a year old and it was amazing she survived, that she must be really special. As it turned she was. She was attacked by a bear, got shot in the leg by a deer hunter, and a bunch of other near misses, and the whole time all this was happening she saved a child that wandered away from his family, led some blind woman around town, and caught a bank robber by grabbing his pant leg. The whole town thought she was some kind of goddess, like Athena or something. Adelaide the Invincible, they called her. The story has it that she lived twenty-one years after that shipwreck, which means she was twenty-two when she died peacefully in her sleep. So her owners invited the whole town over, had some sort of ritual ceremony, and planted Adelaide the tree in her honor. Folks say Adelaide's spirit lives on in that tree, and that sometimes, when there's a mean storm, you can hear her barking inside its trunk, to warn boats to stay off the lake. And ever since, folks have called it Adelaide's tree, and sometime later, the house got named Adelaide House."

Of course I don't believe all this stuff about a tree trunk barking, but I figure it's a good story, like my mom's lessons, and if folks want to tell it, it's their prerogative. "Where is this tree?" I ask.

"Follow me," Butch says.

By now it's dark. He switches on his flashlight, and I follow him and Hannah along the beach for maybe a half mile until we get to a set of wooden stairs, and we climb three full flights to a wide two-story house with a large, second-floor circular balcony overlooking Lake Michigan. It looks like a house where a sea captain might live. All that's missing is a telescope.

"Adelaide's around front, nearer the street," he says. "But be quiet. All these houses around here are summer rentals, so there might be pigeons here."

"Might be?" Hannah says. "Theresa, from South Haven Realty, was at Cisco's last night and said every place in town is rented."

Adelaide is a large sprawling oak tree with heavy limbs, some of which are hitting the metal roof of the house. "Somebody needs to trim it," I say.

Butch hikes me up on his shoulders so I can reach a heavy limb. My climb is slow and steady. One solid branch at a time. Light shines from an open window. The sound of a fan blowing. I make my way toward it. The room has beautiful red filigree wallpaper and a huge, sparkly chandelier. A man and woman sit on the bed, their backs to me. Feeling like a voyeur, I look away, but my curiosity pulls my eyes back. The man wears only a white undershirt. He puts his arm around the woman, whispers something I can't hear in her ear. She turns her head toward him and smiles. There's no mistaking her profile. It's my mother. I immediately think about Amy's dad, wonder if it's him. I lose my footing for a moment, nearly fall, but right myself. And maybe I'm a little in shock because at first all I do is consider, in an intellectual way, how long it's been since I saw my mother with a man, not since I was eleven when one found me taking a bath and told me "what a pretty girl" I was, how when I called for my mother she ran in with a knife and told him to leave, how she promised she would never have a man over again. And then intellect leaves and hurt comes. And forgetting I am on a tree, I back away in anger. My foot slips off the branch. I let out a short scream, catch myself, look back inside the house to see if anyone heard. Her eyes meet mine.

Somehow I get down the tree without losing my footing again. Nobody tells you that climbing down is scarier than climbing up. I scrape my leg on rough branches more than once. It's bleeding in several places by the time I hit the ground.

"Are you okay?" Butch asks. "You almost fell."

"I'm fine," I say.

"Who was in that room?" Hannah asks. "Did they scare you?"

"There was no one."

"Are you sure?" Hannah asks. "The light is on."

"I'm sure." I feel the tears coming, hold them back. "I need to get home."

And perhaps it is the look on my face, or that by then Butch knows me in that way that two halves of love do. "People leave lights on all the time, don't they, Blue?"

"Yes," I say. "All the time."

He takes my hand. "I'll walk you home."

I pull away. "No. I'll be fine. You guys stay. I'll catch up with you later."

"Here," he says. "Take the flashlight."

I walk as slow as I can until I know they can no longer see me, and then I run. And when I get back to our little house, that stupid, *empty*, dilapidated house, I cry myself to sleep.

Scarlet

Week 29.

HOPSCOTCH. BEACH. SMOKE. BOAT.

Those were the words I wrote before Blue and I moved to South Haven. Before we got on our most recent bus. Before the bus before that and the ones before that. The first time I wrote my graph, it had a different ending. It was a confrontation plan, not a murder plan. That was before HE found me that second time.

My daughter was five years old when I saw his black Cadillac drive by, the same age I was when he took me. I had no idea how he found me. We had changed our names, moved far away from Michigan. I was at my studio in Tribeca, the entire second floor of a high-ceilinged loft I shared with three other artists, where my daughter and I had been for the three years since we'd escaped him for good. My studio mates and I kept our windows open on nice days, often sat on the deep ledges, our backs against the frame. I couldn't see through the darkened windows of the Cadillac, but I knew it was him. It was the way the vehicle slowed as it passed, then sped back up. Though I didn't plan to tell Jeremy about him, I felt I had no choice. That's when the running from town to town began. I'd see a black Cadillac with dark windows driving slowly by where we lived (a house or an apartment or a duplex or a room in a boardinghouse), then speeding back up. Generally he drove by at least three times before I was able to pack the two of us up and get to a bus station. I never had a destination in mind, until South Haven, that is.

"You don't care where the bus is going?" the clerk would invariably ask.

"It doesn't matter," I'd say. "As long as it's far away from here."

Up until Henry, Jeremy was the only person I told about my abduction. Unlike Henry, Jeremy believed me immediately. Helped me pack. Took me to the bus station. When I told Henry that I'd been taken as a child, he'd narrowed his eyes in disbelief.

"Did he take you against your will?" he'd asked.

I was tempted to respond with something sarcastic, something that highlighted the asininity of that question, like, *No, he asked my permission first.* Or, *What is it about the word* take *that you don't understand?* I was five, for god's sake. What five-year-old even knows about free will? What five-year-old understands the continuum of space and time? What five-year-old would even consider fighting a grown man? Sometimes I couldn't fathom how Henry ever became an analyst. If he weren't so encumbered by his own crappy childhood, maybe he'd be quicker on the draw. I'd told him some, about the fires and whatnot, and I planned to tell him about the four subjects of this graph entry, hoping that would spark his memory—*Henry, when are you going to put two and two together?*—but I had no intention of telling him about what it was like those first few days. That information belonged to me alone.

First there was the fear and panic, the deep sadness, the missing and wanting, the crying myself to sleep at night, the confusion. Where were my parents? Why didn't they want me anymore? Who was this man? And the question I asked the most, and for the longest time, *Why me?* That question was in fact still embedded in my DNA. The resentment came next, not toward HIM—I was too afraid to be mad at him—but at my parents, especially my father, for not saving me. Then the recognition, the horror of my circumstances. And finally a kind of grace, not to be confused with acceptance; there was never acceptance. Grace was an entirely different state. It involved make-believe—wonderlands and fairies and wizards and sorcery—and magic. If a magician named Houdini could disappear, then I could too. While I was with him, the time I now refer to as IT, I became adept at disappearing my mind from my body. I became a fugitive from myself. And after I escaped, the time I now refer to as AFTER IT, I tried to disappear those years from my mind.

It has been said that time cures all, no matter how painful or awful. It is true that the wider the space between IT and AFTER IT, the longer I could avoid the memories. At first, I celebrated *not* thinking about IT for a few minutes, then a few hours, then a few days, and so on. But IT never completely disappeared. IT still popped up at unexpected times and in unforeseen places. The cereal aisle of the grocery store. Rocking on a porch on a bright sunny day. A flower shop, a bookstore, a walk along the beach. And for no obvious or connected reason, I panicked. I couldn't breathe. I broke into tears. Distraction and diversion became my salvation. When the bad thoughts came, I twirled. When fear crept in, I danced. When magic eluded me, I entered my paintings.

Henry wanted me to *talk* about IT, as if releasing IT into the physical world would somehow diminish its magnitude. He was naïve. He wasn't taken. His innocence wasn't stolen. He didn't understand the distance I needed to keep in my mind.

Four words: *HOPSCOTCH. BEACH. SMOKE. BOAT.*

They were where the road I knew, the life I was meant to have, ended. They were where the road I should never have known began.

HE was the intersection.

Blue

My mother doesn't mention locking eyes with me that day. She's pretending it wasn't her. Hoping I'll pretend too. I'm hoping I'll forget. Forget I saw her and a man sitting on a bed together. Forget I returned to an empty house. Forget I woke to the sound of her stumbling into bed. Forget the smell of alcohol seeping from her pores.

Forget. An inactive verb I activate that year, which results in an activity I will master.

But rumors have the stealth and pounce of a panther. Two weeks or so after the incident at Adelaide House, Hannah tells me people are talking about my mother having an affair with some man. "Do you think it might be Amy's dad?" she asks. Then, the next day, while sipping a malted and waiting on Butch at South Haven Drug, I overhear whispering coming from a nearby table. I don't think much of it at first, but then I catch them stealing looks in my direction. Fearful of what I may hear, I try not to listen, but my already acute sense of hearing allows snippets of what they are saying to pierce my resolve. "Is that the daughter? Where do they meet? Is the man you-know-who?"

I get up to pay for my malted.

"It's on me," Sunshine says loudly, while shooting a disapproving look in the whisperers' direction.

"Will you tell Butch I'll catch up with him later?" I ask.

"You got it," she says.

I walk quickly by them on my way to the door, hoping I'll disappear.

When I can't rely on the forgets, I resort to the so-whats and the what-does-it-matters. So what if my mother is having sex with someone? What does it matter if everyone knows about it? It's not like we're going to be around long enough to care if the entire town is blabbing about us. It's already July. Seven months have passed since we moved to South Haven. Any day now, my mother will say she saw the Shadow Man. Any day now, we will be on a bus heading to another town, starting another new life. But though I practice all these diversions, I've come to understand that the so-whats and the what-does-it-matters, like the forgets, are really no different than the pretends. They are all just ways to fend off hurt.

Two days later, Hannah suggests we sneak out one night. The three of us are sitting in a booth at Cisco's.

"And go where?" I ask.

"Where she meets him," Hannah says. "Don't you want to know for sure that the rumor is true?"

"No," I say, then add, "How can you even be certain it's my mother?"

"I overheard my dad talking to Big Al. He was bartending, and Big Al was perched, like he is most nights, on his usual stool. He said he saw your mother and some guy over at Adelaide House."

My stomach drops.

"Geez," Butch says. "I hope he's keeping this information to himself." He takes my hand, squeezes it. "Sorry, Blue."

"Are you kidding?" Hannah asks. "Since when has Big Al kept anything to himself? Billy says Big Al has the gift of gab. He chats up all his plumbing clients."

Butch starts rubbing my neck. "Yeah, but just because he talks a lot doesn't mean people believe him."

"You two are sickening," Hannah says. "I know what we can do. When she leaves, you could call us. Do something like let the phone ring twice and then hang up. What time does she normally leave?"

"She doesn't *normally* leave," I say.

"Are you sure?" Hannah asks. "Maybe you're asleep when she leaves."

"This is stupid," I say.

"We don't have to do this if you don't want to," Butch says. "Just say the word and we won't talk about it again."

I don't know how long it is before I answer. I'm not sure I want Butch and Hannah to know what my mother is doing, not firsthand anyway. It's embarrassing, and I don't want to see their pity. Before I saw my mother with a man that day, I would have stuck to my earlier no. Like with my mother's voices and Amy's dad's affairs, pretending seemed the better option. But I did see her, with my own two eyes, and she knows I saw her, so we are past pretending. "Lying is against the Rules," she always says. "Breaking the Rules can get us killed." So I can't lie, but she can? What else has she lied about? How long has she been playing pretend?

And in that moment, anger having got the best of me, I say, "Okay. If she leaves, I'll call."

Henry

It was hot, even for August. In an attempt to create a cross draft, I had three fans going, each in a different corner. Scarlet sat across from me looking cool and fresh.

"Can you tell me about the man that took you?" I asked.

"I've told you what happened," she said. "Why do we have to beat a dead horse?"

"You're right," I said. "You have told me what happened. I was hoping you'd tell me how it *felt*."

"Why?"

"Recognizing and reliving painful emotions is how we begin to heal."

"You're wrong," she said. "It will only bring up bad feelings. I don't want to feel them all over again."

"Maybe at first it will, but the more you let yourself remember, the more you let yourself feel, the more power you gain over those feelings and memories. And one day you will conquer them. I know you're scared, but you're safe here. This is a safe place. It's just you and me."

"Safe? Seriously? Do you have any idea how naïve that sounds?" She was getting agitated.

"You're right. I can't presume to understand, but I'd like to."

"You want me to tell you how it felt? Fine. He told me he was my mother's brother, but I'd never met him before that day."

"What day?"

"The day our house burned down."

I waited.

"I was playing hopscotch," she said, her voice childlike, like the day she'd climbed under my desk. "My nanny had just returned from holiday and brought me a set of sidewalk chalks. Twenty-four different colors. So pretty. I drew grass beneath the board, tall skinny flowers either side of it, pink and blue and purple and yellow and red, and above it a bright orange sun. I saw him peeking through the bushes that lined our driveway, watching me, pointed him out to my nanny, but he was gone by the time she looked. I remember her saying he was probably one of the gardeners, but I knew all the gardeners, and besides, gardeners don't wear suits. I told her that, but you know how adults are."

"How are adults?"

"They don't listen to children. Which is ignorant."

"Why ignorant?"

"Because children don't second-guess intuition like adults do. If they see something that isn't right, they just say so."

"What happened then?" I asked, trying to be gentle.

"It was a few hours later. My mother was teaching me to swim while my father was finishing up party preparations. We were walking out of the water when I saw him again."

"The same man?"

"Yes. My mother grabbed the towel, wrapped it around my shoulders, and picked me up. I only remember snippets of their conversation, but I do remember the way it made me feel."

"How?" I asked.

"Scared."

"Why scared?"

"I guess because my mother was. But she wasn't at first. She just seemed surprised. He was friendly, like they were friends. That's what I thought, he was just early for the party. But then she asked if it was him she saw hanging outside her classroom at the church, watching the children play, and his smile went away. She tightened her arms around me and told him to leave."

"Did he say anything else?"

Scarlet sat back, closed her eyes, after a minute or so opened them. "He said she was wrong about it being him at the church. He sounded mad."

"Why do you think he got mad?"

"I've asked myself that question a million times. I went to this spiritualist once, and she said if we just let go, stop trying so hard to control outcomes, the answers will come. She was full of shit."

"You said her classroom at the church. Was your mother a teacher?"

"No. A social worker. She taught children how to play again. That's what she always told me. I asked her why they needed to be taught to play, since I played all the time, and she explained that they didn't have a nice childhood, that their parents were either mean, in jail, or—" Scarlet paused, leaned over, put her head in her hands.

"Or what?" I asked.

"They were lost and found," she said.

"What do you mean?"

"Stolen or missing, but ultimately found. I used to go with her sometimes. Play with this one found little girl who looked a little like me, same color hair and eyes. She was sadder than a lot of the kids, and I remember my mother asking me to try and make her happy."

"Did you ever see the man there?"

"I don't remember."

"Do you think he might have seen you?"

"I said I don't remember."

"Tell me about the fire," I continued.

"I remember coughing. I couldn't see anything. There was so much smoke. I remember my father lifting me from my bed. He took me outside, put me in this small boat he used for fishing, laid me down on one of the seats, started the motor. I was so tired. I fell back to sleep. It was dawn when I heard the motor stop, not at a marina, it was a wooded area along the water and there was another boat there, a speedboat. It was yellow. He took me into his arms, brushed his hand on my cheek. And that's when I saw that it wasn't my father at all. It was the man from behind the bushes and from the beach. I screamed, but he put his hand over my mouth, told me he'd kill me if I screamed again. We got into the yellow boat. There was a rope, he used it to tie my hands and ankles, he put tape over my mouth, then he put me on the floor between the seats and covered me with a blanket. We drove for a while. It was so dark inside the blanket, then the boat slowed and stopped. He took off the blanket and untied me. 'You'll be good, right?' he said, and I nodded. He took my hand and walked me down a long dock to a house on a lake, not a large lake like where I'd lived with my parents, a smaller one."

She paused. There were tears running down her cheeks. I handed her a tissue.

"Are you okay?" I asked.

"What do you think?" she asked.

"What are you feeling right now?"

"Fear, sadness. I don't know what else. Maybe confusion, I guess. I didn't understand what was happening. Or why I was there or where my parents were. Or why our house was on fire."

"Do you believe the man started the fire?"

"Yes."

"Why do you believe that?"

"Because he told me he did. Not that night but later."

I thought about what I was about to ask, worded it first in my mind.

"Do you believe he knew your parents were in the house when he started the fire?"

"He killed them." Then she was sobbing.

After a while, she wiped her eyes, blew her nose.

I waited.

"I can't talk about this anymore," she said.

"It wasn't your fault," I said.

"Of course it was. He killed them so he could take me."

"Think about what your mother said."

"I don't understand."

"Do you think he suspected your mother knew something about what he did to a child, something illegal, and he went there to see how much she knew?"

Recognition dawned on Scarlet's face. She looked at me, her eyes filled with tears, her face and nose red. "Why did he take me? Why didn't he just kill me? I wish he would have. I wish I would have died in that fire with them."

"But you didn't," I said. "You survived. And you're still surviving."

"I need to go," she said.

I urged her to stay, told her that what she'd just revealed was huge, that it would take a while for the child her to catch up with the adult her, told her we could work on that together.

But she left.

My office felt empty. A hole formed in my stomach. My chest hurt. I thought about Lily, my wife. About how much I still missed her. About how I recognized a similarity between her and Lily. A vulnerability. And now I understood why. Lily had been raped when she was a teenager by a boy she went to high school with, an athlete. The school knew and together with his family covered it up. Lily continued to go to school. I couldn't imagine what it must have been like for her, to suffer the bullying and lewd sexual comments thrown her way. Getting away with crimes often emboldened criminals. I spent the years Lily and I had together saving her. Every single day. Because, unlike my dead mother, Lily *could* be saved. My own years of therapy taught me that Lily and I were bookends. The perfect match. The one who needed saving and the one who needed to save. And now I realized, because I could no longer save my mother or Lily, I was directing my energy at Scarlet.

A few weeks ago, when Scarlet brought up the fire and the man, she'd been all over the place, but this time was different. There was no talk of New York. She didn't crawl under my desk. There were details. She was present and coherent. But that was the way it sometimes was with schizophrenia, moments of lucidity. Schizophrenia could be either hereditary or brought on by trauma. If what Scarlet had told me was true, she had certainly been through a major trauma. But to be certain my suspicions were correct, Scarlet would need to be evaluated by a specialist. I knew of someone in Kalamazoo. How could I get her to trust me enough to go through the evaluation? And if it was schizophrenia? I had been hearing about clinical trials using experimental drugs. I sat back in my chair, closed my eyes. My next client wasn't due for an hour. In the meantime, I would think.

Scarlet

I had to get out of there. It felt like the room was closing in on me. I was having trouble breathing. My heart felt as if it was going to jump out of my chest. I felt anxious. Sick to my stomach. Dirty.

I hated myself.

I hadn't meant to tell Henry so much. I went into the bathroom, grabbed my razor, stared at it for several minutes. Pressed it against my wrist where the other scars were. From those other two times. Scars I'd told Blue were birthmarks when she asked about them. Pressed harder. The sharp edge dug into my flesh.

Blood.

I dropped the razor, went out to the kitchen. I needed to get drunk, obliterated. I grabbed a bottle of chardonnay from the refrigerator, the good stuff, unscrewed the cork, took a sip—cool, buttery, oaky—swallowed the entire glass, poured another, and another. The dirtiness was getting murky, oozy, wobbly. I opened another bottle. Sat on the sofa. Refilled my glass.

What I'd told Henry, what he'd made me tell him, what he now knew, was grounds for erasing him. From now on, every time he looked at me, he'd see the real me. The weak, pathetic whore.

The room was spinning. I felt nauseated. I ran to the toilet, threw up, and then sat on the floor. Henry said if I told him, if I let myself remember, I could get my power back, but it didn't feel that way at all. It felt more like I'd given Henry my power. Now what? I had to do something to take it back. Under any other circumstance I'd just throw Henry away, never see him again, I was good at that, but I couldn't do that with Henry. I needed him.

The voices started talking all at once, directing me to perform unspeakable acts. "Stop," I said. I put my hands over my ears, shook my head from side to side, but they only got louder, more insistent. I thought I heard them say "training books," but maybe it was me who said it. I was so confused. Then I remembered the how-to books. When I was creating my graph, I read silly training books that I thought might help with Henry. I'd ultimately dismissed their instructions, finding them myopic. The how-to-catch-a-man book said I should be mysterious and elusive. As if I weren't already expert in such forms of manipulation. I'd spent ten years appeasing HIM so I could survive, and these last several months practicing similar techniques on Henry. The book was obviously bullshit. It didn't even have a section on emergency procedures. But what about the how-to-discipline-a-dog book? I went into the bedroom, retrieved the rucksack from its place under the bed, blew off a layer of dust, unzipped it. Pulled out my winter coat, hat, and gloves. Pushed aside paint tubes. Shuffled through books. Found it. *Puppy Training Made Easy.* I checked the table of contents, opened to the chapter entitled "Curing Your Pet of Bad Habits." There was a list of potential bad habits and recommended cures. One read, "If your pet has an accident in the house, or chews on your furniture or shoes, IGNORE him." It went on to explain that puppies and dogs cannot stand to be ignored. It hurts their feelings and is a surefire way to break their will and bend them to yours.

"Perfect," I said.

It was then I realized how quiet it was. I closed my eyes and basked in the silence.

Blue

I got the last fan from South Haven Drug. Sunshine said she sells out every summer around this time, "when the heat wave comes." She recommended my mother and I close all the windows and blinds to keep the sun from beating into the house and making it even hotter, which I did, and turned the fan up full blast.

Now I sit on the cat-clawed sofa, the fan pointed mostly in my direction so it doesn't blow on my mother's new painting. Lines and shadows and shades of gray characterize it—the underpainting. The book on Impressionism lies open to Renoir's *Luncheon of the Boating Party*. I consider asking her why she is copying yet another Renoir, but decide against it. I just want to sit here watching her as I feel the fan blow. Watching her paint and feeling the goose bumps it inspires is part of our rhythm. Surely every family has its own rhythm, doesn't it? Ours had been struggling since I saw her with the man at Adelaide House. I've pulled away even more since I overheard those women talking at South Haven Drug. I feel stung and humiliated. And yet, despite it all, I've missed her. Missed *us*. At this moment, as I watch her paint, I'm trying to find us again.

She stops. Backs away from the canvas. Begins cleaning her brush.

"I'm tired," she says. "I think I'm going to head to bed early. You should too."

And I find myself praying to a god I've never met. Begging him or her to reward my efforts to overlook what I saw from Adelaide's tree and what I heard at South Haven Drug by making not true what I fear is true at this very moment. The thing is, she never goes to bed early. She's a night owl. But isn't there a first time for everything? Couldn't she really *be* tired?

"Can I bring the fan?" I ask.

"Sure, but face it toward you, okay?"

I drag one of the rainbow table chairs into the bedroom, put the fan on it, and plug it in. Then I head to the bathroom and brush my teeth until my gums bleed. Once in bed, I pretend to sleep. Perhaps a half hour passes before she rises, dresses. She often can't sleep when she starts a new painting. "I can't quiet my mind," she says. I admit to even hoping it is the voices that are keeping her up. Anything but the reason I fear. Even through the whir of the blades, I hear her tiptoe to the front door—there is a downside to exceptional hearing— and turn the knob. Squeak of the hinges. Faint sound of crickets. Door closing. I jump from my top bunk onto the floor, run to the window, see her sprinting through the night, the fabric of her white dress flowing behind her.

I call Butch and Hannah, each time letting the phone ring twice.

I hear a whistle as I approach Adelaide House. Hannah sits on a bench in the small park across the street. I catch a whiff of baby shampoo as I join her.

"The streetlight is out," she whispers. "Isn't that fab?"

"Why fab?" I whisper back. I can't wait until she finds another word.

"Because no one can see us."

We wait. My stomach churns. My mother paces back and forth in front of the house. A few minutes later, Butch shows up. He wears all black clothes. My heart skips a beat. For a moment, I forget why we are here.

"You look like a cat burglar," Hannah says. "What took you so long?"

"It's a long walk from South Beach."

Hannah puts her forefinger to her lips, says, "Shh."

A man walks toward my mother. Tall, thin. City clothes. He carries a large black portfolio. I can't make out his face.

"Who is that?" Hannah whispers. "It's definitely not Amy's dad."

"Why would it be Amy's dad?" Butch asks.

"Forget it," Hannah says.

"He can't be from around here," Butch says. "Look at his clothes."

"Maybe it's a disguise," Hannah says. "We need binoculars."

"I think my dad has some," Butch says.

The man places his hands on my mother's shoulders and kisses her forehead before they walk into the house.

A mix of emotions floods me. Shame. Sadness. Most of all anger.

"Should we wait for them to come back out?" Hannah asks.

"I'm not staying," I say. "I've seen enough."

This time Butch doesn't allow me to walk home alone. When we get to the front door, he looks into my eyes, holds me, brushes my lips with his. I feel a deep sense of desire, imagine burying myself in his arms, his entire body, asking him to follow me inside, to stay with me forever. But then I find myself wondering if these kinds of feelings, these kinds of wants, make me like her, and thinking this way destroys the moment, cheapens my desire, and I say to Butch, "I need to be alone."

"I understand," he says. "But call if you want to talk or just want some company, okay?"

He hangs on the porch briefly after I've gone inside. I watch him through the window, biting his bottom lip. I can tell he is worried about me. Soon he walks down the porch stairs and leaves. Perhaps it's habit, or perhaps I'm hoping if I do what I *normally* do, study her painting, what I've just witnessed will, like a comet, become a momentary flash in an otherwise predictable sky. And so I ask myself the questions I normally ask when I'm alone with her canvases: Why hopscotch boards? Why yellow boats? Why dead men? Why paint-by-number Renoirs? I scan the room, note she's completed several new paintings. Everything in me wants to scream and cry. Tell her I know what she's doing. Tell her I saw her with my own two eyes. Tell her I want a different mother. One who doesn't humiliate me or drag me around the country or rob me of friends or romantic love or bury me in pentimento, who buys me a piano, takes pride in my talent, wants to hear and see me play.

Who loves me.

But I know I won't do any of this. Not because I am above such behavior, or because I value the paintings, art for art's sake and all that, but because I am resigned. Because she is who she is. Because we are who we are. *Not normal.* Because, despite everything, the truth is, she *is* this thing called *life*. She *is* my world. And though I sometimes imagine stealing the entire roll of money from the front pocket of her rucksack, getting on a bus by myself, and running far away, or hiding at Mr. Kline's when the Shadow Man comes and she tells me to pack, I can't picture myself actually doing it. Her hold on me is primal. I am hers through and through.

Henry

On the morning of Scarlet's next regularly scheduled appointment, I found an envelope taped to my office door. Inside was a handwritten note. It read:

> Dear Dr. Henry,
>   Thank you so much for everything you've done for me. I've decided not to return to analysis. Just as you said, telling you what happened, just saying it out loud, brought my power back. I feel so much better. At peace. Cured. Please do not contact me.
>   Sincerely,
>   Scarlet Lake

Blue

The windows and blinds in the music store are closed—it must be a thing here—and the twenty or so ceiling fans are on, but I'm still sweating. Mr. Kline doesn't seem bothered; he's acting chipper. He's talking about Russia. About growing up there. About his favorite meals. Borscht and sweet-and-sour cabbage and knish, none of which sound too good to me, especially in this heat. About his favorite Russian composers, whom he calls the Five. Mily Balakirev, Alexander Borodin, César Cui, Modest Mussorgsky, Nikolai Rimsky-Korsakov.

"I think you're ready," he says.

"For what?"

"Every year in autumn, at the commencement of the new school year, there are competitions at Interlochen Arts Academy focused on new talent in each discipline. There are prizes. I have taken it upon myself to enter you in the piano section."

"What kinds of prizes?"

"Scholarships. To the best music schools in the country."

I feel that cliff in my stomach. Autumn, while for some merely another season, is for me a wavy mirage, a time and place I may never reach. Although in the past I have begrudgingly accepted the limitation of impermanence, now, more and more, I fight it. My fantasies about staying in South Haven have become part of my daily routine. The problem is, I can't square them with reality. Where is my mother in the "marry Butch and raise the children here" fantasy? Where are Butch and my mother in the "become a world-renowned pianist" fantasy? I'm continually shuffling the puzzle pieces and putting them back together in different ways. And so, when Mr. Kline tells me about the competition, my future feels simultaneously wondrous and messy.

"When in autumn?"

"The third week of September," he says.

"That's almost here," I say.

"Plenty of time to prepare," he says. "And there's no need to worry about transportation. I will drive you and your mother. The colors on the trees will be changing. Such a glorious sight."

I see no reason to say I doubt my mother will come, since I can't say whether I will either because who knows when the Shadow Man will show up. Instead I say, "You drive?"

"I do. But we can discuss those details later. Right now, we need to decide which piece you will play. Let's try the *Andante*." He puts the sheet music on the piano.

And so I wipe all thoughts of a future or a competition from my mind, and play. I hear his voice over the music, telling me to feel the piece. "*Spianato*," he says, "means smooth." For a while he continues to impart his impression of the piece and my performance. But it is when I no longer hear him talking that I know he no longer differentiates me from the music. Though I can't see him now, I have in the past, and so I feel him walking around, moving his arms as if conducting, now and then kissing the tips of his fingers in praise or holding his palm parallel to the ground, pushing it up and down against an invisible tension membrane. Soon I no longer feel him, or imagine his movements. He and the world disappear. I disappear.

Afterward, I meet Butch and Hannah on the beach. I don't mention the competition. I don't trust it yet. Neither do I say anything about my mother and Adelaide House. I'm hoping Hannah doesn't bring it up—I know Butch won't—because I'm trying to forget it. Hannah is wearing her new baby-blue bikini; Butch, swim trunks. I roll up my sleeves and shorts, lie back on the blanket. I love the feel of the sun on my face. It steals my worrying. Butch asks if I want to go fishing in the morning, which irritates Hannah. She has never liked talking about things that don't include her, but lately she's been downright rude, going as far as to interrupt Butch and me, sometimes even commenting negatively on our conversations. Like now I'm telling Butch that I've just finished reading *Laura* by Vera Caspary and how interesting the structure is. "It's told in first person by alternating characters, even though it's all about the central character, Laura, who has been murdered. And the detective—his name is Detective Mark McPherson—falls in love with her memory. It's really good. There's this great surprise ending."

"My dad loves mysteries," Butch says. "You got it at the library?"

"Yes. Kelly recommended it."

"I like Kelly," Butch says. "She's really smart about books. Guess that's why she became a librarian."

"I hate mysteries," Hannah says. "And that one sounds especially boring. What's going on with your mom anyway? Has she gone to Adelaide House again?" She doesn't wait for my response. She changes the subject to the "art of macramé," which she has recently discovered.

"It's fab," she says. "You make knots with jute."

"What do you do with them?" Butch asks.

"I've been making hanging pot holders," she says.

His eyes narrow in confusion.

"For plants," she says. "Four separate braids tied into a loop at the top and a circle at the bottom. You put the pot in the circle and hang the loop on a ceiling or wall hook. We should all do it sometime."

"I think I'll pass," Butch says.

"I'd like to try it," I say, hoping she and I doing something together, just the two of us, will make her happy.

"Okay," she says. "How about tomorrow? After you guys go fishing." Said with a mocking tone. "We can all listen to my new album by the Turtles. My dad got it for me. I love that song 'Happy Together.'"

"Turtles?" I ask.

"Are you serious?" Hannah says. "You don't know the Turtles? They're a band." (I don't say that I figured as much.) "You will love them. I'll bet you can play their songs on the piano."

I wonder why pop bands seem to name themselves after bugs and primates and reptiles.

The subject changes then to cheerleading tryouts, which Hannah plans to do once school starts since Amy and Miriam are already on the team (lately she's been bringing up Amy and Miriam and Colleen as if the four of them are buddy-buddy again), and fishing club, which Butch is doing. And then we walk down to the lake, take off our shoes, and play and splash like the children we still are. Soon the sun begins its slow descent, cooling the air. The pigeons leave the water, take down their umbrellas, fold their beach chairs, shake out their sandy towels, gather their coolers, put on their flip-flops, walk to their cars or summer cottages or town. Hannah says she has to get to Cisco's.

"My dad is short a bartender. He called in sick."

"You're going to tend bar?" Butch asks.

"Sure, why not?" she says.

"I need to head out too," Butch says. "Fishing club meets at sunrise tomorrow."

And so we do what the pigeons did, shake out our sandy beach blanket, put on our flip-flops, and when Hannah isn't looking, Butch blows me a kiss.

My mind is on the competition when I arrive at our house, how I'm going to tell my mother about it, but it immediately shifts when I open the door. At first, I don't understand what I'm seeing, there's so much going on. The window is open. The fan is blowing. Multicolored streamers hang from the ceiling. They flutter and sway. The rainbow table has been pushed to the center of the room. On top of it are masking tape, a hammer, nails, and several paint-soaked brushes. On the floor, beneath and surrounding the table, is a disturbing mix of broken stretcher bars, the canvases they once supported in varying states of cut and ripped. The only paintings that appear to have been left untouched are the yellow boats and the Renoirs. Rounding out this display is my mother, her bare feet prancing, white slip shimmying, hair flying.

"Dance with me?" she says.

Something silver glistens in the light. I panic. "Put down the scissors, Mother." I go to her, hold out my hand. "Give them to me," I say with as much authority as I can muster.

She sits on the sofa, hands them to me. "You are such a stick-in-the-mud."

"What happened here?" I ask.

"Nothing," she says. "It's an installation. Everyone is doing them in New York. They call it post-minimalism. Do you know that artist Eva Hesse? Well, she's a pioneer. She studied with Josef Albers at Yale. You know Josef Albers, we had a lesson on him. It's all about anti-form. I was tired of those canvases anyway, so I decided to shred them. Sit with me. Watch them move. Aren't they beautiful?"

"Where are we, Mother? What town?"

She rolls her eyes. "What am I going to do with you? You need to lighten up. We're in South Haven, Michigan, okay? Are you happy now?"

Relieved, I sit down next to her and together we watch the canvas ballet, and after some time, she says, "Don't you dare take it all down. It's an installation, not a mess."

But though I don't tell her this, she is wrong. The scene before me is a mess, not an installation.

Henry

I am not certain what compelled me to spy on her. I would like to say it was out of character, but strictly speaking that was not true. While I had never actually donned a trench coat and dark glasses, I wore my share of imaginary ones. Our fantasies were often our true realities, or at least our preferable ones.

It had only been a week since I got Scarlet's note and two since I had last seen her, but it felt longer, and right now at least I had no intention of filling her time slot. I hoped she would return. I got up and looked out my window, and just then, as if it were destined, I saw Scarlet walk by. I rushed out the door and down the stairs. It was a beautiful day out, the sun shining, and the temperature had cooled to the low eighties. The sidewalks were dense with summer people—I nearly tripped when one knocked into me. I caught a glimpse of blond hair. She turned left on Broadway, then left onto Dyckman, crossed over the drawbridge, passed the park, continued on toward North Shore Drive, where she crossed the street and followed the walkway that fronted the town's most exclusive summerhouses. I kept a safe distance behind her, my adrenaline rushing, until she disappeared into the driveway of Adelaide House. When I caught up, she was nowhere in sight. Adelaide's tree stood grand and sprawling in front of the two-story nineteenth-century house. Everyone in town knew the story of Adelaide the dog, the lone survivor of the 1895 *Chicora* shipwreck. The house was now a popular long-term summer rental. What was Scarlet doing there? I waited for roughly a half hour before I saw her walk out the front door with a man. He kissed her on the cheek. They hugged, and then she walked my way. I ducked out of sight, waited for her to pass. Did I imagine that her hair had a mussed look? Was I so jealous that I'd concocted the whole sordid thing? I waited a few moments to ensure she wouldn't see me and returned to my office.

Throughout my remaining sessions, I thought about how little I knew about Scarlet, about the fires she had alluded to, about her dead parents and the man she said had taken her. As seemed to be my norm of late, I obsessed. Could I be certain the stories she told me were true? Who was Scarlet Lake? A liar? A schizophrenic? A victim? All of the above?

That night, consumed by inappropriate feelings and curiosity, I decided I would do something I rarely did: go to the library.

Scarlet

Henry was the worst detective ever. Sniffing, conspicuously I might add, after me like I was a bitch in heat. Did he think I was clueless? That I didn't notice him weaving between moms and kids and strollers? He almost knocked that one woman down, and then nearly fell himself. I was actually embarrassed for him. Had I ignored him long enough? Was it safe to tell him why I came to him in the first place? The dog-training book hadn't suggested a time period, but even if it had, it wasn't as if you could ignore your puppy as long as you might a person. Maybe I'd give it two weeks more.

Unfortunately I needed Henry. I wished I didn't. Possibly I could do the murder part myself, but I would definitely need help getting rid of the body. In the meantime, I was collecting supplies. This was what I had so far: Bleach. A really sharp butcher knife. A bone saw. Two pairs of gardening gloves, one for Henry and one for me. Pots and pans and other containers. Sleeping pills (I'm going to grind those up and put them in his wineglass). Red lipstick (a temptress should always wear red lipstick, shouldn't she?). And carminic acid. This was what I still needed: A heavy blanket. Garbage bags. Mason jars.

I still hadn't figured out Blue. Obviously she couldn't be home for the murder. What kind of a mother would subject her child to such horror? I'd think of something. Or perhaps the universe would help. Thus far it had been quite supportive.

Henry

It had been several years since I had set foot in the South Haven Memorial Library. It was busier than I expected, even for a Saturday. I knew one of the women behind the desk. Kelly Kirkland. We went out a few times shortly after Lily died, and I did the unthinkable. I stopped calling her without explanation. In my defense, a colleague and his wife, their intentions unbeknownst to Kelly or me, had invited the two of us to dinner at their home, even though I had insisted on more than one occasion I was not ready. I still felt married. Death did not erase a person, nor did it replace those feelings of loyalty and responsibility that accompanied marriage. But that was where any innocence on my part ended. I should have left Kelly and any thoughts of her back at that dinner. I definitely should not have slept with her. But I was hurting and lonely, feelings that often led to bad decisions. What I remembered most about the brief time I spent with Kelly was the guilt. Guilt that I was cheating on my wife. Kelly never had a chance. At least I had taken responsibility for what I did *internally*, which is more than I could say for one of my clients, who had excused his "humping and dumping" behavior with such statements as "I don't owe her anything" and "she knew what she was getting into" and "we're both adults." I attempted to explain to him that women do not view sex the same way men do. There were exceptions, of course, but empirically women attached emotion to the act itself and the decision to do it. Deep down all men knew this.

Kelly was reading a book. I couldn't see the cover. The woman in the station next to her, Eleanor Phelps, was busy checking out a patron. If memory served me, Eleanor was the current president of the Scott Club, the oldest literary society in town. She had a reputation for being disagreeable and less than discreet. Such characteristics were not typical of Scott Club members. *Great*, I thought, imagining the rumor mill cranking up. I waited a bit, hoping Eleanor might become free, but when I realized she and the patron were exchanging pictures of their grandchildren, I was left with no choice but to shake my cowardice.

"How have you been?" I asked Kelly when I reached the desk.

She was obviously surprised to see me. Her face flushed, and she immediately looked down, pretended to shuffle through some library cards, then collected herself and said, "Do I know you?"

"We met some years back? Over dinner with Tom and Beth Hutchinson?"

She stared straight into my eyes as if challenging me. "Funny, I don't remember that, but I'm sure it was a *nice* dinner because Tom and Beth are the *nicest* people. And nearly all their friends are too."

Ouch.

"What can I help you with?" she asked, in a tone that could best be described as icy.

"I'm looking for information on an artist," I said. I thought it best not to provide Scarlet's name. "I was wondering if someone could help me locate any books or magazine articles on her work."

Eleanor was alone now. In contrast to Kelly's youthful, blond, wholesome appearance, she was older, your stereotypic librarian type: gray hair wrapped in a bun, reading glasses dangling from a chain around her neck, fitted gray cardigan sweater over white blouse, stern face. She had always reminded me of Mrs. Blankenship, the secretary at Andrews Academy. Everyone was terrified of Mrs. Blankenship.

"Eleanor," Kelly said, "would you mind helping this person out with the card catalogue?"

"It's pretty straightforward," Eleanor said, without looking at me.

"Obviously not for *some* people," Kelly said.

Eleanor rolled her eyes in a show of disapproval, came out from behind the desk, and walked off.

She turned. "Are you coming?" Thankfully she didn't appear to recognize me.

"I wasn't sure I was supposed to," I said.

"Are you asking for my help, or would you like me to do it for you?" she asked when we got to the card file.

"I admit it's been years since I used one, since medical school," I said. "Can you just give me the CliffsNotes version?"

She provided a brief rundown, asked me if I understood, waited for my nod, and left. Out of the corner of my eye I saw her whispering something to Kelly. I was certain it was about me.

I did not have much to go on, so started by looking up Scarlet's name. The only results were a children's coloring book, a book on color properties, and a magazine article on some lake in Nebraska. I wrote them down and tried another search, Traverse City, Michigan, which turned up travel and local history books. My search for the artist Auguste Renoir yielded the most fruit. A number of books on the artist appeared to be located in the same numbered and lettered aisle, which proved to be the art section.

Eleanor found me back at the card catalogue. She must have noted my frustration. "What are you looking for now?"

Rather than confuse things, I decided to mention only the house fire. "A fire that occurred in Traverse City, Michigan, in 1941." Scarlet once mentioned that she had recently turned thirty-two. If memory served me, that was sometime in the spring, which meant she was born in 1936 and would have been five years old in the summer of 1941.

"You'd probably have better luck with our newspaper archives." Her overly pleasant manner made me suspicious. I glanced at the desk. Kelly was busy checking out books.

"Where are they?" I asked.

"Follow me."

She led me to a microfiche machine. I became immediately overwhelmed. I had memories of using one of these for research papers as a student. The process was tedious.

"Are there any Traverse City newspapers in here?" I asked.

"No. Only the *South Haven Tribune*."

"Do you think the *Tribune* would have covered a fire that happened in Traverse City?"

"Maybe if it was newsworthy. But you'll need to know the date." She smiled and left.

In search of clues, I had reviewed my session notes before coming to the library. But while I knew the years of both fires, based on what Scarlet had shared regarding her age, I had no idea of exact dates. It also seemed unlikely that a house fire in Traverse City would have made the *South Haven Tribune*, but on the off chance I might find something, I decided to try. I was about two months through the year when I gave up. I was proud of myself, actually. I did not let go of anything easily. I got up, went to the soda machine, and got a Coke. Because a makeshift note taped to the machine indicated that beverages were not allowed past the front desk, I gulped down the entire contents of the can. Back at the microfiche machine, I went to the year 1952, the year Scarlet would have been fifteen. To my surprise, the second newspaper of that year included a brief mention of an orphanage fire in Traverse City. The fire had happened in the early morning hours of January 1. The building had burned to the ground, and the police suspected arson. What caught my eye was the description of the death toll: "*All* seventeen children and three nuns perished." It had to be the same fire as the one that Scarlet mentioned. But if so, where was she when it happened, and why wasn't either her absence or her survival noted?

"Did you find something?" I heard someone ask. I looked up to find Eleanor.

"Maybe," I said. "Is it possible to get a copy of this?"

"It's connected to a printer." She reached over me and pressed the print button. "We're getting ready to close up," she said.

"Is it six already? I had no idea it was that late."

"If you would have read the sign on the door, you would have seen that we are closing two hours early today," she said.

"Thanks for your help," I said.

As I passed by the front desk, I saw that Kelly was busy checking someone out. I knew she deserved some sort of acknowledgment, but at that moment, I had no idea what I could do or say that would not result in a verbal lashing or unwanted confrontation. Sometimes, I reasoned, it was better to let things lie. Besides, I told myself, Kelly and I were both adults.

Scarlet

Blue wasn't being as open or argumentative. She rarely looked me in the eyes. When I tried to engage her in conversation, her answers were brief. She wasn't cooking meals like she used to, or reminding me to eat. She hadn't asked about my new painting. Had she recognized me that day at Adelaide House? I couldn't bring myself to ask her.

Today, however, was different. When she got home from piano practice, she told me about a competition Mr. Kline had entered her in.

"Can I go?" she asked.

I was painting, so must not have heard the question at first, because what I did hear seemed unusually loud and insistent for Blue. Perhaps *irritated* was more accurate.

I put down my brush, sat on the sofa. She joined me.

"Tell me more about it," I said.

"It's at Interlochen Academy," she said. "At the music school. Mr. Kline says it's an annual competition. It's very competitive. Not just anyone can go. Someone has to recommend you, and provide a recording of a piece you've played. They get hundreds of applicants, but select only ten finalists for the competition."

"Mr. Kline recommended you?" I asked.

"Yes. The winner gets a scholarship to any music school in the country."

"When do you find out?"

She paused, looked down, like she used to do when she was younger, when she thought she might be in trouble, then said, "I already did. I got selected."

Though it shouldn't have, the pride I felt in that moment surprised me. I'd always been proud of Blue's talent, and loved listening to her play. But I was generally reticent when it came to things of this nature. Competitions and the like. I feared for Blue. Wanted to protect her from potential disappointment. And of course there had always been HIM. The more exposure either of us got, the riskier.

"That's amazing, Blue. Congratulations."

Her smile was cautious. "Would you like to come? To the competition, I mean. Mr. Kline says he'll drive and pay for our room."

"When is it?"

"A few weeks from now. I don't know the exact dates. I'll find out."

"How long will you be there?"

"Two nights, I think."

My mind started working. Of course I wanted to go, but Blue being gone for two nights was a message from the universe, one that couldn't be ignored. Not embracing this opportunity could set my plan back years, or destroy it altogether.

"Can I think about it?" I asked Blue.

Her disappointment broke my heart. Her shoulders dropped, face drooped.

"It's my painting," I lied. "My gallery is supposed to come and pick up some paintings that week. Let me find out exactly when, and you do the same. Okay?"

"What about *him*?" she asked. "Isn't that around the time he usually shows up?"

"There is that too," I said. "But let's stay positive. It may all work out."

"I need to go to the grocery," she said, her voice shaking. "Is there anything in particular you want or need?"

"Not that I can think of."

Blue left then, and I thought how my going to the competition would make her so happy. How it would be the *normal* thing for a mother to do. But the truth was, she and I weren't normal, and she was young. I knew, as sure as I knew that I soon would be mixing a red so saturated it would be the envy of painters throughout the world, that one day Blue would be a great pianist, that she would mesmerize audiences with her command of the keyboard, with the finely nuanced language of her music. There would be other competitions, other concerts, more than I could count. In the big picture, missing one was a small sacrifice. She might not understand this now, but killing HIM would provide us the freedom to reach our fullest potentials. And ensure we would stay alive.

Now, how to get him here.

Blue

I wake to the smell of baking pastries. Fresh apple turnovers, my favorite. It has been a long while since my mother baked. I wonder what motivated her to do so now. Maybe it's some sort of consolation prize, her way of apologizing for not going to my competition. Does she really think I don't know her code talk? Asking whether she can think about it is definitely code for not going. I don't know why I do this to myself. Why I expect different answers from the ones I know I'll get. Mr. Kline once told me that expectations are premeditated disappointments.

I get out of bed, get dressed, and follow the scent of freshly baked pastries. My mother is working on the new Renoir. *The Boating Party.* I scan the room, don't see any of the *Madame*s.

"Where are the portraits?" I ask.

"In the bathtub," she says.

"Why are they in the bathtub?"

"They were dirty," she said. "Why else would they be in the bathtub?"

I turn on my heel, head to the bathroom. There they are in the tub. Luckily it appears she forgot to turn on the water. I take them out, carry them into the bedroom, slide them in between the wall and the bunk bed.

"I washed them," I say to her when I get back to the living room.

"Oh, good," she says. "Thank you. I made turnovers. Just took them out of the oven."

I head to the kitchen, grab one along with a plate and fork. Sit on the sofa.

"Where are you off to today?" she asks.

"Fishing with Butch."

"No practice?"

"After fishing."

Maybe she will ask about the competition since she brought up practice. It seems like a natural lead-in. I feel myself getting more and more anxious. I refuse to ask her again if she's going. Shouldn't she be the one asking me if she can come? Of the ten kids accepted to play, I am the youngest. The others are either seventeen or eighteen. Mr. Kline knows how nervous and worried I am. Surely one of the older kids will win. "Winning doesn't matter," he'd said. "Just to be accepted is what's important." Though I didn't say this to him, winning does matter. To me. Winning would set me apart. Solidify my future. The scholarship would ensure my attendance at one of the best music schools in the country. At some, I could enroll as soon as I turn sixteen. I try not to think beyond that point. To enter those puzzles. None of it is real yet anyway. May never be real. Maybe if I rephrase the question?

"Did you find out when your gallery is coming to pick up paintings?"

"Not yet," she says.

"It's been a week since you asked them."

"They're always slow to get back. By the way, we're out of tea and milk. Do you think you could stop at the grocery on your way home?"

"Sure."

"Can you pick up some mason jars while you're there? As many as you can carry. We're making jam."

"When have we ever made jam before?" I ask.

"It was Jeremy's idea."

My stomach drops.

"You know Jeremy," she says. "Full of surprises."

Maybe it's only Jeremy, I think. Somehow just one imaginary person feels less crazy than several. "Is there anyone else helping?" I immediately wish I hadn't asked.

"Everyone," she says.

"Everyone who?"

"Why are you acting so strange? You know who everyone is. Juliette and Rachel and Otto, of course." Now my stomach hurts. I try to calm myself. Breathe slowly. In and out. She looks at me, her eyes vacant. Then says, "You shouldn't worry so much. Everything is going to be just fine. You'll see."

How will it be fine? If she doesn't go with me to the competition, who is going to watch her? She obviously can't be here alone. She's washing paintings in the bathtub and making jam with invisible friends. I decide not to think on all this, at least not right now. I need to get myself happy, not wallow in self-inflicted disappointment. I need to think on fishing with Butch and the excitement of the days before me. But while I know this is what I should do, I can't shake my feelings of fear and insignificance, so I ask her the one question I really want to know the answer to.

"Do you love me?"

"Don't be silly. Of course I do."

But she doesn't put down her brush or hug me or even steal her eyes from the canvas and look at me. Most importantly, neither does she say the word *love*.

"Go," she says. "And don't forget those mason jars."

Henry

I checked the clock again, which I had come to do toward the end of my sessions with Mrs. Burns. It was not because I was uninterested in what she was telling me. It was because even though Scarlet's session no longer followed, I still felt that old sense of anticipation.

After Mrs. Burns left, I sat at my desk, reread the printout of the newspaper article, and reviewed my official typewritten notes from her sessions. I was looking for anything Scarlet said that I might have missed. Something that would provide clues to who she was. But there was nothing. I retrieved the bottle of Old Forester from its drawer in my desk, poured three fingers into one of my two crystal old-fashioneds (the other was at home), closed the bottle, reopened it, added a splash more, and took a steep satisfying sip. A small epiphany came to me. What about my handwritten legal pad notes? Maybe there was something I had not transferred over to the official notes. I kept them in a separate file, but still under Scarlet's name. The notes were a mess, phrases in margins or written at angles, words triple underlined or capitalized or in quotations. Finally, I found something. Back in the spring, in the same session where Scarlet discussed the two fires, I had scribbled these words: *father* and *district attorney*. I rechecked the corresponding official session notes. I had obviously not transferred this information. A district attorney's identity was public record, so I should be able to find out Scarlet's real last name. I breathed a huge sigh of relief and kissed the notes. "This is why I save you," I said.

Feeling renewed hope, I decided to get serious about my quest and establish a timeline, but in order to do so, I had to commit to a given set of assumptions: 1) What Scarlet had told me about her childhood was true, including her age, and the age she was when her family's house burned down and she was taken; 2) The orphanage fire mentioned in the *South Haven Tribune* and the one Scarlet had told me about in our session were one and the same; and 3) Scarlet would turn sixteen sometime in 1952 but was still fifteen at the time of the orphanage fire. Of course, I could not say with certainty that any of these assumptions were true, but I had to start somewhere.

Timeline:
1936 Scarlet born
1941 Fire at family home (age five)
    Parents perish
    Scarlet abducted
1952 Fire at St. Ann's Orphanage (age fifteen)

Outstanding questions:
    Who was the man that started the fire and abducted Scarlet?
    Why did he set the fire and abduct Scarlet?
    Assuming the fire at St. Ann's Orphanage and the one Scarlet spoke of were one and the same, where was Scarlet and why didn't she perish along with the other seventeen children? And where had she been in between then and now?
    Who was the district attorney for Grand Traverse County in 1941?

I picked up the phone, dialed the operator.
"Traverse City, Michigan," I said when she answered.
"Please hold."
"Traverse City," a different female voice said. "What can I help you with?"
"May I have the number for the District Attorney's Office?"

While she read out the number, I jotted it down.

"Would you like me to connect you?" she asked.

"Thank you, that would be great."

My stomach tightened as I waited through several rings.

"Grand Traverse County Prosecuting Attorney's Office," the woman said.

"Hi," I said. "I'm hoping you might be able to help me. I'm trying to locate the name of the district attorney for Traverse City in 1941. Do you know how I might locate that information?"

"Hold on," she said.

While holding, I was running plausible excuses for why I needed the information through my mind.

"The Honorable Charles Lewis Boudreau served as district attorney from January 1938 to July 1941. He was succeeded by the Honorable Winston Langley Smithson, who served from July 1941 to December 1946."

Scarlet's father passed in 1941, so it must be Charles Boudreau. I decided to verify.

"Do you happen to know why Charles Boudreau's term ended?"

"It appears he passed away," she said. "Birth and death dates are listed where applicable."

"Does it say how he died?" I asked.

"I'm sorry, sir, I don't have that information."

"Thank you," I said. "You've been very helpful."

I hung up, reached for the bourbon glass, took another healthy sip, revisited the timeline and the three remaining questions. Knowing Scarlet's real last name was huge, but there was still so much I did not know. Where did I go from here? I looked at the clock. My next patient was due in five minutes. I opened one of the desk drawers and put the newspaper clipping, session notes, legal pad notes, and timeline inside it. It was what I called my purgatory drawer, a kind of in-between, where notes and files that required further consideration went. I began to slide the door closed when the bulb in my desk lamp buzzed, popped, and blew out. *Where did I put those extra lightbulbs?*

I swiveled my chair around and opened the door of my credenza. There they sat. I picked up the pack, pulled one out, and started to set it back down when I noticed the two books stacked next to it. Raymond Chandler's *The Big Sleep* and Dashiell Hammett's *The Maltese Falcon*. I had read both so many times I could practically recite them. Then it dawned on me. Philip Marlowe and Sam Spade did not sit around waiting for answers to come to them. They investigated the crime scene, interviewed witnesses, and chased down clues.

I swiveled my chair back around, retrieved the information I'd just placed in the purgatory drawer, and started a new file, which I labeled *Traverse City*.

All of it—the house fire, Scarlet's abduction, the orphanage fire—had happened in Traverse City. But who was I kidding? I had commitments. Work. Butch.

I felt a pull. Something was needling me, a lack of resolution that I didn't believe had to do with Scarlet alone. My story with Lily was not finished. From the moment I had met Scarlet, there had been *something*. It was as if she were a second chance. I had always been a responsible, staid—some might say boring—man. Not one to take risks. Though I had traveled for work periodically, I could not recall a time I picked up and went somewhere without thinking through every single detail. Butch included. And yet here I was talking myself into a road trip to northern Michigan. Butch was fifteen, a very responsible fifteen. He would be fine by himself. I would check in with him. I would alert Tom and Beth. Butch had their phone number.

Tomorrow morning, I would begin canceling appointments for the following week.

Blue

Butch and I are fishing on the pier when he asks me, the usual row of fishermen and -women lined up either side of us. The air is crisp. The sky, gray. Autumn is fixing to upset summer.

"Do you want to come to dinner at my house tomorrow night?" he asks. "We can fry up the fish."

It is the third time he's asked. I made up excuses the other two times, but I know I can't keep doing that. I want to go to his house for dinner, but I think meeting his dad may be awkward since he *was* treating my mother (lately she hasn't left the house at their normal meeting time). Surely he'll recognize me. Everyone says we look alike.

"Don't worry," Butch continues. "My dad won't say anything about your mom. He's a professional." (He can always read my mind.) "Besides, I want the two of you to meet before you both leave town."

"He's leaving town?"

"Just for a few days, like you," he says. "Weird that you'll both be gone at the same time. C'mon. It'll be fun."

I feel my resolve melting. It's hard to say no to Butch. It isn't only his cute smile and dreamy brown eyes, which are enough to knock me off my feet and send me all the way to earth's center. It's his outlook on life. I've always been a serious and cautious person. Butch is light to my heavy. Silly to my serious. Fun to my boring. Like my mother.

"Okay," I say and smile.

"Cool," he says. He stands and does a little dance. "We are going to have such a good time. You can play the Bösendorfer while I cook. You'll love my dad. He'll love you too."

Just then a fish pulls at my line. Butch sits, helps me reel it in. Everyone claps, as they do any time someone catches a fish. I stand and bow. Everybody does that too. I know everyone's name and their stories by now. There's Gary, the local butcher. His wife is Gail. They have five kids. Edith, she and her husband, Donald, own the general store. Their hound dog, Moses, is our fishing mascot. Helen is a beautician. She has four cats. She's also a huge Chicago Cubs fan, and something of a celebrity in South Haven. Jack Brickhouse, who does the Cubs TV play-by-play, introduces her and her three friends when they attend games. Tim, he drives a Pabst beer truck. His wife, Cindy, just had a baby, their first. They named her Moonbeam, because Tim says all he wants to do in the world is hang the moon for her. I love all my new friends. I knew I would love fishing the moment I read about it in Hemingway's Nick stories. I love everything about it. Sometimes I think it's even better than playing the piano.

Well, maybe not better, but definitely good.

Henry

I was reading a page-turner Butch had recommended: *Laura* by Vera Caspary. I especially liked Detective Mark McPherson. I identified with his obsession for Laura; it was helping me feel less of a fool about mine with Scarlet.

"Dad, this is my friend Blue," I heard Butch say.

I hadn't heard them come in. He had told me he was bringing home a "friend." They were frying up the fish they caught over the summer. It was the first time he'd brought a girl home. I was happy for him, yet the moment also felt bittersweet. I knew I would never lose him—we shared a unique closeness brought on by loss and the special bond of a single dad and son—but I also understood the total consumption of first love.

My breath caught when I saw her. I collected myself. I could not ask her if she was Scarlet's daughter. I could not mention Scarlet at all.

"Nice to meet you, Blue," I said. "I would like to say Butch has told me a lot about you, but that wouldn't be true. He has been rather secretive where you are concerned."

She smiled.

Scarlet's smile.

"It's nice to meet you too," she said. "Your house is so cool."

Scarlet's voice.

"It was a grade school gymnasium back in the day," I said.

Blue walked over to the bookcase, ran her fingers along some of the spines. "I've never seen so many books in one place, except for a library."

"Do you like to read?" I asked.

"Yes," she said.

"Blue suggested the Vera Caspary book," Butch said.

"That was you?" I asked. "Thank you. I'm really enjoying it."

She went to the large picture window overlooking the water.

"The view is amazing," she said, and, as if she had just processed the space's original use, added, "What happened to the school?"

"Demolished when they extended the road down this way," I said.

"And they just left the gym?"

"I know," Butch said. "Strange, right? Do you want a Coke?"

"Sure," she said.

"Three Cokes coming right up," Butch said.

"Why don't we head out to the screened-in porch," I said to Blue. "It's such a nice night. Butch has already prepared the fish so it won't take long to fry."

"Okay," she said.

"Are you and Butch in the same grade?"

"Yes." She stood looking out over the bluff. "When does it freeze?"

"What do you mean?"

"The lake."

"It's different every year. Usually by February."

"It was already frozen when we arrived."

I took the opportunity to dig a little bit more. "When was that?"

"January. There were these big frozen waves. Bigger than me. I'd never seen that before."

"That doesn't happen every year. It was a harsh winter. Where did you move from?"

"Pennsylvania."

"Did your father get a job transfer?" I hoped the question might lead her to mention her mother.

She turned. Her eyes bored into mine as if she knew what I was doing. As if she knew everything there was to know in the entire world.

"It's just my mom and me."

Butch walked in carrying three cans of Coke. Blue joined him on the wicker sofa.

"How do you like it here?" I asked.

"It's nice," she said.

"And your mother?"

"My mother?" Again, the burning stare.

"Does she like it here?"

"I guess. She doesn't get out much. She's a painter. But she likes the water. We live over on North Beach."

Near Adelaide House? "What does she paint?"

"People mostly. Some landscapes. She sells her work at a gallery in New York."

"Impressive," I said. "What gallery is that?"

Same look. Not so much suspicious as cautious, guarded.

"Blue plays the piano," Butch interjected. "She's really good. She's been taking lessons from Old Man Kline. He says she's a prodigy. I've been trying to talk her into playing for us. I told her we still have Mom's piano."

"Yes, we do. No one's played it in years." I still had the piano tuned regularly, but I had to admit I found the idea of someone other than Lily playing it somewhat invasive. I shook the thought from my mind.

"Time to fry," Butch said.

"I'll help," Blue said.

I loved the smell of frying fish. It reminded me of my father doing it back in Charlevoix. He would fry the fish the day he caught it. Often we sat out on the back deck overlooking the lake to eat. It was a ritual I tried to continue with Butch, but lately he had been stockpiling the fish he caught, no doubt for this very occasion. Soon Butch was collecting plates, napkins, and forks. The dinner conversation centered on Blue's fishing mastery.

"She's already better than I am," Butch said.

"He's exaggerating," Blue said.

"I'm not," Butch said. "It's like she was born to it."

Butch and Blue cleared the plates, and we headed back inside. When finished, Blue agreed to play for us.

"Is there anything in particular you'd like to hear?" she asked.

"Do you know Prokofiev's Sonata no. 6?" I asked. It was Lily's favorite.

Blue looked surprised, but sat down to play.

I shut my eyes, tried to imagine it was Lily, not Blue, but it was not long before my imagination failed me. Butch was right. Blue was indeed a gifted pianist. She did not only command the keyboard; she melted into it. Instrument and child were one. It felt as if my body were leaving me. As if something deep inside me was wrapping itself in and around the sound, wandering through the room, inhabiting every corner, every object, rising above the space. Then I *was* the music, and it, in turn, was me. I remembered Scarlet saying she felt something similar when she painted, and I thought to myself that such talents as Scarlet's and Blue's had to be cherished. Protected.

It took a while for me to find my way back to the present.

"Blue and I are going to take a walk on the beach," Butch said.

"Okay," I said. "Have fun."

After they left, I considered the encounter with Blue. What were the chances that of all the girls in South Haven, Butch would be interested in Scarlet's daughter? I had always been a firm believer in Jung's theory on synchronicity, but had never seen physical proof. And again, I thought about my road trip to Traverse City and I felt certain what happened there would somehow change my life.

I reached for the timeline. Added the new information I had discovered.

Timeline:
1936 Scarlet born
1941 Fire at family home (age five)
    Parents perish
    Scarlet abducted
1952 Fire at St. Ann's Orphanage (age fifteen)
    Scarlet pregnant
    Blue born (Scarlet sixteen?)
1968 Scarlet and Blue move to South Haven

I considered the same questions I had earlier, and added one more: *Who is Blue's father?*

Blue

We walk south, to an area of the beach with which I am unfamiliar. Butch lays the blanket on the sand and we sit.

"This is one of my favorite stretches of beach," he says. "There's never anybody here. The stars light up the sky."

"It's beautiful," I say, shivering.

"Are you cold?" he asks.

"A little."

"Here, take my jacket," he says and wraps it around my shoulders.

He puts his arm around my waist. I feel it before I know what it means, a kind of static electricity, like clinging socks from a dryer, that attraction and spark. Butch puts his hand on the small of my back, traces my spine up to my neck, draws my head toward his, and kisses me, soft and sweet at first, then long and hard. My body feels a kind of hunger I've never felt before, as if it will never be satiated, as if it is doomed to want him, more and more of him forever, and when he takes his lips away, he looks into my eyes and tells me he loves me. And without so much as a single breath between us, I say it back. And though I don't tell him this, I wonder what it all means. What can be next after a boy tells you he loves you? And he must feel the same, because he pulls me down on the blanket with him, and I fall asleep in his arms.

It's still dark when we wake. I have no idea how long we've slept. He shakes out the blanket, folds it, takes my hand, and walks me home. And there on the uneven porch of the dilapidated house he kisses me again. He loosens his hand as he backs away until only our fingers touch, and then he turns and goes on his way, and the emptiness I feel is wrenching. And I know from this moment on I will always search for the smell of his skin, the taste of his lips, the embrace of his arms as I drift into sleep. Not my mother's. And I understand the push-pull I've been feeling comes from her. Her all-consuming love. For she always knew this moment would come.

FEBRUARY 12, 2014

Chicago, Illinois

46 Years After the Murder

The Pianist

A group of children surrounds me. Nine, perhaps ten years old. Some stand behind my smooth wooden bench, some between it and the two *Madame*s. They don't appear to see me: the middle-aged woman on a bench stalking Renoir.

"Can anyone tell me what the difference is between the two paintings?" the teacher asks.

A girl raises her hand.

"Yes, Louise?" the teacher says.

"The colors," Louise says.

"In what way?" the teacher asks.

"The one on the right has a lot of red in it and the one on the left doesn't," Louise says.

"That's right," the teacher says. "Do you know why that is?"

A boy raises his hand.

"Because one is real and one's a copy," he says.

"That's exactly right, Jason," the teacher says. "Does anyone know why there are two paintings?"

"Because the artist decided two is worth more money than one?" another boy asks.

"You moron," Jason says. "Did you see the date on the wall? The artist didn't even paint the other one. He's dead."

"Jason," the teacher says. "We don't talk that way to each other, do we? Apologize to Ethan."

Jason rolls his eyes and offers a less-than-convincing apology.

I smile. I like Jason.

"Jason is correct," the teacher says. "The artist, Pierre-Auguste Renoir, died in 1919. The painting on the left is his original work. The one on the right was made by a computer to show us how the painting looked in 1883, when the artist painted it. You can see how much certain colors have faded, the reds in particular. That's because in those days, colors weren't permanent like they are today. The colors in many of the Great Masters paintings faded over time. You remember who the Great Masters are, right?"

Most of the children nod.

"Like blue jeans?" Ethan asks.

"Kind of like that," the teacher says. "Okay, class, let's go on to the next painting."

All the children except Jason shuffle after her. He stares at the original painting for a while, then turns to me.

"It's called fugitive pigment," he says. "It disappears. Like magic. I read about it in the catalogue."

"Me too," I say.

"My mom says kids don't read these days," he says. "So I always do."

"Your mom is smart," I say.

"She's really smart." He smiles wide, dimples forming at the edges of his mouth. "Did you read about those bugs?"

"A little," I say, thinking about Butch's dimples. All this reminiscing is pushing him and those years in South Haven to the forefront of my heart and mind.

"They're tiny, like five millimeters in diameter, and they have these beak-like mouths that burrow into cacti and feed off their juice and berries. The catalogue says they were the only source of red dye, but that isn't true. There are other natural sources. I looked it up on the internet. Like chokecherries, beetroots, and hibiscus flowers, even animal or people blood. You just need to add salt or oxide to the dye so the color fixes."

"Maybe back then the bugs were the only source they knew about," I say. "Maybe they hadn't discovered those other sources yet."

"I don't think that's why." He pauses as if he's been taught not to argue with adults.

"What do you think?"

"We read in school that kings and queens wore bright red clothes, so I think they didn't want common people to know where they got the red dye from. They wanted to be the only ones that had bright red clothes."

Again, I smile. "That's pretty smart. Do you like art?"

"Yes," Jason says. "I'm going to be an artist when I grow up."

"My mother was an artist. A painter like Renoir."

"Really? Does she have any paintings in here?"

"I'm afraid not."

"I know a secret," he says.

"What's that?"

"It wasn't done on a computer."

"What wasn't?"

"The picture on the right. It's a painting."

"How do you know that?"

He moves closer to me, whispers, "I know you aren't supposed to, but I touched it. Well, I better catch up."

He runs off, leaving me curious. Why would the wall plaque and catalogue say it was a digital reproduction if it was a painting?

THREE DAYS BEFORE THE MURDER

BLOOD: 1. The usually red fluid, consisting of plasma and blood cells, that circulates through the heart, arteries, and veins of vertebrates. 2. The spilling of blood; murder.

Scarlet

I was thirteen when I escaped HIM. My decision to leave was not without consideration. I had become dependent on him. I knew no one other than him. Did I feel love for him? A kind of love, I suppose. A confusion I couldn't articulate in the beginning. He had taken me, yes. Disciplined me. Hurt me. But he also fed me and clothed me and sometimes touched me in a loving way. I wanted to leave; I wanted to stay. I needed to leave; I needed to stay.

He drank too much that night, like so many nights, and passed out. I was staring at him while he snored, his belly hanging over his belt, his thinning hair matted with sweat, seeing everything ugly in him. I remember taking a swig of his whiskey, feeling its warmth seep down my throat and into my belly. It happened in a second. I grabbed a garbage bag from under the sink, stuffed it with what I could carry, put on my only pair of pants (he liked me in dresses) and a sweatshirt with a hood (in case any of his poker buddies saw me), stole money from his wallet, and left. It was spring, still light out. I felt the sun on my face, each step I took bringing me closer to freedom. I hadn't thought about what would happen after that, or where I would go. I just kept walking. It was dark by the time I arrived at a bus stop outside of town. I boarded the first one that arrived.

"Traverse City," the driver called out when we arrived. I was stunned. All this time and *home* had been merely an hour away.

Perhaps I wore an invisible *R* for *runaway* on my forehead, because as I walked away from the station, a group of kids roughly my age asked me to join them. I traveled with them for a few months, ate scraps from garbage cans, slept in a different place every night, abandoned buildings or vehicles, under bridges, on benches in parks. We told one another our stories, watched out for one another. One day, a black Cadillac drove down the road in the field where we were camping.

"It's HIM," I whispered to a girl named Amanda, who had become my friend.

My words spread quickly among us. They threw a blanket over me, stood in front of me. I curled into a ball, made myself as small as I could. My heart beat with fear. The engine hummed as the Cadillac drove slowly by, then stopped. The sound of the window sliding down.

"I'm looking for a girl," I heard him say. "Thirteen years old, tall, blond hair. Unusually pale eyes. Pretty. Have any of you seen her?"

Amanda spoke up. "I saw a girl that looked just like that a few weeks back, at the bus station. She said her name was Mary Ann. She was waiting on a bus to Cincinnati."

"Are you sure she was going to Cincinnati?" he asked.

"Maybe it was Columbus. It was definitely somewhere in Ohio."

"Come over here," he said. "Take this. Let me know if you see her again, okay? There's a reward in it. One hundred dollars."

The car drove off.

"Coast clear," Amanda said. "Do you believe that asshole? All you're worth is a hundred dollars?"

"What did he give you?" I asked.

"His contact information. You want it?"

"Burn it," I said.

Sometimes we stayed in makeshift shelters, a park, a grouping of tents, a church basement. It was at such a place I met Sister Agatha. I'd seen her before. She was young and pretty, had a friendly smile, and I wondered why she had chosen the path she did. She told us about the orphanage, said if we chose to come with her, no one would ask questions about who we were or where we came from.

"What if someone comes looking for us?" I asked. "Isn't an orphanage an obvious place to look for a missing child?"

"If you prefer not to be found, you won't be," she said.

I questioned this silently. She didn't know what HE was capable of, how he could twist words into pretzels, lie with conviction, charm all who met him, hurt without conscience. How he was driven to win at all costs. How conquest was his holy grail. How he had taken me when I was only five, hurt me, tied me to the pink bed in the pink room, how no one could hear my screams, how he molded me to his will with fear. How in order to survive I learned to lie and manipulate, to bide my time until I was old enough to make it on my own, old enough to escape and elude him. How I knew with certainty he would continue to come after me. Because that's who he was. As if I were one of his precious editions of the *Encyclopedia Britannica*, fine leather furnishings, or expensive modern paintings, I was some*thing*, not some*one*, he owned. A prized piece of his perfect collection. Yes, he would come looking to restore what he'd lost, and if he couldn't, rather than allow anyone else to appreciate that which belonged to him, he would destroy me.

"Even if it's someone evil?" I asked. "Someone that hurts little girls?"

She paused, which concerned me, but then said, "Especially then."

I was the only one of the street kids who followed Sister Agatha. It was difficult saying goodbye to them, especially Amanda, but I believed Sister Agatha would be true to her word. You could tell these things. People wear their lies.

Healing proved a slow process. For most of that first year Sister Agatha cared for me, held me when I cried. Cried, I admit, not only because of what I had been through, but also because I missed him, a consequence of abuse I couldn't fully understand. And yet, while sorting out those emotions, I recoiled at the sound of heavy footsteps outside my door. Panicked at the sight of black vehicles in the orphanage drive. Slept in a ball in the far corner beneath my bed. Stayed inside for fear of being found. Sister Agatha urged me to attend the orphanage school. And so, I went to Bible study. Recited my catechism. Sang hymns. Watched the other girls skip rope, play volleyball and Red Rover. One day, I joined them.

It was nearly a year after I arrived at the orphanage before I felt safe enough to walk down to the beach at night. The first few times I went with other girls to one closer to the orphanage, but later I went on my own, wandered farther. One day, I saw boys and girls building bonfires, drinking and smoking and laughing. It was fall by the time I worked up my nerve to join them. I started hanging with one boy in particular. His name was Zach. Almost every night, even as the weather grew colder, we warmed ourselves by the fire. On New Year's Eve, a big party was planned. He was rubbing his hand on my leg and belly, down my back, began kissing my neck.

"Do you want to go somewhere?" he asked.

"I know a place," I said.

He followed my directions to a certain road, down a certain drive. We got out of the car and walked. A light snow fell. Past a cottage. Past the burned-out remains of a house. Down wooden steps to the beach. A section of beach I once knew so well. I was flooded with memories of playing and swimming with my mother on the morning of that fateful day, of listening to the sounds of my father playing the piano that afternoon, and of people talking and laughing behind my closed bedroom door while I lay in my bed that night. Ten years had passed. Those memories now felt more like a pleasant dream. I didn't tell Zach why I wanted to go down that particular drive to that particular area of the beach, and he didn't ask. He'd brought along a bottle of wine and a blanket. He made a fire, kissed me. We took off our clothes, cuddled, and there, under the winter sky, we made love. What I remember most about it was that it didn't hurt. That's when I understood what sex was supposed to be like. That's when I understood HE had not only stolen me from the house that once stood behind me; he also had stolen the life I might have led, every experience I might have had, every experience I still would have. I would forever struggle to achieve those qualities necessary to sustain a healthy relationship—self-love, self-esteem, self-respect—and I would forever know both hate and a sick kind of love. In that moment, in the dreamy, wobbly aftermath of lovemaking, I wanted to tell Zach all this, about HIM, about who I used to be, about the house that once stood behind us, about how my mother taught me to paint, how she made apple turnovers and loved to dance, how my father loved the piano, how he used to take me on piggyback rides all the way from our house to the water, how he built fires and made s'mores. Perhaps in time I would have told Zach all these things. Perhaps in time we would have been together.

If the orphanage hadn't burned down.

If Sister Agatha and the others hadn't died.

I'd walked back alone that night, as I always did. I didn't want Zach to know where I lived. It might not have been safe for him. I took the shortcut through the woods. The snow was so beautiful; it was as if I were inside a forested snow globe. I felt happy, imagined a future filled with love and children.

I smelled the smoke and heard its crackle before I saw the flames, and in that way that you know the route to a familiar destination without thinking, I knew HE had set the fire. Though I hadn't imagined it possible, my hatred grew.

I returned to the streets, to the kids, to Amanda, and all over again, with their help, I learned to survive on scraps from dumpsters, try car doors in search of loose change, look pitiful so the Salvation Army might part with a tattered wool coat and mittens with holes, a restaurant might offer me a plate of warm eggs and bacon, a bakery might have the heart to part with a pastry. Sometimes I watched Zach from a distance. Snow and cold had thinned the bonfire crowd, and yet there he was, wrapped in a blanket or a heavy down coat, sitting alone. So many times, I wanted to tell him I was still there, but I didn't know how to say the words. I feared his rejection. What normal boy would want to be with a girl like me? A girl so broken. A girl so undeserving.

It was mid-February when my breasts got tender. Nausea and vomiting followed.

"You're pregnant," Amanda said.

I tried to do it on my own. But when I was nearly five months pregnant, I got sick. Anemia, the free clinic said. Bed rest and a proper diet were essential to the survival of my child. I had only one place to go.

As if nothing at all had changed, as if I'd never gone, as if I were the prodigal daughter, HE opened his door to me, cared for me. There was something different about him. He'd lost weight, said he'd stopped drinking, promised to be a better man. I wanted to believe this. He built me an art studio upstairs. Bought me paints and brushes and canvases. As my belly grew, he became more loving and attentive, though he never touched me in *that* way. I was no longer a child.

When my daughter was born, I let him believe the three of us were a family.

She was two years old when I noticed him looking at her in the way he once looked at me. There is a moment when every mother knows with certainty that her child is the one true love of her life. That she will do whatever it takes to protect her. No one would believe me. I had chosen to return after all. The very next morning, she and I got on a bus and headed east to New York.

Three years later, I saw a black Cadillac drive by.

We became fugitives, moved again and again, changed our names and our habits. I worked as a waitress, a grocery cashier, a ticket collector at an amusement park, sold paintings where I could. Each time he found us. Then, one day, karma reached out. We were in the waiting room of a clinic, waiting on a pediatrician to see my daughter for her continual stomachaches. I randomly pulled a magazine from a pile, a medical journal, opened it to an article about an esteemed psychoanalyst named Henry Williams. The name was familiar. He practiced in a small beachfront town in Michigan, a town I had been to once, years earlier, on vacation with my parents. There was a picture, a head shot. Dark hair, bottle-thick, horn-rimmed glasses. Details about why he'd chosen his profession, about his own years of therapy, the loss of his father and then his mother, brief mention of an abusive stepfather. Another picture, this one black and white, slightly blurry, of him as a boy standing next to his mother on a dock on a lake. I recognized them. I recognized the dock and the lake. Though I couldn't tell the color of the boat tied to the dock, I knew it was yellow. The rest, the extent of his stepfather's abuse and the cause of his mother's *accident*, I filled in on my own. I'd witnessed both with my own two eyes.

When I was certain no one was looking, I ripped the article out of the magazine, folded it, and put it in my purse.

The thing about karma? You did not want to slap it in the face. There was no denying that the article was a sign. I was supposed to go to South Haven. I was supposed to meet Dr. Henry Williams. It wasn't just that HE had hurt both Henry and me, or that he had killed my parents, Henry's mother, Sister Agatha, and the kids in the orphanage, or even that he meant to kill me; it was my daughter I feared for, and my certainty that HIS actions had set in motion a cycle of destruction that would touch her children and their children. There was only one way to break that cycle.

Blue

The summer people have left. Locals are washing down their boats. Beach talk has given way to school talk. Ladies' clubs are back in session. Leaves are changing colors and falling. Their float to the ground resembles a slow, ritualistic dance, a rite of passage. I feel this as if it's happening inside me, as if I am one of those leaves leaving my mother's tree and going off on my own. Drifting through a wide-open world. It is the afternoon before Mr. Kline and I will leave for Interlochen, our last rehearsal. Though my mother has never said no, it's obvious she isn't coming. It is her way, noncommittal, keeping everyone in her life waiting for a response that will never come. It's selfish and infuriating. I've decided since she's ignoring my feelings, I'm ignoring her state of mind. Why should I stay home and watch her? Besides, Mr. Kline says, "You need to look out for your future." So I'm tossing her crazies out of my mind and going to the competition.

At this moment, I play Mussorgsky's *Pictures at an Exhibition*. Not Chopin's *Andante*. "Shouldn't I be concentrating on the *Andante*?" I ask after I finish.

"I had a dream last night that you were playing the Mussorgsky at the competition," Mr. Kline says. "When I awoke, I recalled your interpretation and how beautifully you played it."

I don't tell him that I've been having continuous dreams about the competition, but in mine, awful things happen. I forget entire bars, stumble over easy scales. "Did I win?"

"In my dreams, you always win."

His words give me hope. "Should I play the Mussorgsky instead?"

"It's always good to know two pieces."

"You mean like a backup?"

"I would call it a comfort piece," he says. "You see, I once knew a student who prepared for a competition day and night. When the day finally came, he slid onto the bench, placed his fingers on the keys, and froze. For the very life of him, his hands wouldn't move. He could not play the piece he had practiced relentlessly."

"What happened?"

"He asked the judges for a moment, left the room, took several deep breaths, returned to the piano bench, and, to his own surprise, played an entirely different piece. The piece he did play was, in fact, one he loved, but hadn't played for weeks. It was what I would call his comfort piece. I believe the Mussorgsky to be your comfort piece. So now, if you freeze, or for any reason feel uncomfortable with the *Andante*, your fingers can walk through Viktor Hartmann's exhibit, tracing each curve of the artist's pen, each stroke of his brush."

"Did the student win the competition?"

"We will never know," he says. "That very night, while the judges deliberated, he left for America."

"It was you?"

"It was me."

I recall what Hannah said about him when I first met her. "You defected?"

"That is the official name for it, yes, but I didn't think of it that way. At the time, there was much persecution. In my country, you see, musicians, dancers, athletes, and others were controlled and held to regimented standards from a very early age. America offered me more artistic freedom."

"How old were you?"

"A year younger than you are now."

"Where did you live?"

"A family took me in. It was prearranged. They were good people. They raised me and my sister, Nadia."

"The one who lives in Schenectady?"

"Yes."

"Do you miss Russia?"

"Yes, the food, the culture, but back then, I missed my parents most of all. I never saw them again. My leaving left them vulnerable. I will never know what happened to them. But I take solace in the fact that it is what they wished. They sacrificed for me. Just as your mother sacrifices for you."

I have never thought of what my mother does as a sacrifice, but right then I see how this may be true.

"Let's play the piece again," he says.

And so I do.

———————

After practice, I meet Butch on the pier. He'd requested that it be "just the two of us." We've been spending more alone time together. Hannah has been hanging out with Amy and Miriam and Colleen, which is fine by me. He is waiting for me at the entrance to the beach, takes my hand, and we silently make our way through the few hearty sunbathers refusing to accept summer's passing. Groups of people still line the pier, some fishing, some hanging out, perched on the edges waiting on sunset. Once at the lighthouse, when we are sure no one is looking, we sneak up the metal stairs to the circular platform. The air is cool, but not cold. "You look pretty today," Butch says. "You always look pretty."

"Thank you," I say and smile one of those shy-girl smiles. I have been smiling those shy-girl smiles a lot lately. I don't know what's happening to me other than life feels more like air than ground these days. Is that what love does to you? Or is it the competition?

"I have something for you," he says,

The box is small. I open it slowly as if I think there is a bomb inside, which in a certain way there is.

"It's a charm bracelet," he says. He points out two charms. "See, there's a fishing rod for me, and a piano for you. Here, let me help you put it on." He fastens it around my wrist. Even a minor brush of his skin against mine turns my insides into mush. More than any-thing I want to feel all of his skin against mine.

"What are the *B*s for?" I smile, this time coy.

"*Butch* and *Blue*." And there is his smile, wide, dimples forming near the corners of his lips, the cutest smile in the world.

"And this one?" A side-by-side *B* and *G*.

"*Boyfriend-girlfriend*," he says. "Do you like it?"

"I love it."

He reaches over, raises my chin with his hand, kisses my lips, and it feels sweeter and more urgent than the last kiss and the kiss before that and the one before that. His hand wanders under my sweater. I want it under my bra. I want all of him. He stops, turns his face away, his expression serious, profile chiseled with a restraint I've never seen in him before. He looks like a man, not a boy.

"Maybe when you get back, we can go somewhere together," he says.

"Where?" I ask.

He shrugs. "I'll think of something. You deserve the best. It's getting late. We should get back."

I'm disappointed. I don't want to leave, not yet, but his resolve is clear, and so I say, "Yes, Mr. Kline says I need to get a good night's sleep."

"He's right," Butch says, looking into my eyes. "You do. I wish I could go with you." He looks like the boy I know again.

"I wish you could too."

"Did your mother decide to go?"

"No," I say. "Her gallery is coming from New York to pick up some of her paintings. She doesn't have a lot of control over when they come." I don't tell him I don't think this is true. Even after everything, her meeting that man at Adelaide House, her not caring one bit about my competition, I don't want Butch or anyone to think badly of her. I want to protect her.

"I'm sorry." He rises, takes my hand, pulls me to my feet, and hugs me tight. "I'll miss you. Call as soon as you get back, okay?"

I follow Butch down the lighthouse stairs. We hold hands as we traverse the pier, the sun disappearing into the lake behind us. The few remaining stragglers are packing up. I steal a look behind me as the orange horizon turns dark blue. The beach is empty, the sunbathers gone, a sandy desert. At the exit to the road, Butch doesn't offer to walk me home. He kisses me again, brushes his hand across my cheek, turns, and walks away, and I stand there wanting him, watching him fade into the dusk. And then, unexpectedly, my body shivers and a painful emptiness forms in my chest and stomach, and I realize I'm scared. Because something about his leaving feels different. Like an ending, not a beginning.

Henry

Obviously I had lost my mind. Here I was going on the definition of a wild-goose chase. I had no clear plan and no logical purpose for doing so. Except for some foggy sense there was a psychic connection between Scarlet and me. That our meeting wasn't random.

Traverse City was roughly two hundred miles from South Haven, and, depending on the route, anywhere from three to three and a half hours by car. I chose the longer route, I-196 North to US 131 North, which ironically was the quickest. It was a gorgeous fall day. Cool but sunny. The trees were in full color. Next to summer, the reds, oranges, and limes of the leaves were the largest draw for tourists seeking a true Michigan experience. This time of year, I was always reminded of hunting with my father. I killed my first, and last, deer when I was eight years old. The sight of it lying there dead filled me with an odd combination of pride and remorse. My dad was thirty-two when he died of an aneurysm. "Born with a ticking bomb in his head," the doctor had said. That shooting lesson and the hunting trip that followed were some of the last memories I had of my father. Though I gave up the deer-killing part, being out in the woods with Butch helped me relive and pass on those memories. Sometimes I imagined I saw my father walking up ahead of us, orange cap, matching vest over plaid flannel shirt, faded jeans, leaves and twigs crunching beneath his heavy Wolverine boots, a blade of grass between his teeth.

The roads were empty. I rolled the knob through radio stations until I got to 91.1, a new National Public Radio station. Pachelbel's Canon was playing. *Perfect.* I needed to consider my game plan. I had called the local police department and talked to a Detective Steve Logan, said I was researching two fires in the area for a book I was working on. Sounded plausible. He was familiar with the orphanage fire, said he had worked the case, that, yes, it was arson, but no, they had not caught the perp. Though off the top of his head he could not speak to a house fire that occurred that far back, since it was before his time, he would see what he could find out. He was busy today, but we made a date to meet the following afternoon. In the meantime, I planned to do some detective work of my own.

My plan was to head to the Traverse City State Hospital first. An old college classmate had recently taken over as superintendent there. I had informed him of my visit. Richard Blake had always been one of those guys who prided himself on being in the know, and he had been orphaned as a child. While it was a long shot, since he had been adopted by a Traverse City family, I thought he might know something about the orphanage fire. At the very least, maybe he could point me in the right direction. After that, I would hit the local library.

I arrived at the asylum just after eleven. The security was tight. I had to check in with a guard at the gate. I remembered Richard being sturdy but trim, with an old-world stately handsomeness that suggested a wealthy upbringing. He was popular with the girls at Michigan, could have had any one of them he wanted, but to everyone's dismay ended up marrying Bitzy Randolph, a shy, plain girl from somewhere down South, who, as it turned out, hailed from one of the wealthiest families in the country. Tobacco money.

Richard greeted me at the door to Building 50, the large campus's main structure, all teeth and coiffed hair, his suit impeccable, Italian wool, I guessed, most likely custom-made. I hardly recognized him. He had gained at least thirty pounds and lost most of his hair.

"Good to see you, old chap," he said. Same pretentious affect. "How was the drive?"

"Uneventful," I said.

"What brings you this way?" he asked. "You're from somewhere up here, aren't you?"

"Charlevoix originally," I said. "But I haven't been back there since boarding school. I've been living in South Haven for years now."

"That's right," Richard said. "You were an orphan, like me. And just look how successful the two of us turned out."

I did not correct him—common ground breeds chumminess—but I never felt truly orphaned, thanks to my trust fund. I found it odd that Richard, given his keen radar for those more fortunate, did not know or remember this detail, since I found out about my trust fund while we were in college.

"I'm wondering if you might be able to shed light on two fires that happened here in Traverse City several years back," I said.

"Fires?" he asked. "Sounds like a complicated subject. Why don't we head to my office?"

I followed him through the large open lobby. The interior of the building, like the exterior, sported stunning Victorian-Italianate architecture. I had done some reading on the asylum. The facility opened in 1885 under the leadership of its first superintendent, James Decker Munson. Munson's "beauty as therapy" philosophy, which forbade traditional straitjackets and prison-like incarceration and promoted a sense of purpose among its patients, was groundbreaking at the time and had since become a model in the field. What stood out to me, in addition to the open, high-ceilinged airiness and the overall beauty of the space, was how quiet it was. I neither heard nor witnessed any of the screaming or erratic behavior often associated with asylums, and on my drive into the premises, I had seen patients working in gardens, raking the lawns, and planting trees.

"It's an amazing facility, isn't it?" Richard asked.

"It is," I said. "It must be a pleasure to be part of."

"I do enjoy my job," he said. "I have a dedicated staff, and our patients are generally well-behaved. There are those, of course, who are, shall we say, in need of more secure accommodations, but by design, they rarely come in contact with the visiting public."

"Where are they?" I asked.

"There's a wing on the top floor of this building that houses the more severe cases," Richard said. "And two of the cottages, the ones closest to the bay, hold those considered dangerous to themselves and others. I'd be happy to give you a tour after our chat if you'd like."

We had arrived at a large office complete with floor-to-ceiling bookshelves, a small round conference table, and a to-scale model of the building and grounds.

"We are here," Richard said. "Back here are the two cottages I mentioned. You can see that this one is quite large, the size of a small mansion. It was in fact such a home in an earlier life. The residence of a wealthy banker. We own all the land surrounding the buildings, over sixty-three acres. The old farm is back here. Patients still work the land, but back at the turn of the century we were a major contributor to the area's agriculture. We even had a world champion cow. Traverse Colantha Walker was her name. The only thing you can't see on this model are the tunnels."

"Tunnels?" I asked.

"Yes. They run throughout the grounds, connect all the buildings and facilities. They also house utilities. Given our lovely northern Michigan weather, they are a must for staff to get back and forth."

"What about the patients?" I asked. "Do they use the tunnels?"

"Only when accompanied by staff," he said. "Although there have been breaches. God knows how they got past the guards."

"What kind of breaches?"

"Back in the early 1900s, a group of test patients hanged themselves from the rafters of one of the tunnels. There have been other hangings, but the number one form of suicide is drowning. They just walk right into the bay. Usually right before it freezes, so their bodies aren't discovered until it melts. I should say 'walked.' We haven't had a drowning since I've been in charge."

"What do you mean by test patients?" I asked.

"Just what it sounds like. During Munson's time, there was a lot of experimentation, mostly on indigent patients or those without families. It's appalling actually, but unfortunately not uncommon back in the day. It happened in most of the asylums."

"I read stories about the hospital being haunted."

"Ah, yes. The ghosts. There have been a few of those Ouija board types. Paranormal investigators, they call themselves. Apparently they found *activity* in one of the laundry rooms, and in some of the halls. Then there's the Hippie Tree, this rotted and twisted dead willow in the woods off Red Drive. Legend has it that it contains the souls of lost or dead patients. The entire thing is painted with brightly colored symbols, and somewhere beneath all those meandering limbs there's said to be a portal to hell. Mumbo jumbo mostly."

I wondered if legend had the tree moaning like it had Adelaide's tree barking. "Why do they call it the Hippie Tree?"

"Because so-called hippies, or what I'd call druggies, did all that painting after they got *enlightened* or some such. Who knows? Makes for good party conversation."

Richard walked behind his desk, sat, gestured to a chair opposite him, an obvious power play. A more secure man would have sat at the round table with me.

I briefly explained my interest in the fires at the orphanage and Scarlet's childhood home.

"I seem to recall something about an orphanage fire, but geez, that was years ago."

"1952," I said. "That wasn't the same orphanage where you lived?"

"No," he said. "Mine was in Detroit, but as in any industry, word travels in the orphanage circuit. If memory serves me, the one that burned down here was all girls. The other fire? What did you say their surname was?"

"Boudreau," I said. "Charles Boudreau. He was Traverse City's district attorney back then."

"Any relation to Mary Ann Boudreau?" Richard asked.

"I'm not sure," I said. "Who is that?"

"A girl I used to know," Richard said. "She wasn't from around here, at least that I knew of, but the surname isn't that usual, so I thought maybe . . . Forget it."

"Why did you think she wasn't from Traverse City?" I asked.

"I saw her at the bus stop a few times," Richard said. "She could have lived just outside of town, I suppose. But it's neither here nor there. I haven't seen or heard of her in years. The only reason I thought of her, other than her surname, that is, is because she was a real looker. Long blond hair. Legs to heaven. Had a bit of a reputation, if you know what I mean. Wish I could have gotten a piece of her. I was shy back then."

I could not imagine Richard ever being shy.

"What do you mean by reputation?" I asked.

"You know, *friendly*," Richard said. "We used to have these bonfires on the bay throughout the year. High school and college kids mostly, but also anyone else who heard about them. Big parties with kegs and weed. I'd see her there with different guys, but mostly with the sheriff's son. Real ass. Kind of guy that thinks his shit doesn't stink. She was younger than us."

"How much younger?"

"Fifteen maybe? Somewhere around there."

"Does this sheriff's son still live around here?"

"Yup," Richard said. "Zachary Ludwig is his name. He married Wanda Sherman. You know, the skier? She made the Olympic team back in the day?"

"Sorry, I don't," I said.

"Well, it was a while ago. And she didn't place or anything like that. They have a son that goes to school with my youngest daughter. Wild like his dad was."

"Do you know how I might be able to get ahold of Mr. Ludwig?"

"He works at the Y. Teaches ice hockey to local kids. He got himself into a snafu a few years back and was sentenced to a community service stint there. He's been there ever since. Or you could just look him up in the phone book. What's this about anyway? You sure have a lot of questions for a guy that's just curious about a couple of fires."

"It's nothing, really. Just gathering some material for a book I'm working on."

I had not planned to repeat the lie, but I did not want to tell Richard, of all people, that I was looking for information on a patient. He never was known for discretion.

"A book?" Richard asked. "I've always wanted to write a book. I think my life is pretty interesting. You got a publisher?"

"Not yet," I said. "I don't have the entire thing formulated in my mind."

"Well, just make sure you put my name in the acknowledgments." He smiled. "You ready for that tour?"

It was past three by the time the tour ended. Although the ghost stories Richard imparted along the way were intriguing, especially those associated with the dank and creepy tunnels, about an hour in, I was kicking myself for agreeing to it. Richard invited me to dinner, but I declined, said I had work to catch up on. Sort of true. I wanted to get to the library before it closed at six P.M. On the way there, I stopped off at the Park Place Hotel to check in, drop off my duffel bag, and make two phone calls. The first was to Butch to tell him I had arrived in one piece and make sure he was doing okay. The second was to Zachary Ludwig. As Richard had indicated, there was only one person by that name in the book. He answered on the first ring and offered to meet me for breakfast the following morning at a Big Boy off US 131.

The Carnegie Library was located on Sixth Street, in a park area overlooking the Boardman River. The women working the front desk—according to their name tags, Suzanne and Virginia—proved much friendlier than Kelly and Eleanor. I mustered up what little charm I possessed, explained why I was there and what I already knew about the fires. I did not even need to ask for help. Virginia popped out from behind the desk and walked me to an uninhabited area of the library.

"So we can talk more freely," she said. "Nobody has asked about that house fire in years."

"I'm doing research for a book." Lies, I thought, are like flannel shirts; they get more comfortable with age.

"Wow, cool," she said. "Everybody knows about the fire at St. Ann's. So sad all those little girls dying."

"Didn't the police think it was arson?"

"Yes, but as far as I know, they never found the guy."

"What about the Boudreau fire? Mr. Boudreau was the district attorney, right?"

"Yes," Virginia said. "I remember because one of my older cousins worked at the cafeteria in the County Courthouse, where the DA's office was. She was always saying how friendly and respectful Mr. Boudreau was, that he remembered her name. My little sister went to kindergarten with the daughter. They didn't play together or anything, but you know how it is. When tragedy strikes, you look for any connection you might have to the victims. One of those not-so-admirable human traits. Poor little girl losing her parents like that. But at least she wasn't there when it happened."

"What do you mean?" I asked.

"We all thought she died in the fire with her parents, but it was later discovered she'd gone to live with an uncle somewhere north of here."

"Do you know where?" I asked. "Or the uncle's name?"

"Sorry, I don't," Virginia said. "But I'm sure the police do. Have you met with Detective Logan?"

"I have an appointment with him tomorrow."

"He's married to one of our librarians. She isn't here today. Some sort of church retreat. They're devout Catholics."

"What about the circumstances of the fire itself?" I asked.

"Folks say there was a big party at the house. The child's nanny lived in the guest cottage. I think she was the one who called the fire department."

"Do you by any chance know the nanny's name?"

"Linda Howard," Virginia said. "Nicest woman you'll ever meet. She lives at the senior home now."

"Which one?"

"There's only one. The Traverse City Senior Citizens' Home."

"You have a good memory," I said.

"Not really," she said. "Traverse City was a small town back then. Everybody pretty much knew everybody's business. And like I said, people don't forget tragedies."

"Do you happen to remember the little girl's name?"

"Sorry, I don't. But I could call my sister later. She might remember."

"Can you give me a call if she does?" I wrote down my name and the phone number of the hotel. "I almost forgot, do you think your local newspaper would have covered both fires?"

"The *Traverse City Record-Eagle*? Definitely. Let me call over there and have them make copies of anything they printed."

"You don't have one of those microfiche machines?"

"Yes, but those things are ridiculous to use. This will be much easier." She left.

When she returned, she handed me a card with a woman's name and the *Record-Eagle*'s address on it. "Just ask for Clara Barnes when you get there. She'll be expecting you. Is there anything else I can help you with?"

"How about a good place to get a bite to eat?"

"The Traverse City Diner is right downtown on Front Street," she said. "Best cherry pie in town, and their spaghetti is to die for."

The Traverse City Diner was one of those establishments with red-and-white-checkered plastic tablecloths, where you can't hear yourself think over the clanging plates and high-pitched buzz. On the way there, I had stopped off at the *Record-Eagle*, where Clara had my articles waiting inside a large manila envelope bearing my name and stamped OFFICIAL BUSINESS. I figured I would look at them when I got back to the hotel. I found a table by the window. A large sign hung over the counter that separated the dining area from the kitchen. It read: *IF YOU DON'T LIKE GARLIC, GO HOME.* I found a table by the window. The waitress—Debbie, her name tag said—was there in an instant.

"What can I get you?" she asked.

"I hear your spaghetti is good?"

"Best in town."

"Sold. What kind of wine do you serve?"

"House red or house white."

"I'll have the red."

"A cherry pie just came out of the oven," she said. "You interested? Traverse City is the cherry capital of the world."

"Sounds good. Is your coffee fresh?"

"I'll brew a fresh pot."

After she left, I marveled at Michigan's berry bests. Here I had been to the blueberry capital and the cherry capital all in one day.

While I waited, I read the paper place mat, which supplied a brief history on Traverse City's cherry notoriety. Who knew that cherry orchards lined Lake Michigan's coast from Benton Harbor to TC, or that the area produced 75 percent of the nation's tart cherries and 20 percent of its sweet ones? Also of note were tidbits such as that it takes 250 tart cherries to make one pie, an average cherry tree produces twenty-eight pies, and the record for picking the most cherries in one day was held by seventeen-year-old Harold Robertson, who, in 1958, picked 1,225 pounds of cherries in a one-hour period.

Virginia was right. The spaghetti sauce was great, which probably had something to do with the heavy-handed dose of garlic, and the pie was sublime.

I was dead tired when I got back to the hotel, but perused the articles anyway. The Boudreau house fire had happened in July of 1941. As with the orphanage fire, the police suspected arson, though in this case they considered it might be a revenge crime, someone Boudreau had put in jail. The obituary was for both husband and wife, but what was said about Mr. Boudreau was so glowing I wondered who wrote it. Little was said about Mrs. Boudreau. What stood out most was there was no mention of a daughter. The fire at St. Ann's Orphanage, as I had previously noted, happened on January 1, 1952. It was a longer version of the Associated Press piece I found in the *South Haven Tribune*. In addition to the death count, it mentioned a "possible witness," though no name was given. And there was something else. Both articles mentioned the respective fires as having started at approximately two A.M. The phone rang just as I had finished reading. It was Virginia calling to tell me that the Boudreaus' daughter's name was Mary Ann, the same name Richard had given for the girl at the bonfires. I added the name to my timeline, along with that of Zachary Ludwig, whom I was meeting for breakfast, and Linda Howard, whom I would call first thing in the morning to set up an appointment. Then I placed everything I had gathered on the nightstand, and went to bed.

Scarlet

A radio hit parade was playing in my ears. "Respect" by Aretha Franklin, "California Dreamin'" by the Mamas and the Papas, and "These Boots Are Made for Walkin'" by Nancy Sinatra, among others. I was having trouble painting with the voices so loud. Blue would be gone for several hours—she'd gone to piano practice and then was meeting Butch on the pier—so I invited Jeremy over. He was sitting on the sofa, oblivious to the loud singing. As usual we were both a bit tipsy, and it wasn't even ten A.M.

"You seriously can't hear them?" I asked him.

"No," he said.

"Do you think I'm going crazy?"

"Aren't we all a bit mad?" He went to the refrigerator and refilled his wineglass. "Do you want more, love?"

"No, I'm fine," I said.

He put back the bottle and returned to the sofa. "You seem a little melancholy today. Is there something bothering you?"

"Blue is upset I'm not going to her competition. I wish I could."

"When does she leave?"

"Tomorrow," I said.

"I have an idea," he said. "Why don't we go buy her a dress for her big day? Since you can't go to the competition with her, you can at least make sure she feels gorgeous. A beautiful dress will elevate her confidence and self-esteem. You, of all people, should know that.

Remember those exhibits in New York? How we shopped for the perfect dress? And you felt like a million bucks, didn't you?"

Jeremy had always been more fashionable than I, and helped me to dress on more than one occasion.

"I know just the place," he added. "In Saugatuck. We could shop and have a late lunch, make a day of it."

"I need to be back before she gets home," I said.

"Then we will be," he said. "You best hurry and change though. There's a bus leaving in twenty minutes. Given the amount of wine we've consumed, I don't think it's a good idea for me to drive."

The bus dropped us off right on Butler Street. Like South Haven, it was busy with late-season tourists. I followed Jeremy to a shop called Polly's Boutique. Inside, he went right to the dress section and began sliding hangers, inspecting each dress. He made a disapproving face at every one I picked out. "Too young," he said. "She's not a little girl anymore." Then, "Look at this one." He pulled out a simple black taffeta shift, handed it to me.

The store owner approached as I was admiring it, said, "That's a lovely dress."

"My friend helped me pick it out," I said.

"Friend?" she asked.

"Yes." I turned to indicate Jeremy, but he was nowhere in sight. "He must have stepped out." I explained to her what the dress was for.

"A piano competition?" she asked. "You must be so proud. Would you like me to help you pick out shoes and stockings?"

"I am proud," I said. And in that moment, I was filled with a combination of pride and regret. Pride in Blue's talent. Pride in the beautiful and talented young lady she had become. Regret that I couldn't go to the competition. Regret that our lives had been what they'd been. "And yes, thank you, shoes and stockings would be perfect."

After we gathered everything, she rang it up. "I have a box I think will work," she said, "and blue-striped wrap, but I think this occasion calls for something a little more festive. I'm sure the drugstore on the corner will have better paper choices. I'd be happy to wrap it with whatever you choose."

I searched for Jeremy on my way to the drugstore but couldn't find him. I picked out shiny silver paper and a white bow so large it would surely cover the entire top of the box. Outside the store, I found Jeremy sitting on a bench smoking a cigarette. "Did you get a card?" he asked.

"Card?"

"You need to write something special to her." He must have noticed my overwhelmed expression because he added, "How about I pick one out and meet you back at the dress shop?"

After the clerk finished wrapping, we found a restaurant on the water, had lunch, and shared a bottle of wine.

On the bus ride home, Jeremy and I talked about those good old days in New York. It's what we always did: reminisce.

"What's with that lady across the aisle?" I said to him. "Why does she keep staring at us?"

"Ignore her, love," he said. "The world is full of nosy Nellies."

Back in South Haven, he walked me home but didn't come inside. Blue would be here soon, and I wanted to take advantage of what was left of the daylight to paint.

Once inside, I sat down at the rainbow table, got out the card, thought about what I wanted to say, and signed it. Then I slipped it beneath the ribbon and hid the package under the sofa. I wanted to give it to her in the morning, when both of us were fresh. Then I selected a brush and studied *The Boating Party*. But instead of painting, I found myself considering what Jeremy had said earlier about Blue at least deserving a beautiful dress. She deserved so much more. She deserved my presence. She deserved my support. What if I pulled the rucksack out from under the bed, the one we'd only ever used to run from HIM, and packed the black dress and pumps Jeremy had helped me pick out for my first group art exhibit? What if I went to Interlochen, sat in the section of the auditorium reserved for the family members of the competitors, watched my daughter walk onto the stage, clapped louder than anyone else, listened to her play? What if, in this moment, I decided to be the mother that Blue deserved?

But I couldn't go. I couldn't be. Not yet.

Just two more days and everything would change.

Blue

That irritating red bird wakes me. Eight claps and chirps. I'd removed the batteries. My mother must have put them back in. I find the clock annoying. Things don't annoy my mother. She has three modes of oblivion: painting land (when painting), crazy land (when outside reality), and cloud land (the rest of the time). It is the day I leave for the competition. My nerves are flashing and firing like spark plugs. I dreamt I broke all my fingers. I don't know how. I bend each in turn to ensure they are intact and functioning. Brush my teeth four times longer than usual to make sure they're clean. Walk into the living area. My mother is still working on *The Boating Party*. She was painting when I got home yesterday. I don't think she even heard me come in.

"Where did you put the mason jars?" she asks. "I've been looking all over for them." Not *Good morning* or *How did you sleep?*

"They're under the kitchen sink." It is the exact thing I said when she asked me the same question two weeks ago when I got them. Granted, she was asleep on the cat-clawed sofa when I got home that afternoon. I remember thinking she must have been really tired because she slept through *Bewitched* and *Peyton Place*, her two favorite TV shows. They're on the one clear channel we get. But the next morning she asked about the mason jars, and now here she is asking again.

"Good," she says.

"Are you still making jam?"

"Jam?"

"You said you wanted the mason jars because you were going to make jam."

She puts down her brush, looks at me, her gaze as vacant as a mannequin's. "That's right. Sorry, I didn't understand the question. I was lost inside my painting."

The response relieves me.

"What time is Mr. Kline picking you up today? The competition is tomorrow, right?"

"Noon, and yes," I say. I'm grateful she remembered both.

"Are you excited?"

"Nervous," I say.

"You'll do great. This is your destiny." A sly smile crosses her face. "There's something under the sofa for you."

It's a present, a large flat box wrapped in pretty silver paper with a huge white bow. Two gifts in two days, I think. From the two people I love most in the world. I open the card. It reads: *To my dear sweet girl. I thought the beauty of this dress nearly matched yours. I hope it helps bring out your inner confidence and charms the dance of your fingers. And no matter what happens, always remember I love you with all my heart.* The words bring tears to my eyes.

"Oh, stop blubbering and open the present," my mother says. "If you don't do it by the time I count to five, I will."

I rip the paper from the box and open it. Inside is a grown-up dress (black taffeta, no girly ruffles), silk stockings, and patent leather kitten-heel pumps.

"Thank you. I love it." And I do, and while I am grateful for the dress and shoes and stockings, I'm even more grateful that she went shopping, that she left the house to do something normal, and since I've never seen a dress like this in South Haven, she must have gone to a clothing store elsewhere, St. Joe or Saugatuck or Holland, and then to another store to buy wrapping paper, ribbon, and a card. And I know how much all of that must have overwhelmed her.

"I'm so happy you like it," she says. "We bought it in Saugatuck. We shopped and had lunch. It was such a nice day."

"Who is we?" I asked.

"Jeremy went with me. It was his idea actually."

I decide not to think about her invisible friends. I decide not to worry about her. I decide to believe she will be fine while I'm away.

"Are you sure you don't want to come? Mr. Kline says there's a nice restaurant in the hotel, the kind that serves wine, and we could stay up late watching a TV that isn't staticky. Maybe your gallery could come a different time?" There are a million other things I want to say, but she interrupts and says this.

"My gallery?"

"You said they were coming to pick up paintings?"

She looks at me, same blank stare, then asks, "Did I?"

"Yes," I say, while thinking I was right to wonder if she'd lied.

"Oh," she says. "That's tomorrow. I thought you meant today. Everything is going to be fine, you know. You'll see."

She picks up her brush, starts to paint again.

I head to the kitchen and make some toast. Soon I will need to start getting ready. Soon Mr. Kline will pick me up. Soon I will be at a fancy hotel. Soon my fingers will be dancing across the keys of a grand piano. Unless, like in my dream, they break.

Henry

Zachary Ludwig was sitting in the last booth on the right, near the window, just as he had indicated. He was a clean-cut, good-looking guy with light hair and eyes, about my age. He motioned me over.

"How did you know it was me?" I asked as I scooted into the booth.

"New face in town," he said. "And you look like a psychiatrist. The tweed and horn-rimmed glasses are a dead giveaway."

"Psychoanalyst."

"Ah. One of those Freudian gurus."

"Jungian actually," I said. "Are you familiar with the field, Mr. Ludwig?"

"It's Zachary," he said. "But call me Zach. Only my father calls me Zachary. And only when he's pissed off, which is most of the time. Used to think I wanted to be one of you guys. But I couldn't afford the necessary schooling. Not to mention I got myself into a little trouble back then. Served a year in the pen."

I was curious as to what kind of trouble but didn't ask.

"Most people ask," Zach said, "so I don't tell them. But since you didn't, petty theft. I stole some first-edition books from a neighbor's house when they were on vacation. Got a pretty penny for them. It was stupid though. I sold them to a used bookstore in town, one of the first places the police checked. My dad could've gotten me off, he was the town sheriff, but thought I needed the lesson. He's a dick. So, Richard gave you my name? Did he also mention my most recent brush with the law? Knowing Richard, he probably did. Loves to put other guys down. Makes him feel superior. But you know that, right? Psychology 101. I got picked up for driving under the influence, so now I teach kids how to play ice hockey. It's been one of those blessings in disguise. I really enjoy it. You got kids?"

"A son," I said. "He's fifteen."

"Mine's ten," he said. "His name is Craig. Yours?"

"Butch."

The waitress showed up.

"Cindy, this is Henry. He's in town doing some research for a book."

"Really?" she asked. "I love to read. When's it come out?"

"Not for a while yet," I said. "I'm in the research stage."

"What did you say your name was?" she asked. "I'll watch for it."

I felt bad enough for lying. The thought of people searching for a book that would never exist made me feel even worse.

"Dr. Henry Williams. But don't look for a couple of years." I hoped she'd forget my name by then.

"What can I get you?" she asked.

I ordered the combo. Bacon, hash browns, toast, eggs over easy.

"The usual, Zach?" Cindy asked.

"Yup."

When Cindy left, I asked Zach about Mary Ann Boudreau.

"She was the prettiest thing that ever walked this earth," Zach said. "And she had the personality to go with it. Sweet. Kind of ethereal. Maybe a little damaged."

"Why damaged?"

"Just the way she acted," Zach said. "She'd look off into space sometimes. And a few times she cried for no reason. I asked her once if I'd done something, but she said it didn't have anything to do with me. Said it was something that happened to her when she was a kid. She didn't say what."

"You dated for a while?"

"Four months. We met at the first fall bonfire. She was sitting there on the opposite side of the fire from me. Richard was sitting next to her. It was obvious he was trying to impress her, he's always fancied himself a ladies' man, but her eyes were wandering around like she was looking for an escape route. That's when ours locked. She and I just talked that first night, but after that we were pretty much inseparable."

"Richard indicated she had lots of boyfriends."

"Richard is an ass. And he was jealous. He tried to talk to her more than once, but she was loyal. She was already with me. And even if she hadn't been, she wouldn't have been with him. She was a good judge of character. I would've kept seeing her, but I guess it wasn't mutual. The relationship ended abruptly."

"May I ask what happened?"

"I wish I knew. She just disappeared."

"Did you try to contact her?"

"I would have," Zach said, "but I didn't have her contact information. She wouldn't give it to me. She was like that, mysterious. I asked around about her, but nobody knew anything. It was like she was a ghost."

Our breakfast came. "More coffee?" Cindy asked.

We both said yes.

"That looks good," I said to Zach.

"They call it a scramble," he said. "Scrambled eggs mixed with whatever else you want. I do the vegetables and cheese. Mushrooms, potatoes, green peppers. I think they put some cut-up apples in it too."

I made a mental note to have the same thing the next morning.

"How did she seem that last night you saw her? Was she nervous? Worried?"

"Happy. We had sex. It was the first and last time."

"Do you remember what year this was?"

"When I last saw her? New Year's Eve, 1951." He paused. "Technically I guess it was 1952, since it was after midnight by the time she left. The same night as the fire. I remember because when I got home my dad was in uniform and on his way out the door. He told me what had happened."

"The fire at St. Ann's?"

"Yes, I was still living at home then. It wasn't right away, but after not hearing from her for a while, and then not at all, I wondered whether her disappearing like that had something to do with the fire."

"How so?"

"I don't know, like maybe she was dead. But then I thought that was just because it happened the last night I saw her and I couldn't separate the two in my mind. And because, you know, when someone leaves you without explanation, when you thought the two of you had something, well, I guess you think the worst. Or maybe you want to. Hurts less than believing the whole thing was one-sided."

I did the math. Blue was born in 1952. Depending on when, it was possible Zach was her father. *I need to ask Butch when Blue's birthday is.* "Do you think if she hadn't disappeared that it might have been a long-term relationship?"

"Who knows. She was a good kid. I was pretty broken up when I lost her."

I noted that Zach had called Scarlet a kid. Did he know that she was only fifteen at the time?

Zach and I talked for a while more. About Traverse City. About Charlevoix. About his wife. About how mine died. About Butch and Craig. I felt a kinship with him. Was it just one of those things when you meet someone with whom you feel an immediate connection, or was it because we shared strong feelings for Scarlet?

"I should get going," he said. "I have a class at ten. Group of six-year-olds. They start them young these days. Hopeful parents, I guess. Thinking of college hockey. Maybe even the Olympics. It was a pleasure."

"Likewise. And thanks. You've been very helpful."

We stood. I noticed he was tall. *Like Scarlet. Like Blue.* Six four, give or take.

"You're not really writing a book, are you?" he asked.

"No."

"What are you doing here then?"

"It has to do with one of my patients, someone who used to know Mary Ann."

"Well, if you ever find her or figure out what happened to her, let me know."

"Will do," I said, then asked, "Do you happen to know directions to the senior citizens' home?"

The senior citizens' home was more like a small neighborhood. There was a three-story apartment building, a recreation room, and a small hospital. People could qualify for placement in the facility at retirement age and live in one of the apartments until they could no longer function on their own, at which time they would be transferred to the hospital.

"They call it graduated living," Linda Howard said. She had just finished explaining how the complex worked. "My husband passed last year and I felt my house was just too large, so I sold it, moved back to Traverse City—I grew up here—bought this place, and now I have a nice little nest egg. We have an event planner. She organizes dances, bridge tournaments, bingo games, and golf and shuffleboard in the summertime, you name it. I especially like that. Never a dull moment here. You said you were here about the fire? Such a horrible thing. The two of them dying like that. You say you're writing a book?"

"Just doing research right now. You mentioned you moved back. When did you move away?"

"After the fire. The memories were just too raw. My husband was able to get a teaching job in Lansing."

"I understand you'd cared for the child since she was born?"

"Yes. As you can imagine, being that she was married to the district attorney, Mrs. Boudreau had a lot of volunteer activities to attend to. And she worked part-time at the Catholic church in town.

She was a social worker by training, worked with traumatized kids. Such a lovely woman. Generous. I made a better income than other nannies in the area, and she always made sure to take care of me at the holidays. One time, she gave me two airline tickets to New York City, along with a paid hotel, and theater and museum tickets. My husband and I had such a nice time."

"What was the little girl like?"

"Mary Ann? Just precious. Near as perfect a child as there ever was. I adored her."

"Did you ever see her again after that night?" I asked Mrs. Howard.

"Well, I know this is going to sound odd, but one time I thought I did. See her, I mean. It was the fall of 1951. I remember because I was in town for my thirtieth high school reunion. I was on my way somewhere, I don't remember where, and had stopped for a red light. She was waiting at a bus stop near the intersection. The car behind me had to honk its horn I stared so long. Once I got through the light, I actually turned the car around and drove back by the stop, but she wasn't there anymore."

"She would have changed quite a bit by then, right? More than ten years later?"

"Yes, that's true, but there was just something about the girl."

"What?"

"Well, for one, she was twirling."

"Twirling, you say? How do you mean?"

"You know, arms outstretched or cupped above her head, hair flying, round and round. Mary Ann used to do that. She loved to dance. But I suppose you're right. Probably I just wanted to believe it was her. I read in one of those grief books that can happen, that you imagine you see lost loved ones. The book called them love ghosts."

"What about before you moved, in the weeks after the fire? Did you hear anything else about her?"

"I did hear she went to live with an uncle. Which was odd

because Mrs. Boudreau never mentioned a brother or brother-in-law. Or any extended family, for that matter."

"Where did you hear that?" I asked. "About her going to live with an uncle?"

"Why, I can't remember," she said. "I do know I didn't hear it right away. At first, we thought she died in the fire, but they didn't find her remains. Then the police said they thought she'd wandered off, got lost in the woods. One of them even mentioned the possibility that wolves got her. Which I found truly heartless. Saying such a thing when you don't even know if it's true." Tears came to her eyes. "It was like losing my own child. My husband, Herbert, and I couldn't have children of our own. She spent a lot of time with us."

"I'm so sorry for your loss," I said.

"Thank you," she said. She reached into her pocket, grabbed a handkerchief, dabbed her eyes.

"Can you tell me what you remember about that night?"

"There was a party. Mr. Boudreau was always having parties. He was a good host. He played the piano, you know."

"The piano, you say?"

"Yes," Mrs. Howard said. "He was a marvelous piano player. Gifted. Everybody thought he should have played professionally. Anyway, I was in bed with my husband—we lived in the cottage behind the house. I couldn't sleep that night it was so noisy. I thought if I couldn't sleep, maybe Mary Ann couldn't either, so I went to check on her. But I had no reason to worry. She was safe and sound in her bed. And then, not even two hours later, the fire broke out. I smelled it first. Then I saw the flames. They were shooting into the sky. My husband and I ran outside to see if we could do anything. You see, at that time we thought, surely, they'd gotten out. I mean it wasn't that long since we'd heard the arguing."

"Arguing? I assumed by noise you meant party noises."

"Oh, no. The party had broken up by then."

"Mr. and Mrs. Boudreau were arguing?"

"Two men were arguing. Mr. Boudreau and another man."

"Man? Do you have any idea who he was?"

"I thought it might be the man in the suit I saw earlier that day. I was taking my daily walk along the beach when I saw him with Mrs. Boudreau and Mary Ann. I might not have thought much about it except who wears a suit on the beach in July? And there was the way Mrs. Boudreau was holding Mary Ann. Tight, as if she was scared or upset."

"Did you recognize him?"

"No. I'd never seen him before that day. I think he was from out of town."

"Why do you say that?"

"Because it was a small town, and I knew pretty much everyone in town at least by sight. And there was the hair."

"Hair?

"Very blond, almost white. Kind of unkempt, like that artist Andy Warhol. Very distinctive. So it would have been hard to miss him if he was from around here."

"Did you tell the police all this?"

"Yes, of course. But they didn't seem that interested. They were busy investigating the fire. You see, they didn't think it was arson at first. They thought it was faulty wiring, or perhaps even, because of the party, that a bottle of alcohol had caught fire, or that a cigarette had fallen on the shag carpeting."

"Do you know when they changed their minds? About it being arson?"

"I'm not sure exactly. It was before my husband and I moved. So maybe a few weeks later?"

"How did you find out?"

"I read it in the paper like everyone else. Can you imagine? No one even came by to tell me."

"You mentioned you were here in the fall of 1951 for your high school reunion," I said. "So you weren't here when the orphanage fire happened?"

"No. I was in Lansing for New Year's. A friend called to tell me about it, so I looked for it in the news, just awful, those poor little girls. She said the entire town was in mourning."

"Did you have any reason to believe the two fires were related?"

"I never thought about it, I guess. They happened so far apart. Do you think they were?"

"Just a surmise on my part," I said. I wrote down my phone number and asked Mrs. Howard to call me if she thought of anything else.

"Well, if you learn anything, please let me know," she said. "The police certainly won't. You know how they are. Tight-lipped. It's all been so sad and frustrating. Like reading a whodunnit with the last chapter missing."

I said I would, and thanked her for her time.

Detective Steve Logan looked to be around forty, so sixteen years ago he would have been in his mid-twenties, and ten years before that, when the Boudreaus' house burned down, he would have been in high school. Meaning, as he had indicated on the phone, he didn't work that case.

"Thanks for fitting me in," I said.

"No problem," he said. "Slow day. We like them that way. You say you're writing a book."

"Yes. About the two fires. As I mentioned on the phone. A house fire and St. Ann's Orphanage."

"I can help you with the orphanage fire. And about the house fire, I did some research and assume you're talking about the Boudreau arson? It's the only high-profile unsolved house fire I could dig up."

"That's the one," I said. "Why high-profile?"

"Boudreau was the county district attorney at the time. He put a lot of bad guys in jail, one of the reasons why arson was investigated. I pulled both files this morning. Refreshed my memory on the orphanage fire, although that wasn't really necessary. It's one of those cases that sticks to you, if you know what I mean. More so for me, I suppose, because my wife and I were in the process of adopting one of the little girls that died in the fire. We can't have children of our own."

"I'm sorry," I said.

"Thanks. It was a bad time, but God blessed us with a precious little girl two years later. Her name is Sophie." He pointed to a picture on his desk. "She'll be fourteen next month."

"She's beautiful," I said.

"Yup, we call her our little miracle. We got her from a Catholic orphanage in Indiana. The mother chose my wife and me from a pool of over thirty applicants. God's will. We weren't the only folks affected by the St. Ann's fire. Several of the little girls were set to be adopted. Not to mention the whole town was shocked. It was a brutal crime. What kind of monster would burn innocent children alive?"

"What can you tell me about it?"

"We got the call just after two A.M. on New Year's Day. It was a real tragedy. Maybe if we'd gotten there earlier, we could have stopped it from spreading, but as it was, the building went up quickly."

"According to newspaper archives, the Boudreau fire started around two A.M. as well. Seems an odd coincidence."

"Yes, I read that."

"Why did you think the fire at St. Ann's was arson?"

"Because of where it started," Logan said. "In the cafeteria. The walls in there were basically kindling. And we found the matchbooks. Not in the cafeteria. Under a tree several yards away. They'd been positioned into one word. *BITCH.* It was like the arsonist had a vendetta against someone inside. We tested them for fingerprints, but nothing came up."

"Any idea who he was targeting?"

"No. It didn't make a lot of sense. Who has it in for nuns and little girls?"

"Seventeen."

"What?"

"There were seventeen little girls inside. And three nuns."

"My point is what kind of a person would do something so cruel unless he had a specific target? We looked into all the nuns, and there didn't seem to be anything in their pasts to indicate someone might hold a grudge against them. And the little girls, well, they ranged in age from infants to eighteen years. We did our best, but none of them were in the system, and any records the orphanage may have had that could shed further light burned in the fire."

"I read there was a witness?" I asked.

Logan picked up one of the files, shuffled through it. "Rhonda Bishop. Mrs. Bishop said she got up in the middle of the night to get a glass of water and saw a man walking by."

"Did she describe him?"

"Average height and build, wearing a dark suit but no overcoat."

"Blond hair?"

"No mention of a hair color. Where'd you get blond hair?"

"I talked with Linda Howard, the Boudreaus' nanny, right before coming over here. She said she saw a man wearing a suit arguing with Mrs. Boudreau on the beach the morning of the house fire. I was just wondering if it might be the same perp."

"We never made that connection. Do you know something we don't?"

"No, like I said, the two A.M. timeline. But also two fires, both arsons, both unsolved. Could I talk with the detective that worked the Boudreau case?"

"According to the file, that would be a Detective Ben Forest. He's dead, sorry. Heart attack six years after the fire."

"You said earlier that Boudreau being the DA was one reason arson was investigated as the fire cause. Were there others?"

"Just the one," he said. "According to the file, there was a gash on Boudreau's head."

"Gash? I thought I read that his body was burned beyond recognition."

"It was," Logan said. "But the coroner was able to see that his skull had been cracked. The shape of the wound matched a fireplace poker found near the body."

"What happened to the little girl?"

"Little girl?"

"The Boudreaus' daughter. Mrs. Howard said you didn't find her body?"

"Not me," Logan said. "My pre—"

"Your predecessor, I know."

"It looks like they dropped the ball. They figured she died there too, so no one checked up on her. Then, when they didn't find her remains, they filed a missing-persons report, but nothing turned up. Too much time had gone by."

"Mrs. Howard said she heard she went to live with an uncle."

"I didn't see anything in the file about an uncle. Could've been her wanting to believe the kid was okay. No one wants to believe the worst about a missing child. Kid was five years old, had smoke inhalation, was probably disoriented. My theory, she woke to the flames and wandered off. Who knows what happened after that?"

"But you never found a body?"

"Not that I know of."

"Did you ever look into the fact that witnesses to both fires mentioned seeing a man in a dark suit?"

"I'm not trying to be defensive here, but just so you know, we really worked the orphanage case. *I* worked that case. We tried to fingerprint those matchbooks. We interviewed all the neighbors within a mile of the site. Rhonda Bishop was the only witness that saw anything, and we weren't too sure about her. I personally went out to her house that night to verify what she said she saw. First of all, it was dark out and snowing, and her house is pretty far back from the street. I had one of my guys stand on the street while I looked out the very window she said she saw him from. I could barely see my guy. Then she said she'd looked through binoculars. It seemed pretty convenient that there would be binoculars right next to the sink, but

I looked through them. And yeah, I could see my guy better, but I'm not sure I would have been able to identify him beyond his basic build had I not known him. Do you know how many guys wearing dark suits there are in the world? Especially on New Year's Eve. For all we knew, if she did see someone, he could have been coming from a party."

"Were there any parties nearby?"

"Several. We checked those out too. What's the deal with this book anyway? Why the interest in two fires in Traverse City?"

"Do you mind if I borrow these files?" I replied.

"These are yours," he said. "I thought you might want them, so I made copies."

I stood, readied myself to leave, then remembered something.

"What did you mean when you said you weren't too sure about Rhonda Bishop?"

"After you do this for a while, you just get a sense of people. She hounded us for weeks, even called a reporter and had them print a story about us not listening to her. A couple of months later, she called to say she saw the same guy down at the marina, said he was getting into a boat. So, due diligence, we checked that out and came up empty. Another few months passed and she saw him again and so we checked that out. Same thing, empty. Then, an entire year later, she calls to say she saw the guy in some other town."

"So you're saying you didn't believe her about any of these sightings?"

"Lonely older woman. Husband traveled a lot. We thought maybe she was looking for attention. Anyway, I'll just let you decide for yourself."

After I left, I considered how Detective Logan had characterized Rhonda Bishop's interest in the case. "Hounded us" was how he put it. The comment seemed unfair. Her desire to get to the bottom of things might be considered tenacious, even admirable, could it not? Or perhaps my defensive posture toward Detective Logan's assessment of Rhonda Bishop had more to do with my own fixation. Here I was, ignoring the majority of my patients' needs, my son's needs, all to chase down the needs of one patient whom I could not even be 100 percent certain was telling me the truth.

I resolved to take Detective Logan's advice and decide for myself.

Scarlet

Not even five minutes after Blue left with Mr. Kline for Interlochen, I checked under the sink to make sure she had gotten the mason jars. Everything else was in the rucksack waiting. Then I washed up, dressed, and headed to Dr. Henry's office. On the way there I walked down to the beach. It was a lovely warm day. Not too hot. Fall was in the air. I stared at the lake, remembered that first time Blue and I were there. It was winter then, white, a different kind of beauty than it was now. Then, the waves were frozen. They were mammoth, majestic. I remembered feeling as if they were announcing their arrival, and ours. As if they knew this was the place where I would meet my destiny.

And at that moment, I felt a kind of release, a euphoria, and I raised my arms above my head, and twirled.

I focused on each step of my walk to town. I wanted to fully experience every single movement I made. And every gift from nature. A soft breeze fluttering strands of my hair. The sun warming my skin. Tomorrow night everything would feel different. Wouldn't it?

I paused when I got to the wood-and-glass door that led up to Henry's office. Paced back and forth. I hadn't meant to stay away so long, but time hadn't been making sense to me lately. I wasn't sure how he'd take to me showing up unannounced. But what choice did I have? I opened the door and climbed the stairs. He shared the second floor, also the top floor, with a dentist's office, which I'd always found kind of funny, one profession limiting talking ability while the other promoting it. I tried his office door, locked, then noticed a note attached to it. It read: *I will be out of the office until Thursday. If you have an emergency, please call Dr. Arlene Volker.* It gave Dr. Volker's phone number. I felt all calmness, all peace, draining from my body. In an instant replaced by anger. What was wrong with the universe? Why was Henry gone at the exact time I needed to tell him the truth? He could be so infuriating. Then I remembered he had recently invested in some new contraption he called an "answering machine." He'd gone into a long, technical explanation on how it worked, not unusual for Henry.

I went home, dialed the phone number for his office. A female voice said, "No one is here to take your call. Please leave your name and number."

I hung up.

I had no idea how leaving a message worked. Could Henry call in and hear his messages from a remote location, or did he need to listen to them in person? Regardless, I decided I had to try. I got out a pen and paper, wrote out what I planned to say. Crossed it out. Rewrote. Did that at least ten times. It was important I get the message right. Even the tone of my voice had to be perfect. A mix of scared and pathetic. Maybe my voice should sound shaky, as if I were about to cry? Yes, shaky.

I called Henry's number again. Waited for the female voice to stop talking, then read the message I'd settled on.

"Dr. Henry, this is Scarlet. Scarlet Lake. I know it has been a while, but I hope you will understand. There is something I have to tell you, something very important, and in all honesty, I haven't known how to. So, I've stayed away, out of fear, I suppose. Please call me when you get this. I need to see you as soon as possible. The information I want to share would best be delivered in person."

I hung up, poured myself a glass of wine, went to the window, and looked out at the street. It would be dark soon.

He'll get my message, I thought. *He'll come back from wherever he is. The universe will make sure he will.*

Blue

I have never been on what Mr. Kline calls a "road trip" before. I've only ever gone anywhere in buses. We are on a freeway that is lined with big trees. Mr. Kline keeps pointing out the pretty colors of the leaves. He's right, they are really pretty. From this distance, at this speed, they blend together, a journey through an Impressionist painting. I wish my mother could see the saturation of the colors, the oranges and reds, especially. I wonder if she has ever thought of grinding leaves into pigment. I wonder what she is doing right at this moment. I wonder if she's wondering what I am doing. The longest amount of time we have ever been apart is when I'm in school or with Hannah or Butch. We've never spent an entire night apart. But though I'm wondering about her, I don't really miss her, not yet. Mr. Kline is talking about the competition. He's been talking a lot. I don't feel like talking. I've never been too good at concentrating on two interesting things at once. It's the leaves that hold my attention right now, their particular story. The brightness of their colors makes them appear happy, and yet they turn these colors because they are dying, because soon they will fall to the ground, leaving all the trees sad and bare.

It's the cold that kills them. Just like the freeze stops the waves.

Why does Mother Nature make them the most beautiful right before they die?

"You're quiet," Mr. Kline says. "Are you nervous about the competition?"

"Yes," I say, though I don't want to think about that at this moment. Right this moment I'm curious about the cycle of death, or perhaps a positive person like Hannah would correct me and say the cycle of life, but I don't want to tell him that's what I'm really thinking about. I need to work it out for myself first, and besides, like I said, I've never been good at working through two things at once.

"That's normal," he says. "Some say being nervous helps sharpen concentration and enhance performance."

"That's good," I say.

"We're almost there," he says. "Are you hungry? We can order room service, since we won't have too much time before your practice appointment. How does that sound?"

"Fine," I say.

A man in a red uniform opens my door when we drive up to the hotel. He takes our bags, gives Mr. Kline a ticket, and directs us inside. The lobby is bigger than ten times the size of my mother's and my dilapidated house. Checking in is tedious. There are people everywhere; the lines are long.

"Is everybody here for the competition?" I ask Mr. Kline.

"Yes," he says. "It is the official hotel."

The nice lady at the counter gives us our keys. "Adjoining rooms, just as you requested," she says to Mr. Kline and smiles.

We walk to the elevator under the tallest ceilings I've ever seen. Huge chandeliers hang from them. The furniture is dark wood. The cushions of the sofas and chairs are pink and black stripes. White wainscot lines the bottom of light blue wallpaper with gold scrolls. The plush carpeting is burgundy with floral medallions.

Another man in a red uniform runs the elevator. He asks us which floor, pushes the button, and opens the door for us when we get there. We locate our rooms (our bags are already there), and within minutes food is delivered. White cloth napkins, silver domes over the plates, and my Coke is served in a glass with a stem. Mr. Klein joins me. And after we eat, a hamburger and French fries for me and a steak for him, he puts our trays outside the door, I brush my teeth for as long as time will allow, and we head to the auditorium.

Now I stand before the grand piano I will play. Each contestant is allowed one hour to visit the stage and practice their piece. I'm overwhelmed by the space: the high-raftered ceiling above me, the tall velvet curtains that separate backstage from main stage, the vast three-story auditorium with its balconies and private boxes like the one where my mother and I saw the *Nutcracker* ballet, and the rows and rows of red velvet seats. My eyes locate the one where my mother would have sat. I imagine her there watching me, smiling and proud. I softly rub the palm of my hand over the piano's shiny surface as if I'm petting a rabbit, but I don't touch the keys.

"Why don't you play?" Mr. Kline says. "Get a feel for it. All pianos are different."

"That's okay," I say. "I'd rather wait." I don't say I fear that playing today will jinx my performance tomorrow.

The rest of the day blends into the night, like the sun blends into the lake when it sets. I remember a stroll through campus, a visit to some shops, a fancy dinner, a very clear TV, trying to sleep but waking several times during the night, sweating, my stomach twisting.

Henry

Rhonda Bishop lived on a barely two-lane road that overlooked the Grand Traverse Bay. It was hard to tell how many houses had once separated her home from the orphanage because the land where the orphanage once stood now held one of those fancy waterfront developments. The Bishop house, white with green shutters, was a veritable mansion. Sixteen tall windows wide and three stories high. But it was not set that far back from the road, and there were no trees obstructing the view.

I parked in the driveway and looked at my watch. It was quarter to three. I had called Mrs. Bishop from a phone booth after leaving Detective Logan's office. Luckily, she had time to meet at three P.M. ("How about tea?" she'd asked), just thirty minutes from then. I planned to grab a quick lunch at the Burger Shack, which was connected to the local putt-putt golf course, but given the timing, I had two choices: get lunch and arrive late, or drive straight to Mrs. Bishop's house and arrive early. I was tired. I had met with three people in the span of a few hours. Rhonda Bishop would be four. I still had questions about Scarlet. For instance, when and how did she escape the man she said had taken her? When and how did she end up at the orphanage? Where did she go after the orphanage burned? It was just like what Zachary Ludwig had said: She was a ghost. I looked at my watch again. Twelve minutes to three. I decided to skim the files Logan had given me. The contents appeared to match the information Logan had shared, but I would look at them more closely when

I got back to the hotel. Seven minutes to. I thought about resting my eyes but worried I might fall asleep.

I got out of my car, crossed the front walk, and knocked on the door.

"You're early," Rhonda Bishop said. "I like a man who is early. So many of your species make a woman wait. Like my husband. He's infuriating. Come in. Here, let me take your jacket." She hung it in the coat closet. "Katrina," she called out. "Our guest is here. We're ready for tea whenever you are." Then, to me: "Let's head to the great room."

I followed her. She was in her early sixties. Tall, dark hair, thin. The word that came to mind was *handsome*. Perhaps because of the way she was dressed. Riding clothes and boots.

"I apologize for my casual attire," she said. "I was planning on going for a ride before you came, but one thing led to another, and now here you are."

The room was indeed great. The ceilings took advantage of the house's entire three-story height. Two deep and worn leather sofas faced each other, their ends perpendicular to a mammoth stone fireplace. A scarred, heavy-wood coffee table sporting a large grouping of lit candles sat between them. One wall of the room was entirely glass. It looked out to a deep backyard complete with stables and a fenced paddock for her horses, and beyond that a stunning view of the Grand Traverse Bay. Wouldn't that mean the orphanage had overlooked the water as well? I briefly wondered why someone who was leaving the scene of a crime would walk away on the street when a boat might be less conspicuous, but then saw that the house and yard were located on a cliff.

"Is there a path or stairway down to the water?" I asked.

"No," she said. "We're up pretty far here, and the terrain is steep and rocky. When we bought this house, it was listed as having a *water view*. Which pleased me at the time, but I do wish we would have found something with better beach access. We have to walk about a half mile to the stairs that lead down to the private beach area we share with other neighborhood residents. But here I am again, being ungrateful. We are lucky to have such an unobstructed view."

"What about the orphanage?" I asked. "Did it have lake access?"

"I don't really know about back then," she said. "The new houses do. The builders cleared a path through the woods and built a meandering staircase that follows the natural terrain. It's quite lovely. It's only for the residents, but I've been known to borrow it on occasion." Sly smile. "You said on the phone that you're writing a book about the orphanage fire? Like a true crime novel? I just love those."

"And another fire that happened ten years earlier," I said, dodging the question. "At a family home."

"I don't know anything about that," she said. "We didn't live here then. We moved to the area just one year before the orphanage burned down. Such a shocking and upsetting thing. I couldn't sleep for weeks thinking about it."

Katrina arrived with our tea and cookies, which contained the largest chunks of chocolate I'd ever seen.

"They're homemade," Mrs. Bishop said. "I thought you might be hungry."

"Thank you. I grabbed a quick bite on the way here, but didn't have dessert." I reached for one, took a bite. It was still warm from the oven. "Wow, really good." It felt good to say something honest.

"You want to know about the man, don't you?" she said. "The one I saw that night."

I nodded. I was still chewing.

"I saw him clear as day," she said. "It's like I told that detective. I'd gotten up to get a glass of water when I saw someone walking on our side of the road."

I swallowed the last bite of cookie. "What time was that?"

Mrs. Bishop held out the tray. "Please have another."

I took one.

"A few minutes after two in the morning," she said. "My husband and I had decided to stay in for New Year's. He's not much of a partygoer. We tried to stay up to watch the ball drop in Times Square but didn't make it past ten. I know what time it was because I purposefully looked at the clock. It just seemed so strange. No one ever walks by our house. There aren't even sidewalks. And the access to the main road is in the other direction."

"It does seem odd," I said. "Why do you suppose he did?"

"I've thought about that," she said. "And I've decided he must have come by boat and parked it in that neighborhood access area I mentioned. There are guest slips there. As I said, it's only a half mile. It wouldn't have taken him more than ten minutes to get back to his boat once he set the fire."

"Interesting theory," I said. "Do you think he might have been coming from a New Year's Eve party?"

"Well, if he did, it wasn't one close by. He was walking away from the orphanage, toward our house. Back then, there weren't any homes over there, just woods."

"Do you remember what he was wearing?"

"A black suit," she said. "Well tailored. Crisp white shirt and dark tie."

"You could see all that so clearly? Wasn't it dark and snowing?"

"Detective Logan asked that very same question," she said. "It wasn't snowing hard like a blizzard or anything, just soft snow. There's a streetlight by the mailbox banks and the light was reflecting off the white flakes. It was lovely that night. Like a winter wonderland. Later, after I found out what had happened, I was struck by how that beauty sharpened the brutality of what that monster did. Oh, but you asked about how I could see him so clearly, didn't you? My husband is a bird-watcher. He keeps binoculars by every window. That made the man I saw closer to me than you are now. I was right on top of him. But that Logan person had me doubting myself."

"When I talked to him earlier, he mentioned coming out here to talk to you that night," I said. "He said he looked through the binoculars and could only make out the outline of one of his guys."

"Unless he needed glasses, there's no way he couldn't see the officer he sent out there. I looked too and could see that officer clear as day."

"He said you saw the same man other times?"

"That's right. Once at the marina and another time at a restaurant downtown."

"Are you sure it was him?"

"It was definitely him. They said they looked into it, but I doubt they did."

"Why is that?"

"I could tell they were just humoring me. They thought I was crazy, or just looking for attention. That's what they always think about women, that we're emotional and unreliable. So I nearly didn't call when I saw him in Charlevoix, but then I figured they would surely believe me, since I had more detailed information, and I admit I wanted them to apologize for having treated me so badly, for not believing me in the first place."

"Did you say Charlevoix?"

"Yes. I'd heard it wasn't too far, and that it was a nice, quaint town, so I decided to drive over for the day, have lunch, do a little shopping. I visited a lot of the small towns alone back then, still do sometimes, because my husband travels a lot for work. I was sitting at an outdoor café when I saw him. It was like I was supposed to see him, if you know what I mean. Like kismet, or some sort of divine in-Logan's-face retribution. I believe in that stuff, you know. I took a class in chaos theory once. The science of surprises and the unpredictable. It sounds as if it would be the opposite of Jung's theory on synchronicity, but if you really study it, the two have more in common than one might think." She paused. "There I go. My husband says I think too much. Oh my, I totally forgot who I was talking to there for a moment. You said on the phone you are a psychoanalyst?"

"I am." I hoped my words sounded clipped. I was too tired for a long philosophical exchange.

"I do apologize," she said. "I'm sure you don't want to discuss the nuances of your profession with a total stranger."

"Why did you think it was the man you saw that night?" I asked, trying to get us back on track.

"The man from the fire? Because it was. He might have looked different, but it was definitely him. I've always been good with faces. And I got that same nervous, fearful feeling. Law enforcement types and shrinks always say you should trust those feelings. Don't get in a car with a stranger. Or if you think someone might be following you when you're alone on a sidewalk, hightail it to the nearest open establishment or group of people."

She was right about trusting your instincts. Many a crime had occurred because people did not trust their instincts. Humans would rather be polite than trust the warning signs their bodies were signaling. "Looked different how?"

"All three times when I saw him in Traverse City, he had dark hair. Very thick and curly. But this time it was gray and thinning. And he wasn't wearing a suit. He had on a flannel shirt, jeans, and loafers. Very casual."

Linda Howard said he had blond hair. "Are you sure his hair was dark when you saw him in Traverse City, not blond?"

"Definitely dark and curly. Nice, well-kempt curls."

"But in Charlevoix it was gray and thinning? Seems odd it would be so different."

"I thought the same thing. But believe me, it was him."

I was starting to understand Detective Logan's reservation.

"It does seem coincidental that you were passing through Charlevoix the same day he happened to be."

"He wasn't passing through," she said. "He lived there."

"Why do you say that?"

"Because someone called out to him. Right by my table. Another man. The man asked him whether their poker game was still on for that weekend. What he actually said was—I remember every word—'Wade, are we still on for poker this weekend? I heard the town is dedicating some park in Christine's name. I can't believe she's been gone—what has it been? Nine years? Ten?' And the man from the fire said, 'That's *next* weekend, so count me in.' And the other man said Elizabeth, his wife, I think, was out of town that weekend, so they could really whoop it up. Those were his exact words, 'whoop it up.' And then the man from the fire crossed the street and went into a dry-cleaning establishment, and he walked out a few minutes later with cellophane-wrapped black suits on hangers and three shirt boxes. The suits looked exactly like the one he was wearing those other times. Doesn't that all sound to you like someone who lived there? I must say I did wonder who this Christine was—bless her soul. I mean, it sounded like it might have been his wife."

I was having a very hard time digesting what I had just heard.

"Are you certain those were their names? Wade and Christine?"

"Dead certain," Mrs. Bishop said. "Some other detective took my call for Logan—he wouldn't even talk to me. I guess he decided it wasn't worth his time because he never called me back. Oh, and there's one more thing. He dropped his lighter on the street. Probably because he was balancing the hangers and boxes. And after the two of them left, Wade and the poker friend, I rushed across the street and picked it up. It was engraved with the initials *WC*."

"Did you say *WC*?"

"Yes, *WC*. I played that letter game with myself so I would re-member. You know, make the letters into words. *Wine Corkscrew* were my two words. It's good to choose words you use a lot. I'm for-ever losing my wine corkscrew, so I'm always asking myself or my husband, 'Where is that wine corkscrew?' If you haven't already, you should try the letter memory game sometime. It really works."

"Do you still have the lighter?" My heartbeat quickened.

"Well, that's just it. He must have realized he lost it, because just as I was looking at it, I heard someone asking for it. 'I think that's mine,' he said, startling me. Deep, menacing voice. I don't know, maybe I imagined that menacing part. But there I was standing right next to a murderer. Wouldn't you be frightened? Luckily, I'm quick on my feet. I said I was just on my way into the dry-cleaning place to turn it in to their lost-and-found, and I was so happy he came back for it."

I felt light-headed. What were the chances there was another Wade with a lighter bearing the initials *WC*?

"Are you okay?" Mrs. Bishop asked. "You're white as a sheet."

"I'm fine. It's just been a long day."

"Do you want me to show you the kitchen window I saw him from, and the binoculars?"

I followed her into the kitchen.

"I was standing right here, in front of the sink," she said. "And see? The binoculars? We kept them in that very spot back then. The lenses are quite strong. They cost a pretty penny, I'll tell you. I saw what I said I did. Here, look."

I looked through them. She was right. I could see the names on every mailbox in the banks across the road. Why had Detective Logan indicated otherwise? My psychoanalyst's brain kicked into gear. Did he have a bias against women like Rhonda Bishop? Wealthy. Assertive. Straightforward. Was he so irritated he had not wanted to give credence to anything she said?

"Do you believe me? That Logan person looked through the binoculars for maybe a second. He had the gall to ask me whether my vision was good. Twenty-twenty, I told him."

"You obviously had a close, unobstructed view," I said.

"I certainly did," she said. "And I was telling the truth about the man in Charlevoix being him. Like I said, I've always been good with faces."

There were times your heart wanted to lie but your brain wouldn't let you. I did not tell Mrs. Bishop that the initials *WC* stood for *Wade Connor*, my stepfather's name. That Christine was my mother's name. That the lighter was a gift from my mother. That my stepfather was vain, and when his hair started thinning he took to wearing toupees and wigs. Why had Detective Logan not gone to Charlevoix to check out what Mrs. Bishop had told him? They had his initials. They had a description. They had the location of the dry cleaner's Connor obviously frequented. But, even if they had narrowed the search to him, how do I know they would not have been taken in by my stepfather's charm, just as his attorney and my school provost had been. As my mother had been. Not just charm, intoxication. I always knew Wade

Connor was one of those men, the kind everyone wants to be around, who sucks you into their web, always seems to skirt societal rules. In the past I had considered him a sociopath, but now I understood he was something much worse. While the *DSM* classified both sociopaths and psychopaths as antisocial personality disorders, the two had distinguishing characteristics. Both were charming and narcissistic, but sociopaths were prone to emotional outbursts. They lacked self-control, and could form attachments. Psychopaths, on the other hand, were cold, unemotional, and extremely manipulative. This, along with their lack of empathy and remorse, allowed them to commit and get away with violent behavior. From both my own interactions with my stepfather, and what I now knew of his criminal history, it was safe to say he fell into the latter category. Although such a disorder was better diagnosed by an *unbiased* professional.

"I believe you," was all I said.

"Oh, thank god," she said, her voice full of emotion. "You have no idea what it's been like all these years, with no one believing me. Not even my own husband. I mean it would be one thing to be right about something minor, but the man set an orphanage on fire and killed seventeen little girls and three nuns!"

I have very little memory of what happened after that. One minute I was at her house, the next I was fumbling my keys outside my hotel room. My heart was pounding. My chest was tight. My throat was constricted. It felt like I was having a heart attack. I threw up as soon as I got to my room. I had never had a panic attack before, but I was pretty sure that was what was happening to me. *Slow, deep breaths*, I thought. I had instructed many of my clients to do this. I took more slow breaths than I could count. About an hour later, once I had calmed down, I chastised myself for blaming Logan for not doing his job. The truth was I had not done mine. I knew the asshole had killed my mother, so why did I think it would stop there? Or maybe the question was, why did I choose not to think? Maybe I could excuse my lack of bravery when I was kid, but I had been a grown man for decades now. The best indicator that a person would kill in the future was that the person had killed in the past. The blood of those seventeen children and three nuns, as well as Scarlet's parents and whomever else my stepfather had murdered, because there were surely more, that blood was on me.

A memory came to me unbidden. My mother had asked me to come home from boarding school. I was twelve. I had not been home since I left for Andrews. I found my mother's invitation odd because my stepfather had made it more than clear he did not want me there, and my mother, for whatever reason—fear of him? fear of being alone? misplaced love?—had chosen him over me. In that moment, I thought of another reason. Could it be that she was trying to protect me? Did she know what he was capable of? Did she fear he would kill her, and me? She was crying when I arrived. I asked her what was wrong. She pointed through the window of the sliding glass doors. My stepfather was pushing a little girl on a swing. She had long blond braids. For a split second the little girl turned her head my way, looked at me pleadingly. I remember feeling unsettled by the look.

"He says she's his niece," my mother said. "But I know he's lying."

"Why is she here?" I asked.

"Her parents died," my mother said. "Convenient, don't you think?"

"She's living here?"

"He's at her," my mother said. "And she's not the first."

"What do you mean?" I asked.

She motioned me away from the sliding glass doors and into the dining room, looked me in the eyes, hers wide with fear, and repeated those words. "He's at her. Do you understand? You need to make him stop."

I remember wanting to ask if she meant he had hit the little girl, like he had my mother, like he had me. I remember wanting to ask what she wanted me to do. Did she want me to call someone, our priest, the police? But there was no time. Her body stiffened as her eyes traveled over my shoulder, and I felt my stepfather's breath on my neck, and just as I had so many times before, I turned toward him and held out my arms, shielding her body from his. But also like before, though I imagined myself as forged steel, he threw me aside like tin, grabbed my mother's arm, and shook her, his face distorted with anger, his mouth spitting, "Stop what? Do you hear me? Stop what?" Her voice so small I could hardly hear it, she said, "Nothing." He pointed and said, "Go upstairs." Watched to make sure she obeyed, then turned to me. "Leave," he ordered. "This is between your mother and me. And don't ever show your pimply face in this house again."

And what did I do? I cowered, slunk away, hitched a ride to the bus station. I just left her there.

My mother died a few weeks later, and I never went home again. I would like to say it was merely grief and anger that kept me from returning to my childhood home and confronting Wade. But it was more than that. It was fear.

After Lily died, I went into therapy to deal with her loss. Through years of patience and care from my own analyst, to whom I will be forever grateful, I came to understand that the extreme guilt I felt about not being able to protect Lily was directly related to the guilt and shame I had been harboring for abandoning my mother when she needed me most. And the debilitating fear and helplessness I couldn't shake? Though Wade had nothing to do with Lily's death, he had everything to do with how I had reacted to my mother's. It is not uncommon for a child who experiences tragic loss to connect all future losses to the initial one. It was also not uncommon for a physically abused child to remain fearful of their abuser into adulthood. "The body remembers" is how my analyst had described it. And now it was Scarlet who was awakening those conflicting feelings of protectiveness and helplessness, and I was again traveling that rough and sometimes dark journey to the most hidden pockets of my psyche. But this time it was different. This time my unconscious had been sending me messages. Messages that to date I had ignored.

Like when I had that vision of Scarlet as a little girl with long blond braids in a swing. She and I had been meeting for a mere three months when I had it. It was the first session in which she had expressed either anger or sadness. She had lamented the fate of artists, especially women, who were misdiagnosed with madness in Carl Jung's time. She had confessed she felt trapped in a tower like Rapunzel in the fairy tale. I still remember her tears and that haunting *pleading* look in her eyes.

The same look I saw in my mother's eyes that day, now so long ago, when she told me, "He's at her." The same look as the pigtailed girl in my vision. I did not understand then what my mother meant by those words, but I did now. I actually understood much more. I understood why I had that vision. My unconscious had known all along that Scarlet and the little girl my mother pointed to were one and the same. Which meant my mother was not the only person who had needed my help that day. My fear had gotten in the way of saving them both.

My mother's words rang in my ears, those other words: "She's not the first." And then I allowed myself to see the entire truth, a truth I would have to live with for the rest of my life. I thought back to what Scarlet had told me about her mother's volunteer work, how she had counseled children who had been taken but were found, about one particular little girl who Scarlet sometimes played with when she went to the church with her mother, blond and blue-eyed like Scarlet, and at that moment it all became clear. Why Wade had been scoping out Scarlet's parents' house that day, why he approached Scarlet's mother on the beach. He had come to see how much she knew, if she suspected him. Perhaps he hadn't intended to kill Charles and Melody Boudreau. Perhaps he thought he could charm her like he did everyone else. But he saw that it would be only a matter of time before she put two and two together, before her husband, the district attorney, knew. He had to get them out of the way.

I knew my stepfather. I knew his psyche. While I did not have proof of this theory, I knew in my gut it was true.

It was too late to save my mother or Lily, but I could still help Scarlet. I believed that was what it had always been about: saving Scarlet. *That* was why she came into my life. It was my destiny and hers. Because my saving her would in turn save me.

Scarlet

I was painting, in the dark, like I often did. I preferred the silence and emptiness. I saw the bright lights first, reflecting off my canvas. I didn't understand they were headlights until I turned around, saw the car on the street. Just sitting there. My initial thought was that it was Henry. He'd gotten my message. And then I remembered he didn't know my home address. I should have included it in my message to him. I put down my brush, peered into the night. The car was stopped in the middle of the road, engine idling. Maybe it was just someone waiting on a neighbor? Or a pizza-delivery service?

I switched on the porch light.

Black sedan with tinted windows. It looked like a Cadillac. I ducked out of view.

What was HE doing here? I hadn't called him yet, *or had I?* Calling him was part of the plan. Telling him I wanted to talk, that I'd missed him. How else could I get him here? On my schedule? But if I had called him, I would have told him to come tomorrow, not tonight. Everything was planned for tomorrow night.

Maybe it wasn't HIM.

The car inched forward, took a right at the end of the street. *It could be anyone.* But out of caution, I checked the doors and windows, locked those that weren't, grabbed one of the dining room chairs, pulled it into the shadows by the front window, and waited.

About ten minutes later, the car drove by again, slowed to a stop directly in front of the house, again sat there.

My heart beat loudly. It had to be HIS Cadillac. How many Cadillacs with tinted windows could there be in South Haven?

I snuck to the phone, dialed Henry's number, got the same recorded greeting. "Henry, it's me again, Scarlet," I said. "It's urgent I contact you. HE is here. He's driving by my house. I'm sitting in the dark—" I got cut off.

Redialed. Waited. "Henry, please call as soon as you get this. The man we talked about, the one that's been following me, that wants to kill me, he's here. I think I called him. You were supposed to be here to help. Just call, okay? Or come by?" This time I left my address.

The car sped up, turned where it had before.

Less than ten minutes later, the black sedan drove by again, slowly, but didn't stop.

I rechecked all the doors and windows to ensure they were secure, then went into the bedroom, pulled the rucksack out from under the bed, unzipped it. Stopped. It was habit. What Blue and I always did when HE appeared. We packed, left town. Perhaps I would have done just that, chickened out, if Blue had been home, but she was up in Interlochen. The universe had handled that.

I wondered how much time I had before he knocked on the door. An hour? Twelve? Twenty-four? I'd never waited long enough to find out.

"Where are you?" I called to the voices. "Tell me what to do."

Nothing. No chanting. No singing. No sound from them whatsoever.

It had always been so easy, so satisfying, so power-inducing, to imagine doing it. But now, faced with the prospect of carrying through on my plan, I was terrified. Wouldn't it just be easier to remain a fugitive? To run to another town? The risk was too great. Not for me, for Blue. What if he killed me the minute he walked in the door? What if I killed him like I planned, but something went wrong and I got caught? Who would take care of Blue? What would she think of me? What would that knowledge, that her mother was a murderer, do to her? Why hadn't I thought about all this before now?

What kind of mother was I? I'd been so scared, so self-absorbed, so preoccupied with HIM, that I hadn't considered how it would affect Blue. And now it was too late. He was here.

I heard a scraping sound, froze for a moment, collected myself, searched the house, even checked my canvas, my brushes. It must have come from outside. Went to the window. The neighbor's dog scratching at their door. Their door opening, dog trotting inside.

"You were the ones that kept telling me to kill him," I said to the dark. "And now you're silent? Cowards."

I refilled my wineglass, returned to the bedroom, calmed myself. Told myself it would be okay. Everything was ready to go. I wouldn't get killed. I wouldn't get caught. When the sun came up, I would write Henry a long letter, tell him everything, apologize for my past behavior, walk to town, all the time looking over my shoulder, climb the stairs to his office, and slide the envelope under his door. Henry would get my phone messages. He would get the letter I slid under the door. The universe was looking out for me. But on the off chance I didn't hear from him, I would move on to Plan B.

I shoved the rucksack back under the bed, crouched in the corner, and waited.

Blue

The phone wakes me the next morning. "Breakfast?" Mr. Kline asks. "They have blueberry pancakes."

I go, but don't eat much. When I get back to my room, I take a long bath using the hotel's free soap and bubble bath, stay in the water so long it gets cold and my fingers and toes wrinkle. I drain it, refill it with fresh hot water and bubble bath, and again soak until the water gets cold. When I finally get out, I wrap myself in the biggest and fluffiest white towel I've ever seen. I dry my hair, stretch it back from my face, roll it into a bun the way Hannah taught me. "Concert pianists and ballerinas wear their hair in buns," she'd said. "It accentuates their long, thin necks." Because I was skeptical, she showed me pictures to prove she was right. I look at the clock, take a deep breath, slip the black dress over my head, carefully pull on the silk stockings so as not to snag them, step into the black patent leather kitten-heel pumps. Survey myself in the mirror. I don't know the girl who stares back at me. She's prettier, more poised than me.

Mr. Kline meets me in the hotel lobby. Tells me I look nice. We take a taxi to Interlochen, arrive backstage, and check in at the contestant table.

"Here you go," the woman at the table says after she finds my name. "Number eight. Sarah will escort you to the waiting room."

On the way there, Sarah tells me that she is my assigned guide. We arrive at a large room with chairs made of leather, a long table of snacks and beverages, and speakers in each corner so all the contestants can hear one another play. "I'll be back to get you when it's time," she says.

After Mr. Kline and I sit, I quietly ask him why I am number eight. I don't want any of the others to hear me. "Was I the eighth person picked?" Which I think must mean I'm eighth best.

"It's a lottery," he whispers. "The practice times were selected through a lottery as well. That way no one is granted preferential treatment over anyone else. Going last could be considered an advantage, because your performance will be freshest in the judges' minds."

A few of the other contestants come over and introduce themselves to me, but while I'm nice enough, I don't belabor the conversations. I can't understand how they're even able to talk. I see a serious-looking boy sitting across the way. Like me, he isn't eating snacks or making small talk. I sit back in my chair, will my nerves to settle down, play the imaginary piano that lives in my mind. When number seven is announced, Sarah comes into the room and asks Mr. Kline and me to follow her. She talks the whole way, says she's currently a student at Interlochen, tells me she was in this competition two years ago and I shouldn't be nervous, and when we get to the velvet curtains that lead to the main stage, she wishes me good luck. The boy before me is playing Beethoven's *Waldstein*. I recognize him as the serious boy. I try not to listen for fear I will get intimidated, but I find myself closing my eyes, allowing the music inside me. His interpretation is so pure, so true. No other contestant I heard play from the waiting room can compare. Confused emotions come over me, appreciation for the beauty of the music and his command of the piece, and sadness because I know with certainty I won't win. And I remind myself what Mr. Kline said about how just being selected is an honor. But what if it's even worse than not winning? What if my fingers get all mixed up? What if I freeze? The boy stops playing, stands, bows. Clapping and cheers. The audience has heard what I did, I think. He will definitely win.

"Blue Lake," a deep voice says.

For a moment, I don't understand why my name has been spoken. I've never heard it said through a microphone. I collect myself, walk slowly onto the stage, shoulders back, chin up, the way Mr. Kline taught me—"correct posture makes you look confident"—try not to click my shoes too loudly, arrive at the piano, bow to the audience, hold down the skirt of my dress as I slide onto the bench. I wait there for a moment, take a long, deep breath, sit tall, but I can't shake the nerves. I fear the *Andante*. What if I don't get it right? And so I stretch my hands over the keys, readying them to play my comfort piece, *Pictures at an Exhibition*, and then something odd occurs. Instead of the Mussorgsky, it's the *Andante* I hear. Resounding. Filling the entire space. My body, my hands, my fingers, moving on their own, as if they belong to the music, not me. As if they belong to Chopin, not me.

Henry

I woke, looked at the clock on the bedside table. It was almost noon. My mind and body were sore. It was as if I had been in a car accident, the kind that robs its occupants, that changes their lives forever.

I was at a crossroads. Did I tell Detective Logan what I had discovered? But would he believe me? He had not believed Rhonda Bishop. Maybe since I was a man, he would. Or did I take matters into my own hands?

My stomach growled. I packed, grabbed the files Logan had given me, went down to the front desk, checked out, and drove to the Big Boy off US 131 where I'd had breakfast with Zachary Ludwig the previous morning. Cindy saw me enter and immediately walked me to a table.

"How's the research coming?" she asked.

"Good." Depending on how you looked at it, that was or was not true.

"What can I get you?"

I ordered the scramble Zach had. While I ate, I read through the contents of the "unsolved" file. Everything Logan had told me appeared to be true, right down to the department's distrust of Rhonda Bishop. There were interviews with other neighbors and workers at the marina. No one recalled seeing a man in a suit. There was no amendment regarding Mrs. Bishop's alleged sighting of the man in Charlevoix. Obviously, Logan's team had not checked into it. But with that exception, it appeared the department had been thorough.

I paid the bill, left the restaurant, put the files on the passenger seat, and started the engine. For a moment, I thought of flipping a coin. Heads: Detective Logan. Tails: Charlevoix. I put the car in gear and headed north.

Charlevoix was roughly an hour from Traverse City. It was a small, quaint tourist town located on the shores of Lake Michigan, Lake Charlevoix, and Round Lake. My mother's house was located on Lake Charlevoix. I had spent the first eleven years of my life swimming and canoeing and water-skiing that lake. It was an ideal childhood. Ideal until my father died and Wade moved in.

Our driveway was long and tree-lined. I heard the familiar sound of crackling leaves beneath my tires. I used to hate chores of any kind. The downside of a beautiful tree canopy was never-ending raking. The house looked exactly the way I remembered, pale blue with black shutters, though it appeared freshly painted. Likewise, the wooden porch that wrapped around it and led down to the water looked newly sanded and sealed. Which was all fine, but what wasn't, what was utterly distasteful, was the monstrosity of a three-car garage that partially blocked the view of the lake. A snazzy paved driveway completed the repugnant display. I backed up, parked in one of the dirt spots in a cluster of trees where my father always had, and turned off the engine. From this vantage point, I couldn't see the house, which meant no one inside it could see me.

My father had kept the guns in a cabin in the woods. He built it especially for that purpose because my mother wouldn't allow them anywhere near the house. I was certain Wade did not know it existed, and it was unlikely he had ever happened upon in it since he was not an outdoorsman. Nor did he like to get dirty. I followed the path along the lake for about a mile until I came to a thicket in the woods that obscured the cabin. I tried the door. Locked. I went around back and slithered through the crawl space and a door in the cabin floor, a practice I had engaged in often when I was young, though I was a bit more agile back then. I spent many a time smoking cigarettes, drinking alcohol, or simply hiding in the cabin after my father died. The furnishings were still sparse, a wrought iron double bed with a bare mattress that smelled like mildew and a couple of old pine chairs. The safes were under the bed, the only reason the bed was there. I pulled them out so I could access the loose floorboard that hid the keys, which were right where I had left them years earlier. I tried one of the rifles—it needed a good cleaning, but worked okay. I grabbed a box of bullets, loaded the gun, put the rest in my pocket, replaced the safes, slithered back through the crawl space, brushed the dirt and leaves off my clothes, and headed back to the house. I had no idea what I was going to do when Wade answered the door.

I stood tall, crossed the walk, pushed the doorbell.

Waited.

No answer.

Tried the bell again. Knocked.

Still no answer.

I walked around the house, peered through windows. Wade had had the place redecorated. White leather and chrome furnishings replaced rustic brown leather and wood. Ridiculously huge and ugly abstract paintings hung in place of Audubon birds and hunting dogs. He had even switched out the stone fireplace for a polished marble-and-glass one. The only parts of the décor left untouched were the bookcases either side of the fireplace. I noticed he still had his three prized sets of *Britannica* encyclopedias. "Don't touch these," he always said to me. "They're early editions. Very valuable." He sold *Britannica* encyclopedias for a living, was a top seller in the company, received awards at fancy ceremonies down in Chicago, where the headquarters was located. Collectible sets like these were only gifted to those who reached major sales goals. When he was on the road, he always wore a black suit, white shirt, and tie. The place was sterile. The countertops bare of household essentials. No crumpled blankets on the furnishings. No lived-in clutter. I was not a violent man by nature, but I had to admit the idea of his blood spewed all over these prissy furnishings gave me great pleasure. I tried the back door.

Locked. Checked the obvious places where a just-in-case key might be (before Wade, we'd rarely locked our doors). No luck. Considered breaking a window. Maybe the asshole had seen me drive up and was hiding in a closet.

Should I wait?

I walked down to the lake, put the rifle down on the dock, sat on its edge, took off my shoes, put my feet in the water. It was cool out, but the sun was warm and bright. The chirping of birds and soft splash of the water hitting the shallow shore was comforting. I was not certain how long I sat there. It was as if I had dissolved into the wood. I was both asleep and awake. Periodically I searched over my shoulder for life, but no one came. When the sun started to set, I put my shoes on, walked back toward the house, and took one last look through the windows. No lights. No life. I headed back to my car.

I told myself that it was probably for the best he was not home. Better to think it through before doing something rash. I had Butch to think about. I had to figure out how to tell Scarlet. Butch would know where she lived. I would apologize. Tell her I had been "obtuse" (her word), that her criticism was apt, and I now knew why she had chosen me. She had given me clues. Said and did things that would make perfect sense to someone paying attention, someone not caught up in their own internal drama.

I checked the time. Too late to head back to Traverse City. Detective Logan would probably be gone by the time I got there, and in any case, I wanted to get home. I would give him a call when I got back to South Haven, tell him everything. It was up to him what he decided to do with it.

I put the rifle in the trunk, got back in the car, turned on the engine, backed out of the dirt parking space, and headed down the long tree-lined drive.

FEBRUARY 12, 2014

Chicago, Illinois

46 Years After the Murder

The Pianist

In my memory, South Haven is a symphony of seasons.

A single harp makes up the winter section. It plays gently, softly, *piano* and *pianissimo*, capturing the quiet of snowflakes. The stillness of ice. The thinness of cold. Opposite it, in the summer section, trumpets and trombones and tubas blast, *forte* and *fortissimo*, glorifying the laughter of children. The squawk of seagulls. The fullness of heat. String instruments, violins and cellos, make up the spring section. A waltz is their composition of choice. The dance of flowers. Scurry of squirrels. Pitter-patter of rain. And then there's autumn. A season I *should* prefer not to remember, but still I do, for it is the sound of my piano I hear. Forever playing the *Andante*, the piece I played in the competition, the piece that changed my life. Unlike those frozen waves, my memories of winter and spring and summer and even fall refuse to melt.

I wish I could say the same about my mother.

For in my memory, she is merely an outline of her former self. A ghost that visits my dreams. An apparition in my mirror. Blond hair, blue eyes, full lips. Like a Cheshire cat, she slowly disappears, leaving only my hair, eyes, and lips behind. Sometimes, after her image has faded, I sit at my vanity for hours, doing what I did that time with Van Gogh and have done with every composer since Mussorgsky. I imagine her entering me, her face becoming mine.

Scarlet in Blue.

No one tells you that no matter how hard you try, you will forget details of those whom you've loved and lost. Or maybe they do, but you don't hear it. Because while someone is alive you can't imagine them gone. Fleeing this earth. Fading like fugitive pigment. Even after all these years, I imagine I catch a glimpse of her sometimes. In a faraway crowd. On my daily walks. Passing by a fruit stand or flower cart. She is older, but still so beautiful. She smiles, twirls, her arms arched above her head like a sugarplum fairy. Of course it isn't her, but I like pretending it is. I like pretending that my heart is a brush that will continually paint her.

And no one tells you that bad memories and anger fade as well. My mother was far from perfect. She could be selfish, self-centered, controlling. She painted more than she mothered. Moved us from town to town. In that final year, she became erratic and unstable. And she did the unthinkable. She lured a man into the dilapidated house, put a sedative in his wineglass, waited for him to pass out, and slit his throat.

Here's the question.

If it isn't the anger I want to forget—if it isn't my mother's image, or her voice, or her laugh, or her dancing, or her crazies, or even the murder—what is it? It is the very thing I would give anything to have again, the thing I didn't cherish when I had it:

Her love.

Because the memory of that is unbearable.

THE MURDER

South Haven, Michigan

MURDER: The unlawful and malicious killing of one human being by another.

Blue

It's dark. Raining. The windshield wipers swish. Back and forth. Back and forth. Hypnotize. I am both here and not here. I both feel and don't feel. It is not a sensation I have experienced before. Happy is how I would characterize the way I felt after the junior state fair competition, but *this* is entirely different. After the state fair competition, my mother suggested we celebrate with a corn dog and curly fries and cotton candy, all of which I ate completely. Now I'm restless. My chest is tight. Appetite gone. Mr. Kline is talking, but I have no idea what he's saying. All I hear is nonsense and gibberish. It's like he's that smoking caterpillar Alice encounters in Wonderland.

Then, clearly, distinctly, resoundingly, as if spoken by a higher power, I hear these words: "You were frozen."

I look at Mr. Kline to see if the words came from him. He is concentrating on the road. "Did you just say something?" I ask.

"I said you were frozen. They called your name twice. I had to push you toward the stage. You got a standing ovation."

And my mind goes to those frozen waves my mother and I saw when we first moved to South Haven, and to the image of her I saw inside them, which I knew I'd only imagined. But still, why did I imagine it? My mother inside the ice wearing her white nightgown trying to scratch her way out, her fingers bleeding, her mouth open in a scream of terror. And I wonder why Mr. Kline chose that particular word. *Frozen*. Not *paralyzed* or *in shock* or *startled*. And for a moment, a darkness washes over me, and a fear I don't understand.

"Why do I feel scared?" I ask him.

"You won a major competition," he says. "Your life is about to change, and you can't imagine how. Nor can you control it. There will be a lot of press. The finest music schools in the country will court you. Matriculation to some—Juilliard, for instance—begins at age sixteen, the age you will be next month. Everything will happen quickly."

I think about this explanation, and yes, I am nervous about what the future has in store and worried about what that will mean for my friendships with him and Hannah and Butch, but I'm not scared about any of this. Not even about how my mother will react. Deep down I know, despite everything, she will be proud of me, and the two of us will figure it out.

It's late when we pull up to the curb in front of the dilapidated house. He leaves the engine running. "Your porch light is off. It doesn't look like your mother is home. Do you want me to stay with you until she returns?"

"The porch light doesn't work," I say. I look at the house, see a very faint but focused glow through one of the windows. The small lamp that clips onto her canvas. "She's home. She likes to paint in the dark. She didn't expect me home until tomorrow, or she'd have more lights on." I hadn't wanted to stay another night. I wanted to get home. To be with her. To share this amazing experience, this victory, with her. No one else.

"You made me proud tonight," he says.

The tears surprise me. First they fill my eyes; then they overflow. I reach over and hug Mr. Kline, and he hugs me back, and we hold on to each other as if we fear letting go, and after what seems an eternity, we stop. Mr. Kline gives me a handkerchief. I wipe my eyes.

"You'll be just fine," he says. "Have some warm milk. It will help you sleep. We'll talk tomorrow, okay? We'll make a plan together."

"I should come to practice?"

"Right now, you need to keep to your routine. It will help you get used to this new you."

I wave at him as he drives away. I can't see whether he waves back. I walk up the sidewalk, nearly trip on the uneven wooden stairs, and open the door.

A new painting of *Madame Léon Clapisson* glows inside the circular halo of the clip-on light. A figure stands just outside this bubble, assessing. It isn't until my eyes adjust that I see my mother is naked except for her apron. I am confused. I know something is wrong with the scene before me, but my mind isn't registering. It's not that my mother is naked. I've seen her that way before. It is something to do with the painting. Then I realize what it is. The red paint. It's saturated. Brilliant. And for a moment, I am happy. Happy she has chosen to live in the present. To explore the limitless color palette of Winsor & Newton.

"Did you use a tube of oil paint?" I ask. "One of the reds?"

She turns to face me. "Of course not, silly."

I see the red on the white apron first. Then on her body. Red in her hair. Red on her lips and face and arms and legs and feet. I see the red footprints. Follow them from the living room to the hallway and into the bathroom.

I remember wishing the scene before me were part of a movie reel I could stop and rewind. Rewind all the way back through the hallway, and the living room, out the front door, back into Mr. Kline's car. Then I would restart the reel again, but this time the porch light would work and the interior lights would be on and the dilapidated house would glow like that Edward Hopper painting *Nighthawks*, and when I skipped up the sidewalk and climbed the crooked wooden steps, I wouldn't trip. I would sail through the front door and my mother would be dressed and she would turn and smile broadly and ask me if I won and I would say yes and she would say she knew I would and we would select music schools together and she would plan to move to wherever I went so we could be near each other, and then she would ask me what I thought of her painting and I would see that same old portrait with the same old dull maroon paint, and content with the mundanity before me, content because I wouldn't know any different, I would go about my nightly routine. I would turn on the staticky TV, mute the volume, play the *Andante* again on my imaginary piano, periodically watch my mother play her brush across the canvas, feel those goose bumps I so often do, and then something glorious would happen. On hearing the beauty of my music, my mother would stop painting and listen, and her face would beam with pride and she would tell me how much she loves me, and afterward we would talk all through the night and somewhere along the way I would lay my head on her lap and sleep.

But you can't rewind life.

Now I stand in the bathroom looking down at a dead man. I can't look away. It is as if my eyes are glued to the grotesque scene. Like my mother, he is naked. His throat is slit from ear to ear, the knife still stuck in his neck. He is awkwardly splayed, the back of his head wedged against the porcelain, one leg and arm hanging over the tub's edge, blood pooled beneath him, his skin scored like those canvas strips that hung from the ceiling, a soup ladle and pots (*blood catchers*) at his fingertips, the drip-drip sound of it all, like a faucet that needs a new washer, the uncaught blood wandering through the tile cracks. And under the sink, in a neat row, their blue glass turned purplish from the red liquid inside them, are the mason jars my mother asked me to get at the grocery store. Nausea overwhelms me. I can feel the vomit rising in my throat, turn away, slip on the bloody floor as I try to exit the bathroom but barely make it to the sink.

"Jeremy helped me." She stands in the hallway. "He went to get the van. So we can get rid of the body. Do you think the blood will keep in the freezer? Isn't it lucky that human blood is so saturated? I thought it might be. Well, I did cheat a little. I added carminic acid. Did you see my canvas? The reds? Aren't they glorious? Artists every-where will be envious, will want to know my secret. But we won't tell, will we? My paintings will be so sought after. And the critics, even that asshole Morris Abernathy, will hail me as the greatest painter of all time. Greater even than Renoir."

It takes me a few seconds to register what she is saying. I move past her. Return to the canvas. And then the full horror of the situation hits me. The red on her palette, the red on her brush, the red on her canvas, none of it is paint. It is the dead man's blood.

Somehow I make it to the phone.

Henry

Butch was waiting by the door when I got home. His face was white.

"What's wrong?" I asked.

"Blue called," he said. "Something happened at her house. Some sort of emergency. She sounded really scared."

"When was this?" I asked.

"Just now," he said. "I told her you'd be home any minute, that you'd called from the truck stop in Grand Rapids about an hour ago."

"She didn't say what kind of emergency?"

"No, only that it had to do with her mother and it was urgent, and you should come as soon as you got home. I asked if I should come, and she said no, only you. Here's the address."

I knocked, but no one answered. Tried the door. Open. The room was dark except for the halo that shone on her canvas. I closed it behind me and switched on the overhead. Scarlet sat on the sofa, naked beneath her painter's apron. As if she were a child playing dress-up, bright red lipstick smudged her mouth and chin. The red on the rest of her body was not paint.

"Scarlet, are you okay? Did you hurt yourself? Let's get you to the hospital."

"I tried to call you," she said. "To tell you. I went by your office, but you weren't there. I left you a note. And a message on your machine. Please don't be mad. You wanted him dead too, didn't you?

What was I supposed to do? He showed up like he always does. It's self-defense, right?"

"What are you talking about?" I asked. "What do you mean, self-defense?"

"I'm so glad you're here. You can help Jeremy put him in the van."

Jeremy? The invisible studio mate?

"No one will know. I bought some bleach to clean the body, and the floors and tub. I told Jeremy we should cut it into pieces, take them out to the lake in one of those canoes that are always parked near the pier. I have trash bags, those heavy-duty ones, and a saw. Jeremy doesn't want to do that. He wants to bury it in the woods. What do you think? Or maybe you have a boat? A boat with a motor? HE had a boat with a motor. A yellow one. Wouldn't that be perfect?"

"Scarlet, who do you mean? Whose body?"

I looked around, saw the red footprints, followed them to the bathtub and the man inside it. There was no doubt he was dead. Even with all the blood, there was no doubt it was my stepfather. So many thoughts swam through my mind, the least of which was the timing. While I was in Charlevoix looking to blow the bastard's brains out, Scarlet was here in South Haven slitting his throat. It easily could have been me who killed him. A strange feeling came to me, a kind of déjà vu. It was as if this moment had been foretold, as if our three disparate souls, my stepfather's (pure evil) and Scarlet's and mine (spoils of that evil), were meant to converge in this house on this night.

I went back to the living room, asked Scarlet, "Where's Blue?"

"In the bedroom," she said.

Blue was curled in a ball in the far corner of the bottom bunk. I called to her, but she didn't respond. I turned her toward me, held up her chin. Her eyes were vacant, her breathing labored. When I tried to pick her up, her arms and head fell to the side, as limp as a rag doll. She needed immediate attention. It happened in an instant. I didn't think. I went to the phone, called for an ambulance.

It wasn't until later that I realized what I had done. In my rush to save Blue, I had betrayed Scarlet.

Blue

THREE MONTHS LATER

I remember very little about that night. "Selective amnesia," Dr. Henry calls it. "The mind shuts down so it doesn't have to face a traumatic event."

I remember being in a *normal* hospital for a week, then a clinic for kids with issues for another five. Days running into one another. Sometime in there turning sixteen. Dr. Henry telling me to think of my stay as downtime. Knowing he is worried about me because I am acting *abnormal*. Detached, apathetic, incurious. Him visiting me daily. Encouraging me to talk about my feelings. About what happened. About what she did.

I remember the hurt and anger and confusion building like a volcano. Then, one day, the words erupting. "My mother was selfish and stupid. She didn't think about what would happen to her. What would happen to me. I am no better. I saw her changing, getting more and more crazy, and I didn't do anything about it. I thought if I told someone, those men in white coats would come and take her away. I've seen them in movies. How their vans drive up to someone's house. How they put people in straitjackets. But the kids of those people usually have another parent, don't they? Or grandparents or aunts and uncles or older siblings? But I don't have any of those people. So where would I go? She was the only person in my life. She figured it just being her and me was okay, but it wasn't, was it? Our lives have always been precarious. If one thing wobbled, everything would fall. Like dominoes." I remember pausing, taking a deep breath. Saying, "Sorry, I didn't realize how mad I was." Him saying, "You need to get it all out, to face your feelings so you can heal."

I remember him telling me about the Shadow Man, who he was, his real name, his other crimes, that my mother wasn't the only little girl he hurt. I remember him asking me if I believed the Shadow Man had been chasing my mother and me all those years, or whether she had imagined him. Me saying I wasn't sure. But inside wanting to believe her, believe he was chasing us, believe we *had* to move all those times, because the alternative was too much to bear.

I remember him telling me about schizophrenia, about my potential risks.

I remember him telling me about the trial, how my mother never showed emotion or spoke a word, not to defend herself, not when the judge read the verdict, guilty by reason of insanity, not even when he committed her to live out her life in a mental hospital. Her only request was that she be sent to the one in Traverse City because it had once been her home.

I remember him telling me about Zachary Ludwig, the man he thought was my father, how he and my mother met and why they parted, giving me his phone number. Saying, "He cared about your mother. She never told him about you. If she had, I believe he would have wanted to be part of your life." Me wondering why I would call him. What good it would do.

I remember him telling me my mother's father, my grandfather, played the piano, that my mother's nanny said he was gifted, that he thought I'd want to know that, that my talent may have come from him.

I remember him mumbling apologies for his failure to protect my mother, for not being there when she needed him, sometimes watching him pace, one time listening to him cry.

I remember telling him I wasn't sure I wanted to visit her at the asylum. That I hated what she did. Hated what I saw. That I wanted the old her back. The her before the crazies. That I would give anything, even give up playing the piano, to get on a bus with the old her right now.

I would give anything to run.

I remember the one subject Dr. Henry didn't talk about: Butch.

I remember not reading even though there is reading hour. Not playing the piano even though there is music hour. Not painting even though there is painting hour. Instead spending a lot of time in my head, always the place I've felt most at home. Writing invisible stories. Playing my invisible piano. Painting with invisible brushes on invisible canvases.

I remember Mr. Kline coming to visit me. Telling me when I leave the clinic I'll be staying with him, that I'll have my own bedroom. That he's in the process of adopting me. That since I am now sixteen, I can begin my music studies winter semester. Me saying I don't want to play the piano anymore. Him saying as soon as my fingers touch the keys again, I will change my mind. About this, he is right.

I remember sitting in South Haven Drug waiting on Butch and Hannah. Everyone staring at me. Whispering about me, unaware that pianists have exceptional hearing.

One asking, "Is that her daughter?" *Truth.*

One saying, "Poor thing." *Half-truth.*

One saying, "Her mother is a whore." *Half-lie.*

One saying, "I hear she's in a mental hospital upstate." *Total truth.*

One saying, "I heard she cut him into pieces with a steak knife." *Lie.*

One saying, "I heard she was naked when she did it." *Half-truth.*

I remember it made the TV news. The front page of the *Chicago Tribune* saying, "Murder in a Sleepy Southwest Michigan Town." The *Herald-Palladium* saying, "South Haven Slaughter." The *South Haven Tribune* saying, "Bloody Massacre in North Beach."

I remember feeling grateful when Butch finally arrived. Him staring down the nosy necks, the whispering stopping. Kissing my cheek. Asking if I'm okay. Apologizing for taking so long to come and see me. Saying, "My dad told me I should wait until you got a little better." Me saying, "I understand" and "Where's Hannah?" Him saying she couldn't make it. That she needs time. Me feeling a profound sadness, even though I have yet to know I will never see or hear from her again.

Time, I remember thinking. In music, a grouping of rhythmic beats that contribute to measures of equal length. Recurring over and over, until the piece's creator alters its intent. In life, a grouping of seconds that contribute to minutes and hours. Recurring over and over until it passes us by. Unless *we* alter its intent. Unless *we* try with all our might to keep those we love. Like Hannah. Like Butch. Like Mr. Kline. Like my mother.

I remember Butch talking for a while more about fishing and school, and other things of little interest to me at this moment. Because my mind is full with getting through life, of taking what Dr. Henry calls those "baby steps that one day will turn into giant strides." And, rather than trying to explain my complacency, pretending to listen intently, smiling blankly when I'm supposed to, standing when he does, hugging him back, and watching him walk out of my life.

I remember thinking that pretending and lying are what I will do until I no longer need to.

I remember Mr. Kline driving me to Juilliard, me looking in the rearview mirror at the cars behind us, thinking that though what happened that night will linger for many, on tongues, in print, as legend, I am choosing to leave it behind.

And I remember believing that one day what happened that year will become a story I tell myself, a story that happened a long time ago, whose details will scatter through the language of summary or past tense.

FEBRUARY 12, 2014

Chicago, Illinois

46 Years After the Murder

The Pianist

For a long while, the events of that night haunt me. I have vivid nightmares. I see the Shadow Man's grotesque, blood-soaked body, those purplish mason jars all in a row, the painting of *Madame* on my mother's easel. I wake soaking wet, my heart beating rapidly, feeling as if it will jump from my chest. Wondering if I am destined to be like her one day. A crazy woman. A murderer. Remembering what Dr. Henry said about the symptoms of schizophrenia. "Rarely do they occur past the age of forty-five."

Rarely.

And so that winter of 1969, when I get to Juilliard, still hearing the echo of that word, I bury myself in my music. Over time, I make new friends—other musicians and dancers and actors—and, for a time, I am able to paint over South Haven and the events of that night, but then, one day, in 1971, the paint beneath me shows through.

Pentimento.

It is just prior to my third year when Butch calls. I hadn't heard from him since that last encounter at South Haven Drug, and after enduring many sleepless nights wondering why and shedding many tears, I resolved not to respond if I ever did. But my heart betrays me when I hear his voice. He is set to leave for college at Michigan within the week, and asks if he can come to New York to see me. He says he feels "bad about the way things ended" and wants to make sure I am okay. He apologizes, says he's been a jerk, asks for my forgiveness, but offers no excuse. And like a nice, sweet girl, a girl who still loves him, I tell him he has nothing to apologize for.

I meet him at the train station. Even through the dense crowd I recognize his gait. He hasn't changed. Same warm, friendly smile. Same dimples. Same dreamy brown eyes. I remember always feeling lucky that a boy like him would be interested in me, hoping perhaps he still might be, but not holding on to that hope too tight. And just like that first time at South Haven Drug, I float toward him.

"How are you?" he asks and hugs me, causing those old butterflies to flutter again.

"Good," I say. "You?"

"Great."

Pleasantries, I remember thinking. Cover for awkwardness.

We have dinner, talk about "old times," his upcoming studies and mine. We don't talk about why "things ended." I think I, at least, am so caught up in the fairy tale of the moment I don't want to break its spell. He stays the night with me in my small apartment, and for the first time, we make love. It remains the loveliest sexual experience I've ever had. The following evening, as he is climbing the steps to board the train, he turns, says, "We could do this, you know."

"Do what?" I ask.

"Us," he says. "People do. We could see each other once a month, trade off weekends. I come here, then you come to Ann Arbor. And when we graduate, you could move back to Michigan and teach music like Mr. Kline."

"Okay," I say, while thinking maybe, like Hannah, he just needed time.

He smiles, wide. The train starts moving; the lights inside glow. I can see Butch moving down the aisle, finding a window seat, opening the pane. "I love you," he yells, and blows me a kiss. The train speeds up. And even though I've never been one to show emotion physically, I skip, all but prance, all the way home.

He calls every week at first. I play the girl's phone-waiting game like we used to in those days. We stay on the phone for hours, talk about everything from our classes to what we will do together when we next see each other. But that monthly visit schedule never does materialize, and over time his calls, which are usually accompanied by an apology and a reference to his busy schedule, come less and less. And one day, a love I once felt I couldn't live without turns into a bittersweet memory.

After I graduate, my career soars. I travel throughout the world, live in places like Paris and Milan and London. I can't sit still. I crave the impermanence. I become recognized as one of the greatest pianists of my time, play and record with some of the best orchestras in the world, including the New York Philharmonic, London Symphony Orchestra, and Vienna Philharmonic. In 1984, when I am thirty-one, the same age my mother was that year in South Haven, I receive an invitation to judge the competition I won at Interlochen, which isn't far from the Traverse City State Hospital. Sixteen years have passed. I have never visited my mother.

A nurse escorts me to her room. "She's having a good day," he says. "She talks about her daughter being the great Blue Lake all the time. She'll be happy to see you." He closes the door when he leaves.

My mother is standing by the window, her back to me, as it so often was, the light shining through her. She looks ethereal. I remember thinking she will always be beautiful. Some people are just made that way. It's one of those tricks of biology.

She turns, smiles. "Beauty is as beauty does." She could always read my mind.

"How are you?" I ask.

She cups her arms above her head and twirls like a sugarplum fairy. "I'm fantastic. Really I am. I always knew you would be famous. They let me listen to your recordings. Pure magic. They say great talent skips a generation. My father used to play, you know."

I don't tell her that Dr. Henry had told me that when I was in the clinic, after the murder. I don't tell her how I've wished I could have known him, wished he and I could have played together.

She walks over to the wall opposite her dorm-size bed. There, in a kind of wallpaper display, is a tribute to me, announcements for upcoming concerts, reviews, pictures of me playing, bowing, smiling. She points to several, talks at length about the emotions each touched in her. My throat tightens as tears come to my eyes. Love, I've come to understand, is a painful emotion.

"Are you painting?" I ask, my voice trembling, but she doesn't appear to notice.

"They only give the murderers one recreation hour a day, but I've managed to complete quite a few. Jeremy still comes and picks them up. He had an exhibit of my work recently. Did you hear about it?"

Still Jeremy. "No."

"Guess what the theme was."

"Yellow boats?"

"No, silly," she says. "Fugitive pigment. He said they sold out. He's stashed the proceeds in an account he opened for me, so I'll have money for my new life in New York." She pauses, smiles devilishly. "Did I mention he's going to break me out of here? 'Like an Old West cowboy,' he says."

I ignore the statement. "Are you still painting Renoirs?"

"Yes, of course," she says. "And I will for as long as there are buyers." *What buyers?* I wonder. "Henry still comes to see me, you know. Every single week. He's my assigned analyst. Does my reports and the like. He's the same. Still wears those ridiculous bottle-thick glasses."

I know this too, of course. While Dr. Henry and I have only talked a few times since my time in the clinic, I get regular reports about my mother's progress that are signed by him. They are never accompanied by even a brief note. Forever the professional.

I hear the key turn in the door lock. The nurse comes in. "Mary Ann," he says. "It's time for your nap." Though I know Mary Ann Boudreau is her real name—she was tried for murder as Mary Ann Boudreau, and referred to as such by the media—it still stops me when I hear it. All these years later, and to me she is still Scarlet. Tragedy freezes time and its details in our minds.

"Fuck naps," my mother says.

"Maybe your daughter will come back tomorrow?" the nurse says. "Would you like that?"

"Lucas treats me like a three-year-old, don't you?" my mother says to him. Then, to me: "Bunch of fucking idiots in this place."

I go to my mother, hug her, tell her I'll see her again before I leave town, begin to back away.

"Wait," she says. "It's Grace."

"What's grace?"

"Your given name. It is what I felt when you were born, such grace."

Grace. And I remember her calling me her "sweet Grace" years ago, the day she suggested the lasagna dinner with Hannah and Butch. And while I do find it lovely, it is not who I am. I will always be Blue. For Blue was my name when I won my first piano competition, which got me to Juilliard, which initiated my career. And though it was my name through the bad of that year in South Haven, it was also my name through so much good, when I made my first real friend, when the fairy dust of first love sprinkled, when I learned to play the piano, when I mastered the art of fishing.

"But Blue suits you," she says, again reading my mind. "It has always suited you. I love you, baby girl."

Again I feel the tears. Again I feel love's pain.

That is the last time I see my mother. Two weeks later, Dr. Henry calls to tell me she has gone missing.

"I fear I have bad news," he says.

My chest tightens.

"They suspect she escaped through the maze of tunnels underneath the hospital," he continues. "One of the access doors, the one closest to the lake, was found open."

"When?"

"Two days ago, I'm afraid. I would have called earlier, but I just found out myself. The local authorities are searching for her, but I'm sorry to say it began snowing this morning. They're expecting a blizzard. They will continue looking, of course, but I want you to prepare yourself for the worst. The conditions aren't such that support survival."

When I hang up the phone, all I can think about is my decision not to go back and see her again at the hospital.

The next day, the lake freezes, and weirdly, just like in 1968, giant crystalized waves line Lake Michigan.

After the spring thaw, the body of a naked woman is found on the shore thirty miles or so from the asylum. Though it has decomposed beyond recognition, the police, hospital management, and, ultimately, I myself agree it's my mother.

And I think about her life, about how she endured tragedy upon tragedy, about how, despite the loss of her own childhood, she did her best to give me one, how she made our constant moves adventures, how I no longer cared whether or not we were being chased because those moves (all those places, all those experiences, all those people we met along the way) are what molded me into everything I am, how she fed me and clothed me and held me when I cried even though no one had held her.

Mr. Kline visits me regularly over the years. At Juilliard, at my apartment in New York, at many of the various cities where I've lived. He becomes more than a father to me. He fills a deep hole inside me. He brings me back to life. Papa, as I come to call him, passes at the ripe young age of 102. I am holding his hand when he takes his last breath. It is the one and only time I return to South Haven. It feels odd being back, as if I never left. I wet my toes in Lake Michigan, go fishing on the pier, enjoy a blueberry malted at South Haven Drug. Sunshine is still waiting tables, still complaining about the winters, still threatening to "up and move to Florida." She catches me up on local news, that Dr. Henry had passed a few years back, aneurysm like his father, which I already know. Papa told me. That Hannah married a rock musician she met at Woodstock and moved with him to California, which makes me smile. And finally that Butch married a girl he met at Michigan, a senator's daughter.

I am surprised how much this information hurts, how flimsy the wall I've built around my feelings for him is. "When did they meet?" I ask before thinking.

"Oh gosh," she says. "His freshman year, I think. He brought her here for a blueberry malted, I think it was Thanksgiving break. Haven't seen as much of him since his father passed. He still owns the old gymnasium." She notes my sadness. "Girlfriend, you were too good for him."

It's what we women always tell each other when a man breaks our hearts.

When Facebook becomes a thing, Butch is the first person I search for. I admit to still reading his page on occasion. At sixty-one, he is still handsome, thinning hair, but he has the same smile, same dimples, same dreamy brown eyes. His profile says he's a practicing veterinarian in Ann Arbor, but that isn't what interests me. I zero in on the woman he chose to marry, one of those perfect wives. Fit. Pretty. Blond and blue-eyed like me, but not at all circumspect. No deep forehead wrinkles from a continuously furled brow. Little sign of the sagging skin that so often plagues those who have endured tragedy or lived hard lives. They have two boys. In pictures, they are always smiling as if they are the happiest couple, happiest family, in the entire world. *This should be my life*, I sometimes think. *These should be my boys.* I often wonder whether he thinks of me, reminisces about the times we went fishing, remembers my smile or my laugh, whether he has followed my career or searched for me at all. Whether he relives that final night we spent together or that moment we said goodbye. Sometimes I find myself inside that night, and I experience the same euphoria I did then, and like a fool, I pine. Pine in the way I suppose we do for first love. For its all-consuming innocence, for the first kiss and the spine tingles and the way our bodies melt at the mere sight of the beloved, and, also, for the time and the space within which it blossomed. Its particular bubble in our memories. For me: a beach, the perforated metal floor of a lighthouse balcony, the concrete platform of a pier, the smell of water, sound of gentle waves. And for a moment, I allow myself to enter that bubble and bask in its sights and smells and sounds, and I catch my breath as the feel of Butch surrounds me, and my chest hurts as the tears come to my eyes. But then I snap myself back to reality, and I remember what he said when he was boarding that train, about me moving back to Michigan and becoming a piano teacher like Mr. Kline, and I repeat his words over and over, while telling myself I wouldn't have been happy. Could I have been happy with a man who didn't *see* me?

I have taken lovers over the years, some of whom I loved dearly and fully, though marriage never has been an option for me. Both because I enjoy my freedom—it suits my nomadic lifestyle—and because I decided long ago against tempting fate, passing on my mother's disease, and potentially mine, to a child.

And Zachary Ludwig? I have thought about calling him many times. Run scenarios through my mind about how it might go, what we might say to each other, but my imagined conversations never progress past awkward pleasantries, and besides, I've had a Papa, one whom no one can ever replace, one who will, like my mother, live forever in my heart.

Recently, feeling as if I needed a break from my frenetic traveling, I accepted a two-year position as a visiting pianist with the Chicago Symphony Orchestra. Traveling does seem to wear on one after a certain age. Admittedly I had no idea the Chicago Art Institute was right across the street. An unfortunate coincidence, given where I now find myself. Sitting on a smooth wooden bench staring at twin portraits of *Madame Léon Clapisson*. *She* is why I entered the museum. *She* is why my knees buckled. *She* is why I both wanted to leave and wanted to stay. Because she was the painting on my mother's easel that night. I study the original, a victim of fugitive pigment. In many ways, she symbolizes those years, now so long ago, when my mother and I were fugitives. What if things hadn't turned out the way they did? Would we have kept running, leaving less and less of an imprint behind, until we faded into the canvas that was our lives?

Perhaps I'll never know the answers to these and so many other questions.

Out of the corner of my eye I see a figure hovering. Fedora and pinstripe suit. Extremely white teeth for a man of his advanced years. I decide to ignore him. He clears his throat. Smiles. "Is this seat taken?" British accent.

Obviously I was right about him the first time he approached me, when he gave me the catalogue. Does he want something from me? Why else would he return?

He ignores my ignoring, says, "She said you would come."

I stare straight ahead, avoiding eye contact.

"She told me to watch for you. That you walk the same route every day on your lunch hour. That you always look at the banners. That you'd recognize the name of the exhibit."

Fine. Just one little question. "Who is *she*?"

"Your mother," he says.

My mother? I feel myself getting angry. I look around for a museum guard but don't see any.

He winks. "When you want to touch a painting, they're everywhere. But when an old man with a British accent pesters you, they're nowhere in sight."

"Who are you?" I ask.

"My name is Jeremy," he says. "Jeremy Jones."

Jeremy?

"You probably don't remember me. You were just a child when we last saw one another. I was a friend of your mother's. We took art classes together, shared studio space in New York with two other artists, Juliette Armand and Rachel Monroe. For almost three years. Maybe you'll remember the flower store on the street below? You loved going there. You loved all the colors. You called them *fowers*."

Juliette? Rachel?

A faint memory comes to me of walking through the stand while holding my mother's hand, of the sweet smell. But then I chastise myself for even entertaining his comments. I've been in many flower shops over the years. So what if his name is Jeremy? It's a relatively common name.

"I took the two of you to the bus station when he showed up."

"He?"

"Her stalker. The man chasing her."

How does he know about the Shadow Man?

"She said you would require verifiable data," he says. "'Conversation over.'"

"What did you say?"

"'Conversation over.' Isn't that what she used to say to you? And you once climbed a tree in South Haven. You peered in the window and saw your mother with a man."

"How do you know that?"

"Because we saw you. I was the man with your mother that day at Adelaide House. I'd rented it for the summer so your mother and I could spend time together. I believe it made her happy. And just so you know, there was no nookie going on. I prefer men. It was such a lovely town. So serene. And the water? Glorious. I could see it from nearly every window in the house. Sometimes I came to your house to pick up paintings, or drop off stretchers and canvas, or just visit. When you weren't there, of course. Your mother didn't want to confuse you. I opened my gallery a year after the two of you left New York. Thankfully I realized early that I didn't have your mother's talent. Some don't, you know. Creator's ego, I call it. Her paintings always sold well. Still, there was never enough money, was there? That's why I encouraged her to paint the Renoirs. I have a client that pays a pretty penny for exceptional forgeries, and Scarlet's are as perfect as they come."

My mind is swimming. I don't know where to begin, I have so many questions. If he knows about Adelaide House, then it's likely at least part of what he's saying is true. I decide to test him.

"Why do they call it Adelaide House?"

"Because of the tree."

"What about the tree?"

"It was planted in the dog's honor. That was her name, Adelaide. She was the sole survivor of a nineteenth-century shipwreck. They say shipwrecks weren't uncommon on Lake Michigan back then."

I stare at him. I don't know what to say.

"Cat got your tongue," he says and smiles. "You hated it when she said that, didn't you? She still goes by Scarlet. The name Mary Ann Boudreau was all over the newspapers, and Mary Ann Boudreau was committed to the Traverse City State Hospital. Few people knew her as Scarlet. And those that did are either dead themselves or think she is." He pauses. "It's hers, you know."

"What's hers?"

"The painting. Digital reproduction, my ass. Whoever makes those tags should be fired. It is obviously paint. All those layers." He looks around. "There are no guards here now. Go ahead, touch it. I'll keep a lookout."

"I don't think so."

"Your choice," he says and shrugs, as if challenging me.

"Fine." I look from side to side. Rise. Brush my hand across the surface of the reproduction. Quickly withdraw it and return to my bench.

"Well?"

"Anyone could have painted it."

He smiles knowingly. "As it turns out, there's a legal market for forgeries as well. May I sit?"

I pull my bag and coat toward me.

"She arranged this exhibit, you know," he says. "They hire visiting curators from time to time. If you flip to the last page of the catalogue, there is verifiable data to that effect."

"You're saying she's alive?"

"Of course," he says.

"But that's impossible. She drowned."

"Oh my, that," he says. "We have a lot to discuss, don't we? First, so you know, she's been living in New York, but she travels to many places. Over the years, she's attended your concerts. When you moved here, she decided to present and curate this exhibit. She followed you on many occasions, knew your route and habits. She had no doubt you'd see the banner the first day it went up. That's why I came today. But if you hadn't, I would have come every day until you did."

"If that's true, if she's alive, why hasn't she contacted me?"

"At first, she feared being sent back to the hospital. Later, after time had gone by, she didn't want to risk upsetting you. She knew your childhood and what happened was hard on you. She wanted you to have a normal life."

"None of this makes any sense. She was crazy. She saw people. Lost time. Killed a man. She couldn't possibly live on her own."

"She doesn't live on her own. She lives with me. I take care of her. She's no crazier than half the people that walk this earth. Sure, she has a vivid imagination, and she might lose track of time periodically, but when she goes into her other worlds, I just watch her more closely."

"But there was a body."

"Ah, yes, the body. We couldn't believe our luck. It all but guaranteed no one would come looking for her. Oh, that does sound rather heartless, doesn't it? Of course I feel for the poor woman's family. They're probably still looking for her. And not only that, the weather. It was balmy and sunny that day, and not two days later, the temperature dropped, it snowed, and the lake froze. As your mother said, the universe was looking out for us. Would you like to know how she escaped from the asylum? You believe that at least, don't you?"

"I don't know what to believe."

"We'd been planning it for a while. I visited her pretty often, under an alias, of course, in case anyone found reason to review the visitor log. Dr. Henry didn't even know. It was essential that no one connect the two of us. We couldn't risk anyone finding the truth. She paid attention to the habits of the nurses and guards. They used to transport the patients through the tunnels. She learned which exits went where. On my last visit, we devised our scheme. Toward the end of his shift, she would entice the day nurse, Lucas, into a linen closet, and while he kissed and fondled her, she'd steal his keys, and then wait for Brenda, the night nurse. Brenda was on the lazy side. She rarely checked on the patients. She preferred crosswords. While Brenda was lost in her puzzle, your mother would sneak out of her room, use the key to access the nearest tunnel door, and exit through the one closest to the water, where I and my rental boat would be waiting. It was exhilarating. We laughed all the way to the dock where I'd parked the car."

Jeremy and I sit in silence while I absorb what he's told me. I notice that the light has changed in the museum. Though there isn't a single window in this room, I can feel that it is late afternoon. It is a consequence of spending your formative years with a painter. Acute sensitivity to light sources. The two of us are alone in the room. Alone with the two portraits of *Madame*, the original and the one this man, this *Jeremy*, says my mother painted.

"What did you mean when you said you couldn't risk them finding the truth?" I ask. "Who? What truth?"

"Ah, well, that is the million-dollar question, isn't it? First, let me say, I didn't choose to leave her, not permanently anyway. I just went to get the van so we could transport the body to the boat. I'd parked it several blocks away so the neighbors wouldn't wonder who it belonged to, and he wouldn't see it. I was probably gone no more than twenty minutes, but when I got back, there you were sitting in a car with your piano teacher. She didn't think you'd be back until the next morning. I held my breath when you went inside. God only knew how you'd react. I had to think fast. Generally I'm good on my feet. I don't know how long I sat there considering, but I was just about to go in the house when Dr. Henry showed up. What a conundrum. I mean, when I slit his throat, I was nervous, I'd never killed anyone, but I was also feeling pretty confident we would get away with it. But you and then Henry? What was I supposed to do with that? What to do? That's what I was thinking. What to do? What to do? Then I realized there was no reason to worry. Your mother had told me about Henry, how he hated his stepfather for killing his mother. He wouldn't turn her in. In fact, he could help. Six hands were better than four. When I heard the sirens in the distance, I thought they were for some other address at first. But they got louder and louder, and closer and closer. Then I saw the flashing red lights. So, I left. It never dawned on me Henry would call the police. At the time I didn't know you'd gone into shock and he was just trying to save you. That all came out in the trial. I attended, you know." He pauses. "Do you believe me now? How else could I know all these details?"

I am reeling. I'm not even thinking about whether or not I believe him. I'm stuck on four all-important words: *I slit his throat.*

"*You* killed him?" I ask.

"Well, she gave him the sedative, but I did the rest. She couldn't do it. She didn't think it was fair to you. She thought you deserved a better mother than that. She knew you'd win the competition. She wanted to support you and your career. So, you see, that's why I used an alias when I went to see her in the hospital, so when I helped her escape, they couldn't find her through me. That's also why I took care of her all those years. Because I owed her. Because I should have gone into that house. Because I should have turned myself in. I told her that, but she didn't want me to confess. She said my confessing would just make things worse. Then we'd both be in jail, so to say. It's not like they were going to just let her out of the loony bin. 'Someone needs to break me out of this hellhole,' she'd said. And so I did."

"How long had the two of you been planning to kill him?"

"The two of us? No, that wasn't me. She meant to do it with Henry, but he was out of town, so she called me. Luckily I was still at Adelaide House. The weather was so beautiful I'd decided to stay one more day." He pauses, looks at me. "Your mother loves you, you know. You and your career are all she ever talks about."

I don't know when I started crying. I'm not even certain why I am crying. Happy tears? Sad tears? And I think to myself that this is exactly where I should be at this very moment in time. This is exactly the room I should be in, exactly the bench I should be sitting on, exactly the two paintings I should be facing when I learn the largest, most important truths of my life. My mother is not only alive; she isn't 100 percent crazy. At least not the kind of crazy that kills people. Or completely makes up people.

"What about Henry?" I ask.

"What about him?"

"Did he know my mother was alive?"

"Not at first. But after she told him, they stayed in touch until the day he died, and he never told a soul. He was in love with her, you know."

I did know that. I saw it in his eyes and heard it in his voice when he cried that day at the clinic. And in that moment, I understand why Dr. Henry had distanced himself from me. Because he was carrying a great secret, one he feared would make any encounter he had with me a lie.

I think about all the secrets being kept. Henry not telling me my mother was alive. Butch not telling me he had married. My mother not telling Dr. Henry that Jeremy was visiting her at the hospital. My mother not telling me she was alive. Were all those secrets necessary? Look at all the time with my mother I've lost.

"Why now?" I ask. "Why did she decide to contact me after all these years?"

"She isn't well."

"What do you mean, not well?"

"I think your mother should be the one to tell you that." He rises. "It's time I return." He hands me a business card. "Here is her contact information." He pauses. "It's uncanny."

"What is?"

"How much you look like her." He tips the brim of his fedora, says, "Cheerio."

I feel a chill, as if a ceiling fan had just turned on, turn to look for him, but just like before, he is nowhere in sight.

"Are you okay, ma'am?" a guard asks, startling me.

"I'm fine," I say. "I was just looking for someone. Did you happen to see a man wearing a fedora and pinstripe suit? Older gentleman with extremely white teeth? He was just sitting with me?"

"Sorry, ma'am, I didn't, but I only just arrived in the room. Doing my rounds. You sure you're okay?"

"Yes, yes, fine."

"I'm off then," he says and walks away.

I set the timer on my phone. My eyes follow the guard until he exits. Two full minutes have passed. Jeremy was gone in less than five seconds. My eyes focus on the second *Madame*, the reproduction. "If you flip to the last page of the catalogue," Jeremy had said.

I open the cover, bypass the dedication, brief history of Renoir, explanation of fugitive pigment, exhaustive information on the cochineal, and the index until I get to the sections titled, "Exhibit Curator" and "Reproduction Artist." Both are listed as Scarlet Lake. Something pulls at me. I flip back to the dedication. It reads:

> *For my daughter, Blue, the love of my life. I dedicate this exhibit to the fugitive lifestyle we once shared, and the brilliance you've brought to the world of music since.*

I stare at the card that holds her contact information. What if I conjured Jeremy because I wanted so badly for everything he told me to be true? What if my mother's madness has finally found me?

And then it comes to me. A test of sorts.

I stick the catalogue in my purse, don my coat and newfangled earmuffs, exit the exhibit, negotiate the maze of halls displaying works by Seurat and Matisse and Van Gogh, dodge the ticket line, walk through the arched doorways, descend the concrete stairs, pass the large green lion statues that flank the museum's grand entrance, traverse the plaza, wait for the walk signal, and cross Michigan Avenue.

When I am safely inside the symphony hall, I head to the restroom and look in the mirror.

And there on my face is my mother's. Blond hair, blue eyes, full lips. I will my eyes to hold her image. To refuse that moment when she, like a Cheshire cat, will slowly disappear, leaving only *my* hair, eyes, and lips behind. But then, I let go. I accept what will come. And in that moment, I realize a greater truth. There is nothing to fear. Her memory will never disappear. Whether or not she is alive, whether or not she answers the phone, she is inside me. Inside my body. Inside my heart. Inside my soul. She will always be a part of me. I will always be Scarlet in Blue.

I retrieve my cell phone, take a deep breath, and dial the number.

ACKNOWLEDGMENTS

There is an African proverb that says, "It takes a village to raise a child." So many people have had a hand in "raising" this novel, from tiny idea to messy first draft to tighter tenth draft to wishful-thinking final draft to ultimate finished manuscript and, finally, to an actual book. Writing *Scarlet in Blue* has been an amazing and fulfilling experience, and I am so grateful to so many. I want to thank my husband, David, for allowing me the time and space to write, gifts that cannot be measured. No way could I have escaped so completely into this story's world without you to help hold down the real one. To my daughter, Madi, for teaching me that nothing worth having or doing comes easily. It feels like, as a single mom and daughter for many years, we grew up together. You are my heart and pride. To my mother, Helen, for taking me to the library as a child and instilling me with a love of reading and books.

Heartfelt thanks to Miriam Altshuler, my agent extraordinaire, for being there with me every step of the way. I am so grateful for you, for your belief in this story, and for your keen ability to get it in the right editor's hands. To Jody Hotchkiss, thank you for your expertise and support in handling the dramatic rights.

To my editor, Maya Ziv, thank you for taking this journey with me. You are truly *the* best! What this book has become is thanks not only to your brilliant editorial skill set, but also to your remarkable ability to "request" deletions and "inspire" additions with kindness, support, and respect. While I won't mention them here, more than a few large revisions you suggested early on made this a better book. To my copy editor, Mary Beth Constant, wow, I am so grateful for your attention to detail throughout the book, but specifically to the timeline and for your help identifying the classical piano pieces Mr. Kline taught Blue in preparation for her competition. Thank you to Christine Ball, Emily Canders, and Natalie Church for your early reads and ongoing support in bringing this book into the world. Thanks also to the many other folks at Dutton who helped make this project happen: John Parsley, Susan Schwartz, Ryan Richardson, Alice Dalrymple, Hannah Dragone, Elke Sigal, Leigh Butler, Sabila Khan, Jillian Fata, and Lexy Cassola.

Thank you to the talented and generous authors Jennifer Niven and Randy Susan Meyers, who read this novel prior to my agent shopping it. Your kind words gave me confidence in this story and its readiness for professional eyes. Amy Blumenthal, flutist and co-founder of Carpe Liber (the best book club in Charlotte, NC), thank you for sharing your knowledge of classical music and the arts, and your discerning reader's eye. Roma Edmundson, thank you for cheering me on. And thank you to my best friend and dedicated companion Brutus, for lovingly sitting beside me as I write.

Special thanks to the community of South Haven, Michigan. Elaine Stephens, retired college professor and community leader, for bringing your knowledge to this story. Lois Howard, South Haven Memorial Library board member, for sharing 1968 information on archives, microfiche machines, and card catalogs. Clark Gruber, longtime resident, for passing on some 1968 specifics. Dick and Pam Haferman, owners of Black River Books, for supporting my first novel and for continuously asking me when they can start selling this one. And to all my other friends and neighbors in South Haven, thank you for welcoming me and offering your friendship, support, and smiles. I thought of you as I wrote this novel, and I hope I've done South Haven proud.

Thanks also to all you readers, book advocates, booksellers, librarians, bloggers, reviewers, and others who support and spread the word about reading and books.

ABOUT THE AUTHOR

Jennifer Murphy holds an MFA in painting from the University of Denver and an MFA in creative writing from the University of Washington. She is the recipient of the 2013 Loren D. Milliman Scholarship for creative writing and was a contributor at the Bread Loaf Writers' Conference from 2008 through 2012. In 2015, her acclaimed debut novel, *I Love You More*, won the prestigious Nancy Pearl Fiction Award. Her love of art led her to start Citi Arts, a public art and urban-planning company that has created public art master plans for airports, transit facilities, streetscapes, and cities nationwide. She hails from a small beachfront town in Michigan and has lived in Denver, Charlotte, Seattle, and Charleston. She currently lives in Houston, Texas.